THE DIVINE COURAGE TRILOGY BOOK 3

# VANQUISHER

## C.C. URIE

Cover by Miblart

Map by Derek I. Schmidt and C.C. Urie

ISBN: 978-1-969115-06-6



Printed in the United States of America

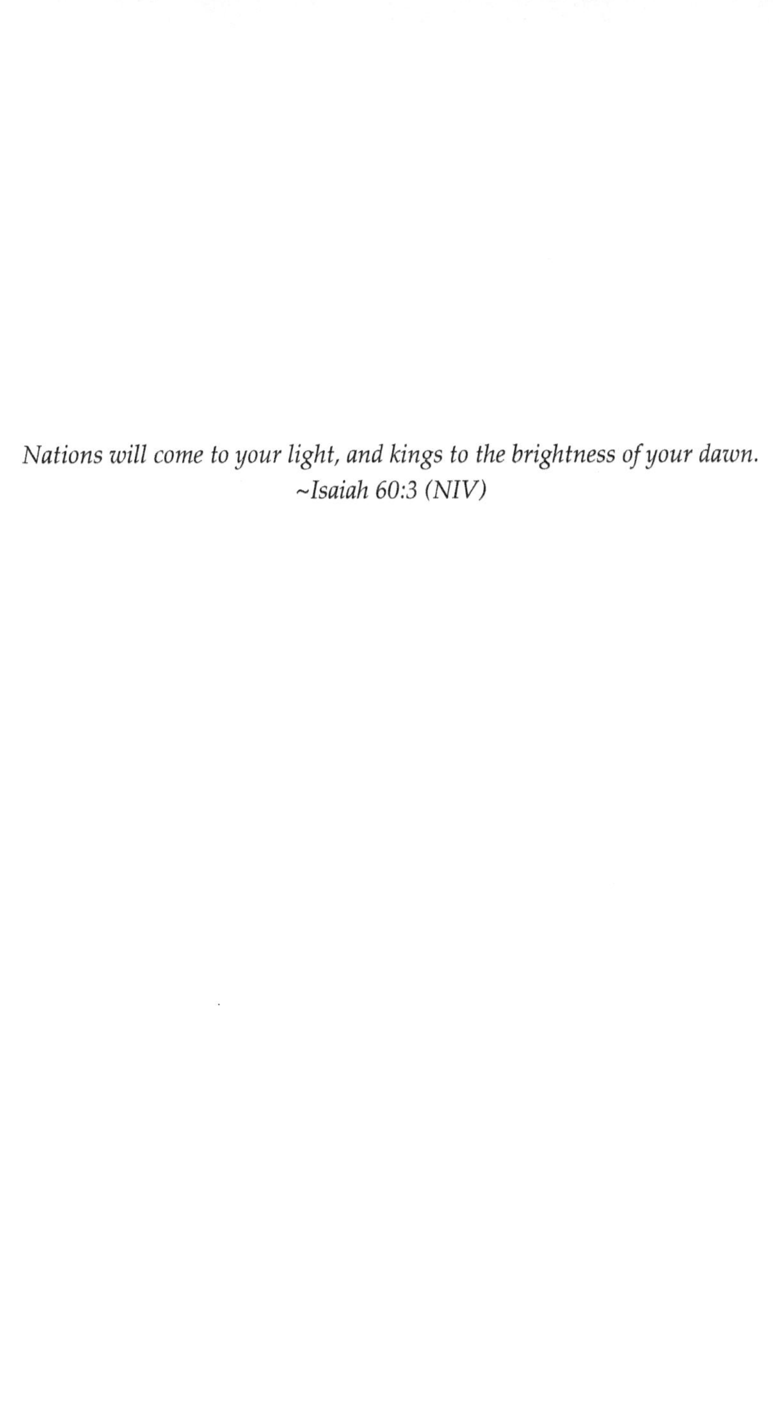

*Nations will come to your light, and kings to the brightness of your dawn.*
*~Isaiah 60:3 (NIV)*

*For everyone who has supported this series.*
*Thank you.*

# TRIGGER WARNINGS
## WARNING: SPOILERS

- Larken is in multiple aircraft accidents and has severe PTSD because of it
- Larken is emotionally abused by her mother and older brother, and her father is an alcoholic
- A war takes place throughout this Trilogy and there is blood, shootings, stabbings, and other injuries
- One character is a narcissistic abuser who becomes obsessed with his victim and has lustful thoughts about her, makes several innuendos, and tries to stalk her which may be upsetting to some readers
- This Trilogy deals with adult themes like abandonment, self-worth, relationships, and other complicated emotions

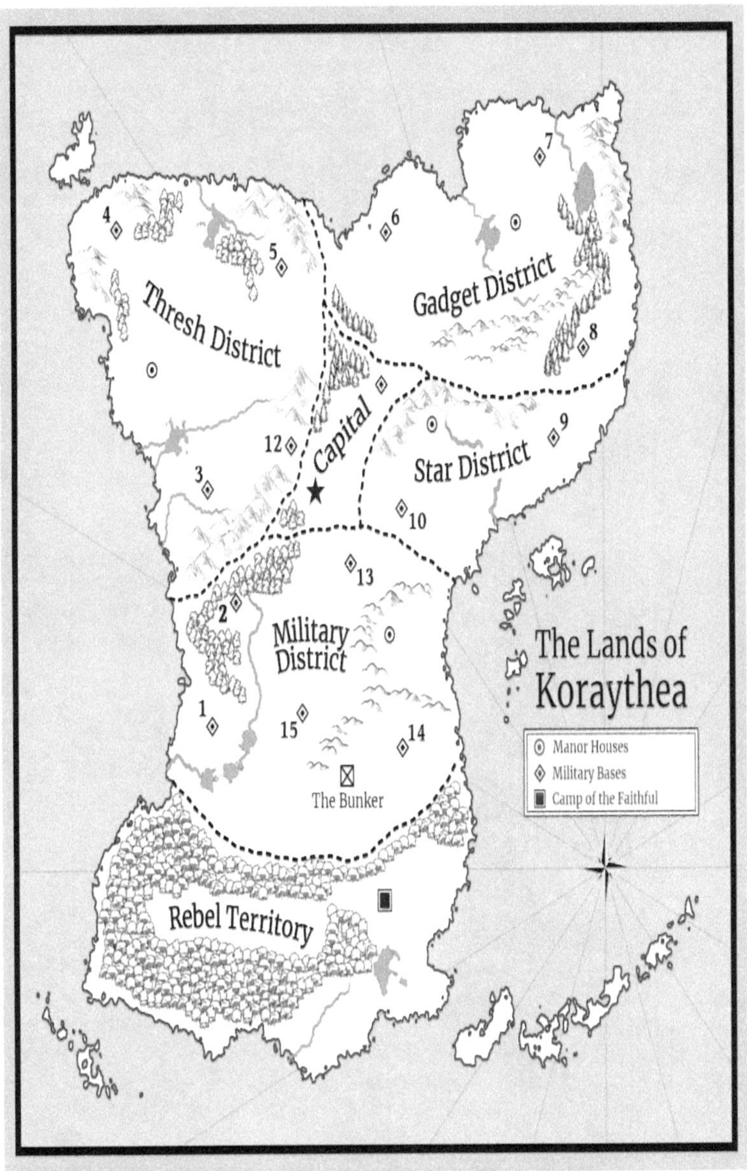

Thresh District
Gadget District
Capital
Star District
Military District
The Bunker
Rebel Territory
The Lands of
Koraythea
Manor Houses
Military Bases
Camp of the Faithful

# PROLOGUE

*Why marry for love when money can ensure your happiness?*

It was the question Cornella Hale had always asked herself. Why have love when she could have a life of luxury, a life of ease, or a life filled with music? She had fallen in love the moment she heard the first note sounding from a pianoforte.

When she was a child, she would sit in front of the television and watch old operas and concerts boasting of forgotten music. As a teenager, while her friends were off galivanting with a new boy every week, she would sneak into the theater and listen in the rafters since she was too poor for anything else. Cornella made herself a promise that she would marry above her station and one day be able to afford a seat out in the open. She would wear fancy dresses, laugh, and cry in the audience. And…she would finally be happy. Then Trogar came along and offered her everything she had ever wanted.

It came as no surprise that Cornella eventually fell in love with a man who made the most beautiful music she had ever heard. Not only was Fisher a skilled musician, but he was extremely handsome, as well. He made her feel like she was the greatest, most precious thing in the world. It was a feeling that Cornella became addicted to. She put everything on the line for him and was rewarded with a heart torn in half. More than anything, she wanted to keep her wealthy life of music, but she was just as willing to give it all up so she could only hear Fisher's.Then, Fisher found his way back to Maxim and broke her heart.

Hating him, and Maxim, for everything that had been done to her, Cornella ruined him and promised to forget him. Music no longer held the same joy it once had, but now she could afford to find new interests. Cornella devoted herself to her son and raised him to demand what the world owed him.

Then *she* came. Cornella had convinced herself that the baby was her husband's, but that wheat-colored hair and those eyes didn't lie. She came and ruined everything. Trogar started drinking shortly after that, and the Magnate began talking about finding a new Luminary. Cornella had already lost music; she refused to lose her life, as well.

She pushed and pushed, forming the Vigilants, and started the war against Maxim. Wardell was an afterthought. What better way to pull at the heartstrings of others than with a baby? Cornella had successfully painted herself as the tragic mother who had to lead the war efforts.

So, with all of the pieces in place, and even more sway than the Magnate himself, why wasn't she happy? Cornella looked out of her window, hands gripping her arms. Captain Braves was sprawled in a chair, smoking those awful cigars that were constantly hanging out of his mouth since Larken's betrayal. The smell only added to her crippling migraine, but she kept her frown firmly in place. This Maxim-forsaken house was getting on her last nerve.

Stagnant air surrounded her, the heat and the blueberry fog making her back sweat. Her heels, though gorgeous, were completely impractical for the task at hand. Not that she had plans to join the men and women running drills outside. Larken was off playing in the woods somewhere, while Cornella had literally been left here to rot. One of the drill Sergeants blew a whistle that had her right eye twitching. All she needed to do was get through this, then she could drug herself on the aircraft and sleep the whole way home.

"Something bothering you, Lumina?" Braves mocked. "The view not to your taste?"

"Perhaps you should get off your lazy backside and join them. What woman will want you if you get fat off drinks and cigars?" she retorted.

He huffed an annoyed laugh, and she saw out of the corner of her eye as puffs of blue spilled past his lips with each exhale. Cornella had to fight not to roll her eyes. The man was a disgusting failure. He had become lazy, *obsessed* with only finding her daughter. Braves was barely useful anymore. If it wasn't for the fact that he was so devoted to tracking Larken, Cornella would have taken care of him weeks ago.

Another breath almost choked her. She needed to get out of this room. Letting her eyes take in the padded wallpaper and old furniture once more, Cornella brushed her hands on her black pants and walked out into the sun. Another shot of pain stabbed behind her eye, but it didn't stop her from walking away from her childhood home. After her parents died, she had considered burning the place to the ground, since it was more land than home. But she ultimately thought up another use for the crumbling farm.

The Sergeant with the whistle still resting in his mouth gave her a nod of respect. Cornella ignored him. She had finished what she had come here for. She'd looked over the soldiers, checked the stats of the Vigilants that had infiltrated the bases of Koraythea, and taken the unpleasant, involuntary trip down memory lane that she always did whenever she saw her childhood home.

Walking as fast as she could while still coming across as elegant, Cornella made her way to her personal aircraft. The pilot was waiting inside for her, probably sweating more than she had been in the small house. She didn't care though. The only thing she wanted was the sweet release hydrocodone could give her.

The aircraft started up as soon as her foot hit the carpeted floor.

Cool air blasted out of the black vents, hitting her in the face and giving her the first sense of comfort she'd had in the last five hours.

Cornella didn't bother to shut the door behind her; the pilot could do it automatically and knew by now to do so. It started to close just as she hit the button to black out the windows. Darkness began to slowly encase her until the only light left shone from the screen sitting above the drink dispenser where she finished imputing her commands. Instead of her usual shot of tequila, a clear liquid of another sort appeared before her. Without waiting for even a second, she knocked the hydrocodone cocktail back. She made a face at the flavor of licorice that coated her tongue but felt the effects almost immediately.

Soon her eyes grew heavy in the darkness, and the last thought she had was of finally extinguishing the yellow light that was Larken Hale.

# CHAPTER 1

Larken huffed out a breathy laugh as she dodged a blow and lunged for Blade. Shadric couldn't take his eyes off her. She had a magnetic pull, something that made him feel like he was losing himself whenever she was around. A sharp smack to his left knee nearly buckled him, and Shadric turned his gaze to Delvon. Delvon glowered at Shadric and rolled his eyes, silently telling him to pull his head out of the clouds and get back to their spar. Reluctantly, Shadric forced himself to pay attention, but the bodyguard still managed to keep the upper hand.

Delvon had taken his job at the Manor seriously, and even though he was back at Camp, he rarely left Larken's side. It pleased Shadric as much as it annoyed him, and he wished more than anything that he could be her protector. But it seemed that he would need to get in line.

The Camp had come alive in a way he had never seen before when Larken stumbled off that aircraft. The people here, the ones that he had grown up with, were drawn to her. She never seemed to have a moment alone, either talking to the families or her friends from base. Shadric couldn't help but feel a little jealous. Their stolen moments together seemed so long ago now, and a selfish part of him wanted to steal her away and go back to his field. There, they weren't a celebrity and the Daughter of the Military, only Shad and Larken. Even though she had been engaged at the time, Shadric still missed those days. And with the uncertainty of what was to come, he almost wanted to go back.

He couldn't forget the way she looked at him the night of her rehearsal dinner, the way she had felt in his arms. She seemed so broken and lost, and he wanted nothing more than to take her away and fix her problems. Now, she was right here in front of him, and so impossibly far away.

With a victorious cry, Larken weakly punched the air and then doubled over, panting as she rested her hands on her knees. Her pale-yellow tank top stuck to her skin, drenched with sweat in places. Blade grumbled bitterly, too quiet for Shadric to hear, his own chest heaving. Larken let her head drop forward, and she rasped a laugh. Her old squad members stood off to the side, cheering loudly. The tall one, Loxly, ran forward and grabbed Larken around the waist. He spun her in the air, hollering something about little birds and them being tougher than they looked. A little girl jumped up and down excitedly, begging to learn how to do what Larken just did. She drove the point home by punching and kicking at the air in front of her.

Delvon muttered something about a shower and a waste of a spar and disappeared. Shadric knew he should follow and let Larken have this time with her friends, but he couldn't. Leaving would just mean that he was willing to give up on her now that she was safe and happy. He didn't want her to think he only wanted her because she was breaking. Shadric needed her to know that he was ready for all of it. The bad as well as the good.

When Larken was once again on the ground, the rest of her friends surrounded her. All of them except for Soren, who stuck out a hand to help Blade to his feet. Shadric couldn't get a good read on the former Captain, but he didn't think the man liked him very much. It was to be expected, though; Delvon had told him that Soren didn't like anyone. The woman, Hinlee, leaned into Larken and whispered something. Larken then turned to find Shadric watching her. She smiled and offered a small wave.

Shadric smiled and waved back.

One of the men next to Hinlee—Shadric couldn't remember if it was Levi or Brecker—muttered something, and Hinlee elbowed him in the stomach as Larken turned to glare at him. The other two men chuckled, and Shadric suddenly felt a little embarrassed. Larken hissed something and then headed his way, cheeks as pink as his felt.

"Hey, Shad," she breathed when she reached him. Larken may have just been in a spar with the Faithfuls' most formidable warrior, but she smelled like the first day of summer.

"Hey." Ignoring a catcall, he asked, "How are you settling in?"

"Good!" She nodded quickly and then hugged her middle, almost as if she didn't know what to do with her hands. "Everything is great. I love my new place, although being so close to the Chin's has been driving me a little crazy."

Shadric's brow furrowed. "Are they bothering you?"

Larken laughed. "No, no, nothing like that." She smiled. "Mr. Chin is a chef."

Shadric grinned. Now knowing exactly which family she was talking about, he could safely assume that the little girl bouncing around Loxly's feet was Jing. "Del did tell me you are easily swayed with a good meal."

Larken's eyebrow rose in defiance. "He did, did he?"

"When I was thinking about what to get you for your birthday."

Her cheeks went pink once more and she sucked her bottom lip in between her teeth. Shadric stared, wishing they could go back to who they were. He wanted to pull her into his arms, wanted to hold her and make her forget everything else. If they didn't have an audience, and he knew Carl or Delvon wouldn't call and interrupt them, he would have. Instead, he had to reluctantly let her go as Blade barked for them all to get ready for their meeting in an hour.

Giving him one last shy smile, Larken turned and headed back to her group. Shadric stood there like an idiot, just watching her go.

He should have been braver; he should go after what he wanted. The person he had been at the Manor had. That man didn't have a care in the world and was open about how he felt. But now that she was here, he was afraid that she wouldn't be his to keep.

Loxly murmured something to her, and she shoved him so hard that he almost fell into a bush. His rich laugh filled the clearing, and Shadric sighed. The open space had heard more conversation and laughter since Larken and her friends joined. This clearing was the one they tended to frequent and had now become his and Delvon's usual place to train as well. The group made their way to wherever they were headed, disappearing through the trees. He would see them all again soon enough; there was no use standing there and looking pathetic.

Shadric headed for the showers and found Delvon walking out just as he was walking in. The man groaned and gave Shadric that look, the one that said he could care less about feelings but would listen if he needed to. Shadric had planned on ignoring his offer, but then asked, "Do you think she's happy here?"

"My answer is the same as the last six times you asked me that."

"I know, but..."

Delvon crossed his arms. "*But?*"

Shadric groaned softly, feeling like a broken record. "She's been pushed around so much in the last few months. I just don't want her to feel like that here."

"I promise, she doesn't."

"How do you know?" Shadric's voice sounded more accusatory than he wanted. "Did you ask her?"

"No, I didn't ask. I don't care enough to." Delvon turned to walk away. He took two steps and huffed out an annoyed breath. Without facing him, he said, "She never used to laugh like that at the Manor, even before Blade tried to make her think he'd been killed. She's happy here."

Shadric didn't want to trust his friend's words. It seemed like there was more not being said. Delvon had told him everything that had happened at the Manor, even about their fake romance. Shadric didn't believe that Delvon had actually fallen for her—the body-guard's heart was too locked away for that—but something about the man seemed different. Almost like Larken had some sort of pull over him, as well.

Sighing, Shadric entered the communal showers and rinsed off. He couldn't dwell on his thoughts; they would only drive him mad. He just had to accept that that's who Larken was. She blew into your life like a missile, and nothing was ever the same again. Even Blade had his own story from when he met her as a fierce four-year-old. She had walked right up to him, tears in her eyes, and demanded that he play with her because she wanted a friend. Shadric didn't have to stretch his imagination very far to see it, and he knew that Larken was just as stubborn now as she was then.

Their conversation in the field about her not thinking she had any worth didn't change his mind about her. How could she see her own worth when she only had Blade growing up? Even now, when she was pushed and pulled like a puppet with an over-eager puppeteer, her doubt was understandable. Shadric knew from experience that she wouldn't just believe what others told her; she needed to learn for herself. She needed to see what she was capable of, and she needed to forge her own relationship with Maxim. No one else could do it for her, and the people that should have shown her how were either too drunk to function or actively trying to kill her. But she wouldn't be Larken if she didn't keep trying. She had befriended Blade, found friends that obviously loved her, softened Delvon, and twisted Shadric up inside so much that he couldn't tell which way was up anymore.

Knowing he would be early but not caring, Shadric made his way to the tabernacle. It was his favorite place in Camp. So many of his days had been spent there praying, laughing, writing music, and singing. He might have grown up by himself, but he was never truly alone. The familiar sounds and smells of Camp followed him, and he thought again about what it would feel like to really be a part of it all. What it would be like to have someone to come home to; to share a meal with someone other than the guys; to have his own children that ran around barefoot through the leaves and dirt. People waved to him, and Shadric waved back, offering warm grins. At least here he wasn't Shadric Barlow, eligible heartthrob. He was just Shad, the guy who led music during service.

The familiar eight-point star greeted him, and a calm washed over him as he walked inside. Letting the door shut softly behind him, Shadric leaned against it and let out a defeated groan. He let his eyes adjust to the dimness of the place, and he spotted a familiar form sitting in the front pew. Heart beating in his ears, he slowly made his way to the worn stage he practically lived on. The same smell of wood and nature filled the room, giving him the strength it always did. Without a word, he took the seat next to Larken and let himself relax.

She seemed tense. Nervous energy rolled off of her as she stared into nothing, nibbling her bottom lip and wringing her fingers. She had changed her clothes, but her hair was still in that same haphazard bun it was during her spar. The olive top complimented her brown shorts and had her skin looking softer than he remembered it being. Without thinking, Shadric reached out and grabbed her left hand. He squeezed it, and her lips twitched up slightly in gratitude. Shadric wanted to ask. He wanted to know if this was a Luminary thing or a Larken thing. But he no longer knew if they had that type of relationship. At the Manor, it felt like she had chosen him to be that person. Here, she had Blade again. Blade and Soren.

Deciding to risk it, Shadric turned to face her fully. They both opened their mouths and said, "Do you—"

He smiled as she laughed. "You first."

"Do you want to talk about it?" he asked.

Larken looked at their hands, and he wanted to know what she thought about him not letting go. She didn't pull hers back, so that must be a good sign.

"Do you think this is all just some big mistake?"

Heart sinking, Shadric asked, "What do you mean?"

"This. *Me*. What if I can't do it? What if I ruin everything? I don't know the first thing about—well, any of this."

He waited for his heart to beat normally again, relieved that she was talking about her future and not him. "You already know what I think."

"Do I?" She met his gaze. "I know that you wanted me to come here, that you thought I could help, that you—" Her cheeks went pink and she looked away.

Her hand twitched in his, and he knew she wanted to pull away and hide. Instead, Shadric felt his lips quirk. "That I *what?*"

Her blush crept from her cheeks down her throat as she mumbled something that sounded like, "*Don't make me say it…*"

"Sorry, what was that?" he teased.

She reluctantly met his eyes again, her teal depths sucking him in like they always did. "*Shad,*" she begged, voice a rocky whisper. Her unspoken plea to not have this conversation was audible in her tone.

Shadric took pity and didn't force her to speak. Instead, he reached out for her, cupping her cheek with his free hand. If she didn't want to talk, she didn't have to, but he wasn't done with this conversation. He made sure his thoughts and feelings were clear in the look he gave her.

*I care for you.*

The color in her cheeks deepened as her eyes took in his expression.

*I know.*

Finding that bravery he had by the fountain at the Manor, he moved his hand from her cheek to the back of her neck. Shadric drew her close, stopping to give her enough time to pull away. When she didn't, he brought her closer still, moving in as well. This was it. He was finally going to taste her. He was finally going to know what she felt like.

Only, the kiss didn't come. Instead, Larken jerked away from him just before the door to the tabernacle flew open and everyone spilled in. The group was laughing about something but stopped when they caught sight of the two of them sitting alone on the pew. Blade pushed to the front of the group, complaining about the hold up, and took them in.

Frowning, he barked, "Larken, upstairs. Now."

She didn't have to be told twice, and Shadric knew he was in for a long conversation with his mentor later. He had pulled Shadric aside once already and told him that she had enough going on. Clearly, he didn't listen.

Loxly started up a too loud conversation about shotguns and Hinlee complained loudly, ignoring him as she pushed her way past him to the stairs. The rest of the men glared his way, and Shadric nervously ran his fingers through his hair. When they started filing up the stairs, Shadric groaned and fell back onto the pew. He scrubbed his hands over his face, feeling stupid.

Delvon kicked the pew, and Shadric's head bounced off the wood at the jolt. "Are you a complete moron, or are you just having a bad day?"

"I don't know," he answered honestly. "Probably both."

Delvon looked over at the stairs, then glared down at him. "She deserves more than this."

"What are you saying?" Shadric accused. "That I'm not good enough?"

"No. I'm saying *you* are a confusion she doesn't need right now."

"We were just talking!" Shadric winced, the words sounding lame even to him.

"Right, and she really was my fiancée." Delvon started walking away and didn't look back as he called, "Hurry up. You're already late."

"Yeah? Well, you're late too," Shadric mumbled.

Pushing himself to his feet, Shadric smiled as his thoughts drifted back to Larken. She had kind of talked to him, and if they hadn't been interrupted, there was a good chance she wouldn't have pushed him away. He almost didn't dare hope that things could be the same between them once more, but he was too stupid to let it go.

# CHAPTER 2

*What am I doing?*

Larken had asked herself this at least fifteen times in the last two minutes. It took that long for everyone to crowd into the little conference room, and she hugged her middle as they took their seats around the long table. She stared at a gouge in the wood, refusing to meet anyone's eye. She didn't want to talk about it, and she felt like if anyone looked at her, they would know how near she was to ripping apart at the seams.

A calloused hand grabbed the back of her shirt moments later and pulled her from her chair. The scent of pine and salt told her who it was before Delvon even spoke. He pushed her gently into a corner of the room, crossed his arms, and frowned at her.

Not wanting to have this conversation, she joked, "What, not going to pretend to kiss me this time?"

He leaned in close. His frown deepened and he rasped, "Maybe if I did kiss you, these idiots would stop chasing after you and take this seriously."

"I don't want to talk about this with you."

"If you had it your way, you wouldn't talk about this at all. You would bury your head in the sand until it all blew over."

"Well, no one asked you."

"No one ever does." He leaned back and sighed as he rubbed his forehead with his thumb and forefinger. "Just, be careful. He's... *sensitive.*"

Larken felt the fight leave her. She hugged her middle once more, a bad habit she had developed over the last week whenever she felt too exposed. "I don't know what I'm doing. I'm..." she mulled over her word choice, "...confused."

"I didn't ask."

She glared at him. "*You* brought it up."

"And I regret that now."

"I just—it was simpler when I was engaged."

"Was it really?" Delvon quirked an eyebrow.

No, it wasn't. She had been just as confused about Shadric and Soren then as she was now. She thought that she and Soren had reached an understanding on the Harpy, but true to form, Soren had fallen into old habits as soon as he was initiated into the Faithful army here at Camp. He threw himself into training, and she was forgotten...again. But Shadric, he made it clear that he could never forget her. She had known, once, what the right choice would be, what the easy one was. Now she wasn't sure about anything in her life. Not about this, and not about her future as a Luminary.

"This is stupid," she grumbled.

"Well, it's your life now."

"If I didn't have to be Luminary, I wouldn't have to look for a future Luminar," she challenged.

"*That,*" Delvon grinned wickedly, "is not my problem, Peach."

"It is if I say to skies with it and choose you."

He choked as she rammed her shoulder into him on her way back to her seat. It probably hurt her a lot more than it hurt him, but she refused to reach up and rub her shoulder. At least her bad one hadn't been bothering her lately. Not only were Ezra and Jodi both here, but the mattress in her bungalow had to be of higher quality than the one back at the Manor. She didn't know who had furnished her new home, because Vallen denied it every time she brought it up, but she had a feeling that hers was more impressive than the ones that surrounded it.

Vallen sat at the head of the table, and she sank back into her seat at his right. It hadn't been that long ago that she walked into this very room, only to discover that she was right about Vallen faking his death. She had been overjoyed, and then that joy turned into hurt. Larken understood that she would have given the secret away by not reacting to his death, but that didn't stop it from bothering her. She'd spent too many sleepless nights worrying if he really was dead, and too many stressful days looking for evidence that he was still alive. It was something she refused to live through again. Vallen had promised that she wouldn't be left out of his secrets anymore, and now it would be easier for him since her mother wouldn't be looking for him.

Loxly, having taken the seat next to hers, leaned in to ask what Delvon had wanted.

"I was proposing."

Loxly laughed, no doubt thinking she was joking, but sobered when he saw the look on her face. He looked over the room quickly and turned back to her. His voice was soft when he said, "Look, Little Bird, I'm not gonna tell you how to live your life, but it will break Jing's heart if you don't marry that Barlow guy."

"And you?"

"I, well—" Loxly looked away from her uncomfortably.

She followed his gaze and found Soren glaring at the sharp-shooter. Larken's heart stopped as she wondered if he had heard them. Soren rose an eyebrow in question, and she could breathe easy again.

"If we could start this today..."

Everyone turned their attention to Vallen. He sat forward in his chair, set his elbows on the table, and rested his chin on his fists. Light reflected off his bald head, making his dark skin shine. He took in the room around him, and Larken let her eyes follow. Sitting near him at the head of the table was her squad, her *family*. Shadric's team sat near the end, a few standing at the back of the room. She had yet to figure out which of them shot her that day they were training in Field E, but none of them wanted to admit that they could have easily killed their only chance at freedom.

Not one for patience, Carl leaned forward and asked, "So what's the plan?"

"Other than to get Larken her new title," Levi added.

Larken rolled her eyes at the field-medic and he winked at her.

"We need to see where the Districts stand," Vallen grunted.

"And how are we going to do that?" Ewan asked. Out of all the members on Shadric's team, he was Larken's favorite, if only because he helped her harass his brother.

Vallen looked to her and raised an eyebrow.

"You can't be serious," Soren growled.

"What?" Hinlee asked.

Larken felt the eyes of her squad on her, but she didn't look away from Vallen. She didn't trust herself, and she didn't want to see the way Soren was glaring at her. She might not know the details of Vallen's plan, but she knew that no one in this room wanted her to be involved more than necessary.

"He wants to dangle Larken in front of them."

"Don't say it like that, Deckard," Delvon sighed, the eye roll evident in his voice.

"Of course *you* knew."

Larken's gaze shifted to Delvon as he leaned into the table, both hands pressed flat on the surface. "That's because it's *my job*. When's the last time you stepped out of the training field long enough to be useful, mate?"

"Enough!"

Both men quieted at the tone of Vallen's voice. Delvon sat back in his chair, crossing his arms and running his tongue over his teeth like he so often did. He met her gaze, and Larken glared at him. He glared back, and she could almost hear his, *"He started it."*

She rolled her eyes, wanting nothing more than to light into him again, and then turned her gaze onto Soren. He glared at her as well, and she huffed and crossed her own arms. The two of them had been going at it like a pair of half-starved wolves fighting over a scrap of meat, and Larken was tired of asking them how they would like her to be cooked.

Turning her focus back on Vallen, she said, "Whatever it is, I'll do it."

"Don't say that, Little Bird. What if the plan is to give you back to Braves so you can spy on the enemy?"

"Better Dominic than others," she mumbled. "At least *he* didn't smother me." Larken didn't mean that, but the two warning growls told her that her jab found its mark.

"We aren't *giving* Larken to anyone." Vallen sighed, rubbing at his temples. He looked more like an exasperated nanny than the leader of a group of rebels. "Half the people in this room were raised in the military, the other half grew up in the woods."

"Not true," Carl interjected. He grunted when Candy obviously kicked him under the table.

Vallen continued on like nothing had happened, "We need to infiltrate the District Manors and speak to the Luminaries. We also need to have someone there that knows how to talk to them and won't threaten to tear their arms off if they don't."

Larken wanted to complain, to refuse to go back to that world, but she bit her tongue. Agreeing was the last thing she wanted to do, but even more than that, she wanted to get back at everyone else who had been telling her what to do. Jumping into the line of fire wasn't her first choice, but it wasn't Soren's or Delvon's either.

Larken chanced a glance at Shadric and found him looking intently at the table like it was the most interesting thing in the world. He never told her what she should or shouldn't do, and she suddenly wondered what he thought of Vallen's idea. Did it make him nervous? Would he ask to go with her? Even more than that, she wondered if she even wanted him to. Delvon was right—he was a distraction that she couldn't afford. But was that what she really wanted? She would have let him kiss her earlier, just like she would have let him kiss her all those times before. Larken just didn't know if it was what she really wanted, or if he was the only option she had left.

Vallen cleared his throat and waited for Larken turned her attention back to him before saying, "We will form a set of teams to go to the Districts with Larken, and from there it will be simple. Get her in to get the answers we need, then get her out. No one will know that we were there, and if we do our jobs right, everyone will come back safely."

"Vallen," Larken swallowed as all the eyes in the room turned on her, "what about—" She couldn't say it. *What about my mother?*

Understanding her unspoken worry, he said softly, "Cornella is on the hunt for you, that's no secret. It's also no secret that your deranged *friend* will stop at nothing to find you."

"*Not helping,*" she muttered.

He smirked. "You'd rather we send Delvon to Thresh?"

Larken's own lips twitched. "With his dark hair and sour disposition, I don't think he would be Alex's type." She raised her eyebrow. "Shad would be the better choice."

"Who's Alex?" Hinlee asked.

Larken opened her mouth to answer, but Carl said, "Morgan and Jinora's son."

"Is *he* an ex-fiancé too?" Jodi's sarcastic words were punctuated by a single raised eyebrow. Her chocolate-colored hair had been pulled back into a single braid that rested over her left shoulder, and she still sported that same onyx stud in her nose. Carl had helped strip the dye from her hair, and Larken thought her natural color looked best on her. If Ezra's shy glances were any indication, he thought so as well.

"*No.*" Larken felt her cheeks heat, then mumbled, "Nothing was ever official."

Jodi barked a laugh as Larken's squad exploded with questions. Loxly's voice rose over them all as he demanded, "Why didn't you tell me?"

"Why would I? He's the son of a Luminary, I'm the second child of one. Of course it was talked about."

"What happened?" Hinlee asked.

Larken looked to Vallen, not knowing the answer to the mechanic's question.

"They follow Maxim, so, naturally, Cornella thought it was a poor match."

"That, and she wouldn't want to risk Larken being happy," Levi added under his breath.

"That too," Vallen agreed.

"So, the plan?" Larken asked over the snickers coming from Shadric's team, trying to get back on topic.

"We get you to Thresh, then Gadget, and then Star. Once we know where everyone stands, we'll take our cause straight to the Magnate himself. We're hoping that if we can get enough Luminaries to back you, he will approve the change in leadership."

"And if he doesn't?"

"Then we'll have to get you in power the old-fashioned way," Delvon said, his grin a little too menacing.

"So we'll…what, take him out too?"

"Of course not." Vallen gave her a look that she knew all too well. "We will just have to be extra persuasive. I don't see it being a problem, though. He's a wise man."

"Can't be too smart if he let Cornella talk him into a war," Brecker observed.

"Things were different then. *We* were different then."

"Well, let's hope he had the same change of heart." Larken stood, exhausted. She didn't know what had taken more out of her—the meeting or the spar. "I'll go. Just tell me what I need to say and give me some time."

Larken didn't wait for the meeting to end. She was sure that there would be more arguing on Soren's and Delvon's parts, and she didn't want to deal with it. She would talk to Delvon later when he broke into her bungalow to eat dinner with her, and maybe she would get a chance to talk to Soren at some point, but she wouldn't hold her breath. Delvon was right in that regard: Soren seemed to be living in the training area now. Estelle would be excited to see her at least, and for now, her android pup was all she needed.

# CHAPTER 3

The meeting went on for two more hours, and both Soren and Delvon were eventually asked to leave. Half the time Soren didn't know if he wanted to strangle the man or thank him for stepping in where he had been failing miserably. Soren had promised himself he would be better, but it would seem that old habits died hard. Why reach out and ask Larken how she was feeling when he could go on a three-mile run by himself? Why talk about what happened on the Harpy when he could lose himself around Camp and pretend it never happened? But he knew this time was different. Before, he could count on the fact he would eventually get the chance make things right; now, Larken had *Barlow*.

Seeing the two of them in the tabernacle did something unpleasant to his insides. It was always the same when he saw Barlow with Larken, and Soren found that drowning himself in whatever Mr. Chin brought him to eat was only a temporary fix. Soren honestly didn't know what to do. Hinlee and Brecker would tell him to stop being an idiot and talk to her. Loxly would make a joke, probably along the lines of Soren leaving her alone so he could have a chance. Levi would tell him to think of Larken and do what was best for her, which would most likely involve him leaving her alone. And with how he felt about Delvon, Vallen was the only one left he could ask for advice.

Vallen was *not* an option.

Soren could see it now, him walking back into the conference room and announcing that he had confused feelings towards Larken. Vallen would then tear him apart and throw the pieces across the room.

This was one of those moments Soren almost wished that Larken never joined Squad 19. He hadn't second-guessed himself before she showed up. He also hadn't entertained silly thoughts or got annoying songs stuck in his head.

Soren sighed, thudding to a halt. His chest heaved, and he felt his ragged breaths rather than heard them. He couldn't run without music anymore; his own thoughts were too dangerous. His headphones blared a song he didn't know, but one that was as un-Shadric-like as possible. Sweat beaded at his temples and ran down the side of his face and neck. Running didn't help anymore, either. Nothing did. Shaking his head, Soren wandered from the forest trail and into the tree line. He stomped through bushes and pushed past branches and twigs, only to find his feet sinking into the loose dirt that quickly transitioned into sand.

Pulling the buds from his ears, the music turned from a menacing guitar solo to a high-pitched whine. Soren pulled out his communicator and cut the sound. Soon he was left with nothing but the gentle surf.

He stomped over to the log he had adopted as a bench and fell to it. The worn, sun-bleached wood was too battered to use for anything other than burning or sitting, but it somehow stood day in and day out against the elements. Soren sighed again, his left calf twitching. His body still wanted to move, but he was no longer sure what he was trying to run from. It wasn't Larken, it couldn't be. They had moved on, moved past his letting her go. They had talked. He had *saved* her from a marriage that would have ended in her death. The two of them had reached an understanding. And yet here he was, in this place she would absolutely love, without her. In fact, he didn't even know where she was. She could be at her place, or she could be back with Shadric. All he knew was that she wasn't here.

Soren set his communicator next to him before he crushed it. How many times had he considered bringing her here? How many times had his finger hovered over her name, ready to call her and give her directions to where he was? The answer was too many. But something inside him wouldn't let him. He wasn't stupid. Soren knew that if he shared this place with her, there was no going back.

He closed his eyes, focusing on the sound of the waves gently caressing the shore. Soon, he was back at that beach, standing in the sun and holding Larken close as the salty air surrounded them. She had been so beautiful in that ruined wedding gown, despite the reason she had to wear it. Soren could still feel her under his fingertips as he leaned in to kiss her. Maybe part of him was afraid that if he did bring her here, Loxly would find a way to ruin that, too.

Soren stood, turning back to the woods. Larken had too much to worry about; he really shouldn't be having these thoughts. She needed to focus on the next part of her life and doing anything to sidetrack her would be selfish. Still, that voice in his head couldn't be silenced.

*She won't wait around for you forever.*

Knowing it wouldn't help, Soren returned his headphones to his ears and started running back to camp. He didn't stop until he reached the first bungalow and only took his headphones out when he was once again around people.

Walking through Camp was worlds different than walking through base. Here, people were happy—happier than he knew people could be. They laughed together and cried together. They shared food and prayed for each other. They were open and honest, and they made Soren realize that Maxim wasn't the one truly in control of the base. Cornella was.

"Captain Deckard!"

Soren stopped and turned in the direction he heard his name from. He knew it was Mr. Chin immediately; no one else referred to him by his title. Loxly still affectionately called him *Cap* now and then, but Soren suspected it was more out of habit than anything.

Reaching the Chin's doorstep, Soren asked, "What can I do for you?"

Mr. Chin held up a little plastic tub. "Delvon never showed up like he said he would tonight. I was on my way to Miss Hale's."

Soren's gut twisted. What did it say about them that Mr. Chin assumed that he was on his way to Larken's? He let his mind wander briefly, remembering the words Jing had so carelessly tossed in his face.

*Soren loves her.*

Forcing a smile, Soren reached for the tub. "I can take it."

Mr. Chin offered him a goodnight and asked Soren to give his best to Miss Hale. Soren slowly made his way to Larken's bungalow, wondering what Jing told her father. He knew that she adored Larken, everyone did, but to Jing, it seemed Larken hung the moon. Soren could see her, sitting at dinner with her father, talking about how Larken had worn her hair that day, how she had let her play with Estelle, who she thought Larken should marry. It wasn't too long ago Jing thought it should be Shadric Barlow. Now Loxly often told him that Jing asked Larken awkward questions about *him*. Soren pushed away the thoughts as he knocked at Larken's door. He immediately regretted that he hadn't stopped to freshen up.

*Stop being stupid. She's seen you like this a hundred times before.*

A flash of her jumping into his arms while he was like this crossed his mind as he heard her on the other side of the door. She pulled it open as she said, "Finally! I didn't think you were going to come. Why are you—" Larken's eyes widened when she saw him. "—knocking?"

Soren didn't realize his mouth was hanging open until it was too late. Soft pink cotton shorts hugged her thighs and hips. They were shorter than the ones that haunted his dreams at night and were tied in the front with a haphazard bow. A thin turquoise sweatshirt threatened to swallow her shorts and hung off one shoulder, revealing a white spaghetti strap. She had pulled her hair up in one of those buns that looked like they would fall out any second, and the pearl he had given her hung around her neck, catching the last light of day.

Larken hugged her middle and looked down at her bare feet. Her toes flexed, gripping the fluffy rug in front of her door, and she nibbled on her bottom lip. She looked unsure of herself, and he wanted her to meet his gaze and yell at him instead.

Gaining control over himself, Soren frowned. "Who wouldn't knock before coming into your place?"

Her cheeks went pink and she still refused to meet his eyes. "No one…just, Delvon doesn't usually knock."

Red-hot anger surged through Soren's veins. "Why not?"

"Oh, come on, Soren. It's not like he barges in anytime he wants. My blinds are open so I'm clearly not naked. He isn't some sort of freak."

"Did he just barge into your room at the Manor as well?"

"That's different." Her face went from an embarrassed pink to a heated red. Her eyes narrowed, and Soren finally felt comfortable for the first time since they had started talking. "There were cameras *everywhere!* Anyone could come and go from my room, and it wouldn't matter. Why are you so worried about this now? I seem to remember you sitting in my room a few times I got ready, too."

Her glare softened the slightest bit, and with it, the ice between them started to thaw. Sighing, she rolled her eyes and stood aside, allowing him to come in. In the week they had been there, Soren hadn't been to her place yet, and the first thing he noticed when he walked in was the photo album he had gotten her for her birthday. It sat in the middle of her wall, the focal point that she had arranged all her other photos around. Soren also noticed that the one Vallen had taken of her mooning over Shadric was missing.

"So, what's that?" Larken asked, nodding to the plastic tub in his hands. Her arms were still wrapped around her middle.

"Dinner from Mr. Chin, if you're hungry."

"How did you end up with it?" She raised an eyebrow, clearly waiting to see if he would lie or not.

"I was on my way back from a run when we ran into each other. He was on his way here, assumed that's where I was going, and asked me to bring it with."

Sighing, Larken turned to her little kitchen. She pulled open a drawer and started fishing around in it. "Go ahead and sit down."

Soren didn't need to be told twice and made himself comfortable on her loveseat. He saw Estelle *napping* on her charging port, the little bundle of mechanical energy curled up and looking impossibly adorable. "She'll be finished by the time you go to sleep, right?"

"Yes, *Dad,* but it doesn't matter. I know you idiots have a schedule set up so my place is always being watched."

"And how would you know that?"

"Because you guys are bad at keeping secrets. It's why Delvon breaks in every night and demands I feed him. He's on first watch." Larken finished in the kitchen and plopped down next to him, holding out a spare fork. "But, I guess I scared him off today so he won't be stopping by."

Soren pulled the lid off and accepted the fork. They dug into the mess of meat, sauce, and rice without a word. Soren finished his first bite and asked, "Scared him off?"

Her cheeks went pink again. "It's nothing, just stupid stuff."

"Stupid stuff is the stuff that bothers you the most."

"You won't want to talk about it."

"Try me."

Larken took another bite, chewed slowly like she was buying time, and then swallowed. "I have certain things that will be expected of me if I become a Luminary, and I'm not looking forward to some of my duties."

"*Like?*"

She sighed and let her head fall back against the loveseat. "*Like* who my future Luminar might be."

Soren choked on a piece of chicken.

"See? This is why I don't talk about it!" She looked away, nibbling on the tongs of her fork, and then said, "Delvon was teasing me about it today, so I got him back by threatening to choose him and we haven't talked since."

Soren's voice was a hard rasp. "Is that what you want? To marry Delvon?"

"Of course not!" She rounded on him. "But it's not like I have many options here."

Soren's stomach soured in a way he never wanted it to again. "What does that mean?"

"It means that—" She cut off, eyes going wide like she just now realized who sat on her couch. Her face went past its endearing blush to scarlet mortification. "Nothing, never mind. It's getting late and I have to be up early tomorrow."

It was a lie. They never had training on Saturdays, and Carl insisted on doing all of Larken's laundry so she wouldn't ruin her clothes. She had no plans, but she was clearly done talking about this with him.

Soren stuck his fork into the remnants of their dinner, no longer having an appetite anyway, and stood. His feet stuck to the floor, giving him a moment to say something, anything, but he pulled them free and walked out of her place. She didn't get up, and he closed the door behind him. He heard a noise that sounded like Larken screaming into a pillow and leaned against her door. He closed his eyes, and the voice taunted him once more.

*Told you she wouldn't wait forever…*

# CHAPTER 4

"*It wasn't until the fire had been doused completely that Byron Hillock was found dead in his study with his wife and three sons. The eldest's son's wife, Harriet, had been out shopping that day with their daughter, and the entire fortune will go—*"

"Can I get you anything else, Captain Braves?" the brunette asked, cutting off the reporter. Not that he really heard what the man was saying; Dominic already knew what had happened. After all, he had orchestrated it.

The woman leaned in closer, spilling out of her top in a way that told him how she wished to be of service. He took a long drag from his cigar and pushed his whiskey glass towards her. The ice clinked against itself, barely having had any time to melt. The brunette pouted, jutting her lip out in way she obviously thought was flattering. Dominic had to force himself not to laugh in her face.

She moved behind him, and he heard the stopper of the decanter being pulled. The trickle of whiskey stopped way too soon, and he almost yelled at her to bring the whole thing. It was too much, this waiting and searching. It was getting to him.

The woman made her way back around, and instead of setting his drink next to his ashtray, she sat in his lap and pressed the glass into his chest. Dominic took it, ignoring her hand as it lingered and started playing with his undone buttons, and downed the drink in one swallow. He hissed at the burn and set the glass aside. The woman muttered something, but he wasn't listening. He didn't care. Cornella had thought it funny to parade women in front of him, knowing full well that none of them would hold his interest. Even now, the woman that sat in his lap had been with him for a full three days, and he still didn't know her name. It didn't seem to bother her though as she pressed herself into him, purring like a cat.

"You've been so stressed, Captain. Please, let me help you relax some." She undid one of the remaining buttons, and he took another drag of his cigar.

Letting the blue smoke blow past his lips, he looked her in the eyes. The shade of dull bronze was so different from the teal ones that haunted his dreams at night. This woman wanted him, and she didn't bother trying to hide it. Before, he would have gladly accepted her offer. Now, he could only smirk at her and ask, "What was your name again?"

The woman pulled away, her eyes going wide. Hurt danced across her features, and she awkwardly pulled herself from him. She didn't say anything as she walked over to the door and let herself out. Dominic pushed away the disappointment, enjoying it much more when they caused a scene that Cornella was forced to clean up. She might be the one pulling the strings, but he was the one who had the final say. She needed him, and she knew it.

An hour passed before she barged into his room, and Dominic didn't even look up from his newly poured drink before saying, "You can keep coming back all you want. I already told you I wouldn't be sharing your bed."

"As if I would trade one pathetic drunk for another."

That one stung, and his grip on the glass tightened. How dare she compare him to Trogar. The man had all but abandoned Larken in his need to drink. Dominic would never abandon her, and it was the inability to find her that had driven him to this state in the first place.

"What do you need, Cornella? Did you want to yell at me about the girl?"

"No, I wanted to know why you let Harriet live."

Dominic looked over at Cornella, taking in her black day dress and red heels with his bleary gaze. Hair up in its usual twist, she looked more put together than a woman who just lost her daughter should.

"It was an arranged marriage. She held no loyalties to the family or to Maxim. She's now Base 10's newest sponsor and will report to us if she hears anything regarding the Faithfuls. Doubt she will though; she said the family didn't trust her very much."

Cornella walked over to him and took his drink, finishing it off without so much a twitch of her lips. "My, my, what a soft heart you have. Perhaps that's why my daughter found it so easy to leave you at the altar."

That's how it had been since the wedding. Always *my daughter*, never Larken. Dominic wondered if it had hurt Cornella, or if she was just as unfeeling as she appeared to be. What would it be like, he wondered, if Larken had looked like her? Would Cornella have even known? How would Larken's life be different? Maybe Cornella wouldn't have hated her, maybe Trogar wouldn't have started drinking, or maybe Liam would be the proud big brother that he never had the chance to be. Most importantly though, would Dominic have wanted her?

He fished out another cigar and lit it, telling himself to drink less. There was no way he would want a clone of the evil woman before him. Larken was smart, kind, beautiful—everything Cornella wasn't. He needed to get her back.

"I can see that this conversation is going nowhere. I'll send someone new to help you soon, but as for now," she looked him over one last time, "take a shower."

Cornella left, leaving his door open. She had been right about one thing: this was going nowhere. Either Larken didn't have access to the broadcasts the fires were being reported on, or someone was keeping the information from her. He needed to start changing tactics. The Night of Masks was less than a month away, and they would be making their appearance as husband and wife there just like he had planned.

Pushing himself to his feet, Dominic stumbled to his bathroom. A cold shower would help clear his mind, and then he could start on a new plan for finding his fiancée. He would need to stop thinking about what would get her attention and start thinking about what she would do next. She wouldn't give in to violence, so he could at least rule out any assassination attempts on her part. This also meant she would try to make as many allies as possible in an effort to broker peace.

Dominic now had a new starting point. Not only that, but he had a whole slew of Vigilants to help. He would call a meeting, demanding that anyone who knew anything about the Faithfuls or Larken seek him out. It didn't matter if it was information he already knew. There was a chance that something might be learned, or that something might click into place.

Larken didn't know what she started the day she left, but she would learn soon enough. Dominic Braves wasn't a man to be played with, and Larken had been teasing him for too long. Their time would come, and when it did, Dominic would be ready.

# CHAPTER 5

"I f your mother is going to do something drastic, it will be at the Night of Masks celebration. That's why we have to move fast."

Vallen's words echoed in Larken's mind hours later, through her dreams and through the landing. Larken startled awake on the Harpy, alone and unsure what day it was. Vallen's jacket had been draped over her, and she only noticed it when it fell to the floor in a heap. Her head pounded, and she needed water. This was so different from the last time she had woken up here, and a pang twisted her heart as she pushed away the memory of Soren's warmth. Had he sat with her, holding her close like before? Or had her team given her a bench to herself?

A shiver worked its way from the bottom of her spine to the back of her neck, and she grabbed the jacket. Stuffing her arms into the sleeves, she brushed at the hair that had fallen from her ponytail and into her face. Not bothering to zip up the jacket, Larken pushed to her feet, stumbling as she did. She was forced to reach out for the bench across the aisle so she didn't land on her face.

Needing fresh air, Larken willed her trembling legs to take her to the door. Leaning into the door, she placed her hand on the handle and it opened easier than she thought it would. Larken almost went flying a second time. Her chest heaved as her heart calmed, and a snorting huff caught her attention. Larken's jaw slowly dropped as three faces looked up at her. Their giant brown eyes melted her, and their pink tongues lapped at the black stairs that had sunk into the soft grass. More huffs and snorts sounded as the creatures took her in, as if her mere presence was the cause of their excitement.

Larken's open mouth turned into a grin as she made her way slowly down the top two steps to the calves. They were on her at once, sniffing her and nibbling on the jacket's hem. She laughed, petting them and letting them lick her fingers. Two had standard black and white coloring, but the third was a caramel brown. The smaller of the black and white ones pressed their nose into her thigh and then sneezed against it, leaving a wet spot.

"That means she likes you!" Loxly called. Larken looked up to find him jogging toward her.

"Where are we?" Larken brushed her hair out of her face again, taking a moment to finally look past the calves.

The Harpy sat in the middle of a vast field. There were cows everywhere, some grazing, others napping in the sun. It would seem that the aircraft only interested these three little ones.

"My farm." Loxly held out a hand for her, and she let him help her down the rest of the steps. He had to nudge the calves out of the way a few times, and they followed closely behind them. "We figured that this would be the best place to get you ready for your hot date."

"Morgan is a married man and very much *still alive.*" Larken reminded him. "I highly doubt I'll even see Alex while I'm there."

"Trust me, Little Bird, he'll know you're there. He'll be able to tell."

"And how could you possibly know that?"

"Because I always know where you are too." He grinned. "Don't see Levi out here, do you?"

Larken scoffed and rolled her eyes. "I'm willing to bet every single token in my suspended account that your Dad sent you out here before asking for volunteers to come check on me."

Loxly brushed away her words with a hand, then reached out

and pulled her close. "Watch your step. Don't think Carl will take too kindly to you ruinin' your boots."

They bickered all the way back to Loxly's home. Larken went quiet when she saw it. High walls, peeling yellow paint, and a giant wrap-around porch. It looked too perfect to be real, and Larken was suddenly afraid to go in. She didn't want to taint it with whatever brokenness clung to her, like just stepping foot inside would cause a rift between her best friend and his father.

"It's just a house, Larken. Nothin' to be scared of," Loxly teased, picking up on her unease. "Dad's excited to see you again. He wants to hear all about Estelle."

"Loxly…"

They stopped, and Loxly turned to face her. Larken realized the calves had broken away at some point, and she wanted to go back and find them. They wouldn't expect her to be someone she wasn't and would be perfectly content with snacks and kisses. Loxly bent forward just enough to look her in the eyes, and she didn't hesitate to reach out and brush his hair out of his.

"You should really let Hinlee or Carl cut your hair."

"You shouldn't change the subject."

"What do you want me to do, Loxly?" She dropped her gaze. "The last time I saw your dad, it was a disaster." Heat rushed to her cheeks at the memory of running to her room on visitor's day because Vallen wasn't allowed to visit, and Soren finding her. He held her as she sobbed, as she asked him why her mother hated her. A rush of emotion too complicated to figure out right now washed over her and Larken regretted not zipping up the jacket.

"That's not how he remembers it." Loxly pulled her in for a hug. "He still talks about that pot roast, you know. Thought it was as good as the one Gran used to make."

"I was a mess, Loxly. I'm *still* a mess."

"We're all a little messy; it's part of life. You aren't gonna ruin everythin' just by bein' here. You gotta stop actin' like you are."

Larken sighed. "Are you sure I can't just stay here and hang out with my new friends?"

"Not if you don't want Carl to have a heart attack."

Larken gave Loxly a tight squeeze before pulling away. "If your house suddenly catches fire, you aren't allowed to blame me. I tried warning you."

"Noted."

A knot pitted Larken's stomach as Loxly stepped behind her and gently pushed her to the porch. The wood used for the steps creaked under their weight, and a cat leapt off a porch swing to wrap around Loxly's feet. Sidestepping with a grace Larken never knew he had, he managed to open the screen door for her.

He grinned wickedly before shouting, "Pa, I found another stray! Can we keep her? She's mighty purdy!"

"Stop acting like an idiot and get in here!" boomed Rich.

Hinlee's laugh rose above the others, and Larken felt a little more at ease.

When she didn't move, Loxly grabbed her hand and pulled her into the house. "Hope y'all saved some of that lemonade for Larken."

She barely got a glance of the yellow and crimson wallpaper in the halls, or a peek up the worn-looking staircase, before she stumbled into the sitting room with Loxly. He quickly abandoned her, falling into a faded purple armchair that looked to be molded to his body. After a quick scan of the room, Larken found the only open seat was a spot barely big enough for her between the arm of a floral-printed couch and a grumpy-looking Soren. She would practically be sitting in his lap, and she suddenly realized that she wanted to be as far away from him as possible. Larken glared at Loxly, and he smirked as he quirked an eyebrow. She could hear his silent, *"You could sit in my lap instead, Little Bird."*

Narrowing her eyes further, she stomped over to Soren just to spite the sharpshooter. But, as soon as she was nestled against him, Larken couldn't help but feel like she was the one losing. She wasn't proving anything, and she felt the parts of herself that she had hidden away seeping out at being so near him again. Levi complained about the amount of room, and Soren was left with no choice but to drape his arm around her so the three of them could sit comfortably on the loveseat. Larken shot a look at the field-medic and grimaced when she caught his smirk. It seemed like they were all out to get her.

Carl leaned in his armchair towards her, offering a pink-tinted plastic cup nearly filled to the brim. She wrapped her fingers around the base as he gasped and demanded, "That better be sweat on your jeans!"

"Tangerine sneezed on her," Loxly said, taking a gulp from a green cup.

"That means she likes you," Rich added, repeating his son's words.

"Larken does seem to have a way with drooling livestock," Carl agreed. "And cute animals."

Levi and Brecker chuckled at the jab toward Larken's romantic life, and Loxly snorted into his drink. Even Hinlee failed to not look amused, but she at least had the decency to avoid Larken's eyes while she hid a small giggle. Soren stiffened ever so slightly next to her, and she was once again reminded of their conversation in the Harpy.

*You don't know how worried I was.*

His words, the hurt in his eyes when he thought he had lost her, they were harder to forget when pressed this close to him. Then Larken realized how unfair she had been to him. He was avoiding her, it was no secret, but that wasn't why he spent every waking moment training. He did it for her, to make sure that she would never be given to Dominic again. Larken leaned in, pressing herself closer. Slowly, the tension eased out of him and he was able to relax as much as he knew how.

Needing to distract herself, she brought her glass to her lips. She could already taste the tartness as an ice cube brushed the tip of her nose. Holding her breath, she didn't stop drinking until the bitter taste of the chamomile extract was no longer in her mouth. Rich wordlessly passed the pitcher to Hinlee, who continued handing it off. Soren took it from Levi, filling her cup to the brim again.

Conversation continued around them, so Larken mumbled, "How bad was it this time?"

"You didn't dance or try to strip, if that's what you're asking."

"Very funny."

"You were fine. You asked Hinlee if she could braid your hair later, and if Levi could make you some fancy cheese and dill soup—"

"Havarti?"

Soren nodded. "But other than that, nothing too bad."

He seemed to hesitate, and Larken felt an unwanted chill settle in her stomach. "What?"

"Nothing, you were just talking a little in your sleep. No one heard you."

"But you did?" That coldness spread, turning her stomach to ice.

His lips twitched, and for a moment he was the old Soren, the one that she had been stolen from all those weeks ago. "You were using my lap as a pillow."

"*I was not,*" she gasped.

"It wasn't my idea; you're the one who sat next to me."

"And you couldn't pawn me off on Hinlee?"

"I couldn't. You said her legs were too boney to make good pillows. She wouldn't have let you, anyways."

Larken took another long drink, not knowing if she wanted to ask the next question that burned her tongue. In the end though, the heat became too much. "What did I say?"

Soren cleared his throat softly, then said, "You asked me if there was a chance the extract would keep you from waking up."

"*And?*"

"*And* if it did, you asked me to kiss you and break the spell like in the old stories."

The block of ice that sat where her stomach should have been cracked and then turned to dust. She looked anywhere but at him, not seeing anything, and mumbled, "Well, if you'll excuse me...I need to ask Loxly to take me out to the pasture and shoot me."

Soren's façade broke, and he laughed softly. He moved his arm from the back of the couch and pulled her closer. The wall that had been built between them since their last conversation came crumbling down, leaving the two of them to be themselves again. Only then did Larken notice the collective breath everyone in the room had been holding. With its release, Larken brought her lemonade to her lips once more and took another sip. She could see Loxly's smug look over the brim.

Rich pulled Larken into a conversation while Loxly gave Carl a hard time about getting his shoes dirty. Rich asked about Estelle, and Larken gladly told him everything he wanted to know, from the temperament she programmed to the color eyes she picked out. Hinlee and Levi both added things they thought were important as well. Even Soren commended Rich, explaining about the security camera that Vallen was excited about.

Larken looked around the sitting room, feeling at home with her squad. It was only right that they were the ones to come with her this time. It was their first mission, and they were visiting Rich. It wouldn't have been fair to bring anyone who wasn't on Squad 19 along. Larken wouldn't have felt right catching up with Rich while the others couldn't. Delvon hadn't liked it, but he had relented once Vallen talked to him.

Something buzzed against Larken's right thigh, and an awkward shuffle followed as Soren pulled out his communicator. Larken peeked at the screen, but she wasn't fast enough to see who had messaged him.

Soren leaned into her and murmured, "You should let Fisher know you're safe. He's worried about you."

Larken lifted her hips so she could pull out her own device. She opened the messaging screen and then stared at it blankly. What should she say? How much should she tell him? She typed something out, thought better of it, and then deleted it. Larken repeated the process twice more before looking up at Soren.

"Just tell him we made it here."

"But what if that isn't enough? I don't want him to worry about me, but I don't want to tell him something he doesn't care about."

Soren offered a small twitch of his lips. "Trust me, he'll be interested in whatever you have to tell him."

"How do you know that?" she narrowed her eyes at him, wondering for the first time what kind of relationship he had with her biological father.

"Because we've talked about it."

Larken didn't know if she should be happy that the two were talking or hurt. Did Fisher think he couldn't talk to her? She thought their relationship had changed since the theater, that he was testing the waters like she was. But if he was reaching out to Soren instead, maybe he didn't want a relationship with her after all.

"Don't do that," Soren ordered. "It isn't like that and you know it."

Larken looked away, hating that he could read her thoughts just by looking into her eyes. "Do what?"

"He wants to be in your life. He just doesn't want to push you into something you aren't ready for."

"So, the Camp…"

"He reached out to me after you met up with him at the theatre. He wanted to help keep you safe from—" Soren's gaze dropped for a second, but he didn't need to mention her mother's name. "I told him that we were moving you, and he wanted to come, no matter where it was."

Larken nodded, unable to speak past the lump in her throat. If she didn't know what to say before, now she worried she wouldn't remember how to type. Taking a deep breath, she wrote a simple message, letting Fisher decide what to do next.

*We made it safely to the farm. Didn't embarrass myself too badly on the way. Hope you have a good day.*

It only took a moment for her to get a reply.

*I probably won't breathe easy until you're back. Glad you're safe. Don't feel too bad about the flying, it runs in the family. At least you have a good reason for it.*

Larken smiled. She typed out a reply, and Soren tightened his arm around her for the briefest second. He didn't have to say he told her so, and she was glad he had been right. They melted seamlessly back into the little conversations around them, not saying another word to each other. They didn't have to, though. Something broken between them had been fixed, and Larken felt the twist she hadn't known was in her stomach ease.

# CHAPTER 6

"I'm not leavin', Lox, and that's final."

Larken paused on the stairs, knowing she shouldn't be listening but unsure what else to do. Hinlee was still in the bathroom, and Larken was practically dancing where she stood.

"Come on, Dad, what're you gonna gain here? Come back with us," Loxly pleaded.

She should turn back and take her chances. Larken didn't want Loxly to get the wrong idea if he found her there. They had barely come up with a plan before Rich pulled her and Levi into the kitchen with him to help with dinner. But what was there to plan? They just needed to get her in front of Morgan. They had no inside information on how his security was set up, and they only had Larken's vague memories of what the Thresh Manor looked like.

"Maxim has kept me safe this far. It's pointless to try and do somethin' 'bout it now. I could die tomorrow, or ten years from now. Only Maxim knows. Me leavin' won't change that. It'll only show my doubt in Him."

"Dad, that's not true." Larken slowly turned and moved up a step. It creaked, stopping her heart. Loxly took a few steps back and looked at her. Instead of the anger she expected to see, his brown eyes begged. "Tell him, Little Bird."

"Oh, um—" She looked at Loxly, her heart beating faster now than it had after the step creaked. "I have to pee."

Loxly sighed, smiling sadly. He shook his head, like he was wondering what he had expected by asking for her help. Waving a hand, he waited for her to come down the stairs and led her to the bathroom. Larken locked herself inside and turned the faucet on. She didn't want to hear what they might be saying.

Once she finished, she crept back out. Loxly was nowhere to be found, but Rich was waiting for her. He leaned lazily against the stairwell, his hands in the pockets of his worn jeans. He offered her a friendly smile.

Neither of them said anything for a minute, and Larken tugged awkwardly at her sleep shorts. Finally, he broke the silence by asking, "Keep an eye on him, will ya?"

Larken nodded, wrapping her arms around her middle.

"He means well, but what'll happen when this is all over and he doesn't have a Camp or a base to return to? I need to stay here, keep this place runnin'."

Her stomach tightened. "How can you be so sure?"

"That things'll work out?" He waited to answer until Larken met his gaze. The corners of his eyes crinkled the same way Loxly's did. "I've been around for a while. I don't need some fancy device to tell me the exact moment the seasons are gonna change, and I don't need to be a genius to know you're made of the same stuff. You're gonna change things, Larken. And with Maxim with you, you won't lose."

Larken couldn't speak. He said the same thing everyone else had been telling her, but in a way that was completely different from anything she had heard before. Could it be possible? Could she be like a season, changing everything so drastically that there was no going back, no avoiding it? Her knees threatened to buckle, and Rich offered her a warm goodnight before heading up the stairs.

She waited until she heard his door close, and then bolted up the steps herself. Her heart pounded in her throat—*her ears*. It was too much. Too much pressure, too much change, too much sitting on her shoulders. She pulled open her door and stepped inside. Forcing herself not to slam it, she fell against the wood and slid to the floor. Someone shot up out of bed and rushed to her. The scent of leather and freshly tilled earth told her it wasn't Hinlee and that she was in the wrong room. She tried to get up and leave, but her limbs shook too badly.

"What happened?" Soren demanded.

"It's too much," she rasped. "I can't do it. We have to go back; they need to pick someone else."

Soren sighed, dropping from his crouch to the floor next to her. He leaned against the door as well and pulled her close. Memories of the garden, the night in the medic-building, and the Harpy had her turning her face into his collarbone. He was dressed for bed and didn't have a shirt. His bare skin and body heat almost burned her, but she didn't care. She needed to be closer, to feel him here in this moment.

Soren gave in to her wordless request and pulled her onto his lap. He wrapped his arms around her tightly, and she only realized she was crying when his skin became slick with her tears. He rested his cheek against the top of her head, her hair clinging to his stubble like velcro.

Before, Soren would have let her work out what she needed to on her own. Now he asked, "Why is it too much?"

"How can I change everything when I don't know what I'm doing? I feel—" How did she feel? Confused? Lost? *Alone?* Her breath hitched, and Soren didn't press her to continue.

"Did you know what you were doing when you waltzed into Base 14, barefoot and scared?"

It was a stupid question that he already knew the answer to. "You know I didn't, as much as I pretended otherwise."

"And somehow, you managed to ruin every single one of our lives with your music and your stubbornness."

Larken sniffed back a few tears. "Ruin, huh?"

Soren put a finger under her chin and brought her face up so she would meet his eyes. They burned a deep green in the darkness that almost made her shiver. She was aware of every spot his bare skin touched hers. Part of her wished for Vallen's jacket to cover her bare arms, but the other part only wanted to melt back into Soren's embrace.

"Yeah, *ruin*." He moved his hand, cupping her jaw and brushing his thumb over her cheek. "What makes you think that this will be any different?"

"It's just...so much bigger this time. It's not just your life I'm *ruining* this time. It's all of Koraythea. What if I mess up?"

"I promise you can't do worse than start a war against Maxim."

The comment would have hurt coming from anyone else, but Larken found herself smiling. Here in this room, Larken wasn't the girl with the insane, bloodthirsty mother or crazy ex-fiancé. She was Larken Hale of Squad 19, just like Soren said. In that garden, he told her who her family was and where she came from hadn't mattered. But here, in this bedroom, she didn't want to think about any of that. She wanted to know what this man thought of her.

What he really thought of her.

As if reading her mind, Soren's thumb slowed to a stop and his eyes heated. The smell of his skin surrounded her, enveloping her in a way she never knew she craved. His gaze fell to her lips, and her breath caught. She had been here before, too many times. And each time, nothing happened. It was different with Soren than it was with Shadric. With Shadric, she felt cherished, but with Soren, she felt safe. Safe in a way she never thought possible. Not only that, but she felt *desired*.

Larken tried to wet her bottom lip, but her mouth felt too dry. Soren followed her tongue with his eyes, his own lips parting slightly. Suddenly their breathing went from a barely-there quiet to the only sound Larken could hear. Soren slipped his hand from her cheek to the back of her neck. He pulled her in, not giving her a chance to back away. He knew as well as she did this unspoken desire between them. Larken sighed and let her eyes close. She didn't have the nervousness she had with Shadric, only the burning anticipation. Their lips barely touched when the door thudded into Soren's back, causing his forehead to bump into hers.

"Hey, Cap? When I said you could use my room, I really meant *share* my room." Loxly tried to get in again, and Soren let his head fall to Larken's shoulder. He laughed bitterly, and she couldn't help but join in.

"How many times does that make?" she asked.

"Too many."

"Cap?" Loxly knocked on the other side of the door.

Grumbling, Soren got to his feet and helped Larken up. "If your shoulder's sore in the morning, Jodi gave a muscle relaxer to Levi. You just have to ask him."

Larken smirked. "You sure you don't want to do it?"

He didn't look at her as he opened the door for Loxly, turning her smirk into a smile. The sharpshoot glanced between the two of them, ears going pink. Larken patted Loxly on the chest as she walked past him and went into her own room. She would leave it to Soren to either explain or let him assume what he would. Soren had been right; Loxly had interrupted them too many times now. She just hoped that if Soren did decide to talk to him, that Loxly's habit of interrupting would soon come to an end.

# CHAPTER 7

Soren still considered reaching over and strangling Loxly as he maneuvered the hovercraft through the streets of the District. Loxly had apologized profusely the night before, more embarrassed at catching them than Soren was at being caught. He told his friend not to worry about it, that he was used to it by now. Loxly, the idiot, had no idea what he had meant. The sharpshooter still wouldn't meet Soren's eyes, and he didn't tease Larken about it like he should have. It was as if the whole squad knew that there was something between the two of them and didn't want to risk ruining it.

*Ruin…*

That was how he described meeting Larken. That she *ruined* his life, as if that were at all possible. She had turned his life upside down and somehow nothing made sense when she wasn't around. Even now, when she was only a hover away, Soren felt antsy in a way that made Loxly's skinny neck look like the perfect distraction.

"Are we sure this is going to work?" Brecker asked.

"No," Hinlee offered simply, adjusting his bottle-green bowtie.

Larken had helped Loxly with his before they set out that morning, but Soren's still hung undone around his collar. It matched the vests and socks perfectly, playing off the cream-colored shirts and grey dress pants. Carl had pulled a few strings to get them each a uniform. They should be able to sneak in with the morning shift unless something went horribly wrong.

They all agreed they probably wouldn't be able to use this plan again, especially once word got out that Larken visited Luminary Morgan, but they would think about that later. For now, Soren had to pray that Carl would keep his promise and make it so Larken wasn't instantly recognizable. Though, how he would do that without hair dye or colored lenses, Soren had no idea.

Soren found himself looking in the review mirror again, watching the hover behind them. Even from where he was, he could see Levi frowning. He hated that he'd been forced behind the wheel. Soren caught occasional glimpses of wheat-colored hair and a cream-colored sleeve.

Thankfully, the Thresh Manor uniform used flats, otherwise Larken would be tripping over herself the whole time. Hinlee had been disappointed, never really getting the chance to wear heels before. Larken had assured her that she wasn't missing much, but Hinlee still seemed a little put out by it.

"What do ya think he's doin' to her?" Loxly asked, forcing Soren to pull his gaze from the mirror.

"I don't know," Hinlee answered, now messing with Brecker's hair. "But I looked into some of Carl's old clients way back when he was getting Larken ready for the opera. I think it'll be fine."

"That makes one of us," Brecker said, pushing Hinlee's hands away and moving out of her reach.

Hinlee huffed and crossed her arms. "Well, we aren't trying to make her look like someone else. Luminary Morgan needs to be able to recognize her. Carl is just making it so someone who doesn't know her as well as us will have to think twice about it."

"That's true," Loxly agreed, moving behind a line of matching brown hovercrafts.

"Do the other staff members drive themselves, or are they brought in?" Brecker asked. He grabbed the headrests of Loxly's and Soren's seats and leaned forward to try and get a look.

"Not sure." Loxly paused a moment and then added, "Some of

them have to drive themselves, right? A Luminary wouldn't pay to have *all* of his staff chauffeured."

"I don't know," Hinlee mused, leaning forward as well. She stuck her hand under Brecker's arm and pointed. "It doesn't look like any of the drivers are getting out."

They stared at where the mechanic pointed, and sure enough, all the hovers were slowing at a gate. Two to four staff members got out and started walking down the drive, pausing only to show what Soren assumed was an ID.

"Fiddlesticks," Loxly cursed. He fished for his communicator and a second later, Larken's voice sounded on the other side.

"What?"

"We need a Plan B. *Now.* All the staff members are hitchin' rides, and it looks like they have to show an ID at the gate."

"Grant didn't say anything about chauffeurs when I asked about the hovercrafts," Carl said defensively, like they were all about to blame him.

"Well, your buddies with the uniforms also didn't mention an ID," Brecker said, his jaw set. His eyes moved over the gate that they would soon approach, already looking for a way to sneak in.

"We're going to have to find another way," Larken insisted. "Take that road up ahead, don't get in line. Maybe we'll luck out and people won't think anything about the brown hovers."

"Seems weird, don't it?" Loxly asked, taking the turn Larken indicated. "Why wouldn't Carl's friend say anythin' when he specifically asked about the hovers Thresh Manor staff might use?"

"Don't ask me," Carl barked through the device. "I told Candy we couldn't trust him. This whole thing is probably ruined now."

"Why?" Soren demanded, grabbing the communicator from Loxly. If he had put Larken at risk, intentionally or not, Soren would break him in half.

"We were here for some harvest festival a few years back. I had to ride with my client, so Candy had to find her own way. This Grant guy ended up seeing her there and said if she ever *needed anything* to look him up." The way Carl said *needed anything* made it sound like Grant had more in mind than a discounted hover ride.

"So now we get found out because some guy wants you to suffer." Levi's statement was distant but could still be heard.

"This isn't helping," Larken reminded them, her voice taking on a Vallen-like authority. "We need a plan, and fast."

"We'll have to hop the fence; there's no way around it," Brecker said. "We don't have IDs and we can't be stopped for questioning. They'll know who you are."

"We can't just *hop the fence*," Levi argued. "What happens when a drone flies by and sees seven people crawling over the gate? It won't work and will be even more suspicious looking."

"What about garbage?" Larken asked distractedly.

"No, we have to pay a cleanin' fee if we leave anythin' behind in the hovers. We can't hide the hovers in garbage." Loxly coasted to a stop, and their group spilled from the hovercraft.

Levi docked next to them, and Larken and Carl jumped out of theirs as well. Larken walked over to Soren, reached up, and started tying his bowtie. Her hair had been pulled back into an elegant bun, and the makeup Carl had used seemed to dull her features. Her big, bright teal eyes looked tarnished, and her cheeks were rosier than usual. Carl had used a dark but professional color on her lips, pulling the attention away from her eyes.

"I don't mean we trash the hovers, Loxly." She gave Soren's bowtie a final tug and then ran her fingers down his vest, smoothing out the creases. Larken turned to the sharpshooter and crossed her arms. "Vallen told me once a long time ago that the best way to break into the Manor would be through the garbage entrance. No one cares about the person clearing away the Manor waste."

"That," Hinlee added, "and it would be hard to get rid of something suspicious if it was being watched."

"Exactly." Larken's eyes beamed. "I don't see why it would be any different here."

"Only one problem," Soren said, moving closer behind her. "We don't know where that is."

"We don't know where it is *yet*." Carl walked away, pulling out his communicator as he did.

While he was occupied, Hinlee turned on Larken, grabbing her hands and pulling them out. "Look at you! I wish I could pull this off as well as you."

Larken blushed. "I don't look that good. I feel like an over-done barmaid in a bad net drama."

Soren silently disagreed. He thought the knee-high bottle-green socks made Larken's legs look long and feminine. The skirt hit mid-thigh and poofed out around her hips. The bottom half of the long vest she wore rested on top of the skirt, nearly sticking straight out. The sleeves of the dress ended at her wrists, hiding her arms completely, but cut off just under her shoulder. The vest was the same color as the socks and wrapped its way around Larken's neck, covering only her spine. The uniform left the tops of her shoulders bare and instantly reminded Soren how soft her skin was.

He wanted to pull her away and ask about her shoulder, and if she had needed Levi's help with it this morning. Soren hadn't gotten the chance before. From the moment Carl turned on the lights in Loxly's room, demanding a shower and shave from all of them, Soren had been on the move. Somehow, Carl had gotten his hands on seven uniforms that fit every single one of them perfectly, just like he promised he could. The uniforms also had a few pockets they could hide small knives or firearms in without being too suspicious, though Larken didn't think they would need to utilize any of them. Then it was a blur of getting ready, being stuffed into a hover, and thinking about all the ways this could go wrong.

Carl walked back over. "Candy says it's about a mile north. We enter through the garden and then take a left turn. Then we just follow the cobblestone instead of the dirt."

"Right." Loxly used his communicator to pull up a street map. "Let's go. Don't wanna keep Alex waitin'."

Larken blinked as if it took a second to realize that Loxly was back to teasing her, and then smacked him in the chest with the back of her hand.

# CHAPTER 8

They walked in relative silence, Larken chafing her arms every now and then. Soren stayed as close to her as he would allow himself, wishing that he had a jacket or something to give her. She always seemed to be freezing, no matter what the temperature outside was. Only during a workout did she ever complain about being too hot. It was a quality that he found both endearing and incredibly annoying.

Larken brought her hands up again, wrapping her arms around herself to suppress a shiver. She failed, and he asked, "Can you stop?"

She turned her gaze on him, that spark of a challenge in her eye. "I seem to remember telling you that I don't stay as warm as you." She smirked before adding, "Macho toes or otherwise."

Soren's lips twitched at the memory of their first real day together. He had tried to belittle her for wanting to order a rug. Now, if they were back at base, he would give her whatever she wanted. She could rip everything out of the dorm and style it however she pleased, just as long as they could stay together. Soren couldn't lose her again...not when it had almost destroyed him.

Reaching out, he pulled her to his side. He let one hand rest on her bicep, and he could feel her warmth even through his vest. Her cheeks turned a pleasant shade of pink, and Loxly must have decided the previous night was enough for him because he moved all the way to the other side of the group. Soren didn't really care. It was a nice change, walking next to Larken instead of behind her. Soren certainly hadn't minded the view it afforded him, but there was something about being able to look down and see her there. He thought of the last time they had been like this, and his communicator burned in his pocket, reminding him of the picture saved on it that shouldn't be.

Larken eventually relaxed enough to start up a conversation that almost didn't sound forced. It would seem that she was either remembering the opera as well, or actively trying not to think about the night before. But it didn't matter. Soren would never bring something like that up in public. What happened between him and Larken stayed between him and Larken.

Eventually, the gate came into view, and Larken stiffened as the scent of roses danced on the breeze. Soren couldn't blame her and offered her an encouraging squeeze. Roses were common enough flowers, and just the scent alone didn't mean that the Thresh District had ties to the Vigilants. At least, that's what Soren kept telling himself until they reached the gate and made it through. Only when they took the left path and saw the barely contained blooms of pink and white did Larken's back muscles relax. Even Soren felt some of his own tension ease. They still had the risk of sneaking in and cornering the Luminary, but the fact that he didn't grow yellow roses in his garden seemed to have everyone breathing a little easier.

The seven of them followed the path, moving through the gardens and watching as the roses slowly turned into irises, and then into daffodils. Soren had no idea if any of the flowers were in season, but Carl's comment about being rich enough to control when flowers grew had him doubtful. Aside from that, the garden was the most magnificent that Soren had ever seen, even more so than the one he had walked through to get to the opera. Loxly started up a hushed conversation with Carl about the types of fertilizer that the Manor most likely used, and Soren learned that Candy had started a small garden behind Carl's bungalow.

Larken's breathing changed, fast enough that Soren noticed her growing apprehension. The group approached a green door the same shade as their uniforms. Larken stopped, hugging her middle.

Soren turned to her, grabbing her arms and squeezing them gently. She met his eyes, her teal ones unsure and scared. "What do I do?" she asked, her voice a strained whisper.

"You go in there and make them listen, just like you would if it were me."

Her lips twitched and she huffed a nervous laugh. "I don't think they would side with us if things got physical."

"Yeah, please don't beat the Luminary into submission," Carl called behind them.

Soren allowed himself a small smile. "You can do this."

Larken sighed, looking away. He wished he could take some of the load she thought she had to carry herself. Soren would do whatever he could to make this easier for her, to help her realize that she wasn't alone.

"I guess it's now or never."

"That's the spirit," Levi muttered. "Let's go start a revolution since we don't have anything better to do today."

Larken looked around Soren to Levi, grinning. "Maybe we can stop for ice cream on the way home too."

Levi chuckled and opened the door. A waft of warm air blew out their way, and that seemed to be the only reason Larken needed to walk into the Manor. They piled into the little room, Brecker shutting them in. Larken shivered and made a disgruntled noise as she did. Loxly teased her, and then they all looked to Carl.

The stylist messed around on his communicator for a moment before glancing up at Larken. When he caught her staring, he looked at the rest of them. "What?"

"Where are we supposed to go?" Hinlee asked, messing with the hem of her skirt.

"How am I supposed to know? I've never been here before."

"Fantastic," Brecker muttered. He flicked his eyes to Larken, a silent question there they could all hear.

"I've been here *maybe* three times."

"So we're basically lost," Loxly stated.

"No." Larken's back stiffened, and her eyes took on that look she always had when she thought she was disappointing everyone. "We can figure this out. I kinda remember my way around. We just have to find the front entrance."

"Is there a floor plan we could look at?" Levi asked Carl.

"No, all of that information is classified to prevent assassinations. Unless one of you is a master hacker that I don't know about."

"Master hacker…" Larken repeated, staring off into the distance for a moment. She fished her communicator out of her vest and placed it to her ear after tapping it a few times. A muffled grumble sounded from the device and she retorted, "Good morning to you too, babe."

Soren fought his eye roll.

More grumbles came through and then Larken explained what was happening. A single vibration sounded from her device and then Larken grimaced as she pulled the communicator from her ear. Scoffing, she muttered, "Thanks for the help."

Larken held her communicator down in front of her. Everyone crowded in around the device, wanting to get a good look. Hinlee was pulled in front of Brecker, and he wrapped his arms around her before resting his chin on the top of her head. Carl offered an apology as he bumped into Larken. She stumbled, unsurprisingly, and Soren put a hand on her lower back to steady her. He stepped in as well, looking over her shoulder at the floor plans she had pulled up on the device. Only when his thumb started brushing across her vest did he realize that he hadn't moved his hand away. But now that it was there, he didn't intend to.

They decided to split into groups, moving around the honeycomb floor plan and hopefully cutting off the Luminary in his conference room. It was their best bet since that was where Cornella spent her days. It was decided that Carl would go with Brecker and

Hinlee. Loxly and Levi would set out together shortly after them, leaving Soren and Larken to make their way there together. The two of them had the quickest route and would have to hang back for a few minutes.

Larken sent copies of the Manor layout to Carl and Loxly with strict instructions not to use them if they could help it. She didn't want them to get in trouble when they were supposed to pretend to be Manor staff. None of the staff members at the Military District Manor ever looked at their devices on the grounds, and there was no telling what would happen if one of them were caught. They could be just as easily admonished as fired and removed from the premises.

Larken wrapped her arms around her middle, and Soren pulled her closer. He didn't say anything, just gave her silent assurance as they waited. Either they would succeed, or they would fail. There was no use worrying about it until they learned which it would be. It would only distract them and make it easier to slip up.

In the quiet moments, Soren thought not of the night before, but of the conversation they had about the future Luminar. He didn't want to, but horrible images of a married Larken danced in his mind, taunting him. Things were starting to move fast again, and as he held her, he panicked. Soren was standing there in his mind, watching Larken ask him to be honest with her again, wanting him to tell her to stay. His heartbeat picked up, telling him to leave. He shouldn't be offering her comfort like this; he shouldn't be letting her get close to him when he knew that he wasn't an option. Soren wasn't that kind of man. He wasn't ready to offer her what she needed. He was good at distracting her, but that wasn't the kind of person she would need...and he didn't know if he was capable of more.

Her arms let go of her middle and her hand traced its way from his elbow to his hand. Even through his shirt, he could feel the heat of her skin, and even though he knew he shouldn't, he entwined his fingers with hers. She looked up at him, hopeful and ready to leave. Without thinking, he cupped her cheek and she leaned into his touch. Her eyes fell closed for a moment, taking the feeling of him in, and he knew that he couldn't just give her up, either.

"We should go," she whispered, eyes still closed.

"We should," he agreed instead of saying any of the other things that burned his tongue. There would be time later, either at the Camp or in a cell.

She stepped out of his grasp but still held his fingers until they walked through the door. A polished pine floor and dark walls the color of tilled soil greeted them with. A pleasant aroma clung to the air, smelling like a mix of fresh vegetables and other vegetation. Giant windows showed off the outside world, giving Soren the feeling of standing in a greenhouse. It was leaps and bounds different from the cold and sterile Military Manor. Larken's eyes roamed over everything, and she breathed out a sigh. Soren was grateful for the calming interior of the Manor since he knew she was still nervous about messing up.

He fought not to take her hand in his again and instead set off in the direction that they had agreed on. Their footsteps were the only sounds, and they seemed to be the only ones around. It made Soren both relieved and wary. Every turn they took, every door they passed, they should have seen some sign of life. Cornella had a strict policy on the staff staying out of sight, but their presence was still felt, their work still seen. This place seemed almost too quiet.

Larken started to get nervous again and wrung her fingers. Soren adjusted his gait, moving to walk as close to her as he possibly could.

Without looking at her, he asked, "Which one do you like better?"

"This one, obviously."

His gaze flicked to her, and she took her bottom lip in between her teeth. He looked ahead. "What are your redecorating plans?"

"Get rid of the white tile. I felt like I could never hide growing up."

"Will you need to hide anymore?"

He felt her sneak a peek at him. "Depends on who my security team is."

Soren grunted. "I would hide from Loxly too."

Larken snorted just as a door opened and she collided with someone. She gasped and Soren watched as a pair of strong arms caught her.

"I'm so—" Larken's voice cut off with a squeak as she tried to take a step back.

The massive redhead tightened his grip on her, and Soren's muscles tensed. But he couldn't even get single step closer to her before the man's face broke into a crooked smile.

"Hey, Larken."

"A-Alex," Larken breathed, color flooding her cheeks.

Soren's stomach tightened in the worst possible way as the man's eyes roamed over Larken appreciatively.

"What're you doin' here? And why are you dressed as a staff member?" Alex asked, his crooked smile turning into a charming grin. "Come to see me?"

"I—I, well..." Larken trailed off, her confidence growing smaller with her voice.

Alex seemed to think that it was him that was causing this reaction, not the fear of being caught, and moved a hand from her waist to her cheek. Soren envisioned slowly breaking every single one of his fingers as the man said, "I've been worried about you since you disappeared. Dad said that you might show up, lookin' for help. Don't worry, you're safe with me."

Soren had enough of sweet-talking men from Thresh trying to flirt with Larken. He cleared his throat, and the two of them looked his way. Larken's eyes held a silent cry for help, whereas Alex's widened in confusion.

"Did you bring friends?" Alex grimaced. "Shoot, I should have said sooner..." Larken looked back at him. "I'm so sorry about General Maxwell."

Larken's lips parted and the only thing that came out was another squeak. Soren sighed and stepped forward, pulling her to his side. She went willingly, and Alex's eyes landed on where Soren held her elbow.

"Alex, can I talk to your dad?" Larken asked softly.

"Of course." Alex's eyes shot up to Larken, his smile back in place. "He's in the garden with Mom. I'll walk you to his rooms and let him and security know that you're here."

"*His rooms?*" Soren murmured as they followed Alex.

"It's the only place without cameras." She took a few quick steps forward. "Alex, I brought more than one friend with me."

Soren didn't miss the way the redhead's eyes momentarily dropped to Larken's hips before saying, "I'll have them brought in as well. No worries."

The two fell into conversation, Larken visibly relaxing as they did. Now that she knew Alex wouldn't turn them over to her mother, she didn't seem to have a reason to worry. Soren, on the other hand, only grew more impatient the longer he watched them. Alex clearly had a thing for Larken, even if he was too much of a gentleman to be overly obvious about it. The only thing that Soren understood as they walked together was that if he wasn't ready to give up, then he needed to get a move on. Larken wouldn't wait around for him forever, and the world wouldn't wait for a Luminar.

# CHAPTER 9

Larken sat on a comfortable purple paisley sofa. Soren had taken the seat next to her, pressing her into the armrest. Alex sat across from them going back and forth between offering her curious glances and trying to get a good look at everyone else. The rest of the team stood around the room and waited anxiously for their fate to be decided. They, like Soren, weren't ready to trust the sincerity that Alex had always shown. If he said that she was safe here, then Larken believed him. It would seem Vallen was right and Morgan wouldn't be that hard to convince.

The Manor's gardens were huge, and they all sat there for a half hour before Morgan walked into the sitting room, hand-in-hand with his wife, Jinora. Age touched her dark brown locks, but not as much as Morgan's vibrant red. Thick streaks of blond cut through his hair, showing what Alex got to look forward to. Morgan gestured to the couch to Larken's right. Jinora made to sit but startled when Eudora barged in. Everyone turned to face her, but she didn't seem to care. Alex's sister scanned the room until her eyes landed on Larken. Eudora grinned and offered a quick smirk. She melted into a corner as much as she was able with her curly red hair and rosy cheeks. Larken knew that she was only there to eavesdrop, but she didn't mind. Eudora might be a bit more brash than her brother, but she was incredibly kind.

Morgan gave his daughter a look before helping his wife. The two of them seemed just as in love as ever, and Larken could remember wishing she had parents like that. She could also remember admitting that to Alex on one of their visits, and him telling her that she could come live with him and his new baby sister when Larken got older. Well, she was older now, and Alex's eyes didn't leave her long.

She wasn't the only one who had grown though. The mountain of the man across from her was the spitting image of a young Morgan. With his broad shoulders and easy smile, it was no wonder that a few of the Star reporters had fallen for him. But as Morgan sat and got comfortable, it would seem the Luminary had his own plans for his son. Morgan's eyes moved between Larken and Alex as a small smile pulled at his lips.

"Larken, how are you, sweetie?" Morgan's voice was that same melted chocolate baritone that she remembered, causing a smile of her own to tug at her lips.

"As well as can be expected, Luminary Montgomery."

Morgan lifted his hand as if to brush her words away. "Morgan, please." He put his feet up on the low coffee table and crossed his ankles. Flecks of dirt fell from his boots, and it only made Larken like him more. "What brings you out this way?"

"To see me again, obviously," Eudora said.

"*Eudora,*" Morgan warned.

The girl made a motion of zipping her lips shut.

Larken forced her hands to unclench and spread her palms out on her knees. The knee-high socks she wore dug into her skin, the itch almost unbearable. "I need some help." She looked up at Morgan, ignoring the heavy weight of Alex's eyes and Eudora's intense gaze. "*We* need help."

"*We?*" Morgan rose a red brow.

She swallowed thickly. What should she say? Larken looked to Soren for help, but his blank expression and dark gaze told her that what she did next was her choice. She was on her own, so she took a few seconds to think about what Vallen would do.

*Be vague, let him figure it out on his own.*

"My-my friends and I."

"The same friends that have been hidin' you, I assume."

Larken nodded. "Yes. Together we've worked out a plan and are hoping to gain your support."

Morgan sighed and clasped his hands over his stomach, leaning back into the sofa he occupied with his wife. Jinora squeezed his bicep once before relaxing as well. She offered Larken a warm smile as Morgan stated, "So you're not here for shelter."

"No."

"We'll do whatever we can to help," Alex insisted, finally speaking. "Right, Dad?"

"You bet we will," Eudora answered for Morgan.

"We'll do what we *can*." Morgan glared at his daughter again before his eyes fell back on Larken. "What's your plan, honey?"

"My Mother needs to be stopped. She started the whole war as a way to stay Lumina. V—someone told me that there was talk about finding a new family to reside over the Military District before the war started. That's what we want to do now."

Morgan's eyebrows rose in surprise, as well as Jinora's. "And who would you pick?" he asked.

Larken's eyes fell back to her hands as she balled the hem of her dress. Heat stung her face, and she couldn't get the words past her lips. Loxly saved her by saying, "Larken, of course."

"Hmm," Morgan mused, lips pursing as he thought. He turned his attention to Alex. "What do you think, son? It'll be you workin' alongside the future Luminary."

Alex looked torn, his eyes darting between his father and her.

Morgan sighed. "We had decided that if you came lookin' for help, Larken, we would take care of you. We would have offered you a place in our home, makin' it so your mother couldn't touch you."

The realization of what he said hit her the same time it did Soren.

He stiffened next to her, the hand resting between their thighs balling into a fist. Slowly, the rest of the team understood as well.

Morgan continued as if he didn't notice any of the groups' reactions. "I think it best we give you two time to think about it. Just know that you have options, sweetie. I know you've never been a fan of the spotlight, and I think the adjustment to Lumina would be an easier one than Luminary. But we'll support whatever you decide." Morgan grabbed his wife's hand and the two of them got to their feet. "It's nearly lunch. Why don't we go try and find somethin' for you lot?"

Reluctantly, the group followed the Luminary out. Eudora didn't want to leave at all but Morgan came back for her and ushered her out. Soren didn't make a move to leave until Larken nudged him. If she were being honest, she didn't want to be left alone with Alex and have this conversation. But more than that, she didn't want to have this conversation in front of Soren.

Soren grunted in a very Delvon-like way and said, "I'll be outside."

"Don't be stupid," Larken whispered. "Go get something to eat."

Soren frowned. "I'm *not* leaving you alone."

"And I don't want you eavesdropping."

The two stared at each other for a few seconds before Soren rolled his eyes. He pushed to his feet and made his way to the door. Loxly stood there and clapped him on the shoulder. He started up a loud conversation with his friend after sending Larken a look that said *be careful*.

They closed the door, taking all the oxygen in the room with them. Alex sighed and hunched forward, running a hand through his hair. Larken only tensed, hugging her middle and trying to make herself small. Part of her wished she would have let Soren stay, but she had enough of embarrassing herself like this in front of him.

"Of all the times I pictured proposin' to you, I didn't think my dad would end up doin' it for me." Alex laughed in a self-deprecating way.

"You thought about proposing?" Larken asked, not knowing what else to say.

"I always sort of figured that we would end up together. The arrangement made sense, and I thought you would prefer Thresh over Star."

He wasn't wrong. Larken would have chosen Alex over that slime-ball Charles, Luminary Narcissa's son. Larken didn't belong in Star, but she didn't belong in Thresh, either. She wasn't really sure where she fit in.

"Please say somethin'."

Larken looked up to find Alex giving her a sad smile. She tried to give him a smile in return, but it came out as more of a grimace. "I need to fix the mess she made. I can't just run away, Alex."

His smile turned a little more sincere. "Thought you might say that."

"Are you mad?"

"No, just..." He trailed off, running his hand through his hair again. "I never wanted to get involved with anyone because I didn't want to have to break it off if an arrangement was agreed on. It wouldn't have been fair to whomever she could have been, or to you. Now I'm not really sure what I'm gonna do."

Larken shrugged. "Just do what I'm doing. Take it a day at a time."

Alex stood and crossed the room, offering a hand out to her. "That's all I can do, I guess. Besides," he offered her that crooked smile again, "I'm not the only one stuck in this boat, having to start over."

"No," Larken agreed. "You're not."

"Although..." When Larken was standing, Alex offered her his elbow and led her to the door. "It would seem that you already have more options than I do."

Larken gave him an uncomfortable shrug. He had no idea.

"Don't worry, he'll come 'round."

"I wouldn't be so sure." Her cheeks heated.

Alex insisted all the man needed was time, but he didn't know exactly how much time Soren would really need. Time that Larken didn't have. If they managed to pull this off and at least get Gadget on their side, the Magnate would need a well-thought-out plan. That would include a Luminar that wouldn't try to take power from her like what her mother did to her father. She knew that the Magnate would lean more towards Shadric; he was charismatic and strong in his faith. Again, he was the easy choice. Larken just didn't know if she was ready for easy yet. Or, at least…ready to give up on the hard one.

They walked into the kitchen, greeted by loud noise and lots of laughter. Morgan was regaling everyone with the story of how Larken had gotten lost in the gardens as a child. It was the first time she had visited, and she could still remember Alex finding her. She had run off, embarrassed by the way Liam had talked about her. She thought her chance at a new friend had been ruined, but Alex had sided with her in the end. It was also when he had made his promise that she could come live with him someday.

Slices of bread and mounds of meat and fresh vegetables sat on large platters. Larken's stomach rumbled at the scent of food, having been too anxious to eat that morning. She let go of Alex's elbow and joined the fray. Alex moved to Morgan's side, and the older man pulled him into a one-armed hug. He seemed to know the choice Larken made without having to be told and gave her an encouraging wink. Relief flooded her at knowing she hadn't ruined things between them, and she quickly turned her attention to the food.

Before she could gab anything, though, a warm body pressed against her back, and a plate was thrust in front of her. A sandwich piled high with roast beef and lettuce sat on it, with hunks of cucumber and carrots on the side. There was even a dollop of some sort of dip. Larken could see the dill in it, and her stomach growled again. Carl sighed somewhere in the kitchen, and she knew he only held back his comments about her *unladylike* noises because the Luminary family of Thresh was there.

Soren dipped his head, his breath teasing a strand of hair that had fallen from her bun. It would be so easy for her to tilt her head, for Soren to press his lips to her jaw. Her face heated at the thought, and Larken pushed it away, deciding it best to ignore him instead. It would seem that he had other plans, though.

"You ditching your boyfriend at Camp for the one in Thresh?"

Larken's stomach fell as her heart stopped. It took her a moment to realize that he meant Delvon, not Shadric, and guilt twisted her in a way she didn't know was possible.

"You know I'm not," she huffed, voice barely a broken whisper.

His sigh had goosebumps breaking out across her skin. She thought again about his lips, of how close they were to her throat. Images of her dream all those weeks ago came flooding back. Larken couldn't help closing her eyes as she remembered the way he felt in the dream, kissing the pain away from her shoulder and working his way up to her lips in that world of sunset glass.

"Don't be such a baby." The words tumbled from her lips before she could stop them.

Soren stiffened behind her, no doubt thinking of the first time they almost kissed, and Larken's eyes shot open. Mortification had her stepping away from him and hiding behind Loxly's gangly length. He rose an eyebrow at her, giving her a smile that said he knew she did something to embarrass herself. Larken only picked up her sandwich and tore off a too-big bite.

# CHAPTER 10

"Will you relax?" Delvon grumbled, rubbing at his temples with his thumb and forefinger. "You having an aneurysm won't get them here any faster."

Shadric sighed and stopped his pacing, forcing himself to take up a spot on one of the fallen trees the Faithfuls had repurposed into a bench. Doing so seemed to help Delvon relax as well, but he tensed again when Shadric shot back up at the sound of a motor.

He had been worried about Larken for the last three days; he couldn't help it. Both Delvon and Blade insisted that she was fine, but he wouldn't personally believe their words until he saw her. Not until she stood before him and he could pull her into his arms and say everything he should have told her before she left.

"I told you I talked to her last night. She's *fine*."

"That was last night. What about today? What about now?"

Delvon groaned and pushed himself to his feet. "I'm not doing this again, mate."

A frustrated sound worked its way out of the back of Shadric's throat. He knew he hadn't been easy to get along with since she left. Their separation wasn't like before. Then, she was tucked safely away at the Manor with Delvon and Blade to keep an eye on her.

Now, any number of things could go wrong. What if they had been found out? What if they were captured? What if—

A soft rumble pulled Shadric away from his dark thoughts and brought his attention to the sky. The Harpy was in sight, and Shadric let out a breath, only now able to fully release it. He turned to his friend and apologized.

"I know you're sorry, but that doesn't stop you from being annoying."

Shadric smiled as he followed Delvon from the clearing they were sitting in to keep watch. They hurried to the spot designated for the beast of an aircraft Blade had designed. A small crowd formed around the patch of dirt serving as a landing pad. Delvon and a few others in their team encouraged the people to move on. None of them knew what state Larken would be in, and they all knew she would never leave her bungalow again if she embarrassed herself in front of so many of these people.

The last few stragglers begrudgingly returned to their tasks as the door opened and the black stairs unfurled. Loud laughter drifted out of the Harpy, and Shadric felt the individual muscles in his back relax. One by one, the former members of Squad 19 made their way off the airship. Hinlee grinned and looked over her shoulder and shook her head at the man who had to be Brecker. He smiled back and murmured something too soft for Shadric to hear. They were followed by Carl, and then the man Shadric always confused Brecker with, Levi. Levi was followed by a laughing Loxly, and then Soren.

He grumbled something, and Larken nearly shouted, "I said I can do it myself!"

Hinlee and Loxly laughed again, now on the ground, and Brecker snorted. Levi smirked and shared a look with Delvon that Shadric didn't understand.

"Rough flight?" Delvon asked.

"She didn't sleep a wink," Loxly answered, grinning.

Soren waited impatiently at the bottom of the steps, and Larken appeared. Her wheat-colored hair hung loosely around her face, and she kept trying to blow it out of her eyes. When it didn't work, she brushed the strands away roughly. She had on a black jacket that hung off one shoulder, and she demanded to know why Estelle wasn't there to greet her. Shadric smiled, unable to think her anything other than adorable.

Soren didn't seem to agree because he demanded, "Will you hurry up?"

"I'm coming, I'm—" Larken shrieked as she tripped over her feet and fell down the few steps. She landed against Soren, laughing.

Unable to help himself, Shadric pushed forward. Larken's eyes lit up when she saw him, and she snaked her way out of Soren's grip. She stumbled up to Shadric and beamed.

"Larken."

"Shad!" Reaching a hand up, she patted his thick stubble a few times. "Look at your face! It's so scruffy!"

Shadric laughed and reached his hands out to her. She didn't push him away and stood steadier with his hands on her waist. "You okay?"

She snorted. "Of course I'm okay. We have a new ally, and I don't have to break up with Delvon."

Shadric was going to ask what she meant when she caught sight of the man in question. She pulled from Shadric's grasp and teetered over to him. Larken tripped at the last second and Delvon had no choice but to catch her.

"I thought Jodi knew your dosage."

"Delvon, I missed you."

"Don't lie. You missed my body."

Larken snickered and swatted him. "Don't say it like that." She stepped in close to him and pressed her cheek to his chest. "Where's Estelle? Did you watch her like you promised?"

"She's an *android*," he reminded her, trying to get her to stand steady. When that didn't work, he bent and hoisted her up into his arms.

Larken's excited chatter turned to musical nonsense as Delvon carried her off in the direction of her home. He would never say it, but Shadric knew that his friend had missed her as well.

Shadric stared after the two of them, but then a gruff voice pulled his attention away by asking, "Where's Vallen?"

"At the tabernacle. He was trying to wrap up a few things before you guys got back."

Soren stalked off before Shadric could offer more information or ask any questions of his own. He looked over at the remaining members of the group, hoping they would be a little more understanding of his plight.

Hinlee offered him a kind smile. "Everything went really well. We were able to get Thresh on our side without a marriage alliance."

"What?" Shadric asked, the ground underneath his feet suddenly unsteady.

*That was a possibility?*

"Alex was a little dejected, but we left on good terms. Soren probably just wanted to check in with Vallen before throwing himself into a workout. The ride here wasn't easy for him."

Shadric wanted to ask but didn't at the same time. It wasn't lost on him the looks Larken gave Soren when she thought no one else was watching. But she looked at him the same way, too. Shadric knew she was confused, but he couldn't give up on her when there was still a chance. Especially when marriage was now on the table.

He hadn't even thought about that side of Larken becoming Luminary. Shadric had never pictured himself as a Luminar, but for her, he would do it. She would just have to choose him. That, and it would have to be where Maxim called him. Shadric just needed to do his part and let Larken know he was still an option. She would have the final say, and he would respect it no matter what.

The group started to disperse, going to wherever they might be needed. Carl wondered aloud where Candy might be hiding since she hadn't been there to greet them. Brecker took Hinlee's hand and suggested they find some food. Loxly asked Levi where he thought Fisher might be, and the two went in search of Larken's father.

All too soon, Shadric stood alone. He was always alone it

seemed, though he'd never felt that way when Larken was around. She understood. She knew what it was like to have everyone know intimate details about her and still feel invisible. But it wasn't just Shadric that needed her now—it was everyone. She was doing what Maxim had called her to do, and Shadric couldn't be upset about that. And he couldn't help but feel like every day in this new life of hers was another day she was slowly leaving him behind. He didn't know how to stop it, but he wasn't ready to give up, either. He just needed a little more time, but trying to stop time was like trying to hold water in his hands.

Eventually, it would run out, whether he was ready for it or not.

# CHAPTER 11

The man before him was weak. He sat there, trembling as he fretted over what he was about to say, swallowing thickly over and over. Dominic could see the words the man tried to choke back. He didn't want to be the one to say them. The man rubbed the thumb of his right hand over his knuckles as his jaw ticked. The display only made Dominic irritated, and he eyed the decanter full of whiskey in the corner of the room. He hadn't touched the stuff since Cornella's visit, but that didn't stop it from beckoning to him now. Only the fact that he didn't want to turn into Trogar kept him from going to it. Dominic had seen what the man's drinking had done to Larken, and he refused to be that man. He would be the one Larken needed…whether she wanted that or not.

"Spit it out." Dominic brought his cigar to his lips, taking a deep breath of the blue smoke. His fingers never seemed to be free of the cigars for long, Larken's absence making him insane. At least *this* he could control.

"Captain Braves, I've just received word that there's been a sighting."

Something snapped inside Dominic at the man's words. He wanted to leap over the desk that his feet were propped on and demand to know why he hadn't been told sooner. Slowly, he parted his lips and let the smoke leave his lungs. A blueberry fog surrounded him, and if the man's widening eyes were any indication, it gave him the menacing look he was hoping for.

"You *just received word?*"

"Yes, sir. Not even a minute ago." He added the last bit as if it would keep Dominic from finding him at fault.

It didn't work.

"Where?" he demanded.

"At the Thresh Manor, Captain."

"*What?*"

The man fumbled for a tablet, dropping it on the ground before placing it on the desk. Dominic let his feet fall from the polished wood and grabbed the device. Pulling it close, Dominic ignored the man's stuttered explanations as he swiped through the pictures of Larken in a staff uniform. The dress hugged her body, reminding Dominic of how much he missed the feel of her. His eyes caressed her shapes – her hips, her breasts, the curve of her neck. Fingers burning, he touched the photo, dragging his finger down one of her legs.

The next photo he brought up had him freezing. Larken reached up to a figure Dominic knew all too well from his time in the gym at Base 14. She smiled warmly, touching something that hung around Deckard's neck.

"When was this?" he snarled.

"Yesterday." The man showed no sign that he cared about being interrupted.

"She was in Thresh *yesterday* and no one knew?"

The man gulped audibly, his uniform swallowing more of him by the second. Soon his face would be completely hidden behind his shirt. "We only received an update this morning that all of the footage for the Thresh Manor had been deleted. The whole day had disappeared. Lumina Hale found it suspicious, so we were tasked with finding out whatever we could about it. I'm not sure who it was that suggested looking into the hover feed at the staff entrance, but we found them." The man dropped his gaze from the tablet to the floor. "We can only assume Miss Hale came into contact with Luminary Montgomery."

Dominic took three deep breaths before taking another drag of his cigar. He flicked through the photos until he was once again looking at the one of her standing alone and hugging her middle. He splayed his hand over her.

*What are you up to, Lark?*

"What's our next course of action?"

The man started shaking more, another few inches of his chin disappearing underneath his collar. "That's why I'm here, Captain Braves. I am to report your decision to Lumina Hale."

*So I can be the one to take the fall if this blows up in our faces?*

A growl worked its way out of the back of Dominic's throat. His hand balled into a fist as he thought fast, trying to find something broad enough to keep them informed, but strategic enough to please Cornella. Sighing, he gritted out, "Keep an eye on the other Manors. If she is willing to brave this one, she might try to sneak into the others as well. We'll just have to watch until we know more."

The man nodded quickly, clearly eager to leave.

"Send someone out to Thresh, but don't announce it. See if they can get something out of a staff member. If Thresh decided to ally with Larken, we won't be able to trust Montgomery's word."

The man jumped to attention and saluted Dominic. Turning, he rushed to the door. He had just reached it when Dominic stopped him again.

Dominic took another long drag of the cigar and waited until his lungs were empty before continuing, "Burn some of the outlying farms to ash. Make an example of them and show the rest of the country what happens when they try to keep Larken hidden."

The man reached out for the doorknob, and he missed it twice before gripping it tightly and fleeing from the room. Dominic turned his eyes back to the photo.

"See what you're making me do, Lark?" His thumb brushed against the curve of her jaw. "See what's happening the longer you hide from me? This is all *your fault,* and it won't stop until you come home."

# CHAPTER 12

L arken woke up with a horrible taste in her mouth. Estelle puffed warm air into her face, curled up and using the same pillow as her. Smiling, Larken reached up and rubbed at the spot behind the android's jaw. Estelle only groaned and cracked a bleary, blue eye at her.

"Missed you."

Estelle's rubber tongue reached out and dragged across Larken's palm. Larken debated between rolling over and going back to sleep or making something to eat. She was pulled from her thoughts by a gruff, accented voice asking, "You always talk to that thing when you think you're alone?"

"You always watch women while they sleep?" she retorted, not bothering to look at Delvon.

A grunt was his response. Larken sat up and stretched. One of her arms was still in Vallen's jacket, while the other sleeve hung down to the floor of her bungalow. She reached for it and stuffed her arm back in. Getting out of bed, she made her way over to where Delvon had gotten comfortable on her couch. The sun shone through her windows, making the room look cozy and warm. Delvon stuck a fork into a tub that held the remnants of the lemon chicken she had made for her and Vallen before she had left.

Taking up the seat next to him, Larken folded her legs up under her and took both the food and the fork from Delvon. He grabbed for it and said around a mouthful of chicken, "I believe I was still eating that."

"And I believe that they are still *my* leftovers." She took a bite, letting the thick lemon glaze coat her tongue. "How long was I asleep anyway?"

"You got back yesterday afternoon. You're just in time for breakfast, so give me mine back and go get your own."

Larken paused in her chewing and thought about spitting what was in her mouth out and handing it back to him.

He grabbed the chicken from her with a growled, "Don't even think about it."

She glared at him as he took the fork back as well. Larken shoved to her feet and walked over to her little fridge. Of course he would pick the best thing in there. Larken had to settle for making herself a sandwich, and memories of what had happened in the Thresh Manor kitchen nearly had her putting the roast beef back on its shelf.

"Want me to tell you what happened on the way back?" Delvon asked.

"No."

"You sure? You didn't sleep the whole time you were in the air."

"That only makes me want to know less," she muttered.

Larken looked over to see the former bodyguard shrug. As if to spite Soren, though he would have no way of knowing what she was doing that exact moment, she made the sandwich and ate it. Once her stomach was satisfied, she could move on with the next task of her morning. She took up the spot by Delvon again.

"What next?" she asked.

"You have a few days off, then we're shipping you out to Gadget."

"Who's going with me?"

"Soren, Levi, Loxly, my brother, and me," he grunted.

"Great. I'll get to listen to you and Soren bicker the whole time."

Delvon ignored her, choosing instead to poke fun at her appearance. "You should shower, or at least change your clothes. You smell like a farm."

"I made some new friends while I was away. I'm sure they'd be offended by your words."

"Only if they're cows, like I'm assuming they are."

"You know me so well."

He smirked. "Almost like we dated or something."

"Or something." Larken returned his smirk with a smile.

The two finished their meals in silence, and Larken was grateful that Delvon didn't bring up her stay in Thresh. She didn't know if she would be able to handle his teasing about *another* proposal. She was at three now, if she counted Delvon's promise to marry her before Dominic could. That was three more than she'd ever expected receiving, and three that hadn't come from anyone she truly loved. And as time slowly ticked by, Larken started to realize that maybe Shadric did make the most sense. He obviously cared for her, and she cared for him. Could she learn to love him the way she had always dreamed she might love her future husband? Or was she a lost cause? Too damaged to love anyone romantically?

Larken got to her feet, taking Delvon's container from him. "Hurry up and get out. I need to get ready."

"You've changed in front of me before, love. Why so shy all of a sudden?"

"Because suddenly I find myself without a curtain to stand behind, or a closet to lock myself in." She gently kicked his calf, knocking his feet from her coffee table. "Get out."

Delvon laughed softly and got to his feet. "What are your plans for the day?"

"I'm going to train until I'm not thinking about my future. Then, I'm stopping by the Chin's and stuffing myself until I have to be rolled back here."

He raised an eyebrow, grey eyes glinting. "Will I be doing the rolling? Or would you prefer Deckard?"

"*Delvon*," she warned.

He took on a look of mock innocence. *"What?* It's not my fault you compared him to a *grumbly hero in a love story."*

Mortification rolled over Larken, and she shivered in embarrassment. "I *told you* that I didn't want to know!"

"And I thought it would be more fun if you did." He chuckled before turning to the door. "Now we're even from when you woke me up on my only day off in the last five years."

Larken grabbed a mint-colored pillow from her loveseat and chucked it at Delvon. It hit the back of his head, and he continued on as if he hadn't even noticed. He left, closing her in her bungalow with her thoughts. Now what was she to do? She'd planned on possibly seeking Soren out and training with him since things were starting to feel a little normal again, despite the sandwich incident. But after knowing she had said that to him, Larken didn't know if she could ever look into those hazel eyes again.

Annoyed, she snatched the pillow off the floor and tossed it back onto the sofa. Estelle's pale blue eyes followed her, and Larken made a face. "You're lucky you don't have to deal with any of this nonsense."

Estelle huffed like she was saying, *you'd be surprised*, before burrowing deeper into the bed. What Larken wouldn't give to trade places with the android. All Estelle had to worry about was when she was going to be charged next. Larken, on the other hand, had only a couple weeks to find a future husband that the Magnate would approve of, convince the Magnate that she wouldn't completely ruin everything if he were to pass Liam's title onto her, and overthrow her mother.

Piece of cake.

Larken changed into some workout clothes, not bothering to shower off the day of travel before. She was only going to get sweaty anyway. The black tank top reminded her of the ones she had been issued during her time at base, and she longed for that time of ease again. Back then, her only worry had been how Soren would annoy her during the day and how she could get back at him. She never would have thought that he would be in the running for her future husband.

Not that she wanted him to be, of course. He was just an infuriatingly handsome guy that *happened* to be her friend. Dating wasn't even an option for the two of them, much less marriage. Not to mention, he couldn't make up his mind. Soren kept going back and forth between the brooding grump and the man that pulled her in close as if to kiss her. His unpredictability drove her insane, so why couldn't she just let him go?

*Because if you did, you'd be losing the only person you care about as much as Vallen...*

Larken pushed the thoughts from her mind as she left her bungalow. She took up a steady jog to the training area, trying to outrun her fears and doubts. Thankfully, it was empty when she got there. Larken set her communicator on a fallen tree that served as the viewing area and blared some music. Her playlists were getting thinner by the day since she couldn't listen to anything that reminded her of Shadric or Soren. She readied three practice droids that had been commandeered from one of the military bases and set them for hand-to-hand combat. Larken didn't even think as her body went on the defensive. Her goal wasn't to overtake the androids but to draw out the fight. She wanted to exhaust herself, not prove how quickly she could win.

Larken didn't know how long she had been lost in the fight when her music stopped. The distraction cost her, and one of the practice droids landed a blow to her gut. She groaned and quickly danced away from the android that grabbed for her. Thinking on her feet, she bobbed in and out of their reach until she thought she could join in the fight again. After a couple well-placed kicks and jabs, the practice droids were stunned, and Larken was able to shut them down. Reeling, she turned on whoever had distracted her, only to find Soren frowning.

"What?" she demanded.

"We need to talk."

Delvon's taunts rose to the surface of her mind and Larken felt her cheeks heat. "I don't think we do."

He ignored her. "What happened on the Harpy can't happen again." A chime sounded from her communicator, and Soren picked it up. He glanced at it for a second before adding, "Vallen wants to see you."

Heart beating even faster than it had during the fight, Larken walked over and snatched the device from him. She didn't even thank Soren before turning and making her way toward the tabernacle. Vallen seemed to live there lately, and she missed seeing him as often as she had before he took up his role as leader of the Faithfuls.

Soren grunted and followed her. "This isn't something we can just ignore, Larken."

"Sure it is," she argued. "We ignore stuff like this all the time."

He grabbed her elbow and forced her to face him. "Not when it could mean you getting hurt."

"Wait—what?" she pulled her elbow from his grip. Did he really just say that? Was this conversation really happening? "What are you talking about?"

"The chamomile extract isn't working anymore." Soren rose a dark eyebrow, his eyes flashing green. "What are *you* talking about?"

"*Obviously*, I am also talking about the extract," she said, her voice sounding strained and incredibly awkward. "What else?"

"Mmhmm," he grunted out.

Larken started towards the tabernacle again, praying her face wasn't as red as it felt. "Why do you think it isn't working anymore? I don't remember the flights, and I haven't had a panic attack, either."

"We won't have anywhere we can stay in any of the other Districts, not like in Thresh. You slept for a while after we landed on the farm, but on the way home, you never even fell asleep." He caught up to her, matching her pace. "What if that happened again? What if we get to Gadget or Star, and you're still all...*loopy*?"

Larken's stomach sank as it twisted with nerves. "No, I'm not flying without it. I'm willing to take that risk. We can just make sure that we land somewhere well hidden, and we can all stay on the Harpy. It might not be a luxury aircraft, but it's still built for extended travel. We'll be fine."

"Larken—"

"No." The tabernacle was in view, and she picked up her pace, embarrassed by her fear. She so badly didn't want to be the girl who weighed them all down with her fear of flying anymore.

Soren grabbed her elbow again but didn't force her to turn around this time. "Can we please just talk about this? There have to be other options. We just have to talk to Jodi—"

"Don't you think either she or Ezra would have mentioned other options? Or Levi?" Larken pulled her arm free and hugged her middle, ashamed and nauseous. "Please stop, Soren. I can't. I just… *can't.*"

He was close enough behind her that she could feel him stiffen in agitation, and Larken knew that it wasn't the last time he would bring this up. Ignoring him, she walked into the tabernacle to find an annoyed Shadric standing on the stage. His guitar rested against his back, the strap clinging to his chest. Both Vallen and Delvon stood with him, and the three appeared to be arguing. Larken cleared her throat, and all three of them turned her way.

Stepping further into the tabernacle, Larken pretended that Soren hadn't followed her inside. She stopped when she reached Vallen and asked, "What's going on?"

"Don't—" Delvon tried, but Shadric cut him off.

"They don't think I should go to Gadget with you."

"Why do you want to come with us to Gadget?" she asked.

"Because I can help," the singer insisted. "I can help keep you safe and—"

"She doesn't need any more help," Delvon interrupted, his tone saying he was repeating himself. "She's got me."

"But *I've* been to the Manor before! At least," he quickly amended, "more than once."

"It doesn't matter how many times he's been," Soren said,

joining the conversation. "Delvon can get us floor plans like he did last time."

"Thanks, mate." Delvon turned back to Shadric. "See? We've got it covered."

"Just let me come. I can be useful."

"You can also be recognized," Soren grumbled. "Didn't you just say you've been there before?"

Shadric's cheeks turned pink in anger. The level of animosity in the room grew by the second, bringing with it Larken's anger. The three men continued to argue around her like she wasn't even there, Vallen adding his own thoughts now and then. It was becoming too much, and they didn't even notice how she silently fumed.

"Let me help!" Shadric pleaded.

"How about you just drop it?" Soren sneered.

"How about," Larken barked, reminding everyone she was there, "you all stop treating me like I'm some breakable tool that needs to be protected and let me make my own decisions?"

Larken glared at all four of them, her gaze lingering on Vallen the longest. Out of all of them, he should know better. He'd always let her make her own choices before; now shouldn't be an exception.

"Since agreeing to this, I've had no say in anything. I've just been told what to do, and then when I needed help, suddenly it's all *my* problem that I need to figure out. I'm sick of it." She turned and didn't look back as she called, "Don't talk to me until you can figure out what part you want me to play. Luminary, or ambassador."

It wasn't fair, and she knew it, but they hurt her. She was tired of being pulled at, and she no longer knew which direction she was supposed to go. Soren didn't need to be so overbearing, taking it upon himself to decide whether she could handle flying or who was good enough to help protect her. And Shadric didn't need to fight to prove his abilities. Larken trusted in Vallen's plan, had always trusted him, but he needed to start treating her like he had before he faked his death. This new side of him seemed concerned only with results, not whether Larken thought she could handle all of this. Though, Delvon didn't help matters by still playing the part of her bodyguard. Larken needed less of those. What she *did* need was for her friends to start acting like themselves again.

Larken walked about a hundred yards before the sound of thudding footfalls began catching up to her. She knew it was Delvon without looking. Soren would be on his way to burn off his aggravation in a workout, Shadric was probably beating himself up and would give her space, and Vallen would wait for her to cool down before she gave in and found him later. Delvon was the only one bull-headed enough to chase after her and finish a fight.

"That was uncalled for, love," he said, falling into step beside her.

"No, what's uncalled for is all the men in my life thinking they know what's best for me more than I do."

He sighed. "You need to be fair. This isn't a normal situation we're in."

"Because I have so much experience being the face of a revolution," she deadpanned.

"Yes, this is new for you." He grabbed her elbow, and she almost yanked it away, sick of being held there. "But it's new for us too."

"I just want things to go back to the way they were before," she admitted, not meeting his eyes.

"That would be nice, if it were possible." He tugged on her arm a little, and she fell against his chest, the fight starting to leave her. "Blade just wants what's best for you. We all do."

"I know, but it wouldn't kill you to ask what I want too."

Delvon took a deep breath. "Do you still want to do this?"

"You know I do," she grumbled. "I just need a little more time."

"We don't have that."

"Then maybe be a little more understanding? You have to remember, I thought I was going to have a different life. First I thought I would live in my brother's shadow. Then I had to get used to the idea of going to the frontlines to die. Once I was used to that, I was brought back home and forced into an engagement. Now I'm doing this." Larken pulled away and looked up at him. "It's too much. I can't keep losing control of my life, Delvon."

Things were obviously getting too serious for him, because he scoffed and let go of her before saying, "We're letting you pick who you marry. Isn't that enough?"

"No. It's not."

Delvon grunted. "Fine, I'll include you more." He stuffed his hands into his pockets and started walking. "But you have to apologize. Shad's blaming himself for dragging you here and ruining your life, or whatever. And Deckard's liable to destroy every practice droid we have."

Larken sighed, knowing he was right. "Just as long as you three stop acting like overprotective nannies."

"No promises, Peach."

# CHAPTER 13

Instead of making her way back to the tabernacle or going into the forest to search for Soren, Larken decided to go visit Fisher. If he hated flying too, then he might have some tricks that she could use. It would be better to approach Soren with a peace offering, or at least a solution to his current fixation. She wasn't sure what to do about Shadric, having never fought with him before.

Larken couldn't quite remember the way to Fisher's bungalow though, so she had to stop and call Vallen to ask for directions. Over the call, they apologized to each other and were completely over the incident before the conversation ended. Vallen had always been good about understanding her, reading between the lines and seeing what she was really upset about. He didn't have to be told that she was stressed, scared, and confused. Just like she didn't have to be told that he was trying his best to adjust to this new life. He couldn't be blamed for their lack of time together. At the Manor, being with her was his job. Here, he had a lot more responsibility.

Knocking on the door of a bungalow at the edge of Camp, Larken waited with bated breath. She didn't even know if Fisher was home, or what she would even say if he was. She still wasn't quite sure how to act around him, and even though Soren had insisted that he wanted to be in her life, a part of her still doubted it.

She gave it another three seconds before deciding that this was a stupid idea and turning to leave. The door opened, and Larken straightened her spine, only just thinking that she should have stopped and cleaned up first.

Fisher smiled when he saw her. "Larken, good to see you!"

"Hey, Fisher." She moved back around and stared at her feet for a second, nervously. "Do you have some time to talk? I can come back if—"

"No, no. Please, come in." He took a step back, welcoming her into his home.

Larken waited a second before she was able to talk her feet into moving. Slowly, she walked into the bungalow, the smell of spearmint wrapping around her. Where her bungalow was decorated in shades of light blue, Fisher's was made up of tans and golds. The colors seemed to fit him, making her think of the decadent decorations one would find in a theater. Red accents could be found around the place, only persuading her further.

"Can I interest you in some tea?" he asked, already making his way to the small fridge.

"Sure. Just as long as it isn't too sweet."

He looked over his shoulder, crinkling his nose in disgust. "I don't understand how people can drink something that's basically sugar."

Larken smiled, unnerved by his expression and statement. How could she have spent her whole life never knowing that this man existed when they were practically the same person? Each time Larken was reminded of who exactly Fisher was, she was surprised. She had heard of people that were basically miniature clones of their parents, but she just thought she wasn't one of them.

Fisher handed her a glass filled with ice, tea, cucumber slices, and sprigs of mint. He ushered her into the sitting area and took a seat in a gold armchair, leaving the tan loveseat for her to stretch out on. She didn't though, and tried to take up as little space as possible, not wanting to accidentally ruin anything.

"So, what brings you out this way?" he asked, getting straight to business.

Larken was grateful and instantly felt more at ease. This was how Vallen talked to her. This was the kind of conversation she was used to.

"I need some help," she admitted.

Larken explained the situation, even including her experiences with the various crashes she'd been in. Fisher listened the whole time, not interrupting once. He assessed the situation as a director would, his fingers steepled and pressed against a frown. Larken could easily imagine him sitting through auditions or rehearsals like that.

It was only when she finished speaking that he sighed. "Well, your Grandmother never flew. She would take hovercrafts and ships wherever she needed to go, much to the annoyance of everyone around her. It took her two months to get to a show once. But we don't have that kind of time."

He smiled and Larken returned it with one of her own.

"I personally can't sit next to a window. As long as the aircraft isn't too jerky, and I can't see the ground, I do alright."

Larken nodded slowly, trying to picture that. She imagined she was in the air, unable to see the ground. A sudden fear gripped her at not knowing if the Harpy was crashing to the ground or not. She stopped and shook her head. "No, the Harpy flies too smoothly for that. I wouldn't know where we were or what might be happening."

Fisher looked out his window, his frown back. Larken didn't know what to do while he was thinking, so she took a sip of her tea. It was fresh and crisp, reminding her of the summer days that were quickly turning into autumn.

"What about tea?"

"Tea?" She looked at her glass, not understanding.

"Some valerian tea. It won't be strong enough to completely knock you out, but it should keep your heart rate low."

"Maybe."

"Or, perhaps, if you have your heart set on sleeping through the event, maybe your young medic friend will have some valerian extract. Or even a shot of the hormone melatonin. I know a few cast members that used that to overcome their insomnia."

"I'll bring those ideas up to Jodi. Thanks, Fisher."

"Anytime." He gave her a look that she had gotten from Vallen on more than one occasion. "Anything else you'd like to discuss?"

"No." She dropped her gaze back to her glass, not wanting him to see the lie.

"You sure? I know we don't know each other all that well yet, but I would like to change that, Larken." She looked up at him and he quickly amended, "When you're ready, of course."

She *was* ready, but she didn't know if she was ready to talk about her love life with her father. She didn't even talk about it with Vallen. She sighed.

*What do I have to lose?*

"About being Luminary..." she trailed off, not knowing how to continue.

As if sensing her confusion, Fisher asked, "Does this have anything to do with your ever-growing number of admirers?"

"*Yes!*" The words were out, and she couldn't pull them back in if she tried. "After we're done trying to get the Districts to side with us, we're going to have to convince the Magnate. He'll want a plan, a guarantee that I won't mess up like my—" Larken caught herself, feeling awkward.

She dropped her gaze back to her tea, and Fisher finished, "Like how Trogar messed up by choosing Cornella."

She nodded. "That means I'll have to let him know who I plan on eventually having as my Luminar, but I don't know if I can."

"Is it the men, or something else?"

"Both?" Larken sagged back into the loveseat and looked up at him. "I don't know who to pick—who would be best for the District, that is. And I don't know if I'm even capable of being a Luminary, let alone a good wife. I never thought I would have this life. It was always Liam's future. And because of that, I never thought I would get married. Every time a match was talked about, my mother rejected it."

"All except for the young Braves boy."

"Right. And we both know how well that worked out," Larken grumbled.

"Well, you know my thoughts on the matter. Or, at least, who I prefer."

Yes, she knew. Fisher hadn't done a good job hiding his feelings toward Soren back in that theatre. Not only that, but the two men had to have grown somewhat close since arriving at Camp. Especially if Fisher was messaging Soren to see if Larken was safe. She just wished the choice was that easy.

"The thing about Soren is…" Larken paused to gather her words. She didn't want to make Soren look bad, but she needed to be honest as well if she was going to figure this out. "He's like me."

"As in you're both stubborn to a fault, or that you have trouble letting yourselves be happy?"

*Maybe Fisher knows me a lot better than I thought…*

"Both." Her cheek heated. "We have this thing where we *don't* talk about things. If that makes sense."

"It does, and neither of you are at fault for that. I understand where you're coming from. Having Cornella as a mother would twist anyone up on the inside. And would it be safe to assume that his issues stem from a life of abandonment? He spent his whole life in the military, yes?"

Larken nodded.

"And the Shadric boy, how does he fit into this?"

"He actually tried to kidnap me while I was at base." Larken smiled at the memory. She had been shot, but thinking back to the bumbling fool that Shadric had been before that, Larken couldn't help but find the memory endearing. "He didn't know who I was when we first met."

"Hence the song."

Larken's cheeks heated. "Yeah."

"And then?"

"And then I was pulled back into life as The Daughter of the Military, and we met for real. He's been honest about how he's felt since the beginning, and at the time, I thought Soren and I wouldn't ever see each other again." Larken bit her lip and then quickly added, "Not that I was hoping Shadric would pursue me while I was engaged."

"You don't have to try and explain away your heart to me, Songbird. I, of all people, would know how easily a heart is swayed."

"It's just, back then I didn't have an option other than Dominic. Now, I have too many. I already turned down Alex, Luminary Morgan's son from Thresh, and lost my only chance to get out of being Luminary. I feel like I really only have two choices with the time I have left, and one *looks* better than the other. At least, the Magnate would think so." Larken clicked her index nail against her glass. "I should just hurry up and accept it, but I—" she couldn't finish.

"You're not ready to give up on him," Fisher said for her.

Larken nodded so slowly she didn't even realize she was doing it until she looked back up at Fisher.

"Well, Songbird, maybe there's a way around this after all."

"How so?"

"Maybe don't go in with a full plan. If you're too sure of yourself, it might seem like you are trying to do this for your sake, not the Districts'. Perhaps it would be better if you only went in with half a plan and asked the Magnate for his advice on the matter." Fisher steepled his fingers again. "After all, Trogar was pressured by his father to find a wife at a young age. Perhaps if he had waited a little longer and let his heart guide him instead of his father, he would have chosen different."

Larken sat there at a loss for words. She hadn't known that this was an option. Vallen had always taught her to plan ahead, just as the military had taught him. She was to have a plan for when everything went right, wrong, and every instance in between. It had been so ingrained in her upbringing that not having a plan never even crossed her mind.

"Maybe that will work," she said hopefully. "It would give me a little more time, at least. I don't want to be unprepared, but I also don't want to rush things and make a mistake."

"My advice, then, is to step out of your head and listen to your heart a little more. Ask the Magnate his opinion on what would make you a worthy Luminary, but be praying for Maxim to show you the right man in the meantime. That way, if the Magnate demands a plan from you, you might have an answer for him. Just be open to what Maxim has to say."

Larken grinned, and the two fell into comfortable conversation. She finished off her tea, and Fisher invited her to stay for dinner. She accepted, then sent a message to Mr. Chin letting him know that she wouldn't be by after all. The nerves that she'd had standing on Fisher's doorstep were forgotten, and she was happy she came. Not only did he help fix her problem, but she got to know her father a lot better, too. She held onto these moments with him, knowing that things could change very, *very* soon.

# CHAPTER 14

*Braves...*
    *Alex...*
*Shadric...*

The list just kept growing, and Soren didn't know what to do about it. He just knew that he couldn't add himself to it. That moment in Loxly's bedroom never should have happened; he understood that now. So if the choice was so easy, why couldn't he just let it go? Why couldn't he just let *her* go? Let her be happy?

*Because you're selfish. You've always been selfish.*

Soren couldn't remember ever feeling so torn over a decision. One moment he was willing to do whatever it took to keep Larken, and the next, he was ready to let her go. He knew he needed to make up his mind—that it wasn't fair to Larken—but he couldn't. He also couldn't be the man she would need him to be. Soren was adopted by the military. He wasn't Luminar material. That had been made clear to him when he was a part of Larken's security detail back at the Manor. It was the one aspect of his life where he would always come in second to Braves, and Soren *hated* it.

Levi tried pulling him aside the night before after a workout, but Soren ignored him. Soren was acting like he had after Larken left base, even though she was closer now than she had ever been before. Here at Camp, she wasn't a solider, she wasn't an heiress, and most importantly, she wasn't engaged. They were finally free to be together, but Soren didn't see how it would work out. It wouldn't be fair to her to chase her, only to pull back at the last minute. The right thing to do would be to step back and let Shadric make her happy…but the thought of that had him feeling like he was set on fire. Slow heat at first, then agonizing pain.

And yet, even with all of this going on, Soren still found himself walking to his secret spot. With a towel in hand and black swim trunks on, Soren planned to make the most of the last hot day for a long while. Before crossing through the trees, he pulled out his communicator and called Larken.

She picked up on the second ring, and her ragged breathing could be heard immediately. "Soren? Everything okay?"

"What are you doing?"

"*Running*," she grumbled.

His lips twitched, picturing how annoyed she must be. "How about cardio of a different sort?"

"What did you have in mind?" she asked. "I'm not sparring with you. I'm still upset that you distracted me and that practice droid hit me."

"Swimming. You game?"

"No way! There's a pool here?"

"You want in or not?"

Soren imagined her slowing to a stop and bending over. "Of course I'm in. I need to change, but you have to give me directions. The trees still confuse me."

He let her use the trees as an excuse and didn't tease her about her poor sense of direction. Soren didn't get off the call with her until he saw her walking his way in sandals and a pale pink cover-up. A bag with rope straps and thick peach and cream-colored stripes hung from her good shoulder. Her hair was pulled back into two braids, and she looked him over skeptically.

"No comments on the bathing suit. Carl packed it, and it's the only one I have."

Soren didn't agree to anything, knowing that if he did and then made a comment, she would be annoyed.

"So, where's the pool? It doesn't seem like there should be one this far out into the woods."

"I never said it was a pool," Soren said, already turning to the trees.

She caught up to him. "A pond then?"

"Nope." He pulled her in front of him and led her out of the forest.

Larken gasped at the sight of the calm waves. The trees had blocked the scent of salt and sand, but now there was no hiding the vast ocean before them. She looked up at him, beaming.

Soren felt like he could take on the world.

Together, they took off their shoes and stepped into the sand. Larken held onto him, letting her feet get used to the shifting earth underneath them. Soren dropped his stuff onto the log that he had sat on when he got there, and Larken followed suit. They stood uncomfortably for a moment before Soren made the first move. He pulled his shirt from his body and caught her eyes staring at his abdomen. When her gaze met his, he smirked. She turned away, blushing hotly.

He pretended to look away as she grabbed the hem of her cover-up. Slowly, she pulled it up over her legs, then her torso, then her head. Soren's jaw ticked and he swallowed thickly. The two-piece covered what it needed to, but it still revealed more of her than he had ever seen in all their time together. He couldn't keep his eyes off the curve of her lower back, hypnotized by her pale skin. How many times had he touched her there? How many times had he thought about what her bare skin would feel like?

Too many.

Far too many.

She turned to him, hugging her middle and doing a poor job of covering her stomach. "Carl thought I might want to sunbathe. I know it's not very practical."

What had happened in Soren's pathetic life that would demand he only consider the practicality of a swimsuit? The teal fabric was the same color as her eyes, and he was so thankful that she had it instead of any other.

Before he could do something stupid, Soren marched up to her. Grabbing her waist, he hoisted her up over his shoulder and ran for the water. Her screams and laughter filled the open world around him, bringing a smile to his own lips. He waited until he was waist-deep before tossing her and diving under the warm water. Air bubbles ran down his body as he cut through the waves. He kicked out a little deeper before resurfacing, shaking the water from his hair. Larken bobbed in the waves, sputtering and coughing not too far away. He grinned and swam for her.

Larken wiped water from her eyes, and then splashed him. "You stay away!"

Soren felt his grin turn predatory. He lunged for her, and she squealed. Catching her easily, he pulled her against him. Her hands grabbed onto his shoulders as if that alone would keep her latched to him if he decided to toss her into the water again. Their chests pressed together as a wave knocked her into him. Her face was turned down as she refused to meet his gaze, and Soren couldn't pull his eyes off her.

She was beautiful, devastatingly so. Despite himself, Soren had given her the power to destroy him, and she had no idea. She still only saw herself as the small raindrop, not the ocean he knew she was. Her hair smelled like grapefruit, even standing in the waves. Soren found himself leaning in to bury his nose into the wet strands when she spoke.

"I'm sorry…for yesterday."

He froze, realizing what he had been about to do. "Why are you apologizing?"

*It should be me, not you…*

"I was upset and was unfair to you guys. I know you're trying your best."

"We also didn't need to be acting like you weren't standing there," he admitted, the words he needed to say not coming.

"I talked to Fisher. He actually had some pretty good ideas about —" She blushed. "About a lot of things."

Soren wondered briefly if she had brought up the weirdness between the two of them. "What did he say?"

"Well, he gave me some advice about flying. I have a couple of things I was going to talk to Jodi about later. You can come too, if you want."

She still wouldn't look at him, and it was starting to get on his nerves. "What sort of things?"

"He suggested a valerian tea or a shot of the hormone melatonin. He knows some old cast members that used those. Maybe they could work for me, too."

This was wrong. This wasn't how today was supposed to go. He brought her here so *he* could apologize and make up for the way he had been acting. But Larken, being her ever-compassionate self, had not only apologized but offered up a peace offering as well. It only confirmed how much of a jerk he had been since they got here.

"Larken, don't apologize. Please."

Her teal eyes slowly moved up his chest and met his own. The uncertainty there nearly killed him. This wasn't who they were. They were Larken and Soren, two people who had found each other despite their circumstances. They weren't the type to avoid each other and tiptoe around what needed to be said. He didn't know when their silent understanding and acceptance had turned to second-guessing and doubt. It needed to change, and he was the only one who could fix it.

"I haven't been myself since base. I know. You don't have to apologize and try to make things right when it's my fault."

"To be fair, a lot of what happened at base was your fault too," she teased, giving him a way out.

But the way she bit her lip and looked at him with wavering eyes made up his mind. This wasn't a fight he would be backing down from. He looked deep into her teal depths that seemed bluer when she was surrounded by sea and turned serious. "I know. And I've been paying for it since."

Another wave crashed into Larken's back, and she wobbled. She slowly sunk a few inches as the sand covered their feet. Shifting, Larken used him to steady herself while she pulled her foot free. Her knee brushed against his shin and then she stepped on the top of his foot. Larken slipped, and Soren tightened his grip on her. She met his gaze again, eyes questioning. Soren moved in, shifting a hand from her waist to her cheek.

He pressed his forehead to hers as he murmured the words, "I'm sorry, Larken."

"I forgive you. I'll *always* forgive you."

*You shouldn't*, he wanted to say. *You should move on and never spare me a second glance.*

But he couldn't say it. He was too selfish.

"Thanks for bringing me here, Soren."

He pulled back, and she smiled up at him. Letting go of her, he grabbed her hand and pulled her out to deeper waters. They would spend the day like that, just the two of them. Then they would go find Jodi and put this mess behind them. Soren had made up his mind, and he knew he would do whatever it took to stay in Larken's life. Even if she only wanted him as a security guard.

# CHAPTER 15

Larken hadn't been to the med-area of Camp yet, and she was excited to see what it looked like. She was impressed with everything else so far, and she didn't know how this would be any different. Soren pulled the door open for her as she teased him about his soft stomach. He grumbled something about rock-hard abs that had her blushing, remembering how he had looked at the beach not even an hour ago. They had cleaned up before making their way to the med-area, but the scent of the sea still clung to him.

They meandered to the room Jodi told Larken to meet her at, and Soren opened the door for her again. She sent a smile his way, and then stopped when she looked into the room. Ezra had a hand pressed firmly atop the table he looked to be holding himself up on. A wicked grin twisted Jodi's lips as she looked up at him. His red tie was wrapped around her hand, and she was using it to pull him in.

Soren didn't notice right away and walked into Larken. He steadied her before she was knocked over, and both Ezra and Jodi looked their way. Soren snorted quietly enough for only Larken to hear, and Ezra cleared his throat uncomfortably. He stammered out an incoherent excuse and bolted from the room. Larken walked over to the table, keeping to the side opposite Jodi.

"I thought you said you liked your men big and scary?" Larken teased.

Jodi shrugged, not at all embarrassed that she had been caught. "I thought I'd try a nice guy this time."

"Well, you couldn't have picked better. Ezra's great."

Jodi waggled her eyebrows. "I know."

Soren interrupted their banter, asking Jodi about other sedatives that might be available for Larken. Jodi seemed to think that both of Fisher's suggestions would work and even had a few more of her own. Of course, she said that they would need to be tested first before they flew out to Gadget. Larken's stomach flipped at the thought, but Soren placed a gentle hand on her lower back, silently telling her that she wouldn't face this alone. She was grateful for him, for the comfort he offered her. And she was glad that they were finally starting to feel normal again. There was still the matter of her future husband to be discussed, but she thought that, at least for now, this was something that they could handle ignoring.

"I also have a confession to make," Jodi said in a tone that had Larken's heart falling. She didn't wait for a response before continuing, "I've asked your guard dog to do some digging for me, but I didn't want him telling you or General Maxwell until I knew for sure."

"If this is something I'm going to regret hearing, I'd rather wait until I get back from Gadget," Larken joked, trying to keep things light despite Jodi's frown.

"Cornella doesn't know this, but I stumbled across a folder in the medic wing's system that was marked confidential. It had a lock on it and could only be accessed by a passcode that not even Ezra had."

"And Delvon did?" Larken asked.

Jodi shook her head, the stud in her nose glinting in the light. "No. If it were that easy, then General Maxwell could have looked years ago."

"I thought he led the Vigilants before Braves," Soren grumbled. "Shouldn't he know everything about them?"

Larken elbowed him in the stomach.

"He said the only one Cornella would trust with information like that was Liam, and even that was a jump since he's an idiot."

Larken snorted. "So, why are you bringing this up if you don't have a way to access it? We aren't going back to the Manor."

"No, you aren't. But we have a master hacker and someone who knows very *personal* details about your mother." Jodi gave Larken a cat-like grin.

"You were able to look in the folder."

"I was able to look in the folder," she agreed. Jodi pushed over a tablet with a list opened on the screen.

Larken's heart fluttered in anticipation but sank again as a bunch of numbers and complicated-looking words stared up at her. "What am I looking at?" Larken asked.

"It's a list of all the things the Vigilants fused their bullets with."

A true grin broke out across Larken's face and she turned to find a matching one on Soren. This was the first good thing to happen to them since Larken's departure. Yes, Thresh was siding with them, but Vallen had been sure that they would. But *this* information could change the course of the war. They could have antidotes at the ready to use on the battlefield. They might actually stand a chance now if the other districts decided not to help. Larken suddenly felt light and like she could run for miles on end as she asked about what the next step for Jodi was.

Eventually, the conversation of antidotes and field medics died down and Larken had to leave. She needed to apologize to Shadric for how she had acted. He was probably still beating himself up over what had happened. Delvon had told her when they talked earlier that morning that he hadn't brought up going to Gadget again. Jodi shooed them out of her lab with a box of caramel chocolates that she snatched from the fridge. She injected them with valerian extract and gave Larken strict orders to report back to her after the trial run. That left Larken with two days to test them. And if it didn't work, they would have to try again.

Soren walked with her all the way to the tabernacle, occasionally bumping into her. He claimed each time it happened that he hadn't seen her, and she had to fight a smile every time he did. When they got there, it was almost like he didn't want her to go in. He never said anything, though, and turned away with a promise to stop by later with dinner. She was excited to try dinner with him again, and this time, she would keep her fat mouth shut about Luminars and marriage altogether.

Larken hugged the box of chocolates to her stomach and walked into the tabernacle. A sad melody floated from the stage, though not sad enough to be depressing. Shadric sat on a stool in the middle of the stage, playing his guitar and humming along now and then. It was a song Larken didn't recognize, and she was almost nervous about it. His last two songs had been about her, and she wasn't sure if she wanted to know the words to this one.

Light poured in from the windows, bathing him in sunlight. He was beautiful, all things golden and bright. He was the sun, whereas Soren was the moon. She had always been drawn to the warmth inside Shadric. It was easy to forget how strong her feelings were for him when they were apart, when she had so many other things to think about. But there was no denying the way her heart fluttered standing there, watching him play.

Eventually, he looked up. Shadric offered a shy smile, a blush touching his cheeks. "How long have you been standing there?"

"Not long," she assured.

He let out a long breath, visibly relaxing. He crossed his arms, wedging his guitar between his forearms and knees. "Those chocolates for me?"

Larken smiled, realizing she was crushing the box. "No. They're for me."

"Another admirer?" he asked, his smile dipping the slightest bit.

"No. Just an over-eager medic. I need to try something other than the chamomile."

"Chocolates seem like a good idea to me." His smile was back, and they were quiet for a while before he said, "I'm glad you stopped by."

"Me too." She walked towards the stage and sat in the pew she had the last time they were alone here. "There was something I wanted to talk to you about, actually."

Shadric set his guitar down and joined her, making her remember what had almost happened the last time.

"Before you say anything, though, I need to apologize."

"No, Shad, you don't. I'm the one that needs to apologize. You didn't do anything wrong; I was just upset because I felt like I didn't have a say in anything. I shouldn't have said what I did. I feel awful about it."

"And I should have asked you if you even wanted me to come instead of going behind your back and getting Blade to agree to it." Shadric reached out and covered her hand with his. "I'm sorry, Larken."

They were back in that moment, and Larken's stomach flipped. She wondered if he might try to kiss her again, or if he had given up. Part of her wished that he would try, but the other part that had always belonged to Soren wanted him to take his hand back. It wasn't fair to Shadric, or to Soren either. Larken needed to leave; she needed to figure out what she wanted.

What Maxim wanted.

Her emotions were too twisted, too raw. And she knew that if Shadric leaned in and closed the distance right now, she wouldn't stop him.

Shadric must have seen the confusion in her eyes, because he leaned in and said, "I don't want to make things difficult for you, Larken. But I have to tell you…you need to know…that I'm an option."

Larken's breath caught. She already knew that, but somehow his admission complicated things more. He was there when she thought she'd lost Soren forever. Larken had unknowingly given a piece of her heart to the singer, thinking that, since Soren was gone, he could be her future if she was able to break her engagement. Then, miraculously, she was able to escape Dominic. But instead of living happily with Shadric, Soren came back. Her heart was such a tangled, confused mess that she didn't know if she would ever figure out what she wanted.

"I don't need an answer right away, but I thought you needed to know," he said softly. He gave her a bashful smile. "You know, in case I hadn't made it clear before."

Larken's lips twitched. She looked away, sighing. "Shad…what's your favorite color?"

He laughed. "Why?"

"Because all of our conversations have either been about me becoming a Faithful or a wedding that never happened. I don't know anything about you."

"I doubt that. Don't forget, Blade said—"

"We're not talking about whatever embarrassing stories Vallen told you about me. We're going to get to know each other like two people who haven't lived in the spotlight."

He squeezed her hand. "I like that." He huffed a small laugh again, and then asked, "Would you believe me if I told you I've always liked blue and green?"

"Why wouldn't I?" she teased. "We've just met. It's not like you're some famous singer that wrote a song about my blue-green eyes, or something."

"Right, well, when you put it like that…"

Larken dropped her gaze. She couldn't look at him as she said, "I know everyone is running out of time, but *this*—this can't be rushed."

"I like that," he assured.

Feeling a bit braver, she met his eyes again. They were completely sincere.

"Take all the time you need. Trust me, getting to know you won't be a chore."

"I like dogs," she offered. "Though, you probably figured that one out with me keeping Estelle and Delvon around."

Shadric barked a laugh. "I thought you said he was like a bear?"

"How did you know that? I didn't think that was the kind of thing he'd talk about."

The singer's ears went pink. "I may have asked him what you thought of him back when the media—" his voice caught. "No, not the media. You said that you two were—no, I don't mean that either." Redness spread from his ears to everywhere. "I'm just going to shut up.

"You asked when you heard that we were together?" Larken smothered a laugh. "Did he tell you about the engagement, too?"

"You—what?"

Larken couldn't hold it back anymore and brought a hand up to cover her laughter. When she regained control, she said, "It's a joke. He said that he would marry me himself before he would ever let Dominic come near me."

"So there's nothing—"

Larken shook her head. "No."

"That's a relief. I thought he'd been lying to me for a second."

"What do you mean?" she asked.

"He's just *different* with you. It's like he found his life calling or something. Before, he could only focus on what the next job was. Now he seems almost…I'm not sure how to describe it, but I do know you make him happy."

Larken's heart filled with so much love for her friend in that moment. As irritating as Delvon was, he made her world brighter. She was glad she could do the same for him, too.

Larken changed the subject to something a little less serious and they talked for a while longer. The questions that passed between them were mostly ones they should have already known the answers to if they'd met under normal circumstances. It was nice, until her rumbling stomach ruined the moment. Then she remembered that Soren was probably waiting for her by now.

Shadric grinned at her expense. "Want to go grab something to eat?"

"I should."

"Great." He set his guitar down. "We can go together."

Larken winced before she could help it.

"Something wrong?" Shadric asked.

"I kinda already have plans with someone tonight."

He smiled. "No worries. We can go out another time."

Larken's stomach flipped at the way he said *go out*.

"Absolutely," she agreed.

Shadric picked the instrument back up and strummed a lovely melody as she turned and walked out of the tabernacle...feeling much more confused than she had been before walking in.

# CHAPTER 16

"Well, here goes nothing."

Larken lifted the piece of chocolate to her lips and chewed slowly. Shadric watched her jaw work, praying that whatever she just ate would help her instead of hindering her. He also prayed for safe travels.

"I hope that things go well for you," Shadric said.

"Thanks, Shad. We should be—"

"We'll be fine," Delvon interrupted, bumping into Larken and almost knocking her over. He looked back over his shoulder as Shadric helped steady her and said, "I'll be there, remember?"

Larken's lips twitched as she rolled her eyes, making Shadric smile. She took a step closer and murmured under her breath, "I hate that he's right."

"Me too," Shadric agreed. "Del's always been like that though."

"I couldn't tell." She huffed a small laugh.

Shadric forced himself not to say how much he wished he was going. From the sounds of it, they would all be going to Stars together when she got back. He just needed to be patient. Though, reminding himself to be patient and actually doing it were two different things.

Larken brought her hand up to her mouth to cover a yawn,

showing him that the chocolate was at least making her tired. Soren appeared at the top of the steps then, just over her shoulder. He barked her name across the little clearing the Harpy was docked in, and she looked back at him. Signaling that she would be there soon, she turned back to Shadric and smiled.

"See you soon?"

How he wanted to pull her in and kiss her just then.

"Yes," he rasped, throat dry. He cleared it, saying, "Have a fun trip."

Delvon joined Soren a moment later. "Peach, get your big butt in here."

"You too," she said, ignoring the remark about her rear end. "I mean, not a fun trip, but—"

"What's the hold-up?" Ewan asked, though he didn't quite fit in the doorway.

Larken's cheeks went pink as she stumbled over her words of farewell. Shadric saved her by saying, "I know what you meant."

She nodded once and then scampered the short distance to the Harpy steps. As soon as her booted heel hit the landing, the steps lifted from the ground and folded away. Then the door shut and they jumped into the air. Dirt, pine needles, and dead leaves whipped up around Shadric as a gust of hot air hit him in the face. It was quickly followed by a cold autumn one, and with one last blink, they were gone.

Stuffing his hands into his pockets, Shadric stared at the sky for longer than he would willingly admit to anyone. He kicked a small rock and turned to the tabernacle before he knew what he was doing. Reaching up, Shadric scratched at the stubble coming in thick on his jaw. He should probably shave sooner than later since he wanted to look somewhat presentable for the press conference he had two days after Larken was supposed to get back. However, when he walked into the tabernacle and saw his favorite guitar waiting for him on the stage, he just couldn't bring himself to go to it. Playing felt different now that Larken was at Camp.

Instead of the fun melodies that he usually spent time writing and throwing lyrics to, everything had turned to *her*. Each song, each lyric, each *note* started and ended with Larken Hale. Shadric couldn't get her out of his mind, and because of it, he was making a fool of himself. When he wasn't doing that, he was in a state of worry over her safe return. And to make matters worse, Delvon wasn't there to talk him down this time.

Turning to the stairs, Shadric decided to talk to the only one who knew what he was going through. He was sure Blade was going just as crazy since he had to stay here and pretend to be dead.

Shadric cracked the door at the top of the stairs and found Blade hunched over the table. He tapped furiously at a tablet and a computer. Shadric had offered more than once to bring back better equipment each time he left for a concert or a publicity thing, but Blade insisted that too many purchases would raise an eyebrow or two and they needed to save his arii.

He was just about to back away when Blade looked up with a severe gaze. "What?"

"I—" Shadric's voice caught. "I don't know."

Sighing, Blade leaned back in his chair and closed his eyes. He rubbed at his temple as he motioned for Shadric to come in. He didn't know why, but whenever he talked to Blade, Shadric always felt like a child. Why couldn't he just speak his mind like Delvon? Why couldn't he joke around with Blade like the other members of his team could? It wasn't like Blade was the one who'd raised him. No one really did. It was a group effort from Camp.

"Don't do that," Blade ordered.

"What?"

"That look you get when you think too hard. It makes me feel like I need to step up my game."

Shadric relaxed some and even cracked a small smile.

"So, you don't know why you came to visit this old man, huh?" Blade rose a brow in challenge.

"I—well..."

"I'm sure it has nothing to do with the fact that a certain annoyance has just departed our camp."

"Del's bull-headed, but I wouldn't call him an annoyance."

"I wouldn't either," Blade agreed, making Shadric's feeble attempt at a joke feel pathetic.

Shadric sighed, feeling like the action told Blade everything he needed to know without actually having to say it.

Blade returned his sigh with a grunt. "If this was easier, son, then I would have been down there to see her off too."

"Why weren't you?" Shadric wished he could take the words back when Blade met his eyes.

There was a long silence. Shadric considered getting up and leaving, but Blade finally admitted, "The last time I told her good-bye, I had to turn right around and bring her home. I guess part of me thinks staying up here will keep me from having to do that again."

The dark realization of what Blade meant crept over Shadric like cold water. He didn't want to see her off because he didn't want to be the one to collect her body.

"I'm sorry. I didn't—"

"Don't be sorry. Superstition is useless and we both know it. I'm being stubborn and that's all it comes down to." Blade cleared his throat and sat up straight again. His muscles almost creaked audibly; the man clearly wasn't used to sitting all day. "Now, was there anything you wished to discuss?"

"No. Thank you, but no. I've figured out what I need to do."

"Good. Shut the door on your way out." Even though his words were gruff, they weren't unkind.

Shadric did what he was told and made his way back down to the stage. This time, though, instead of walking over to his guitar, he dropped to his knees in front of the alter. He had been an idiot, thinking about only himself all the while Blade was upstairs purposely keeping his distance in an attempt to keep Larken safe. If something happened to her, Shadric's life wouldn't be the only one that was ruined.

So, he prayed. He prayed for himself. He prayed for Blade. And he prayed for everyone who Larken had touched since joining

Squad 19. Not only did the future rely on her convincing the Magnate, but their hearts relied on their friend making it home safe and whole.

# CHAPTER 17

Larken woke from her hazy dozing when Soren gently murmured her name. She only had a vague recollection of the journey, and from what she could remember, Soren hadn't talked much. Ewan and Delvon had gone after each other in a way only close siblings could. It reminded her of her relationship with Loxly more than the one she had with Liam. She thought she heard talk about a plan, but when she could only remember Ewan asking where they would stop for doughnuts on the way, Larken realized that may have been a dream and she should probably ask about the exact details instead.

*"Larken,"* Soren murmured again, pulling her back into reality.

She groaned, wanting to ignore him and lose herself in the fog once more.

Her pillow moved, nudging her, and she became more aware of her surroundings. Vallen's jacket covered her, and something warm and heavy encircled her waist. Slowly, Larken realized that Soren had his arm around her, and her pillow was his chest.

Groaning again, she sluggishly sat upright. Blinking her bleary eyes, Larken rubbed at the corner of her mouth with the back of her wrist. It came away wet, and her eyes came into focus. Soren smirked at her and she looked away—gaze landing on a drool spot on his shirt. Her cheeks heated and she made to stand after clutching the jacket closer around her.

Soren grabbed her elbow and gently yanked her back down. Her backside hit the seat as he said, "Not so fast."

Larken stuffed her arms through the jacket sleeves and tried to zip it up.

Her fingers fumbled over the zipper, and Soren placed a hand over both of hers, stilling them. He used his other to lift her face. He waited until she met his gaze before asking, "Do you feel any different?"

She shrugged with one shoulder. "The same as I did on the trial run."

"Do you feel alert?"

"More than I did on the extract."

"And your anxiety?"

"How about we *don't* have this conversation," she said, breaking eye contact. Her gaze landed back on the spot of drool. Larken fought to keep her mortification from her cheeks but felt them heat anyway.

Soren sighed, unable to berate her for not wanting to speak. Instead, he pulled her close once more. Her cheek came into contact with the chilled wet spot on his dark shirt, and she was forced to listen to the rhythmic beating of his heart.

She let out a breath, relaxing into him. "I'm fine. The flight was fine. Everything is fine."

"You aren't just saying that to get away, are you?"

She snuggled into him more. "Wouldn't dream of it."

They sat like that for a moment before Delvon could be heard shouting for them to get a move on. Reluctantly, Larken got to her feet, stretched, and then waited for Soren to join her by the open door. She pulled her hair out and fixed it, unable to help herself as she combed her hair up into a bun with her fingers. She looked back at Soren and asked, "Got a brush?"

"I left it behind with your gold eyeshadow."

"Gold-*infused*. If you're going to tease me then do it right," she jabbed, smiling as she finished tying off her hair.

"Sorry. I figured the joke would go over your head. You know, because you're so short." His lips quirked, making her want to kiss the corner where they tilted up.

"Get out here, Peach! We need to get to the safe house!"

The moment ruined, Larken tucked one last flyaway behind her ear and let Soren leave the Harpy first. Nothing but grey greeted them, and after looking both ways, Larken found that they had docked in some sort of giant tunnel. Every step the two of them took to the group had a slight echo to it, the sound as smooth as the walls and floors. There were no lights, yet everything could be seen clearly. It was weird, and Larken decided that she would trust Delvon to take point on this since he seemed to be the one in charge. Despite that, she still pulled her flashlight free, just in case.

They reached the others just in time to see Delvon smack his brother in the back of the head while the man suppressed a laugh. Levi and Loxly shared a look and both snorted when she asked what she missed. Ewen couldn't hold it in any longer and burst out laughing when he said, "Seems my brother's inside source is a spurned ex."

"*What!?*" Larken asked with a laugh. "Delvon's too rude to have an ex."

The group cracked and all ribbed Delvon. He frowned deeply and grunted, "I explained that to her multiple times. She still insisted on growing attached to me." He looked at Larken. "She was even more of a parasite than you are."

"Should I take that as a compliment?" Larken asked.

"Absolutely. She was a nightmare."

As if on cue, Delvon's communicator went off three times in a row. Larken gave him a small smile and changed the subject. "Where are we?"

"In Gadget."

"Clearly."

Delvon gave her a wink before addressing the group as a whole.

"The Military Manor didn't have one because it always had the force of the military behind it, but Gadget has four safe houses. We are about to break into the oldest one that hasn't been used in over fifteen years." He held out his wrist and tapped it. A hologram exploded out of the hidden bracelet he wore and he pointed at a little image of a fat peach. "We're here."

"Obviously," Soren grunted.

Delvon ignored him. "The safe house is here." He pointed to a green square. "And the Manor is here." Delvon pointed to a red triangle. "Unless I brought a bunch of idiots along with me, you can all figure out that our primary objective is to get Peach to the Manor."

"Are you going to share the *how* with us, dear brother? Or are you just going to take her yourself after calling us idiots a few more times?" Ewan asked.

"I'll stop calling you an idiot when you stop acting like one," Delvon shot back.

"He's got a point, though," Loxly said. "You haven't told us what the plan is."

"Or why we needed so few people," Levi added. Larken could tell by the slight tone in his voice that he was irritated that Brecker and Hinlee weren't there. She was sure Soren and Loxly could hear it too, but the field medic's face remained impassive.

Soren stood silently to her left. He might have been keeping his mouth shut, but Larken knew it bothered him that he wasn't in charge.

Delvon sighed and stretched out his hand. He grabbed the hologram and pulled, bringing the street map into view. Tall buildings and electrified skyscrapers filled the holographic space. Larken was just starting to wonder if this was real-time when a small aircraft shot between two buildings. Delvon continued to pull on the image, bringing the Manor into view. Whereas both the Thresh and Military Manor looked like actual manors, the Gadget one was nothing more than a perfect black pyramid. Larken wasn't sure how people got in or out of the place, and the hologram was too granulated to make out fine details.

"So, this tunnel leads to the Manor?" Soren asked, pulling Larken from her thoughts.

"Yeah, can't we just head there now?" Loxly agreed.

Delvon gave his brother a look and Ewan was forced to admit, "It's not that simple."

Levi opened his mouth, no doubt to ask what they were talking about, but was cut off by a loud screech. Metal clashed against metal and the whole tunnel shook, making the weird invisible light flicker. Larken's hand grew slick and she dropped the flashlight. She ignored it and grabbed Soren's hand. The sound was too reminiscent of the multiple crashes she had been in. Soren squeezed her palm, silently telling her he was there. She met his gaze and his eyes shone a fierce green.

*I won't let go.*

Finally able to take a breath, Larken waited to speak until the tunnel stood still. "What do you mean it's not that simple?"

"The reason no one has been to the safe house we're going to is because no one can get to it," Delvon grunted.

Larken made to ask Delvon what he was talking about as she crouched down to grab the flashlight, but her words evaporated on her tongue. She stared in horror at her hand as the ring Brecker gave her shifted and tried to get closer to the ground despite it resting on her finger. There were magnetic strips in the ground and Larken knew where they were without having to ask Delvon.

Her stomach fell as she rounded on the bodyguard. "You brought us to the mag-way!?"

"The what?" Loxly asked.

"The underground traveling system," Levi answered, head snapping to the left so he could stare down the tunnel.

Larken jumped to her feet before grabbing Loxly's elbow and Levi's shoulder. Ushering them back toward the Harpy, she demanded, "What were you thinking? Do you know how dangerous—"

"This one isn't active anymore so just untwist your panties." Delvon glared at her as if this whole thing was *her* fault.

"Delvon," she tried reasoning, "there was a huge cave-in like ten years ago. These tunnels aren't safe."

"Fifteen."

"What?" she asked.

"Fifteen years. Not ten." Then, as if he couldn't help himself, his signature smirk that was equal parts cocky and condescending turned his lips.

"So, the safe house…" Loxly started.

"Was separated from the Manor by the cave-in," Ewan finished.

"Lucky for us, I had someone on the inside who was able to check for Peach-sized holes. We should be able to get into the safe house to clean up and use the track to get to the Manor," Delvon said.

Larken looked over her team, realizing now why Brecker, Hinlee, and Carl had been left behind. Delvon and Ewan were the muscle, and they would serve as scouts since they'd been to Gadget before. Loxly was the pilot, but since he was also a sharpshooter, he would also be useful in a tunnel that hadn't been utilized in fifteen years. Levi was there to keep anyone from getting an infection if they were to get hurt in said tunnel. And Soren would be trading places with Delvon for the mission, acting as Larken's bodyguard. It was a good team, and she hoped that they were able to use everyone's skills except for Levi's.

"What first?" she asked.

Delvon gave her a feral smile. "We rest up and get you ready to plead our case to Luminary Kinslee. Then, we sneak you in and out before leaving this Maxim-forsaken District."

"Worst case scenario?" Soren demanded.

"We get to use our guns," Delvon grunted as he and his brother lifted their firearms in unison.

Larken didn't think Gadget was going to go as smoothly as Thresh, but she suddenly had a very bad feeling that this wasn't going to go as planned at all.

# CHAPTER 18

The safe house was nothing more than a shack, and Soren couldn't help but wonder how the Luminary's family was supposed to fit inside it. The place was clearly the very last resort, what with its three sets of cabin-style bunkbeds and single shower. At least the bathroom had a door and the small kitchenette seemed to be functional and stocked.

It was Delvon's turn in the small shower and Larken sat on the floor by the open front door, furthest from the steam. She leaned against the doorframe, resting her eyes as she waited for her turn to wash up. Hopefully, the way to the Manor was less disastrous than the way the safe house had been from the Harpy. Soren had already showered, but Larken still had black smudges on her face. Her hair had mostly fallen out of her bun and laid in snarled knots around her shoulders.

Soren only just now realized how long it had been since she'd had a haircut, and the length of her wheat hair caught him off guard. She looked so much older than she had the day she first arrived at base, even though it wasn't even a year ago.

Loxly murmured to Levi and Ewan jumped into the conversation every now and then, waiting for his brother to get out of the shower. Delvon had assured them all that his source had turned off the usage links to the Manor so no one would know that they were draining the water and food supply. They could only pray that he hadn't been lied to.

Larken readjusted so the doorframe was more in the middle of her back instead of her shoulder, and Soren immediately felt guilty about the sleeping arrangements. Maybe he should sleep on the ground and give his impossibly thin mattress to Larken so she could use two instead of one. He also felt guilty because he had been so concerned about getting her into the air that he hadn't once thought about her shoulder. The last time he had asked about it was long before their trip to Thresh. It wasn't that he hadn't tried, but he never ended up getting the chance. And now he felt like a jerk because of it.

Soren walked over and dropped to the ground. Larken didn't move and he had to fight not to stick a strand of her hair behind her ear. He stared at her long enough that she cracked a bleary eye at him and raised a brow.

"Your shoulder," he grunted, the words sounding nothing like he intended them to.

"Is fine."

"The beds…"

"Will suffice for the night. Both Jodi and Ezra are on standby for when we get back, but one night shouldn't bother it too much."

Lie.

She was lying. Loxly had told him how much her shoulder had bothered her those first few nights in the dorm.

His concern for her seemed to be having the opposite effect, though, because she turned her head and glared slightly. "If you're that worried about my well-being, maybe you should think up something for me to tell Kinslee instead of focusing on something inevitable."

Instead of rising to the challenge she was presenting, Soren grabbed her hand. The anger in her eyes didn't match the way she squeezed the life out of his fingers. She was scared. Larken was worried about breaking into the Manor, yes, but she was also afraid of this place. It was the reason she was putting off her shower. She didn't want to be crushed to death, not that he could blame her. That's what happened after all; the wrong pipes were laid into the street and the magnet pulled the tunnel ceiling down. She was probably also worried about the water after Ewan's careless joke about being electrocuted this close to the magnetic strip in the ground.

"We'll be in the sky again soon," Soren assured.

"Yippee," she deadpanned, resting her head on his shoulder.

Soren leaned in closer so his shoulder wasn't as much of a stretch for her. She needed whatever comfort he could offer her right now. Larken would shower – she was too stubborn not to – just as she would sleep on the single mattress on her bunk and climb through the tunnels all the way to the secret entrance of the Manor. Larken would hold her head high and pretend her anxieties weren't eating her up inside. The least Soren could do was be there for her. Especially since that was the promise he had made to the both of them.

---

Sweat stuck Larken's shirt to her back, making the shower she had forced herself to take pointless. No air moved in the tunnel, and she hoped that once they were past the second barrier that things would cool off. Part of the blockage that separated the safe house from the Harpy had crumbled away, but Delvon assured them that the one separating the safe house from the Manor would be much worse.

Delvon's communicator had been going off all morning to the point he needed to silence it. Even now the vibrations could be heard from where he walked in front of her. Delvon led the group, Levi and Loxly flanking her. Soren was behind her and Ewan behind him. Weapons were drawn and Larken wished she had her sword. Her gun was in its holster, but the group agreed it would be best if she at least appeared to be unarmed. She was to go in showing signs of peace, not shooting at everyone that came towards her. But all that did was make her fingers itch.

Darkness and light fought to make themselves seen in the tunnel, just like the day before. Delvon said it was early morning when they left the safe house, and Larken's communicator confirmed it. Now though, she had no way of knowing how long they'd been walking. She was trying to save the battery on her communicator, just like everyone else, and was under strict orders to only pull it out in an emergency. And as much as checking the time felt like one, it really wasn't.

Finally, Delvon slowed and put his firearm away. "We're here."

A shudder ran through her as she took in the mound of rock and hanging wires. The reds, blues, and greens dangled there like vines with little copper tongues. Glass, stone, and metal stuck out of the heap in dangerous juts, ready to slice open an unwary hand. And all the way up in the right-hand corner was the hole.

Delvon shot off a message and a chirp sounded from the other side, telling Larken his informant was here already. The earpiece she wore binged to life, reminding her yet again how underprepared they had been for Thresh. They were lucky that Morgan had always planned on siding with them.

Larken pushed the ideas of what could have happened from her mind as Delvon started the climb. He turned, holding a hand out for her. Larken grabbed onto him, meeting his grey eyes as he ordered, "Only where I step."

She nodded, not knowing how she would possibly see past his bulky frame to where he placed his hands and feet. He went back to climbing, Larken trying her best to do what he said. She only missed a few times, the third opening her palm as she grazed a piece of metal.

Delvon reached the top well before the rest of them, Larken holding everyone up, and he looked down at her. "Not sure if your big butt will fit through here."

"Probably easier than your fat head," she muttered, grabbing onto a rock.

Pushing herself to go faster, Larken reached Delvon's boot and used it to pull herself up. He helped and pushed her towards the gap between the rubble and the wall. When Larken reached it, a face poked through and took her by surprise. Big, bright green eyes crinkled at the corners as a smile broke out across the young woman's face. Dark green hair that was almost black hung just past her ears in a curled bob, reminding Larken of the day she first met Jodi.

"Hi! I'm MaryJo!"

Larken could feel Delvon tense at her back and she couldn't help but give a small smile herself. "Hi, MaryJo. I'm Larken."

"Figured. Why don't we get you over here and into the Manor?"

Larken nodded and let the two people help her through the hole and down the other side of the rubble pile. The others didn't wait for her to finish the climb before they started after her. Once everyone was on solid ground again, MaryJo beamed at them. "This is so exciting!"

"Sure," Delvon agreed as Ewan snickered under his breath.

She turned on Delvon, her grin growing even wider. "Oh, Delvon. It's so good to see you again! How have you been?"

"This isn't a social call, MaryJo."

Her face fell slightly. "I know…I just thought we could catch up a little while you're here."

"We're trying to start a revolution. I don't think there's going to be much time for catching up."

"Okay," MaryJo reluctantly agreed. "After then." She turned and started walking, either ignoring Ewan's smothered laughter or just not hearing it.

Larken felt a little bad for the woman, but knowing Delvon, he wasn't lying when he claimed to have told her he wasn't interested. Larken had to admire MaryJo's persistence, though, and could only pray that it wouldn't come back to bite them. Maybe she should tell Delvon to be nicer until this was over. But it would seem that she didn't need to because the man quickly caught up to MaryJo and started talking business. Gone was MaryJo's bubbly demeanor and in its place, a soldier.

Then, it was happening. The rest of them set off before Larken was ready. Her feet pleaded with her to stay put, but with everyone except Delvon and MaryJo surrounding her, Larken had no choice. They were counting on her. The team, her Squad, Vallen, Shadric, Thresh, and everyone back at Camp…they were *all* counting on her.

*"I don't need some fancy device to tell me the exact moment the seasons are gonna change, and I don't need to be a genius to know you're made of the same stuff. You're gonna change things, Larken. And with Maxim with you, you won't lose."*

Rich's words came floating back to her, reminding her of the power she held, of what was at stake. It was too big of a burden for her. Larken stumbled under the weight and was forced to try and pay attention to where she was walking.

"I'll tell you what," Loxly said, interrupting her thoughts. "I'm not sure which is more stressful. This, or your flyin' exam."

An invisible breeze washed over Larken and she wasn't sure if she'd imagined it or not. Images of the grass underneath the Pumpkin and how the sky looked that day had her breathing slowing down. She was stressed then, too. Stressed enough that she had to mentally run through an exercise that had long since stopped working for her.

"I don't know," Levi added. "I think Larken coming after me about fresh starts when we first met was more impressive. Especially since she didn't stop with me."

That was also true. She had put on a brave face and taken on Base 14 all by herself. She even broke someone's face after he tried to mess with her.

"I think taking on a group of Vigilants singlehandedly while her date was bleeding on the ground was the most impressive," Soren said, jumping in on the unspoken agreement to distract her.

Then her heart skipped a beat.

*Oh, I did call him my date that night, didn't I?*

"Let's not forget the engagement we just got her out of. I'm just glad I was on the kidnapping side and not the marrying one," Delvon grumbled.

"You would have made a horrible wife to Dominic," Larken teased.

Delvon didn't say anything, but Ewan barked a laugh at his expense.

But they were right. She made it through her time at base, had overcome her fear of flying for just that little bit, survived an unwanted engagement, and already went up against the men they were trying to take down. She'd faced them twice and lived.

*"You're gonna change things, Larken. And with Maxim with you, you won't lose."*

Rich had been right, at least so far. Maxim had seen her through every obstacle. She made Him a promise in that little chapel that if He saved her from the wedding, she would do whatever He asked. Well, He was asking now, and Larken just needed to trust Him enough to say yes.

Breathing easier, she slowed her steps. Soon, they were all looking at a trap door at the top of a ladder fused to the wall. The tunnel shook again as a tram somewhere around them flew by. It was good thinking on Delvon's part to use the mag-ways. Trams wouldn't be using this route, and the trapdoor at the end would spit them out in the Luminary's study.

*This is it*, Larken thought as her sweaty palms grabbed ahold of the ladder after Delvon. *There's no turning back now. Either she helps us or we run. But, Maxim, I beg you…please let it be the first.*

# CHAPTER 19

Dominic brought the cigar to his lips, the cool early autumn breeze pulling at the embers on the end. The smoke he breathed out did nothing to stifle the smell of manure and dying crops. Dominic could only hope that this time, they got it right.

He wasn't stupid. He knew that burning down the farms in Thresh would cause problems for the country, so he kept the blazes contained to the houses. The house he sought out seemed to have disappeared, though. Every record of the members of Squad 19 had been wiped out, even though Dominic knew for a fact that they existed—that they ruined *everything* for him.

Now…it was his turn.

The sun dipped lower and lower beyond the hills of rolling farmland. The occasional bird or bat flew overhead, either beginning their day or ending it. Browns, oranges, and reds colored the world so much more up here than they did in the Military District. All it did was remind Dominic what he was missing—of how much time was running out.

He needed to move faster but he couldn't do anything until he knew for sure. Dominic had an idea of what she was trying to do, but couldn't confirm it until Larken made her next move. Luminary Morgan played the fool, pretending that he hadn't seen Larken during her trip to the Manor. Apparently, neither had his wife, son, or daughter. But if Larken was trying to be civil about this civil war, then she would need to reach out to another District soon. Thresh was already under lockdown, which left Stars and Gadget. Once she was sighted, they could lay a trap for her at the remaining location.

Dominic took another drag. He faced away from the direction that their home had been built. The land was so free of anything aside from crops that he could almost make out the white roof and plum-colored walls. He was foolish to think that Cornella hadn't known about the house. At least he knew Cornella had no idea that, when the time came, Dominic would help Larken kill her mother.

His pocket chimed and he pulled out his communicator, releasing the build-up of blue smoke from his lungs. His lips turned into a cruel smirk when he read the two words that lit up his screen.

*Found him.*

Feeling lighter than he had since Larken left, Dominic sent the order. He watched as, in the distance, a shot was fired at a large yellow house. It erupted into flames, causing the livestock surrounding the fire to cry out in fear.

Dominic didn't care if the old man got out of the house or not as he pushed off his aircraft. He tossed the butt of his cigar into the nearby grass and opened the door. It could be that Larken was living under a rock now, or that whoever she was with was trying to protect her, but he was sure that this would finally reach her.

After all, Loxly Beau was like a brother to her, and he would be more than betrayed that she was the reason he no longer had a home to return to.

# CHAPTER 20

The trapdoor thudded against something solid and refused to open. MaryJo, still on the ground, swore in a way that would have even Vallen blushing.

"MaryJo," Delvon barked under his breath, his tone leaving no room for interpretation about how he was feeling.

"No—no, i-i-it's not my fault," she stuttered out, turning a deep crimson. "Jarr was supposed to move the coffee table. He—"

"No, it's your fault for not picking someone more trustworthy," Delvon reprimanded.

"*He is trustworthy!*" she hissed. "He's just running behind, is all. He has to be."

"Or he's already turned us in," Levi said from the ground.

Larken's hands slipped against the rung that she held, her eyes leaving Levi and landing on Soren. He changed his grip from the ladder to her ankle. She felt his silent, *remember what I said, I'm not leaving.* Larken gave him a nod and started climbing up.

Delvon grumbled until he realized what she was doing and then freaked out. "*Peach,*" he grunted as she passed in front his legs and climbed up to his chest. "This is my *personal* space here."

"Oh, shut up."

Larken let go of the ladder and turned to face the man. He glared at her as she grabbed onto his chest.

"Flashlight?" she asked.

"Where's yours?"

"I left it back in the tunnel, I think."

Delvon grumbled as he let go of the rung he held onto and pulled a flashlight from his utility belt. Larken took it and turned it on. She shined it at the hinges, praying they were within reach. They were, and Larken quickly got to work.

Fishing a dagger out of Delvon's belt, Larken climbed him until she could reach the hinges. There was more grumbling about his discomfort, but he held the flashlight for her when she started to struggle. Soon, one of the bolts clattered to the tunnel floor, then the second followed. Slowly, Larken let the trapdoor fall, latched at the lock.

A wave of accomplishment washed over her but was doused when she looked up to find only a very solid darkness covering the doorway. Unable to help herself, Larken glared down at MaryJo. Delvon and Soren both joined her, and MaryJo bit her lip.

"Okay, it's less of a coffee table and more of a motherboard."

"What?" Loxly asked.

"Well, you see, the thing is—" MaryJo bit her lip again and sighed. "Okay, so the Manor is all connected by one device that the Luminary alone has access to."

"And she's usin' it as a coffee table? Talk about arii to burn," Loxly said, pointing out the obvious. One spill, one wrong move, and the whole Manor would be shut down.

Delvon stiffened and looked up at Larken, a feral grin splitting his lips. "Told you I got the right person for the job, love."

"Uh-huh, sure." Larken didn't point out that MaryJo was likely the only person that would have taken his call, or that they were now able to shut down the entirety of Gadget Manor because she was an idiot.

Delvon took his dagger back and waited for Larken to climb down to Soren. Ewan replaced her on the ladder and climbed up to his brother. Delvon signaled with his fingers by wrapping them around the dagger one at a time. When he gripped the gold hilt fully, he thrust the weapon upward.

Larken wasn't sure if the device was made of a soft metal or just didn't have any protection underneath, but the dagger went through. The invisible lights in the tunnel turned off with the same slow whirring sound as a dying fan, and the men were quick to pull out their flashlights.

The two brothers reached up, balancing on the same rung, and pushed the device out of the way. Slowly it scraped against the floor. By the sound alone, Larken could tell that the floor was made of wood. When there was a gap large enough for Delvon to get through, he climbed up and stuck a hand back into the tunnel. Ewan mimicked his brother on the ladder, and Larken grabbed onto his hand. She quickly made her way up the ladder, accepting Delvon's help when she reached the top.

Larken barely peeked her head up over the doorway when someone cleared their throat. Stomach lurching, Larken's head snapped around to the sound. Luminary Kinslee sat in an uncomfortable-looking chair, ankles and arms crossed. The room was dark, but not so much that Larken couldn't make out Kinslee's features. Her darkly painted lips tilted down in a frown, and Larken honestly couldn't tell if her lipstick was purple or black. Her severely upturned eyes had a thin cat eye that made them look even more pointed. Everything about the woman's features was hard except for the elegant slope of her neck and the roundness of her jaw.

"I wondered if you would be dumb enough to show up here, *Daughter of the Military.*" The way Kinslee said her title made Larken blush.

Every part of her wanted to wilt away and ask if Kinslee was going to turn them in, but Larken lifted her chin. "You can either hear what we have to say or decide not to. We don't have to stay."

"Oh," Kinslee said as a group of guards walked into the study, "I think you do."

Larken's hands grew slick in Delvon's so he used the back of her shirt to haul her up instead. The black tee bunched, and she pulled it down over her black leggings when she was once again on solid ground. One by one the guys climbed up out of the mag-way tunnel, faces set into stony frowns. When Loxly got into line, the last set of guns was pointed at them. MaryJo joined them, trying to slip into the guard line. Kinslee glared at her but said nothing. She only nodded to one of the guards. He broke from the line and walked MaryJo out into the hall.

Kinslee shifted in the soft purple chair she sat in, crossing her legs instead. She placed her chin on her fist and took them all in. While she did that, Larken looked at the room around her. Everything was dark, the windows all covered by a black, see-through film. None of the monitors or screens were on, and the room appeared almost dead. The motherboard looked to be nothing more than a dark grey wooden trunk. Not even the white walls served to brighten the room. Everything was shadow and darkness.

The four guards that stood at the ready didn't move, and Larken recognized one of them as the Luminar. She couldn't remember his name at the moment, but that wasn't her biggest concern. What she needed to know was if Kinslee planned on having them killed or not.

"Tell me, dear. What made the Military's Sweetheart trade her crown for a gun?"

"We thought me bringing a sword would give the wrong impression."

Kinslee's lips twitched. "And what impression are you trying to make?"

"One that says even though I have people who care and want to protect me, I'm only armed enough to protect myself in case this doesn't go well. Please, I only want to talk for a little while."

"My dear girl, I fear the conversation you would like to have will take more than a few minutes."

"More than a few?" Larken asked in a rush of air.

Kinslee finally allowed herself a small smile and Larken sagged in relief. The Luminary would listen instead of turning them away. Or worse.

"Anyone smart enough to break into Gadget is worth that much, don't you think?" Kinslee asked, an impressed glint in her dark eyes.

"If I agreed, would that make me sound pretentious?"

Kinslee chuckled and stood. "Oh, I like you. You aren't at all the quiet mouse they painted you to be. Nor the rage-induced hormonal woman." Kinslee walked over and patted her husband on the chest. He lowered his gun but didn't acknowledge his wife. "Follow me, please," she said, heading for the door.

The group followed, not needing to be stealthy since the power was out. Kinslee led them a little ways down the hall and into a sitting room that looked the same as the study. The only difference was that instead of monitors, the room was decorated with stiff-looking minimalist white couches. Kinslee took the only chair in the room and reclined as much as the stuffed back would let her. She still managed to look elegant and in charge of the situation, though.

Dim shadows still surrounded them and Larken sat sandwiched between Levi and Loxly. Both Ewan and Delvon flanked the couches, and Soren stood directly behind her. Knowing that they were safe for the moment meant Larken was able to relax enough that she noticed how much of the shoulder pain her anxiety and adrenaline had been covering. She reached up to grab it but let go after only one squeeze when Kinslee's eyes followed her movement. Larken didn't want to give away her one weakness…even if Gadget was a new ally.

Once Kinslee's guards entered the room and took up seats of their own, Kinslee snapped her fingers. An older woman who'd been waiting unnoticed in the corner came forward. She placed a steaming mug of something in Kinslee's hand, and the Luminary didn't wait to take a sip.

"I'd offer you some oolong lavender tea, but you cut the power. This mug was already waiting for my relaxation time. All I can offer is water or chilled cucumber lemon tea."

Larken was torn between wanting to seem gracious and not wanting to be poisoned if this was all just a pretense. Delvon saved her by grunting, "No thanks."

Kinslee nodded, unfazed. "Tell me your plan, Larken. Best not to waste time. If your mother is trying to find you, she'll notice the power outage."

Larken went into as much detail as she could, explaining that some things were still undecided. Kinslee kept a straight face the whole time, watching Larken as if she were a cat deciding whether to pounce. The only time she moved was to sip at her tea.

When Larken finished, Kinslee stared at her long enough for her to start fidgeting. Kinslee pursed her lips and, after what felt like forever, spoke. "So, in short, you want to take your mother's place?"

"And Liam's," Loxly added.

Kinslee nodded. "So what do you need from me? Money? Technology? *Permission?*"

"Only your support—if you care to give it."

Larken started picking at her thumbnail as she waited. Kinslee set her tea down and steepled her fingers. She pursed her lips again, staring at Larken with dark eyes. Never before had she felt so much like a tiny, helpless bird. And Kinslee was the lioness lying in wait.

Finally, the Luminary's demeanor broke and her lips twitched again. "Lucky for you, I'm tired of shipping off tech-guns to the bases."

Larken didn't bother to hide her grin. She reached out and grabbed onto Loxly's hand and squeezed. He squeezed back.

"I think it might be time for Gadget to switch from their more neutral stance to an honest one. We will accept Maxim's call to support Larken Hale and renounce Cornella." Kinslee looked back at her husband and only then did his expression change.

He offered his wife a small smile.

"Right." Kinslee clapped and stood. "Get out of here before the power comes back on. Which, by my calculations," Kinslee looked at a black band on her wrist, "should be in about twenty minutes."

They were rushed back to the trapdoor as Kinslee muttered

about having to fix the motherboard so there wouldn't be technological evidence of their visit. One by one they said their goodbyes and gave their thanks before climbing down into the mag-way.

They waited until the door was closed before looking at each other. Every single one of them gave Larken a grin and she felt lighter than air.

"You did good, Little Bird," Loxly said. "You did good."

"Right," Delvon grunted, not seeming to care that he was leaving his *friend* behind. "Let's get out of here."

He bumped into Larken on his way past, and that was as good a compliment as any from the grumpy bodyguard. The best one came from Soren though, as he gave her a quick wink that had her stomach flipping over. And Larken was forced to admit that maybe, just maybe, things would work out for them after all.

# CHAPTER 21

Soren could still feel the way Larken had clung to him three days later. He should have been focusing on the task he'd been given, but he could only think about the way her hand had balled his shirt up in her fist. Soren wanted to ask what she'd been dreaming about, but he hadn't been brave enough. Not only that, but she seemed fine when he roused her and said they'd landed.

It had been a whirlwind of Ewan getting Larken to Jodie and Ezra, Delvon marching off to find Vallen, and Hinlee and Brecker demanding to know how things went. Of course, Loxly did most of the talking at the time, but now Soren found himself barely having a moment of silence. He even considered ignoring Hinlee's invitation to meet for a small picnic.

He was going to be in charge while they were in Stars, and the idea of it caused his stomach to knot up. Soren would be lying if he said he wasn't apprehensive about the fact that Delvon would be staying behind again. As much as the man got under his skin, it made sense why he had to stay. After Larken ran off, her bodyguard had disappeared as well. This left the public to assume he was a Faithful, and if Delvon was to be seen in Stars with Shadric...well, it would ruin everything for them.

Soren didn't have much of a plan, but the bit that he did have sounded solid to Vallen. Shadric would go with his team in a separate aircraft—minus Delvon and Ewan—and get ready for a charity concert he would be holding at the Stars Manor. There would be no safe houses and no time. Larken would need to get into the Manor study and out before anyone noticed she was there. They wouldn't be able to stay the night or recuperate; Loxly probably wouldn't even have time to power down the Harpy. Soren and Levi would most likely have to get Larken in, and Hinlee would have to stay and watch Loxly's back, which meant that Brecker would have to pose as a guard and tell the Luminary that she was needed back in her study for an urgent matter—all while the concert was happening.

Soren rubbed his temple, stuffing a groan down into his gut. This was all getting to be too much. Not to mention that he felt like an idiot after running a mission with Delvon. Soren had trusted too easily that Morgan would side with them. They hadn't even taken any weapons bigger than a pocketknife into the Manor. Yes, they were trying to impersonate staff members, but that didn't mean they shouldn't have been better prepared. Soren stuffed his fists into his pockets and changed direction. They would be ready next time. Nothing was going to happen, and Larken would be fine.

Soren walked out of the thicker part of the woods and past his bungalow, deciding he would ask Larken if she was going to the picnic. The sounds and smells of Camp hit him in the face as well as a cool breeze. It was good he had taken Larken to the ocean when he did. Autumn was now fully upon them, the change happening while they were in Gadget, and a sea of orange and brown had welcomed them home. There would be no more spikes or random hot, sunny days. Just cool breezes and crisp earthy scents.

Soren let his feet carry him all the way to Larken's bungalow. It sat conveniently near the center of Camp in case there had to be a quick evacuation. Or, at least, Soren assumed that was the reason Vallen chose that one for her.

He knocked on the door and waited for her muffled, *"Come in!"*

Using his shoulder more than his wrist, Soren pushed into her place. He didn't bother to hide his smile as he saw her curled up on her bed, swaddled in a blanket almost as big as her bedspread, book in hand. He recognized the tablet by the deep gouge in it. Soren was the one who packed it for her the night of her rehearsal dinner.

Larken looked up briefly and gave him a quick smile. "I'm almost finished with the chapter; hold on a second."

Soren walked over and sat on the edge of her bed. He didn't even know what he was doing there, but when she lifted the blanket and offered him a spot next to her, he didn't turn her down. They got comfortable and she went back to her book. He could see the tablet clearly, but instead of the words, he followed her eyes as they moved across the screen. He'd missed so much time looking at them since they got to camp, his workouts taking precedence over quality time. Soren regretted so many of his choices, but avoiding her was probably the biggest one.

It took him a while to notice that she had put her book away and now stared up at him.

Soren felt his frown relax some and she offered him a small smile. "Token for your thoughts?"

His lips twitched. He'd asked her the same thing right before they all went gunning together for the first time. Funny that they were worried about the same thing.

"What if I mess up and we lose?" he asked, repeating her words from what seemed like so long ago.

She smiled fully now. "I doubt you will, but if you mess up that badly in Stars, you can buy us all steaks."

Soren snorted. "Thanks."

"No problem."

A corner of the blanket huffed and shifted, revealing where Estelle had been hiding this whole time.

"Tell me about your book," Soren said, drawing the conversation back to the present.

"What do you want to know about it?"

"Tell me about the part you just finished."

Larken shifted her head from her pillow to Soren's shoulder. Her mood changed just enough for him to be able to tell, and she sighed. "The Princess just had to make a difficult choice. She needed to decide between doing what was right and what was easy."

"And?"

Larken met his gaze once more, her eyes holding the same emotion in them that they had at the opera. "She made the hard choice. She decided it would be better to die standing up for her people and going against her new husband than letting everyone else die."

Soren was back in his dorm room, sitting on his bed and wondering why Maxim brought Larken into his life. He had concluded that perhaps it was because they were meant to help her in this time of darkness. And sitting there with her now, he knew that this was the moment Maxim had prepared for them—that together they were to take on her mother and bring Maxim back to the Military District.

Soren opened his mouth to speak, but instead, a feminine cry sounded outside. Both Soren and Larken were off the bed and out the door in seconds. Words of disbelief drifted over to them from the center of Camp. The two of them rushed over and stopped dead in their tracks.

Hinlee clung to Loxly, who sat on his knees, looking whiter than a ghost. Gone was the boyish twinkle in his eye and playful turn of his lips. Hinlee rubbed her hands up and down his back, promising everything was going to be okay as her tears became harder and harder to control. Brecker sat beside her and had a firm grip on Loxly's bicep. Levi flanked him on the other side, grasping his shoulder. Soren's heart stopped. Everyone was here, everyone except—

*No...*

The picnic basket sat forgotten on its side. Food spilled from one end, already attracting bugs. Vallen stood in front of the group, face as expressionless as the day he came to get Larken from base. "We did everything we could, but we just didn't get there in time. I've already sent Medic Lattic out to the scene. He should be arriving in the next hour to assess any damage the Thresh medics may have missed. Rich will be coming back with him and they should be back by tomorrow afternoon."

"Loxly?" Larken asked, her voice small. Soren looked at her and saw that whatever the sharpshooter said next held the power to completely break her.

"He got the farm, Little Bird," Loxly croaked. He looked up at her with unfocused eyes. "Braves burned down dad's farm."

"*No.*" She shook her head and took a step back.

Soren could see her mind racing, her world crumbling. She was blaming herself. Soren reached for her, but she took a step out of his reach. She was a doe in that moment, fighting between running and hiding or staying to comfort her friend. In the end, Loxly won.

She took trembling steps forward. Sinking to her knees, she rasped, "Loxly, I am so, *so*—"

She didn't get to finish as Loxly crushed her to him and buried his face in her neck. His shoulders started shaking, as did Larken's. She would probably be mortified over her show of emotion later, but right now, she needed this. She needed to grieve with her friend and to know that Loxly didn't blame her. Soren's throat went tight and he turned away. His eyes burned and he choked the tears back down. He needed to be strong for them. He needed to be the steady, unmovable Captain they could all lean on. The thing was, Soren didn't feel steady right now. The only man in his life that ever came close to being called father was out there somewhere, possibly injured or dying.

It was all Braves's fault.

Soren glanced back at his friends, fueling his anger instead of giving into his other emotions. He knew for a fact that Braves either went after the Beau Farm to try and cause a rift between Larken and the others, or to hurt Larken's family. Maybe it was a bit of both. Soren turned fully and faced Vallen. The man was already watching him and Soren gave him a firm nod. Braves could do whatever he wanted to try and tear them apart, but what the Star didn't know was that Squad 19 was unbreakable. He would regret coming after them, just like Braves would regret ever messing with Larken in the first place.

# CHAPTER 22

The water ran in rivulets down his back. Dominic pressed his hands into the tiled wall, head bent, letting the jets hit him. His hair hung in his face and the moist air made it hard to breathe, but he didn't dare move.

At least the hot water made him feel something.

Dominic breathed deeply from his mouth. The water running down his face changed direction so it could drip from his parted lips instead of his chin. Without touching his face, Dominic knew he needed to shave. It had been a few days and he was starting to look rough. Though, perhaps Larken would prefer that. She did seem to have a type.

Deckard.

Barlow.

Tanner.

Dominic shook his head under the spray and hit the button to stop the water. He wiped his eyes and grabbed a towel. Dominic was nothing like those men. That's what made him better. He wasn't weak or emotional or whatever it was that made them all so different. Dominic was superior to them in every way. That's just how it was. He was better than them, and he was better for Larken.

*So why did she run off?*

Dominic shouted, hating the voice that sounded in his head whenever things started getting too quiet. He balled his fist and swung at his reflection. The mirror spiderwebbed, sending splits across the reflected dark emerald tile and gold grout. He pulled his hand back, slowly. The humid air stung his open skin, but Dominic ignored it as he wrapped a towel around his waist and walked out of the bathroom into his room. The curtains were still drawn, putting the dark interior into shadows. Sunlight tried to beat its way through the thinning cloth, but the feeble light didn't make a difference.

Dominic walked over to the bed but kicked the trash bin next to his desk on the way. He ignored it, leaving whatever was inside on the floor for the help to clean up. He snatched up the pants laying on the bed and fished around in the pocket for his cigar case. He placed one of the blue sticks between his lips and was just about to light it when his door flew open.

A frazzled Vigilant ran in, eyes wide in either crazed determination or complete terror. "Captain, we found her!"

Dominic rushed to his desk and sat, soggy towel still around his waist. He reached for the tablet in the man's hands and let his eyes dart across the screen. There were no pictures, only a report of a power outage at the Gadget Manor.

"You're even worse than the last soldier they sent. How was there a sighting if there are no pictures?" Dominic demanded.

This soldier was either stupid or fearless because he stood up straighter, squared his shoulders, and said, "Forgive me, sir, but I never said there was a sighting. I simply stated that we found her."

"You found faulty wiring, idiot!"

"For the whole Manor?" the Vigilant challenged.

Dominic froze. His knuckles started to burn, but he ignored them as he looked over the report again. The man was right. The entire Gadget Manor had been without power for over two hours. It was the perfect window for Larken to do whatever she was doing. And because she went to Gadget, Dominic could safely assume his theory was right.

Larken was trying to gain followers by attempting to get the Luminaries on her side.

"Leave!" Dominic barked.

The Vigilant didn't need to be told twice and left without even nodding his respects.

It took Dominic a moment to realize the thin cigar still sat unlit at the corner of his mouth. His mind danced, and he couldn't stop it from jumping from one idea to another. There were three big events happening at Stars that Larken would think to take advantage of.

The yearly District-wide fashion show.

Holly Gold's second wedding that she wanted to be even more extravagant than her first, since she was now a net star as well as a singer, and making twice as much arii.

And the benefit concert Barlow just announced.

Dominic balled his fists and half-grimaced, half-smirked. He knew keeping that conversation between Barlow, General Maxwell, and Tanner in the maze a secret would benefit him in the end.

A woman came in with a dermis gun grasped in her fingers. She didn't say a word as she patched up his knuckles after making sure there wasn't any glass in them. Dominic just let her. He was done fighting the women in Cornella's employment…at least for now.

He had bided his time, and now Dominic would be rewarded. He would share his theory about Larken visiting the Manors with Cornella and have teams scouting the Star Manor every second until the concert was over.

Four days.

That was all there was.

Four days until he would be seeing her again.

And this time…she wouldn't be getting away.

# CHAPTER 23

They didn't have time to say goodbye this time around. Shadric only caught a faint glimpse of Blade giving Larken a hug before he was ushered onto the aircraft. A nervous feeling settled over his stomach, and he wished that Delvon and Ewan were coming with them. Even if they were just hanging back on the aircraft while he performed.

Shadric took in the familiar ratty orange carpet and worn brown leather benches. Someone had cleaned recently. Even though the carpet looked the same as it always did, the pine-fresh scent of the cleaner still lingered in the air. The drink dispenser was already going, too, filling glasses of sweet tea that held slices of lemon.

Instead of taking up his usual seat on the bench that was splitting at the corner, Shadric decided to close himself off in the little bedroom in the back of the aircraft. His friends all gave him his privacy, probably assuming that he wanted to run through his setlist again.

They were wrong.

Everything was fine on his end. He planned on playing all the songs from his first two albums, and he knew those inside out. There was no need to practice. As for the rest of his band, they would be meeting them at the Manor so there wasn't a chance that he would be getting there late. It did make him a little bit nervous that his team was going with him to act as security, even though they had done it before. Blade had suggested they do security for Larken's birthday party, and no one seemed to recognize them as Faithfuls then—not even Larken. But that still wasn't quite what was bothering him.

Shadric just had this feeling that something about this trip wasn't right. Maybe it was because during his last visit to the outside world, there had been whispers about possible Larken sightings. Or perhaps he was worried that someone had managed to put together what they were doing. Whatever it was, Shadric felt restless.

Despite that, he let himself fall back onto the bed. He didn't move as the aircraft took off, and he managed to wait until they leveled out before his fingers started drumming against his chest. He worried about Delvon and Ewan. He worried about Blade. But mostly, Shadric worried about Larken.

She was only one aircraft over, but still…what if something went wrong? What if something happened to her and he didn't know because he was goofing off on a stage instead of helping? What if he could be the difference between them getting out safely and something happening to one of them?

*What if you're just overthinking everything…again?*

Shadric groaned and sat up. He reached for the guitar that always sat in this room and plucked at it. His face twisted at the sour note that spilled from the instrument. Shadric spent a few minutes tuning the guitar before starting to play *Nuovo Amore*. For a second, he was back at the fountain, singing with Larken. It was a moment he would always treasure.

Lyrics came to him, not from *Nuovo Amore*, but for a new one that hadn't been written yet. The melody to *Nuovo Amore* would be the bridge, and the chorus would voice all the fears he had. It would say how scared he was to lose Larken, how impossible it was not to think about her. Shadric would be putting his soul into the lyrics for this song, and still, he wasn't sure if Larken would realize what she was doing to him. He could only do what he always did.

Pray things would eventually work out the way they were meant to.

# CHAPTER 24

Something was wrong. Larken had known it the moment she opened her eyes on the Harpy, just like she knew it now. Something was horribly, horribly wrong.

Her earpiece sat like a lead weight in her ear as a bead of sweat trickled down the back of her neck. Her hair stood on end, goosebumps covering her skin despite the sweltering heat of the room. Soren's face glistened and he wouldn't meet her eye. A hot spike of rage shot through her, causing her to overheat.

He was doing it again.

Him, Vallen, and the rest of her team.

They were all treating her like that fragile doll who would break any second. It drove her insane—even more so because it was true. She wanted to run away from the news about Beau Farm. She wanted to hide away and wallow in her shame. But she didn't. Instead, she had gone back to her place and started digging. She soon found out why she should have stuck with Vallen's unspoken rule of keeping her in the dark—it was no different from when she watched Liam's last interview at base. She should have listened.

Her fault.

It was all *her* fault.

Rage still pricked her eyes at the thought of all the fires, of all the families that were destroyed because of her. Not only had a fourth of the Maxim-following Military families been wiped out, but Gadget had also suffered serious damage. And after their visit, the fires seemed to be solely focused on Thresh. A new farm a day, sometimes even two. Then they all stopped once Rich was covered in the news.

It meant Dominic had been searching for him.

All because of *her*.

Larken glanced back over at Soren, hoping he would just *look* at her. He didn't and she couldn't decide what the stronger emotion inside her was. Fury or guilt. Whichever it was, it kept her moving forward. It was the reason she now stood, melting, in the Star Manor's boiler room.

A suffocating layer of heat worked its way into all the crevices of Larken's tactical gear and covered her face like a damp goose feather pillow. She wasn't sure how, but she thought the gear was the same that she used at base. It would make sense, using the same thing that the other military guards swarming the area would be wearing, but without the bullet hole from her last time in it, there was no way for her to know.

Another bead of sweat crawled past her hairline down her neck. She hoped that it was clear and that her hair dye wasn't melting down her back. Carl had covered her fat Jodi-esque bun in a burnt-scarlet dye. He promised that it was easily washable, but now she worried that she would sweat it out before she got the chance to shower.

Thick false lashes sat on her lids and a heavy layer of stage makeup covered her face. Carl wasn't originally going to come, but he volunteered, saying that if anyone could turn Larken into a Star, it would be him. Levi pointed out that Jodi could since she did all her own hair and makeup on base, but Larken was glad that it was Carl. He was with her when she went back home, through her sham of a wedding, and now. It seemed only right since this was their last chance to approach the Magnate peacefully with complete support.

Carl waited on the Harpy with Loxly and Hinlee. Brecker had

given Hinlee a quick kiss, almost daring fate to keep him from returning to her, and then headed in the direction the concert was being held. Soren explained that Brecker would get the Luminary and Luminar to them, and that Soren and Levi would get Larken to the study. Larken wasn't sure where they docked, but they were able to get into the Manor after walking a mile and taking the boiler room entrance.

It was the complete opposite from when they went gunning together. The locker room had been freezing and Levi made snide comments about Loxly's aim up until the moment they started. Now, there was no teasing. Loxly's near perfect aim was a Maximsend, and they were all melting in this room. A red emergency light sat above the door Soren had his ear pressed to. It was a giant red bulb covered by a small cage. A tiny box sat under the bulb, and Larken could only assume it was a siren.

The Star Manor kept to its original roots as much as possible. It was probably the oldest building in all of Koraythea and looked like something from a net drama about a period long since forgotten. Dresses and lace gloves once moved through these halls and danced with their tuxedo-clad partners in the ballroom. Carpets lined the halls and mosaics covered whole walls in some places. And at the moment, Larken didn't care about any of it. She just wanted Brecker to send Soren his signal so they could finally leave the room.

Then, her earpiece crackled to life. The sound of a single breath came through, followed by a whispered, "Luminary in sight. Path ahead clear."

Soren's and Levi's faces both set into fierce frowns. Soren nodded once sharply. "Songbird moving forward."

Larken pursed her dark plum lips and shot a glare toward the men. Levi smirked and winked. Larken started to roll her eyes but stopped when she worried that the motion might make her lashes fall off. It was irrational. Carl said she could rub her eyes black and they would stay until he used the special serum to remove them, but that didn't stop the thought.

Soren slowly cracked the door. He waited and pushed it a little further. A cool waft of air fought its way into the sweltering room, and Larken couldn't help but gravitate to it, needing to feel it on her face. She only realized how close to the crack she'd gotten when Soren elbowed her in the chest. A loud stomping atop a rug sounded down the hall. Larken's breath caught just as the door did. Soren stopped pulling it shut, and she could assume he didn't want the movement to draw attention. She could only watch in horror as three security guards hurried past. Larken could make out the colors of their eyes, they were so close, but they only stared ahead, not noticing the door.

Or, thankfully, them.

Only when the stomping stopped did Larken draw in a full breath. Soren waited for the span of three breaths before pushing the door open again. He surveyed the area and then opened the door the rest of the way. Quickly, Larken and Levi spilled out into the hall and shut the door behind them. Soren led the way, not needing to announce the all-clear since they were next to him. Even though he was at the head of their little trio, he and Levi still managed to flank her. Larken hoped they didn't look too obvious.

They had spent the previous night in the tabernacle studying the floor plans since they were open to the public. They used the link suggested for people taking tours, only their tour was probably illegal. Mr. Chin provided a large spread of food, and both Shadric's team and Squad 19 demolished it. Even Delvon and Ewan were there, despite the fact they would be waiting on standby with Ezra and Jodi in the docking area for the Harpy. Hopefully they wouldn't be needed when the group returned in the morning.

It was early evening, and Loxly had been flying for most of the day. Larken didn't know how, but he said he was going to take a nap while they did what they needed to do inside. She herself had been sleeping for most of the day, but instead of the blissful unawareness she had to and from Gadget, Larken had fitful dreams of running through Star Manor in her wedding dress. It had her jumpy and looking over the hallways too fast. She would then have to force her eyes to slow down and take everything in again. It didn't matter though; nothing made it past the fog of worry.

*Something's wrong,* the little voice in her head said again. *Something is very wrong.*

The hairs on the back of her neck stood straighter as she reached up and touched her earpiece. Larken slowed, grabbing Soren's tactical vest. He rounded on her, eyes hard with worry.

She waited for Levi to stop before asking, "Where were the guards going? What's over there?"

Soren's brows furrowed as he thought. "The security room?"

Larken dumped her tech gun into Levi's arms and pulled at her vest until she could get at her communicator. There was only one reason extra guards would be going there with everyone out at the concert. She tapped at the screen furiously, hoping it would light up.

Nothing.

Larken looked up, mouth open to say they needed to turn back. Instead, a shot sounded outside. Screams were muffled by the Manor walls but could be heard clearly. The sharp sounds of amps and dropped microphones punctuated the fear, and Larken realized what was happening.

They knew.

It was as if a bucket of cold water had been dumped onto Larken as she turned back the way they came. They were over halfway to the study, trapped like mice with no way to call for help. Larken fastened her vest the best she could with fingers that didn't want to work. She felt sick, *actually* sick. A wave of nausea rolled over her and she almost doubled.

Her fault. All her fault. Someone was hurt—one of her friends could be *hurt*—and it was all her fault.

"Get it together, cadet, and move!" Soren barked, trying to bully her into getting her head on straight.

Larken swallowed it all down – her fear, nerves, nausea, guilt – and moved. Her sword was a comforting weight at her side, but she didn't reach for it. Nor did she take the gun back from Levi. Instead, she chose the handgun Vallen had gifted her for her birthday. She had loaded it before getting on the Harpy.

Fire.

Shock.

Smoke.

Nightshade.

They were there in case she needed them, but she hoped she didn't. Larken rounded the corner, her gut wrenching as she found the last man she wanted to see.

He stood waiting for her half way down the hall, two helmeted guards standing a few feet behind him. His lips twitched and the action reminded her of all the times he tried to kiss her. He had dark bags under his brown eyes and his hair appeared almost oily, like he hadn't been taking care of himself. Moving a step forward, he looked her up and down slowly. When their gazes locked, his smirk turned to a snarl.

"Miss me, Lark?"

All of the emotions that had been boiling inside her since learning about the Beau Farm bubbled up and spilled over. Soren grabbed the back of her belt to keep her in place. Larken hadn't even known she was moving until she couldn't. The guards noticed though and moved in closer to their commander. She gave Dominic a snarl of her own, pulling fury from her Jodi-like look and years of getting beaten down by her family.

"Be smart," Soren ordered softly in her ear. "We don't know his plan yet."

Larken glared up at Soren, not caring that he was right.

Levi stiffened next to her and she knew his gun was aimed at Dominic, finger already on the trigger.

Dominic took another step forward, pulling out a gun. "I've missed you, you know. You left without a word and no way to contact you."

*"You've said plenty for the both of us!"* Larken rasped, her voice sounding more broken than strong.

"The fires, yes." He brought up a cigar she hadn't noticed to his lips. In a breath of blue, he continued, "Well, you see, when I couldn't find you, I was forced to get a little...*creative.*"

Soren tugged Larken back half a step and she was about to break his finger in an effort to get at Dominic. The guards moved in even more, lifting their guns and aiming them at her. Soren tightened his grip on her but stayed calm. He and Levi were waiting for the perfect moment.

Larken was done waiting.

"What do you want?" she demanded as another gun sounded outside.

"What I've always wanted, pet. To take you away from here. To *save* you."

Her stomach soured at the admission.

His snarl was back on his lips, and he tossed away the still burning half of the cigar. "You took advantage of my good nature."

"I did n—"

"You ruined me, Lark. You destroyed me!"

"I never—" she tried, but he cut her off.

"These men took you from me! These people thought they knew what you needed more than I did!" He was shouting. "Not anymore!"

Dominic tightened the grip on his gun and fired off a shot. Larken screamed, turning to Soren in horror. Only, it wasn't her old Squad Captain that cried out.

The tech guns toppled out of Levi's hands as he grabbed at his chest, at the finger-sized hole that was now in his vest. The color drained from his face, making his blond beard look darker than it really was. Larken snapped and was on Dominic before he could finish his silent gloating. Two shots rang out as she dropped her gun. Larken barely registered the two guards falling before she tackled Dominic to the ground. Soren shouted at her, telling her to let it go and move so he could take the shot, but she was too far gone.

Vallen's constant warnings about controlling her emotions sounded at the back of her mind, but she didn't have time to listen.

Not when she was punching and scratching the stupid, smug face of the man underneath her. Larken didn't care that she was straddling his chest, or that she had given him exactly what he wanted. Only that she was *finally* able to pay him back for all the hurt that he'd given her.

The surprise engagement.

*Punch.*

The table dancing.

*Hit.*

The interviews and public embarrassment.

*Whack.*

*Taking her away from her home.*

*Scratch.*

Dominic jerked his head back with a snarled wince. When he looked at her again, three angry red lines marked his left cheek. Blood pebbled up in a few spots, and she knew she'd pushed him too far. Larken was suddenly afraid for herself as she sat there, almost half his weight. She scrambled for the gun she'd forsaken in her rage, but Dominic kicked it out of reach. He grabbed onto her bicep and sat up, sticking his face in hers. He glanced away only long enough to lift his gun and shoot Soren's out of his hands. Soren lunged for the other one by Levi's feet, but the Field-medic convulsed and unintentionally kicked the gun toward Dominic.

"Please, don't do this," Larken pleaded. "You don't have to—"

"Kill him?" Dominic mocked, lips to her ear. "Don't worry, I won't. Well, at least not yet." Dominic put his gun away, a crazed, self-assured smile spreading across his face. "I promise, Deckard's death will be nice and slow. I'll pay him back for everything he's ever taken from me."

"You're a *monster!*" Larken accused, bringing her free hand up.

Dominic caught her wrist and used it to yank her close. He got in her face and demanded, "Fire for fire, right, Lark?" His grip on her tightened. "You have no right. You did this. Look around you. You did *all of this.* You left, and now you're suffering as I have. And soon, you'll have no one left in the ashes."

Larken pulled, fighting him.

"Look at what you did!" Dominic shouted.

She didn't want to, but slowly her head turned to her friend. Levi gasped for breath, still clutching at his chest and writhing. Soren knelt over Levi and assessed him, panic causing Soren's eyes to dart franticly over his friend. Larken knew that despite his stony expression, Soren was struggling. Not only was his Second dying before his eyes but there was just *so much blood.*

Her fault.

Dominic chuckled darkly.

Her fault.

He stood, still holding her.

Her fault.

Dominic yanked her into his chest, pointing his gun at her jaw.

*Her fault.*

It resounded inside her, echoing her every heartbeat. She was to blame. Larken didn't know what was happening outside with Shadric or Brecker, but she didn't think it was good. And here...

Levi cried out again, the veins in his forehead and neck bulging. Her knees threatened to go weak, but she forced herself to stand strong. In the far-off distance, at the edges of the haze she now found herself in, Dominic called for backup. Larken looked around her, trying to find some way out of the mess she made. She couldn't go back to her mother—not like this. She wouldn't give up on seeing the trees again, the ocean, Vallen, her friends.

Her friends that were now dying.

*Stop it!* Larken clamped her eyes shut. *Stop it and remember what Vallen told you!*

She dug around in her memory until she found the right words.

*You go out there and prove that you were born for this.*

And she was.

Larken took a deep, calming breath. Her eyes snapped open and she took in everything around her. Guards shouted somewhere close by that they had found them and were moving in, Soren still kneeled over Levi, and Dominic had relaxed his grip just the tiniest bit. What could she use? What did she have?

*Note to self: next time wear the knife-heels Jodi got you.*

She sent out a silent prayer and moved. Dominic was just distracted enough that she was able to stomp on his foot and flip him, giving herself a few seconds. Another shot rang out in the hall, but she didn't dare look around until she had her gun in her hand. Soren had thrown himself over Levi, but there was no need. The hole in the wall just above them told Larken Dominic's shot had missed.

Guards rounded the corner to the left of them, leaving their only hope for escape to their right. Larken didn't think as she pulled the trigger, aiming for the light fixture above the guards. The whole thing exploded in a shower of glass, and then again as the bullet stuck in the ceiling blew up. Dominic had been trying to get up but hit the floor and covered his head as bits of rubble and plaster rained down on the guards. The destruction gave Larken just enough time to shout at Soren.

"Grab him!"

Ever the soldier, Soren moved, the order sending him into action. He grabbed Levi's arm and hoisted him up over his shoulders as if the man was nothing more than a sack of potatoes. Soren ran for their escape route, and Larken glanced back at Dominic. He quickly took aim at Soren, but Larken beat him to it. She pulled the trigger again and purple shocks jumped and danced around Dominic's arm and torso like little arcs of lightning. His handgun dropped, and as he thrashed, he hit it with his knee. It skidded over the rug-covered floor, and into the mess the guards were trying to climb out of.

"No!" he half-shouted-half-grunted. "They can't have you!"

Larken aimed her handgun at a spot between Dominic and the destruction. As soon as the bullet hit, thick white smoke erupted from it in thin plumes that quickly filled the area. She only had one bullet left. She didn't want to use it—whoever she hit would be paralyzed until they were either found or their heart stopped. Larken turned to leave, running after Soren.

"You're mine!" Dominic shouted.

Larken ignored him, trying to catch up to the men, but another shot went off. Pain exploded across her right thigh as she was hit in the back of it. She glanced back to see Dominic holding one of the tech guns Levi had dropped before he was shot, a look of feral rage on his face. His eyes were crazy, wide and staring. Fear chilled her blood as she started to wonder if Dominic would rather kill her than let her go.

Larken raised her gun one last time as he staggered to his feet and shot him. He stumbled twice before dropping to a knee. His body shook with labored breaths as the paralytic agents of the nightshade took effect. He reminded her of a dying lion, once so proud and strong, now reduced to nothing but a golden shadow. Larken didn't know if the guards in the rubble would be able to help Dominic or not before his heart stopped—but right now, she didn't care. Dominic's lips moved, forming her name before he reached out and caught himself before he hit the floor. Then, the smoke overtook him and he was gone.

# CHAPTER 25

Larken forced herself back into action, fear clutching her heart —or maybe it was something else. She didn't know if it was Soren's or Levi's tech gun Dominic used, so she didn't know what the bullet was laced with. Or if even *was* laced with anything. Jodi and Ezra had taken it upon themselves to experiment with different plants, but it was the Faithful's tech team that made the bullets. Larken's tech gun held bullets that would somehow incapacitate someone, but she didn't know what was in Levi's.

Her heart was a pounding bass line, echoing throughout her entire body. She didn't know if it was a side effect or if she was just working herself up. The only thing she could think about was taking one excruciating step at a time.

*Vallen is going to kill me.*

Larken thought back to that day in the field. Vallen had been shot in the knee and still managed to power through it. She would just have to do the same now, even if she was drugged. Pushing on, Larken ignored the pain and managed to catch up to Soren. He made it easy for her by stopping and waiting. His breathing was labored—more from adrenaline than exertion—and his gaze dropped to her lips.

"What's wrong?" he demanded.

"Nothing," Larken lied, taking the time to reload her gun. "Let's get out of here."

He looked her over completely, eyes landing on the ground, no doubt finding a small puddle of blood. It didn't matter that Levi was trying to break free, or that he was unintentionally kicking and punching Soren as he fought the pain. Soren looked ready to drop him and go after Dominic himself.

"I heard that gunshot."

"We need to go," Larken reminded him.

"He hurt you."

"I'm fine."

"You're grimacing."

Larken didn't know what to say, but they couldn't stay there. She grabbed his elbow and started back in the direction of the boiler room. Soren fumed as he fought Levi, and Larken wracked her brain, trying to think of what might be wrong with him.

He'd been shot. Her friend had been *shot* because of her. She'd sworn to herself after Soren was hurt the night of the opera that no one she loved would be hurt because of her again. And who knew what happened to Brecker? To Shadric? They were still outside with the growing screams. Shots fired, glass shattered, and smoke caught whatever air current it could. Chaos surrounded them, and Larken was having more trouble blocking out her guilt by the second.

Every time she chanced a glance back, Soren picked up the pace. She didn't know if he figured out where her thoughts had turned, or if Levi was just getting to be too much for him, but it didn't matter. Him hurrying didn't stop the thought from coming.

*Turn yourself in.*

They reached the door to the boiler room just as another group of guards did. The guards shouted, raising their weapons. Larken took aim at a spot in the wall to the left of the group and fired. Within seconds the wall exploded, as did the window a few feet down. The group collectively brought their hands up to protect their faces and chests, and the trio used the diversion to slip into the boiler room just as the siren under the light started going off.

Heat greeted them once more and dizziness washed over Larken. She stumbled, bumping into Soren. Levi had gone rigid, and Soren used the opportunity to grab onto her.

"What are you doing?" she asked, her voice sounding far away.

"Helping," he grunted.

"You can't carry us both."

"If I can run with a four-hundred-and-fifty-pound pack for five miles, I can carry the two of you to the Harpy."

She was about to protest again when another wave crashed over her. Soren balanced Levi on his shoulders and wrapped Larken's arms around his neck.

"Besides," he grunted as he lifted her, "you can help me hold him."

Larken met Levi's eyes and they screamed silently for help. He wouldn't ever say it out loud, especially to Soren, but he was scared. Larken's throat grew tight and she sought out Levi's hand. He gripped it tightly just as another spasm worked its way through his body. They needed to get him back, and soon.

Soren didn't wait for Larken to wrap her legs around him before he started running again. He turned the corner as the door was broken in. Grunting, he moved faster, needing to get them back but not wanting to lead everyone where they were docked. Larken buried her face into his neck and blocked everything out, praying as she did. The red light of the room was covered by the darkness behind her eyelids. The scent of hot metal was replaced with one of leather and freshly tilled earth. And even though they were being chased, and even though Soren held onto Levi instead of her, for a moment she was safe.

For a moment…nothing could hurt her.

Then, the moment ended. Soren kicked the door out and autumn air greeted them. He didn't wait around for the shock of it to wear off and just kept running. Larken shivered, not knowing if it was the drastic change from hot inside to chilly outside or a new side effect. It took so many hours for Soren to reach the Harpy, but at the same time only seconds. The world tilted and turned, causing Larken to fall into the side of the Harpy when she eventually got down.

Carl greeted them with a frenzied, "What's happening!?"

Larken tried to answer him, but when she opened her mouth, only vomit came out. She gagged and sputtered, doubling over and coughing as she was ill. Carl squealed in a very unmanly way as she caught him off guard. He still rushed to help her even though his face turned green, and he rubbed her back until she was finished. When he was able to get Larken onto the Harpy, she found Levi thrashing on the floor again.

Soren panted as he sat over his friend. Loxly rushed into action, jumping into the pilot's seat and shifting the Harpy from rest mode to flight mode. Levi gritted his teeth but couldn't hold in his cry of pain any longer. He pulled at his gear, struggling to breathe. The bullet glinted in the cab light, a sliver of silver visible in the blood just past Levi's vest. Sweat covered his brow and slicked his hair. Larken stumbled over to him, fingers already brushing against the vials Levi had gotten her for her birthday. She dropped to her knees —hard—and he reached for her hand.

"Pheno—" he tried, but another convulsion cut him off.

It didn't matter, Larken knew what he meant. She grabbed the syringe that held the phenobarbital and stuck him with it. Nothing happened—not that it would—and she worried that they were too late.

"He has strychnine poisoning," Larken rasped.

"What does that mean?" Soren demanded.

"It means—"

Levi's eyes rolled into the back of his head just as another wave of nausea hit her.

"Start compressions. NOW!" Larken practically shrieked. Soren tore off Levi's gear as Larken explained, "There's no cure, only treatment."

"That's not any more helpful," Soren argued.

"I gave him treatment, but if it was too late..." She swallowed back her stomach. "Look, we just need to give the phenobarbital time to work."

Little lights danced around the edges of her vision and Larken tried to blink them back. She already felt useless, forcing Soren to help Levi. Blood seeped out with each compression, making a fair-sized puddle. She should mention that they needed to stop the bleeding at some point too. Only, Hinlee stood up from the spot she was sitting in while they worked.

"Soren?" she asked in a small voice.

He ignored her as he pushed down on Levi's chest, eyes hard.

"Soren…what happened?"

Still no response. Larken thought she might be sick again.

"Where is he? Where's Brecker?"

Larken was taken back to the day in the garage when she asked Hinlee if she ever got nervous about Brecker being the Scout. She told Larken that she trusted Maxim to take care of all of them and Larken wanted so badly to believe like that. Larken couldn't look at her. Hinlee was too small, too near breaking.

"Cap?" Loxly called out, waiting for an order.

Soren didn't stop compressions as he said, "Get us back to Camp."

"No!" Hinlee cried out. "No! We can't just leave him!"

Larken's eyes stung as she fell from her knees to her hip.

Hinlee made for the door, but Carl stopped her. She fought him, pleading, "Please, Soren! We can't leave him! He could be hurt or—Soren, please! PLEASE!"

Soren didn't respond and she dissolved into a fit of tears. Carl held onto her as they took off into the air, Hinlee's sobs filling the cab. Larken felt another wave of dizziness as the little lights started spreading. She swayed again and threw her hand out to catch herself, catching Soren's attention.

"Larken?" he asked, pain coloring his voice.

She shook her head, trying to tell him she was alright, but the earth moved again. No, that wasn't right. She wasn't on the ground. It was *her* moving. Her head hit the floor of the cab, a strand of red hair falling just in front of her eyes. She'd forgotten that Carl had dyed her hair that morning. She was forgetting a lot of things.

"Larken!" Soren shouted, unable to stop the compressions and help her.

She couldn't respond; her tongue wouldn't work. That was when she noticed the small puddle of blood where she'd been kneeling. Larken didn't know if it was hers or Levi's, but as her eyes fell shut, she realized that it really didn't matter.

# CHAPTER 26

She shot him.

She actually shot him.

Dominic still couldn't wrap his mind around it, even days later. His inept guards almost didn't get to him in time, his heart had almost stopped, and it would have been at his sweet Larken's hands. Yes, he shot her first, but that was only to try and stop her. Larken did it so she could get Deckard and Jameson away—away from *him!*

Dominic shook away the memory of the white sheets and beeping monitors and pushed forward. He ignored the stares that followed him through the halls of Base 14. He honestly never thought he would come back to this place, and yet here he was. Before, women would have been unable to help themselves from looking him up and down and men would have considered him their greatest competition. Now, his fellow soldiers only saw one thing. He couldn't blame Larken for the scars—not when he'd been pushing her so hard. Dominic should have known how she'd react when she was backed into a corner.

So, did he get rid of the marks, or keep them as a reminder?

On one hand, she'd have to see what she did to him every day for the rest of their lives. On the other, he could use it to prove himself to her. Prove that he was willing to give everything up for her—even his good looks. He'd already forgiven her for shooting him, even though he was still shocked whenever he thought about it. That was what she wanted in the end, after all—to be put before everything in the world.

And he would put her first.

Always.

Even if it meant destroying everything around her so she had no other choice.

Even if it meant saving her from herself.

Dominic didn't regret his actions. That whole Squad had it coming. *Larken* had it coming. She had her time of wild rebellion, and enough was enough. It was time for her to stop playing in the woods and come home. He'd only encouraged her to understand that. Dominic would never hurt her, not on purpose.

*What else could you have done?* he asked himself.

Dominic let out a breath, relaxing some as the tension in his back started to lift. But another voice—one that he didn't know was inside him—had him tensing again mid-breath.

*You could have let her go.*

Dominic made a fist as he rounded the corner. There were people everywhere but he still thought about punching the wall. His knuckles popped as he stayed his hand. He wasn't stupid—he knew what everyone was saying behind his back.

Unhinged.

Insane.

Obsessed.

No, he wouldn't feed their fires anymore. Just as he would no longer feed Cornella's. He was done with it. What had the fires gotten him? Not Larken. He'd give the task to someone else and focus on something else…or someone else.

Dominic glared at a group of slacking cadets and barked an order for them to *move it*. They rushed off and he plowed ahead. He wouldn't stop until he found who he was looking for. Dominic had checked the schedule and knew that Xander was around here somewhere. Dominic didn't know why he didn't think of him, or his other squad members, before.

*Cornella wanted them as Captains, that's why.*

The conversation came flooding back to him now. Cornella suggested Dominic break up his old squad and make them all Captains so they could take on a set of Vigilants of their own. Only now did he realize the real reason—she didn't want Dominic to have any allies close by.

Dominic rounded another corner and found him. Xander had a solider with pink hair and wide hips pressed up against a section of wall in the back corner of the hall. Dominic walked over and cleared his throat.

Xander broke away only long enough to look over his shoulder. He smirked when he found Dominic standing there and let the girl go. She met Dominic's eyes and blushed as she dropped her gaze. They got together a few years ago and she was no doubt embarrassed at getting caught with his friend.

Dominic didn't care.

He was only there for one thing.

His old squad could do whatever—or *whoever*—they wanted once this was all over.

"Dominic Braves," Xander drawled.

A spark of anger ignited in Dominic's chest and he growled, "I'm still your superior, Fig."

"Okay, *Captain* Braves, what do you want?"

"I have need of my Second."

"I'm not your Second anymore. You might be Cornella's dog, but I no longer answer to you."

The girl tried to sneak away, but Xander wrapped an arm around her and held her there.

"Look, titles are the last thing I care about right now—"

"That much is obvious." Xander's eyes dropped to the scratch marks on Dominic's cheek.

Dominic frowned and rage filled him. "Help me get what I want and I'll give you whatever you want. My aircraft, my hovercraft, my fortune, whatever. Just get the team back together and help me."

It came out as more of a threat than a promise, but Xander took the bait. His dark eyes lit up, a greedy gleam in them, and he smirked. "Consider it done, Captain."

Dominic nodded.

"Now, if you don't mind, I have other matters to see to."

Dominic didn't bother to hide his scowl. "Let me know when everyone's ready to ship out."

Xander didn't bother confirming his order. He pushed the girl back into the wall and made a sound that mimicked a hungry animal, causing the girl to squeal. Dominic's face twisted in disgust and he walked away. He reached for his cigar case and opened it, only to find it empty. Irritation bristled through him, making his skin itch. Nothing, it would seem, was going right today.

He rushed down the old familiar halls and ignored everyone he passed on his way out. They didn't matter—no one did.

Only Larken.

It was a thought that kept repeating itself over and over again in his mind. He couldn't think about anything else. Not when she was out there—hurt because of something she'd made him do. Dominic fought the images of the bullet hitting her leg as he hurried to the hangar.

The fires could wait another day.

He didn't stop until he reached his aircraft. Dominic hopped in and pulled out into the sky, ignoring the call for clearance that came through the radio. He flew all the way to the beach where she'd left him and docked in the sand.

Dominic rooted around in the compartments until he found his travel case of cigars. He got out and leaned against the aircraft. Dominic stared into the ocean as he opened the case, and grumbled when he saw there was only one left. He lit it, burning his thumb in his haste. The smoke filled him, and on the exhale, he forced out all of the thoughts trying to eat at him. The water crashed onto the shore nearby, and he knew that this would be the last time he would come here. The last time *anyone* did. He didn't care how long it took, but he would destroy this place.

This place…and everything she loved.

Larken could keep running as long as she wanted, but he was able to find her once. He could do it again.

The sun dipped, and Dominic still stood there. The small shadows stretched into larger ones as the sun quickly sank in the sky. He took his last drag as the sun touched the water, turning it gold, then flicked the butt of the cigar into the sand and turned to the aircraft. He placed his hands on top of it and took his reflection in. The window showed a man with three red marks on his cheek and a determined set to his jaw.

Yes, he would keep the marks, just as he would find her again. And the next time Larken was in his grasp, he would not be letting her go.

No matter the cost.

# CHAPTER 27

"And I don't care what you think! I'm telling you she would want to be woken up now that we have an answer!"

The voice startled Larken out of her pit of blackness. It was far away at first, then right next to her ear—shouting.

"I think what my colleague is trying to say—" an accented voice tried but was cut off with a, "He knows *exactly* what I'm trying to say. He's just being difficult."

*Jodi.*

The name swam to the surface of Larken's thoughts.

"He's just trying to do what he thinks is best."

*Ezra.*

"What's best is that she *knows*. You know that as well as I do," Jodi grumbled.

"I really don't think you should be trying to wake her—"

Larken cut the masculine, unknown voice off by groaning. She couldn't open her eyes, and her body weighed a million pounds, but a spark in her memory lit.

Dominic.

Levi.

Brecker.

Shadric.

Larken gasped and bolted up, breaking whatever feeble bonds held her down. The rush of air started a coughing fit and machines screamed all around her. Hands rushed to get to her—rubbing her back, touching her face, and trying to force her back down. She fought them, yelling and crying out. Jodi was right; she couldn't go back under. She needed to know what happened to her friends. She couldn't be the reason they all died.

"Everybody back off!" Jodi shouted.

The only sound in the room was the hectic beeping of the monitors and Larken's ragged breathing. The blinding light slowly changed from a white nothingness to shapes and screens. Three people stood around her. Ezra had his hand on her back, and Larken didn't recognize the other two people. She could assume that the man was the one that wanted to keep her asleep since the other person was a small, dark-skinned girl. All three of them stared at Jodi.

The medic fumed. She stood there, brown hair in flowing waves, black stud sparkling in the bay's lights, and arms crossed. She looked more furious than Larken had ever seen her. The usually aloof medic glared daggers into the people around Larken with her copper eyes until they all took a step back. Though, Ezra stayed as close as he could get away with.

Slowly, Jodi made her way forward and turned the machines off one by one. Larken didn't rush her, not that she thought she could speak. Her throat still tickled, but she tried not to cough anymore. Eventually, Jodi made her way to the bed and sat on the side of it. She grabbed Larken's hand and the weight of what happened in Stars hit her. Larken didn't know if it was a reaction to the anesthesia or something else, but a fat tear welled in her eye and slipped down her cheek.

"*They're okay,*" Jodi whispered. "They're all *okay.*"

Larken crumpled into her friend, sobbing in relief. She tried to stop it—tried to fight the emotion, but her sluggish mind wouldn't allow it. All of her energy was spent on keeping her awake, and she couldn't spare anymore to fight the emotional effects of the drugs and recent events. Not that Larken ever handled anesthesia well. She wished that everyone would leave as she hid her face in Jodi's shoulder.

Jodi only held her and spoke over her embarrassing show of emotion. "Brecker caught a ride back with Shadric's team and they were all fine. Brecker was shot in the shoulder, but it went through and wasn't laced with anything. They had some problems with their aircraft too, but that was it."

"And Levi?" Larken rasped, voice weak and watery. She managed to stop the tears enough that she was willing to risk meeting Jodi's eyes.

"You gave him the phenobarbital in time. We were able to purge the toxins out of his system. His bullet wound was cleaned and fixed up as soon as you all landed. Once you guys were in range again, Carl was able to call, and we talked Soren through everything. He stopped the bleeding and helped fix you up, too."

"What was wrong with me?" Larken asked, remembering how sick she'd felt.

"Tranquilizer. Super embarrassing on your part," Jodi answered with a wink and a poor attempt at her usual attitude.

Larken couldn't help a small chuckle, relief flooding her and making her suddenly lightheaded. She needed to get out of this place. She couldn't take it anymore—the groggy feeling from the drugs, the open stares, the white sterile room. She could have been there for two hours or two weeks, it didn't matter. Jodi, anticipating her next move, helped her pull the machine attachments and IVs free.

Larken stood when she was able after several ragged breaths and saw a mess of red stains on the white pillow. She panicked until she realized her hair must still have the temporary dye in it. Bringing her hand up to her face, she felt around. The lashes were gone, but her fingers still brushed over some residual makeup.

Larken swayed slightly, and Jodi reached for her. The medic offered only silent support, helping her to the door.

The man in the room tried again. "I really don't think—"

"Can it," Jodi barked over her shoulder. She stared ahead and whispered none too quietly, "He's been up my butt about every-thing." Jodi rolled her eyes. "Like Ezra and I haven't been taking care of you for your whole life and career."

Larken nodded, agreeing but not quite present in the conversa-tion. Jodi kept it up, speaking so she wouldn't have to, all the way to the showers. The now-familiar yellow-tan stone passed by in a blur. Larken could only focus on putting one foot in front of the other.

Jodi walked Larken into a stall and helped take her paper-thin gown off. Every sound and movement echoed off the stall walls that came all the way up to Larken's shoulders. She was encased in a tiled square with nothing more than a white curtain that hid her body from the rest of the bathroom. The pale blue tiles clung to the cool moisture from previous showers and caused goosebumps to break out across Larken's skin.

Jodi helped her take down the half of her hair that was still up in a bun before stepping back. She sighed, looking Larken over. "Here's the thing. The reason the other medics were so upset with me was because of the gunshot."

"What's wrong with it?" Larken worried, suddenly afraid that Jodi lied to her about it just being a tranquilizer.

"Both Brecker and Levi took a leaf out of Soren's book. They kept their scars."

Larken looked over her shoulder and saw the ends of a pink spiderweb on her thigh.

"They were going to remove it, but I said you needed the chance to decide for yourself. Brady made sure you were as unscarred as a baby, but..." she trailed off.

"What did Carl think?" Larken asked.

Jodi opened her mouth, but the man in question answered with, "Carl thinks that if you want that badge of honor, then you should wear it proudly."

Larken turned to the doorway and saw Carl holding her bath-room tote, a towel and washcloth, and a set of clean clothes.

"Should you be in here?" Jodi mocked.

"I've already waxed her; it's not like we could get any closer." Carl turned his gaze past Jodi and nodded at Larken. "Ezra said you were awake."

"For the most part." Larken's rasp bounced off the tiles, sounding even worse now that it was louder.

Carl walked up to the shower opening and set her things down. He hung the towel on the hook outside her stall and set the washcloth on top of the tiled wall. Carl held the curtain until Jodi walked out, and then pulled it closed, hiding Larken's body from view.

Turning to the corner of the stall, Larken took two steps over to a knob that resembled a ship's helm. Briefly, her eyes followed the pipe that poked straight up out of the tile wall. Four heads stuck out of the top and each one pointed into a different stall. Thankfully, she was alone and wouldn't have to wait too long for the water to warm up.

Larken twisted the knob and jumped as soon as the water hit her skin. The freezing water chased away the last of her grogginess before it heated to a scalding temperature. Larken messed with the dial until it was perfect, then she glanced down and nearly screamed. Red water the same shade as blood pooled around her feet. Again, she had to remind herself about the hair dye. Larken closed her eyes, unable to look at it. Carl and Jodi murmured in the distance, probably talking about what they were going to do about getting everyone presentable for the Magnate in the coming days. They were running out of time, and the Night of Masks would be here before they knew it.

Larken just started to relax as she scrubbed at her scalp when a voice startled her out of her reverie.

"Peach!" Delvon barked.

Larken's eyes snapped open, and her mouth followed when she saw Delvon standing in the doorway, glaring at her, arms crossed.

"*Do you mind?*" Larken demanded, hands dropping from her hair and arms wrapping around herself—not that he could see anything over the curtain.

"No, I don't. If you're dumb enough to get shot when I'm not around, then I'm going to be around."

"Delvon—*I'm naked!*"

"Not from where I'm standing, you're not," he said, indicating the shower curtain with his head.

Larken bristled. Carl was one thing—he was right; that first day they met back on base, they had gotten *very* personal. She was about to point this out when another voice echoed down the little hall.

"Del, why are you shouting in the girl's—" Shadric froze, looking from a blushing Larken to a fuming Delvon. He clapped his hands over his eyes, turning a shade of scarlet that would have been funny literally any other time, and turned. "I'm sorry!"

"Sorry about what?" Hinlee asked, joining the conversation.

Candy came in on her heels, biting her bottom lip as she took in the situation. The redhead glanced at Jodi and a joke danced between them that Larken could hear as clear as day.

*Should we invite Soren too?*

Larken wanted nothing more than to lay down in the shower and die.

"Everybody out!" she ordered.

Hinlee and Carl, taking pity on her, started ushering everyone down the little hall to the front door. Delvon grumbled and complained while Shadric mumbled apology after apology. Carl was the only one that came back once the door shut, and Larken let out a long breath. Her face still burned and thankfully, Carl didn't bring attention to it.

Larken rushed through the rest of her shower and accepted Carl's help when it came time to dry off and dress. The anesthesia had mostly worn off, but Larken was glad for his help since her hands still shook slightly. She didn't complain as he sat her down on one of the benches by the lockers and worked a comb through her hair.

Neither of them said anything until he was almost done with the second braid he worked her hair into. He tied it off and grunted the same way he did whenever he impressed himself. Then he sat next to her and didn't wait for her to look at him before saying, "You really scared us, kid."

She glanced at him. "But Levi—"

"Was able to be cared for after you explained what he had. No one knew what was wrong with you. Do you know how many different things cause vomiting and unconsciousness? Because Ezra and Jodi do. I've never been on a more stressful flight."

Larken tore her gaze away, ashamed.

"Hey." Carl gently touched her jaw and brought her face back around. "I'm not telling you this to make you feel bad. I just want you to be more careful next time, okay?"

She nodded—it was all she could do—and swallowed thickly. "Where's Vallen?"

"He's with Fisher and Rich. I messaged him when I was on my way here. They're already waiting to see you."

"Are they close?"

"Everyone is under a lockdown order until the media stops talking about Stars. No one will see you."

Larken nodded again. She felt bad that she had a hand in taking away some of the Faithfuls' freedom but was glad no one would be staring at her. She thought back to when she first got there and wondered if everyone was disappointed in what they saw. Surely, if they weren't then, they were now.

"Come on, kid. Let's get you out of here."

Carl grabbed her hand and pulled her to her feet. Larken let him guide her, not paying attention to where they were going. It wasn't until they stepped onto a familiar path that Larken stopped lagging a step behind. The tabernacle stretched up to the sky, the familiar eight-pointed star giving her comfort. Together they walked in and that feeling of home washed over her once more.

Candy and Hinlee looked over their shoulders and smiled at her. Brecker sat to Hinlee's right, the small group taking up the back pew. Levi lounged on the one in front of the trio by himself. His legs took up more than half of his pew and a pillow propped him up. Someone had turned the pew in front of the field medic around so he could comfortably talk to Rich, Vallen, and Fisher. Loxly sat on a stool he must have taken from the stage with his shotgun across his lap. The two Beau men were laughing at what looked to be Levi's expense, and gave her a pair of matching crooked smiles.

Larken looked around and found Soren brooding in the corner. She met Vallen's gaze, and he narrowed his eyes at her. Larken was torn, but Vallen made the decision for her when he went back to the conversation he was having with Fisher. Carl squeezed her hand and joined Candy. She snuggled into him, and he gave an exaggerated groan as the phrase *wildflowers would be perfect* drifted over to Larken.

She smiled softly, knowing that Candy didn't mean any harm in her dreaming and that Carl was only giving her a hard time. Those two were so in love that the only discussion about a proposal was if it should happen before or after this mess was taken care of.

Larken made her way to Soren—who wouldn't meet her eyes. Just like he wouldn't look at her in the boiler room. She tried to muster up the energy to be irritated with him, but she was too exhausted. So instead, she said, "Can we skip the argument this time? I'm too tired."

Soren only grunted.

"What happened wasn't your fault."

Another grunt.

Larken sighed, unable to do this right now. "Fine. I like my steak medium rare."

"This isn't funny," he snarled, forcefully enough to cause a lull in conversation. Loxly covered it by holding up his shotgun and talking about it loudly.

Larken turned to face him fully. "You think I find this funny? You of all people should know that I don't."

"I messed up, Larken. I get it, okay?" Hurt danced in his gold eyes, making her miss their hints of green.

"This is *not* your fault."

"Then who's is it?"

"It's mine," she admitted, the edges of her world starting to crumble. "It's all my fault. Everything that my mother did was to get back at Fisher. Everything Dominic is doing is because I left him. I should have just—"

Soren yanked her into his arms, clearly not caring that they had an audience. "Don't say it. *Please* don't ever say it. You're never allowed to go back to them. You hear me?"

Larken choked and nodded into his chest, clinging to his shirt. They stood like that for a while before a set of arms wrapped around Larken from behind. Hinlee laid her head on her shoulder. Brecker, Loxly, and Levi joined them shortly after. For the first time in her life, Larken lifted her face and was unashamed of the tears that clung to her lashes. She offered everyone a small smile as the love of her family filled her.

Eventually, Squad 19 broke apart and found their seats again. Another stool was pulled up to the group and Larken found herself sandwiched between Soren and Hinlee. Loxly squeezed in next to Rich, and Candy insisted that Brecker sit next to Hinlee. Carl held his girlfriend's hand atop his thigh and shot Larken a conspiratorial wink. This time, she didn't blush at the implications of her sitting so close to Soren.

Everyone got comfortable, and despite trying to relax, Larken found it difficult to look at Rich. She still blamed herself for every-thing that happened to him—even though she *knew* it was all Dominic's doing. And it wasn't until the group grew silent that she chanced a glance.

Rich smiled softly at her, something not quite pity and not quite sadness in his eyes. It took her a moment to realize it was hope. He cleared his throat harshly before saying, "Look at all you've done, sweetheart."

Larken blushed, uncomfortable and unsure of what he was going to say next.

"You succeeded in Thresh, managed to talk some sense into Gadget, and kept your promise to me. You brought my boy home safe."

Larken's throat went tight, but Loxly ruined the moment by saying, "Technically, I brought her home safe."

"Shut up, Loxly. Can't you see I'm tryin' to compliment the girl?" his father chastised.

Larken felt her eyes burn again. She needed to apologize. She opened her mouth *to* apologize, but nothing came out. Nothing she could possibly say would be good enough.

Rich shook his head. "You didn't do anythin' wrong, sweetie. The farm's safe. It's just the house that needs to be fixed up."

"But—"

"No buts. I told you why I chose to stay, and I was right. Maxim delivered me, just like He'll deliver you. Try to keep your head held high and remember who you're doin' this for."

Rich changed the subject, but Vallen watched her. He frowned, asking with his eyes, *You okay, runt?*

Larken nodded.

*I will be.*

They all talked and laughed until Levi was struggling to stay awake. Reading the situation, Fisher was the one who stood first and said he felt like he could use a small rest before dinner. Loxly handed his shotgun off to Rich and moved to help Levi up.

"I'm *fine*," the field medic insisted despite the shaking of his arms as he pushed himself up off the pew.

"Let Loxly help you," Hinlee chastised. "Jodi said you still had some PT left before we ship out for the Capital—don't be a hero and make it worse."

Levi reluctantly accepted the help. He also couldn't hide the way his furrowed brow relaxed a few degrees.

Larken waited until everyone was up and out of the tabernacle, then she looked back to the stage—to the altar—and closed her eyes.

*Please don't let anyone else get hurt because of me. I can't lose them.*

A cool waft of air blew over her, and Larken didn't know if it was a breeze that found its way into the tabernacle through a crack somewhere, or something else. She only knew that it comforted her in more ways than she could say.

Larken left the tabernacle, letting the door fall shut behind her. She took a few steps before announcing, "Bodyguard or not, stalking is still a crime."

Delvon fell into step with her and huffed a grunt. "You know, we're still technically engaged, Peach. I'm just looking out for mine."

"Unfortunately, after much consideration, I don't think we'd be a successful love match."

"You're breaking my heart. How will I manage to go on?" Delvon deadpanned.

"Figure it out."

Delvon grabbed her elbow and yanked her to a stop. They were alone—everyone already having gone off to where they were needed. Even Soren had said something about needing to have a conversation with Vallen before they all left the tabernacle. Larken was stuck dealing with this ugly, uncomfortable emotion sitting between her and her friend. She knew it needed to be addressed, but ignoring it would be so much easier.

Eventually, Larken's gaze found its way up to Delvon's cold, grey eyes. Her lips parted, an apology for scaring him on the tip of her tongue, and his eyes hardened.

*Don't you dare apologize, Peach.*

Larken huffed a frustrated grumble and threw her hands up into the air. "Well, what do you want from me then?!"

"I want you to be more careful! Don't apologize, just do it!"

"How in the world am I supposed to be in control of that?" Larken demanded. "Dominic—"

"Just—" Delvon's jaw clamped shut and then ticked in that annoyed way of his. "Just figure it out."

He turned to leave, but Larken stepped around him and poked him in the chest. "This was your idea to begin with. You *Faithfuls* wanted me to come here and be the face of the new Military District. Remember?" Larken's chest heaved as if she just finished a four-mile run.

"Just because I was the one who asked for your help changing the District doesn't mean involving you was my idea, Princess."

An imaginary bucket of cold water was upended over Larken's head, and her insides shriveled up with icy guilt. "What do you mean?"

Delvon sighed, all of his stress escaping in his breath and washing over her still-damp hair. That action alone told Larken so much more than Delvon would ever give voice to. But he surprised her by admitting, "Look, if everyone wants you to be Luminary—fine. I'll stand by you just like I planned. But if getting to that point means you're going to get yourself killed…"

He trailed off with a frustrated glare, but Delvon didn't have to finish. None of this was his idea. Delvon didn't want her risking herself. He'd been pretending to be okay with everything that was going on around him, all the while hating that he'd been in the dark. Larken only now realized how stressful that must be for him. He was the head of security back at the Manor. He literally knew everything about everything. Now Larken was getting sent off on missions and he couldn't always follow. Delvon truly cared for her and didn't want his friend to be killed for a cause.

Larken ignored the glare he was leveling on her and wrapped her arms around his middle. Resting her head against his chest, she breathed in the scent of pine and salt that always clung to him. He stiffened but eventually returned her hug.

How far they had come. It still amazed Larken that the meathead that held her at gunpoint had become so important to her. Delvon had somehow become one of her dearest and closest friends, and he clearly thought the same about her. They could stand there and talk about their fears and what could go wrong, but Larken decided that she would spare him his moment of embarrassment.

Instead, she asked, "You know…back before my great-great-grandfather put a stop to it, the Military District used to have this thing called a Luminary's Champion. They were pretty much just a glorified personal bodyguard, but they got *way* more job perks."

Delvon waited a beat then grunted, "That's not a question, Peach."

Larken smiled, staring at a tuft of grass blowing in the breeze just past Delvon's bicep. "I'm thinking it might be cool to bring it back. What about you?"

"It sounds like a lot of work. I'm considering an early retirement after this."

Larken snorted and let go of him. "Whatever you say."

"Taking care of you is turning me grey."

"Uh-huh." Larken started off, where to she didn't know.

The tension was finally gone between them and the muscles in Larken's back loosened. They didn't need to argue to reach an agreement. Delvon would be accompanying her out of the Camp from now on. He wouldn't be leaving her side unless he was desperately needed elsewhere. Larken was fine with that. All that was left now was getting her to the Magnate.

The idea of it made her stomach knot and there was no way she would turn away Delvon's help. Especially if there was a chance that Dominic would be waiting for her again.

# CHAPTER 28

Everyone shouted around him, fighting to be the one that was heard. Soren couldn't do anything—couldn't *say* anything. It was just like in his dreams, and he had to remind himself that he was still awake. In all of his years fighting in this war, nothing had prepared him for the nightmares that now haunted him every night. These were worse than the ones from before. Then, he and Larken were only crashing into that field. Now—well, now everyone he loved and cared for was getting shot, bleeding everywhere, and dying.

Hinlee stood screaming and sobbing over a lifeless Brecker. Loxly was covered in bleeding burns as he flew them away from a fire-engulfed farm, crying silently as they left Rich behind. Soren himself was covered in Levi's blood, pushing more and more out with each compression as Larken lay only a few feet away, staring at him with her red hair and lifeless eyes. Every night it was the same, and not even waking stopped the images swirling around in his mind.

"And I say it's too dangerous for us not to!" Ewan bellowed at a rat-faced Faithful that Soren hadn't seen before today.

After the drama of the last outing, quite a few *interested* and *concerned* Faithfuls came out of the woodwork to share their opinions on how they thought the mission to visit the Magnate should be handled. Soren wanted to yell that this wasn't some sort of public forum, but kept his mouth shut. Brecker was doing a good job of speaking for the Squad. Even Levi and Loxly shared their opinions now and then. The only people aside from Soren that remained silent were Fisher and Vallen. Fisher watched the arguments bouncing from one person to the next, his fingers steepled against his lips. Vallen followed the shouting as well, his brow furrowing even more with each stupid idea.

The rat-faced man tried again, the look on his face saying that he thought he would be the one to come up with the perfect plan. "You'll no doubt be recognized. It's clearly a bad—"

"We're going this time and that's that! Del won't let her out of his sight, and frankly, I don't want to either."

"That sounds like more of a 'lack of boundaries problem' than a 'well thought out plan'. We all know that Delvon has an unhealthy obsession with the girl. We need to focus on taking down Cornella, not your brother's love life."

Ewan stood, knocking the chair he sat in to the floor, and looked ready to leap over the table. The Tanner brother was twice the size of the little Faithful and would have him out cold with one hit. Ewan's team members were in action, standing as well to hold the man back. Ewan tried to fight them off, surprising Soren with his show of emotion. Usually Ewan and Delvon were pretty level-headed.

"Listen here, you little pervert!" Ewan shouted. "Just because you steal panties from the communal clothesline doesn't mean—"

"Enough!"

Everyone stopped to stare at Vallen. Well, everyone except Ewan. He still fought against his friends, who ultimately had to drag him out. No one dared to make a sound, but Brecker and Loxly shared a look that said they would need to warn Larken and Hinlee about their underwear.

Once the room cooled off a few degrees, Vallen leaned back in his chair. He rubbed at his temples and said, "Anyone who isn't on the prayer committee or hasn't been considered for any of Larken's teams, get out."

The rat-faced man's expression of triumph fell. "But Blade—!"

"OUT!"

No one needed to be told twice. Chair legs screeched and boots pounded across the floor to the stairs. The only ones that remained were Brecker, Loxly, Levi, what was left of Shadric's team, two old women and Mr. Chin, and Rich. Fisher looked out of place sitting at the head of the table with Vallen, and Larken's, Shadric's, and Delvon's absences were very much noticed. Shadric thought it might be a good idea for the three of them to go over the floor plans again—this time in more detail. Soren would be heading there with Brecker and Loxly next after this. They just all needed to agree on a plan first.

Even Hinlee was off somewhere playing with some new invention Delvon created. The idea was that she would install a holographic device on the Harpy that would cover the aircraft in whatever shape needed. They would be flying under the disguise of one of the Magnate's aircraft. The only issue would be that, since it was a holographic image, Loxly would have to fly *perfectly*. If he was to clip a building with the image, the building would go right through it instead of causing any damage.

Soren was exceedingly relieved he wasn't the pilot.

Once the door closed, Vallen slumped deeper into his chair. Soren had never seen the man look so old. Not only was leading the Faithfuls weighing him down, but Larken seemed to be getting injured more and more lately. Even Soren felt decades older than his twenty-five years. Unable to help himself, his eyes drifted over to Levi. They'd all been through a lot lately—Soren needed to remember that he and Vallen weren't the only ones suffering.

Vallen cleared his throat and sat up. He ran his palm over his mouth, pausing to scratch at some stubble he'd neglected to shave within the last few days. Then, he moved his hand up to massage the back of his neck for a few seconds before letting it fall to his side. Vallen shifted, fishing around in his pocket, and produced a large coin-like device he dropped on the table. The metal was denser than it looked and clattered loudly. Vallen didn't make a move to stop it. Instead, Fisher reached for it and stilled the device with gentle fingers.

The man took a long, slow breath, a habit Soren noticed he shared with his daughter, and ran his finger along the side of the coin. The top opened in the center, spitting out a hologram that nearly took up the entire table. Soren could reach out and touch it if he wanted, but kept his hands where they were.

"I know whoever is going will be taking turns going over the floor plans with young Shadric, but Val—Blade thought it might be good for me to give a brief overview of the Manse before he gets into the plan we've constructed."

Surprise danced over all the soldiers' faces for the briefest of seconds. Soren knew that Larken had sought her father out for advice once before and it was sound enough. Vallen must have thought the same thing if he let Fisher in on his plans. The man had surprising insight for someone who was a director and not a tactician. Although, Soren had to admit that he wouldn't have had the patience or the brainpower to direct the jumbled yet deliberate execution of *Libri E Beaus*. Perhaps a director was what they needed, after all.

Soren took in the building before him. It resembled a long-forgotten governmental-type estate. A dusty cream-colored brick stood strong and tall against columns the same shade. Soren couldn't help but think the building looked dirty compared to the bright white of the Military Manor. It was a great, windowless box of intricate brickwork. A small section of wall jutted out in the front, providing a grand entryway that went all the way up to the top of the estate.

"The Manse of the Magnate," Fisher said. "I've only been there a handful of times, but I at least know how it's set up."

Fisher placed a single finger atop the coin and slid it, moving the hologram so it was more centered. He then traced a light circle around the edge. The Manse took up a slow turn, showing off every angle of the outside of the building.

"There are only two ways into the Manse. Through the front doors and the hangar."

Just as Fisher spoke the words, the hangar passed in front of Soren. It was a diluted grey that went all the way to the roof just as the entryway did. Soren frowned, not liking the solve-a-puzzle feeling he got.

"I'm sure you've all noticed by now that there doesn't seem to be much difference in the appearance of the outside structure from floor to floor. That's because there isn't." Fisher continued, "The inside isn't any different. The Manse has three floors, and they are all built exactly the same."

Vallen stood and walked around behind Fisher. Soren followed him with his eyes and watched as he grabbed an obscenely large stylus. Vallen approached the table once more and used it to tap the back right corner of the Manse. It glowed a pale red, reaching up all three levels.

Fisher waited until Vallen was ready before saying, "These are all of the guest quarters. If you were to receive an invitation to stay for a special circumstance—say, performing in one of the most popular operas in Koraythea—you'd stay here. My room was on the first floor."

As Fisher spoke, a single box in the middle of the first story glowed red as an ember.

Vallen went on to stab the tip of the stylus into the corner in front of the guest area and to the right of the entryway, turning it green.

Fisher cleared his throat and said, "This bit of area right behind the entryway is a massive hallway with open spaces and perfect acoustics. Not very good for hiding, I'm afraid. To the right, you'll find a sort of sitting room or recreational room for the guests. I remember one of my cast members lost quite a bit of arii in a billiard game with a security guard. Anyway—" Fisher motioned Vallen to move to the next spot on the hologram, "—here are the office areas. I don't know who uses them, only that the Magnate doesn't."

The yellow of the offices faded as blue filled the back left of the Manse.

"And this is the library."

Fisher leaned forward and drummed the fingers of his left hand on the table next to the coin. Nervous energy trickled off of him at first, then quickly turned into crashing waves.

"Blade, if you would—yes, thank you."

Vallen skewered the entryway. A pale purple filled the section and Soren narrowed his eyes on a box that grew six steps high.

"What's that?" Brecker asked.

"Unfortunately, it's the only way to the second story."

"Meanin'—" Loxly started but was cut off by Vallen when he said, "Meaning you'll have to get from the hangar to the entryway without being noticed."

"I'm sorry, Blade, but there's something I just don't understand," one of the two old women interjected. Her grey-blue curls clung tightly to her scalp, making her crow's feet more prominent. "Why not just take the front gates? Last service we were informed that the plan for Stars was already known to the Vigilants. Why not just march in?"

Mr. Chin cleared his throat then. "I believe it's because Miss Hale has too high a profile. She would be noticed before they even hit the Capitol."

"Exactly," Vallen agreed. "Our *false Camp* isn't going to hold forever. The only reason we've avoided being found out here is that the army posing as the Camp keeps moving around on the front-lines. We'll have to fly Larken out over the ocean and down south through Thresh. The Harpy will hit the hangar before the front door. Plus, it will be easier to disguise the aircraft instead of docking it on the front lawn."

The woman nodded and muttered to her neighbor, "Add Miss Hale's flying nerves to the list, Dania."

Dania nodded and scribbled on her tablet.

"So, get Larken to the stairs and get her to the second story," Loxly said. "Easy enough. Where's the Magnate? There in the middle?"

"Not exactly," Fisher sighed. "Remember when I said that each level of the Manse was the same? That's because they want to trick anyone who might try to break in. It's true that a simple web search could probably tell you most of what you wanted to know, but even as soldiers, do you know how the Manse is set up?"

Soren's stomach sunk in inadequacy. As a Captain, that's probably something he should have thought about before now. Fisher was right. No one would ever think to investigate the Manse if they didn't have to. It was a stuffy old government building. Soren's job had him focused on the war, not the politics. And since Cornella had control over the war, and no doubt the media on it as well, the Magnate had been gently pushed to the side in favor of Larken's ruined wedding and the fires.

"The first level of the Manse is for guests. Since the front door is only on the first story of the entryway, guests would only have access to the other levels from this staircase." Fisher indicated the dark purple boxes with an open hand. "This ensures that no one can get to the second level who isn't supposed to. And before you ask, no, there are no windows."

"How do they get air?" Brecker asked.

"Through mouse-sized pipes that run through all of the walls and floors," Vallen grumbled, clearly put out that they couldn't break in through the ventilation system. Soren was willing to bet that was the first thing he and Delvon looked into before calling on Shadric and Fisher.

"I don't know what's in the entryway sections of the second and third levels. I never got further than getting stared down by the two security guards working the stairs. And as I understand it, neither has Shadric. Whoever ends up going will be on their own in that department."

He shook his head and Soren waited for him to continue.

"Anyway, the staff occupies the second story—at least that's where they told me they stayed. Shadric said he was told the same thing on his last visit to the Manse. And Ewan managed to find out that all of the security guards live up on the third level."

Soren's eyes flicked over to the man's empty seat. He wondered if the Tanner brother was able to calm down and how exactly he'd managed to come by this information. The two brothers seemed to know an awful lot about everything without having to do much digging.

Fisher stood then, pulling Soren's attention to him, and joined Vallen. He paused the hologram so the library stilled before him. Blue once again filled the section and pushed up against the grey of the hangar. Soren watched as Fisher raised his hand. With a single finger, he tapped the hologram in the far corner of the room, on what had to be where the second level started. Another set of boxes appeared before he could pull away.

"Here is where we believe the second staircase is." He pointed at the general area. "It makes the most sense, but we can't be one hundred percent sure."

Vallen used the stylus to reach the right of the office area. A cylinder of white filled the center space, dimming the rest of the hologram. A black block appeared at the tip of the stylus. "Here you will see the only elevator in the place. It will take you back down all three levels," Vallen paused to stab the center of the hologram on the first level, "and spit you out in the Magnate's personal study. We don't yet know the security situation on the study, but while Delvon works on it, we have to assume that there are cameras to prevent any assassination attempts."

"Exactly," Fisher agreed. "This won't be like any of your other trips out of Camp. This is the Magnate—everything from security to danger will be doubled if not tripled."

Soren's eyes caught on Dania as she mouthed the word *tripled* as she wrote it on the tablet.

He couldn't take it anymore and his own anxious energy bubbled out in the form of a question. "When this is over—and we're still alive—how are we supposed to get out?"

Fisher and Vallen shared a look that had Soren's stomach shriveling up into a tight leaden ball.

The two men shared a silent conversation that Soren couldn't follow before Fisher finally admitted, "We don't know."

The room took on an energy so intense that it was disturbed even by sitting still. No one knew what to say—but what could anyone say to that? Either they died or they were on their own. There was no answer this time.

Rich gave everyone a mild heart attack by clapping his hands and rubbing his rough palms together. The action was reminiscent of digging into a feast, not almost certain death.

Everyone stared at him, and he grinned. "Guess this is where we come in. Wondered why you had us stay."

Vallen gave him a short nod.

"Look, Soren," Rich paused to look at the squad members that were there, eyes staying the longest on Loxly. "Thinkin' back, it's easy to see where you went right and where you went wrong. But try not to think about that. Instead, remember the feelin' you had in the moments like this, the ones where you didn't know if your plans would work or not. It's always the same and you all seem to pull through just fine."

Soren didn't respond. He didn't know what to say.

"Oh, what's that old sayin'?" Rich asked, rubbing at his hairline. "The one about Maxim not needin' to care about songbirds but givin' them resources and a song all the same?" He waved the thought off, saying, "Oh, the words don't matter. The point is that this—*us*—we're more than songbirds and Maxim will see us through. You just need a little faith."

Not much was said after that...not that there was much to decide. Soren had to wait for a message saying Delvon and Shadric were ready to talk, so there wasn't a rush to get to the music room. He waited as Rich, Mr. Chin, and the two women all took turns praying over them and the hologram, asking Maxim to see them through. Soren followed along the best he could, but his heart was still too tight to do more than rapid, shallow beats.

He needed to hit something.

The sounds of gunshots, puddles of blood, and his friends crying found him again. Soren tried to focus on Rich's words instead of the memories as he stood and made his way outside. Chilled autumn air hit him in the face, and Soren took the long route to where he was supposed to be meeting Shadric and Delvon. The memories of the ride back from Stars kept catching him, and Soren was forced to stop and drop against a tree.

Memories and dreams bled into each other in a dizzying vision of horror. He closed his eyes but it only made things worse. He was back on Field E. A gunshot sounded and he watched as she fell to the forest floor. Soren called out her name over and over as her eyes grew heavy and closed. He kissed her forehead and held her as she bled. Then their aircraft was hit and they fell out of the sky. Larken screamed in his ear and he prayed the sound wouldn't stop. Next she was leaving the dorm to go be with Braves—only, he shot her and she was lying on the Harpy floor as Levi bled out under his fingers.

Soren's hand found its way to his side of its own accord and he didn't try to stop it. He was there again, in that field, getting shot. Heavy pants shook his chest as he felt like he was losing air. He panicked and scrambled for his communicator. Something was wrong—he was having a heart attack or something. This wasn't normal, this wasn't—

Soren's breath caught as he realized what was happening. No one was around and he could have a vulnerable moment in the peace of the forest. No one would ever know that he had to take a moment to stop a panic attack. What would they think if they knew how truly afraid he was of losing them all? They were the only family he'd ever known and this could all end in a split second if something went wrong. They could all die if he messed up again…

*Maxim, I'm not strong enough for this. I'm not strong enough to lose them—to lose* her. *Please, be there for them in the ways I can't.*

A message came though, startling Soren and telling him it was his turn to speak with the men.

Rich's words warred with Soren's memories as he took a deep, steadying breath and stood. He loved the man like a father, but Rich just didn't understand. Yes, Maxim cared for His people more than songbirds…but Rich wasn't there in the Harpy. He didn't watch as the only songbird that mattered fell and went unconscious. Soren had, and his greatest fear was that *his* songbird would fall again. Fall…and not get up this time.

# CHAPTER 29

"And I want to know why something wasn't done with this information before!"

In the entire time Shadric knew Soren, not once had he ever done more than growl in his presence. Now—well, now he was shouting and raging at what seemed to be his full capacity. The music stands in the corner almost rattled as Soren raised his voice. Shadric was only now aware of how tiny and fragile the music room was.

"Listen, mate—"

"No!" Soren cut Delvon off. "You listen! We've been busting not only *our* rear ends to pull your plans off, but we've been shot, attacked, and Maxim knows what else! And you've had more information on the Magnate and the Manse the whole time?"

Shadric felt so *incredibly* small sitting between the two men. Like a sapling between two butting rams fighting for the alpha spot of the herd. Levi sat silently across the table from Shadric, eyes boring a hole into the wood and not speaking. He didn't need to, though—his frown and crossed arms said enough. Even the happy-go-lucky Loxly seemed to disapprove of the situation. On top of that, Brecker sat taking mental notes. His eyes darted from person to person, absorbing everything he could to pass onto Hinlee…who would ultimately tell Larken.

*Do something!*

Shadric wracked his brain. As stupid as it was, he wanted to be the one that Hinlee and Larken talked about. She only left a bit ago, just as shocked as her team members were now. But what could they do? Broadcast across camp that a security guard left the Manse and joined the Faithfuls the same week Larken joined the military? It wasn't their secret to share. Especially since Isaiah was the Magnate's illegitimate son.

"We couldn't just—" Shadric tried, but was cut off by Soren growling, "Shut it, Barlow."

"It was—*is*—a delicate situation," Delvon grumbled.

How he was keeping his cool, Shadric had no idea.

Soren glowered at him, nostrils flaring like a charging rhinoceros.

"We swore our secrecy to Blade," Delvon said.

"Then why did we have to sit through that whole spiel just now when we were just going to come down here and learn that you know everything about everything?" As Soren asked the question, his words grew louder and louder. "Does Fisher know he wasted his time today?"

"No one wasted anything!" Delvon barked, finally reaching the end of his rope. "Shut up and sit down! You may have been a Captain back at your base, but here you're no more than an idiot Cadet. I outrank you *ten-fold*."

There was a moment of silence and then the sound barrier cracked. Soren lunged over the table and took Delvon to the ground. None of his friends tried to pull him off and Shadric didn't have any idea what he should do. This fight had been building—Shadric knew that. Probably since the night the two of them first met. Shadric heard that Delvon had been a little rough with Larken. The two men had been going at it like two dogs fighting for the same scrap of meat ever since.

Only, now that they'd come to blows, the dam completely broke between the two.

Both Delvon and Soren were equally yoked, and no clear winner was in sight. Shadric stood and did the only thing he could think of.

He ran out of the music room.

Racing through the door, he burst out onto the stage in the tabernacle. Larken couldn't be too far away—maybe Hinlee would even be with her. The fighting wasn't as loud out here as Shadric would have thought, but then again, Delvon and Soren were using their fists instead of their words. Shadric pushed on, sprinting out of the tabernacle and down the path that led to Larken's house. He was about halfway there when he caught her.

Gasping, he said, "Larken, we need you."

Her eyes went wide with fear. "Is Vallen okay?"

Shadric waved her words away. "Del and Soren are fighting."

"Oh. Well, they always fight." She shrugged her left shoulder. "That's okay."

Shadric shook his head. "No. They're *fighting*. Now. In the music room."

The color drained from Larken's face, and she sped off. Shadric followed after her. They made it back to the tabernacle quickly and hadn't even shut the front door behind them when they heard a loud crash. Blade thudded down the stairs leading from the conference room, demanding to know what was happening. Larken didn't answer him and skidded around the pews.

She got to the doorway before demanding, "What are you idiots doing?!"

She didn't get an answer—not that Shadric expected them to say anything—and ran in. Both he and Blade moved, getting to the doorway themselves just as Larken reached for Soren's sleeve. Delvon lay sprawled atop a crushed table with blood running in two rivulets from a split at the corner of his lips. Soren loomed over him, a gash at his temple bleeding and his own lip busted open. He punched Delvon in the jaw, only adding to the bloodshed.

"Soren, I said stop!" Larken half-pleaded-half-ordered as she tried to get a better hold of his sleeve.

Soren, not noticing her, pulled his arm back for another punch.

Larken caught the recoil full in the face and fell backward on to her rear end as she clutched at her nose.

"Little Bird!" Loxly cried out, the crooked smile falling from his face.

The man rushed to her side and crouched as Soren dropped to his knee and released Delvon. The former Captain turned to find Larken lowering her hands enough to inspect the damage. Blood poured from both nostrils, dripping onto her pumpkin-colored shirt.

The room went completely silent as everyone took Larken in. She gasped in pain as she poked and prodded where Soren's elbow hit her.

"Oh no!" Loxly murmured. "Larken—" a devious glint crossed his eyes as he asked, "—are you...*hale?*"

Larken glared and shoved Loxly in the shoulder so hard that he fell over. He snickered, eliciting a round of groans from his friends.

The sigh Blade released sounded as though it had been pent up for the entirety of Larken's life. "I don't care what happened here and I don't want to know. Just fix it." He turned and didn't even look back as he ordered, "Tanner, stop sniveling on the floor and get Larken to Medic Lattic. Shad, take Deckard to Medic Brocklin."

The door shut behind Blade and no one moved for a moment. The only sound came from Larken as she tried her best to breathe past the blood. She moved her hands tentatively, frowning as she did. She tried once more to check the damage, but she barely pulled her red fingers away from her nostrils before more blood streamed from them.

Delvon grunted as he shifted. He knocked Soren out of the way as he closed the few feet between him and his charge. Tugging her hands away, Delvon grabbed the hem of her shirt and pulled it up. She lifted her arms to help. The movement revealed a toned stomach and a deep emerald sports bra. Shadric quickly looked away, a blush hot on his face as they muttered about Carl and the shirt.

Shadric decided to focus on Loxly as his best friend saw to the girl of his dreams. Out of the corner of his eye, Delvon helped

Larken to her feet while he smothered her face with her shirt. Loxly made his way over to Levi, who leaned against Brecker for support. As far as Shadric knew, Jodi wanted at least two more days of rest and physical therapy out of him. Just by glancing at the man, anyone could see that the Field Medic worried that he wouldn't have enough time.

Everyone was running out of time, it seemed.

Soon, the five others filed out of the room, leaving Shadric and Soren behind. Only just now realizing what an inept moron he must seem, Shadric rushed to Soren's side. He still knelt and Shadric held out a hand to help the man up. The former Captain only knocked it out of the way.

"I don't need your help."

"And I'm not going to ignore orders," Shadric countered.

Soren got to his feet slowly, as if he were some great tree lifting its roots. Shadric could almost hear the man's abused joints creak with their movements. He'd never felt so inadequate before. Soren was a true soldier, whereas he was nothing more than a pretty singer.

"Whatever."

"Look," Shadric tried as Soren made his way out of the room, "it wasn't up to us. Okay?"

Soren rounded on him, staring down into his soul with the golden eyes of a lion. "We're not going to *talk this out* or whatever it is you Faithfuls do. You had information that Larken needed, and you kept it to yourselves. Simple as that. As far as I'm concerned, the only people Larken can trust is her Squad."

"You needed to know the Manse's blueprints while you were in Stars?" Shadric challenged.

Soren's glare turned murderous.

"Or maybe you needed to know them when you lived at the Military Manor before you even knew Blade was leading the rebellion?"

Soren said nothing, but his temple ticked violently.

"We don't have to talk this out and be best friends and sing around a campfire, but you do need to understand that not every-thing is an immediate danger to Larken. You were brought to the music room to learn classified information. You can throw as many punches as you want, but you also have to accept that without Larken, those blueprints are just blueprints. Larken is the only one who has a chance facing the Magnate."

Soren waited a beat before turning and storming off. Shadric followed, more afraid of disobeying Blade's direct orders than a sour Captain. Soren stomped all the way to the med-area with Shadric close behind. He would probably be turned away upon delivery, but it didn't matter. Shadric would see this through and then be done with Soren. He wasn't going to the Manse, so he wouldn't have to speak to him for a good long while.

The familiar white building greeted them, and Soren blew through the double doors. Shadric kept up as they walked past empty room after empty room. They rounded a corner and Jodi stood waiting for them down at the end of the hall. She stared into the room across from hers where Delvon could be heard complaining loudly and Larken laughing.

*Good. At least she's fixed up.*

As the two of them got closer, Jodi noticed them. She shook her head and pointed the way they came from. Soren didn't wait for Shadric as he turned around the hall and backtracked. Shadric only apologized for his companion's behavior, not sure what else to do.

"I'm used to it," Jodi grunted.

The two of them reached Soren and she said, "We're going to fix you up somewhere else."

Soren didn't respond. He just waited for Jodi to lead him to their destination. Jodi went back the way they came for a bit but then took them down a different hallway that spat them out on the oppo-site side of the center from Larken and Delvon. She scanned a purple wristband across a monitor and a door unlocked and swung open. Soren followed the Medic inside and Shadric nodded.

"Well, I'll be going then—"

"Not so fast, bub," Jodi cut him off. "You're the help today."

"Oh, I don't have any med-training."

"Not what I mean. Mr. Tough Guy here isn't a fan of artificial recreation. I'm gonna have to drug him up and sew him together like in the old days. It's going to be your job to get him back to his place when I'm done."

*Blade…*

Shadric sighed, trying not to be too loud and let Soren know how much this inconvenienced him before walking into the room. Soren dropped into a chair, leaving only the exam bench for Shadric to sit on. He did so, silently complaining about how much of an annoyance Soren was.

Shadric honestly couldn't see what Larken saw in him.

Jodi didn't waste any time getting to work. She pulled out a tray loaded with the things she would need and tugged on a set of gloves, letting the left one snap against her wrist just as the bubble she blew popped across her bottom lip. Shadric wondered where she managed to find the gum since it wasn't something they could grow. Their smugglers didn't usually bring it back, either.

Soren's grunt of pain cut off his line of thought as Jodi dabbed at the wound with a rich, alcohol-smelling cotton ball. He kept trying to pull away from her, forcing Jodi to grab his hair and hold him in place.

"Stop moving."

Soren glowered at the medic but kept his mouth shut. The man was clearly looking for a fight. Shadric wondered what it was about Jodi that held his tongue.

Jodi released him only long enough to grab a small syringe. She poked a needle into the spot just above his open gash. Soren hissed and tried to pull away.

"Quit it," Jodi ordered as she emptied the syringe's contents and grabbed a second one. Jodi stuck that one just under the gash and added, "Her nose was broken, if you were wondering."

"I wasn't."

"Of course you weren't." Jodi smirked and dropped the second syringe on the tray. She grabbed her needle and thread and muttered, "She's never going to let you forget about this."

"*Not now,*" Soren growled, looking anywhere that wasn't Shadric.

Shadric felt like he was missing a lot of the conversation and was annoyed yet again at how Larken's friends from base had a way of communicating with each other without actually speaking. He and Delvon didn't act like that—well, Shadric didn't. Delvon had managed to somehow perfect the strong and silent type personality.

After a few very long, silent, and uncomfortable moments, Jodi tied the stitches off and dropped everything onto the tray. She pulled the right glove off before tugging the left up over her hand and knotting the gloves together in a little ball. They landed on the tray with a soft rubbery splat, and she crossed her arms.

"You have two options. You can walk out of here right now and I can cut the stitches out next week, or I can give you something that will have you all healed up by the morning."

"And you chose not to mention that before you stabbed several needles into my face?" Soren rumbled.

"I'll still have to check you in the morning. It's just your choice how long you want the stitches." To emphasize her statement, Jodi scooped up a tiny cup and shook it so the pills inside clicked together.

Soren reached for them, but she pulled them away for a moment.

"These are some pretty intense drugs. They're why I made Barlow stay. You'll heal faster, but you'll definitely need him to keep you from falling over."

An internal conflict that Shadric couldn't understand danced behind the ex-Captain's eyes. He didn't know what there was to think about—or why he got stitches instead of using a dermis gun. Either way, the battle ended when Soren snatched the cup and knocked the pills back.

Jodi supplied him with some water while muttering, "This is going to be so fun to watch."

Soren handed the empty cups back over and resumed his stance of crossed arms and an unfriendly frown.

"I'll be back in twenty to make sure you aren't having a negative reaction." Before she left, Jodi winked and added, "Have fun."

As soon as the door shut, Shadric broke the silence and asked, "What was that about?"

"I don't care," Soren grunted and rested his head back against the wall.

Shadric shrugged and pulled out his communicator. Soren obviously wasn't going to help him pass the time.

"Why was the information confidential? I thought everyone was privy to everything here."

"Huh?" Shadric peeked up from the article he'd just been scrolling through. "Oh, well, it was a pretty sensitive subject."

Soren cracked an eye open and rose an eyebrow in Shadric's direction.

Shadric looked at the door, checking that no one stood outside. He lowered his voice and said, "The person who shared that information with us was the Magnate's illegitimate son."

The other eye opened, and even though he didn't lift his head from the wall, Soren turned his face fully to Shadric. "What?"

"Yeah. Apparently, there was a small scandal that involved a maid. As far as I know, she died when he was young, and he was raised by one of the head security guys."

Soren blinked and shook his head slightly. Regaining his faculties, he asked, "Where is this guy? Does Larken know about him?"

"I'm not sure. It may have come up in her schooling since she would need to know the family trees of the Luminaries and Magnates, but we didn't tell her."

Soren closed his eyes and shook his head again. This time when he met Shadric's gaze, his eyes were glossed over as if he'd been drinking for a few hours. "Great. Someone *else* who'll want to marry her."

The statement took Shadric by surprise so much that all he could say was, "He died."

"Oh." Soren reached a shaky hand up and rubbed at his face. "I think you need to get Jodi. Something feels wrong."

Shadric pushed off of the table and cracked the door open just enough that he could peek his head out. Jodi stood at a table not too far away, scribbling something on a tablet. She glanced up after a moment and blew another bubble.

"Soren says something's wrong."

The grin that split Jodi's face was pure evil. "Wonderful!"

She dropped what she was doing and barged into the room. She pulled a little light from her breast pocket and flashed it over Soren's eyes. He kept trying to follow the light, so she reached out once more and held his head still.

"Looks like somebody skipped lunch today."

"I didn't have time," Soren agreed. "I wanted to get to the meeting."

"Mmhmm, I'm sure."

"Jodi, how's Larken? Is she okay? I feel really bad about what happened."

Shadric stared, openmouthed, at the brooding giant of a man.

Jodi's grin deepened. "She's fine. Ezra fixed her up. Want me to get her so you can tell her how pretty her new nose is?"

"New nose?" Soren frowned. "I liked her old one. It crinkled when she laughed."

"*What did you do?*" Shadric gasped.

Jodi glanced over her shoulder at him. "Weird, right?" She turned back to Soren and asked, "Any tingling in your fingers?"

He stared down at his hands, pulled his head from her grasp, and wiggled his fingers. "Nope."

"I know it's only been fifteen minutes, but you can leave. You're fine."

Soren nodded. "Thank you for helping."

"Why am I not recording this?" Jodi muttered as she helped Soren stand. She dumped him on Shadric and waved them out of the room.

Shadric bore most of Soren's weight as the man stumbled

through the med-center. He'd stop often to look at random paintings or plants. The same thing happened outside, all the way to Soren's bungalow. Shadric half-wanted to be done with him for the day, half-wanted to show him off in this state. He would have deserved it for starting the fight with Delvon. Not to mention, Larken would love to see him like this.

Soren teetered as he climbed up onto the slightest step in front of his door and almost fell. Shadric threw out a hand, but Soren knocked it away. The movement sent his shoulder flying into the door and he collided with a deep *thud*. Shadric only rolled his eyes and joined him on the step. He twisted the knob, but the door didn't give.

"Why is your door locked?"

"Don't want no one stealing my stuff."

"Yeah, but," Shadric paused to take a calming breath, "no one here has any reason to steal. We share everything."

Soren fished around in his pocket for something only to come up empty. Then he chuckled as he pulled a wristband free from a belt loop. "Bet you lock up your guitars, don't ya, Barlow?"

Shadric kept his mouth shut, not wanting him to be right. He also decided that he liked this version of Soren even less than the other one.

Soren finally got his door open and stomped inside. Shadric didn't wait for the invitation to follow and walked into the bungalow. Closing the door behind him, Shadric was hit with the same uncertainty he always had when he visited a new place. Dark furniture cluttered around a dark room. Soren's kitchenette appeared untouched, as did the stiff recliners. Shadric wondered for a moment if he was the first visitor Soren ever had.

Shadric moved on from the furniture and turned his attention to a struggling Soren. His arms and head were caught in his shirt, exposing a scar-riddled abdomen. His pants already sat around his still-booted feet and Shadric barely blinked three times before Soren's little wiggled, undressing dance tripped him. He fell forward onto his bed and then bounced once before falling onto the floor. Shadric sighed heavily before moving forward. He crouched down by Soren and put a hand on his bicep to still him. Soren only groaned.

"Want me to call someone else?"

Soren wiggled some more inside his shirt and adjusted so he could see Shadric. "Whose number you got?"

"Just Larken's."

"No!" he barked, his brows creasing together. "No, I don't ever want her to come here."

Shadric was about to ask why when Soren's eyes flicked up to the nightstand just above him. Following his gaze, Shadric found a down-facing tablet. He reached out, and when Soren didn't stop him, he lifted it up. A picture of the two of them filled the screen. Larken slept peacefully on a crimson couch and Soren stood over her. The man stared at her with a frown much gentler than his usual one as he placed a large black jacket over her frame.

"I don't want her to see me like this," the ex-Captain admitted.

Shadric turned to him once more, finding that he'd gotten control of his shirt.

"I don't want her to see me at all."

"Why?" Shadric asked, his stomach sinking.

"Because I don't deserve her. I can't share her life and she doesn't understand."

The sinking turned to falling, and then the falling turned to nothing at all as Shadric's stomach landed at his feet. He'd always suspected but wasn't sure until now.

Shadric helped him into a sitting position and checked to make sure his stitches weren't bleeding before helping him to his feet. "What do you mean?"

"The Magnate won't want me," Soren said around his shirt. When he was free of the fabric, he dropped it on the floor and fell back onto his bed. "Not when he can have *Shad Barlow*."

Shadric didn't say anything as he untied Soren's boots with one hand and pulled them off. Soren kicked off his pants and socks before rolling onto his stomach. He reached out and took the photo from Shadric and placed it next to his pillow.

"I'm just an unwanted son of the military that fought for this country's demise. I can't give her the life she wants. I can't give her what she needs."

Shadric stared down at his feet, not knowing what to say. This whole situation had gone horribly sour, and his stomach matched the mood. Shadric thought up a lame excuse that would allow him to leave and a snore cut through his thoughts. Soren was already asleep.

Taking a small step back, Shadric realized his stomach was still laying on the floor where he'd been standing. He needed to get away from the ex-Captain and his thoughts of worthlessness. Quickly, he left the bungalow and headed back to the music room to clean up from the fight.

Shadric didn't want to face the truth—didn't want to acknowledge that Soren's reasoning was what made him perfect for a future Luminar. And Shadric knew that despite all of the uncertainty behind Larken's eyes, all of the shy blushes and the almost kisses, he needed to give up.

Someone already held Larken's heart. It wasn't him and it never would be.

# CHAPTER 30

Larken swayed gently as she stared out across the sea. Grey clouds rolled overhead, not quite blocking out the sun but telling the story of rain to come. Salty ocean spray knocked into the bow and misted over her. Larken let her head fall back as she breathed in the humidity and the feel of the water around her.

The yacht dipped again, and Larken reached out to grab the bars in front of her. She didn't know why they were going so fast. To beat the storm maybe? Hinlee yelled across the deck at Loxly to slow down and Larken had her answer. Loxly always drove fast—though she wasn't aware he knew how to drive a yacht.

The electric engine purred so softly that Larken couldn't hear it over the crashing waves. Laughter sounded behind her, and Larken tried to make out the voices. They started out clear but then blurred and grew muffled. Another wave crashed up into the bow and caused Larken to stumble back into something warm and solid.

Strong arms reached up around her and murmured, "Easy now."

Larken turned in Soren's arms without even bothering to look up at his face. His body heat encased her, chasing away the chill of the ocean spray. She could stand here forever with him—right on the edge of this storm. Here, things were safe. Here, she knew what to expect. Larken was afraid of the other side of the clouds and what the passing storm would mean for her. Another dip rocked them, but Soren stood as strong as ever. He may have let her leave base, but he was here now and not willing to let her go.

Until…he did.

The beautiful ocean turned black, and a cruel and familiar laugh cracked through the clouds like thunder. A masculine voice cut through the sound, saying that it wouldn't let them take her. She belonged to this voice and Larken reached for Soren, only to find him just out of reach. Their fingers twisted but a black wave shot up out of the ocean and wrapped its cold tendrils around her. Soren cried out for her, but she was helpless against the undertow. Over the railing she went, and she watched in horror as the sea yanked her closer and closer until—*thud.*

Larken gasped as she shot upright, only to cry out as her head hit something metallic. She whimpered and whined, cradling her forehead with one hand and trying to find freedom with the other. There was an exasperated sigh before Soren muttered, "Someone hit the lights."

Runners dimly lit the cab of the Harpy as Soren got off the bench and onto the floor. Larken stared at him blearily for only a second before he cupped her around the waist and pulled her out from under the bench.

She sat up when she was able and rubbed at her face. Yawning deeply, she asked, "Where are we?"

"Somewhere in the ocean above Thresh. We've been trying to outfly a storm for about two hours now."

"We're still flying?" Larken whispered. Her heart didn't kick into overdrive like it usually did.

"Yes. We're only halfway there. Jodi said your dose would be wearing off around this point. I just didn't think it would be because you fell off the bench."

Larken looked around and found everyone stretched out and sleeping. The benches had been pulled out in true futon style and housed the members of her team. Ewan, Delvon, and Levi all utilized the smaller benches that would only hold one person, while

Brecker and Hinlee snuggled on the one across the floor from where Larken sat. Red hair spilled off the side of the one behind them, and Carl shifted and got comfortable again. He must have been the one to grab the lights. There were no more empty spots and Larken's whole body heated with embarrassment as she realized she'd been sharing a bench with Soren.

Sickly sweet strawberry and kiwi danced under Larken's nose, and she jerked her head back. Soren grabbed her head, but not fast enough to keep it from grazing the side of the bench.

"Drink," he ordered.

"No, it smells gross."

"I don't care. Jodi said to make you drink this before your second dose. We don't have much time before you actually realize we're flying over the ocean in the middle of nowhere."

"I know we're flying over the ocean," Larken hissed. "You just told me that."

"Just because your brain knows something doesn't mean your anxiety understands it. Just shut up and drink your protein juice."

Larken grumbled and insulted Soren before taking the bottle and downing the contents in one breath. She shuddered violently as Soren took the bottle back, then she demanded water. Soren obliged and Larken drank half before realizing her stomach was fit to bursting from all the liquid.

She hunched forward and groaned. "Oh, I feel seasick."

"Well it's your own fault. No one told you to ingest 30 ounces of fluids in ten seconds."

Larken peeked up at Soren. The runners cast shadows on his face, turning him into a soldier of the night. He frowned but couldn't hide the concern in his eyes. He'd been acting weird since he and Delvon had it out. Everyone had been weird, actually. Delvon started tiptoeing around certain topics even though he had no problem speaking his mind before. And other than a quick good-bye, Shadric hadn't spoken to her. Even Jodi seemed to be keeping a secret for once. It was like they all knew something Larken didn't and were actively trying to keep her out of the loop.

She didn't like it one bit.

As if sensing what she was going to ask, Soren used the moment she opened her mouth to cram a chocolate in. She glared but Soren only grunted, "Don't spit it out. You won't get any more until we leave."

Larken didn't lessen her gaze as she chewed and swallowed. Soren offered her the water again and she only sipped enough to wash the sticky caramel down. Once she handed off the bottle, Soren scooped her up and placed her back on the bench. Larken snuggled into her pillow, already feeling drowsy again. Soren covered her up with the blanket and got comfortable next to her on the bench.

"Why are we sharing?" she whispered sleepily.

"I wasn't going to bunk with Delvon."

Larken snorted. "What about Loxly?"

"Him either."

She reached out to smack him, but her hand grew heavy and just landed on Soren's chest. "No, I meant how is he sleeping?"

"The pilot for Shadric's team is in there with him. Those two have been switching every few hours or so."

"That's good. I'd hate for him to fall asleep and crash us," Larken mumbled, her eyes growing heavier by the second.

"I'm glad Jodi was able to find something that worked for you. Could you imagine what people would say if you were trying to take your clothes off right now?" Soren teased.

"That was uncalled for and you know it. You'd want out of that wedding dress, too."

"Don't be such a baby."

Larken's lips twitched as his words washed over her. Soon she was back on the yacht, but this time the world was made of sunset glass instead of storm clouds. No voices shouted or laughed in the sky, and Soren's lips were far too busy to be teasing her about being a baby.

# CHAPTER 31

Soren's eyes snapped open. His back twinged uncomfortably, and he tried to sit up to correct it. A warm body shifted next to him, and he stilled. Right, they were still on the Harpy. The engine was silent and the cab still dark, so Soren allowed himself a few more moments to enjoy Larken sleeping next to him.

Her hand rested on his chest but shifted across it to touch his shoulder. She snuggled deeper into his side and Soren allowed himself to tighten his hold on her. Before they left, he'd awkwardly apologized to her. She wouldn't hear it, saying that tension has been high for a while and that everything would change when this was all over.

Larken had no idea how right she was. After they got back from this mission, Soren would have to tell her that despite what he wanted, nothing could ever happen between them. It killed him—it killed him that he was finally admitting to himself that he wanted her, only to realize that he was too late.

He should have gotten over himself—should have pulled her to him in the dorm room in front of everyone and never let go. He should have spent every waking second trying to figure out how to get back to her instead of sitting in his room bitter about what he couldn't change. And when he got to the Manor, Soren should have asked Vallen about the kind of man that he needed to be for her sake. Pride had killed this relationship before it even had the chance to start, and it was all his fault.

Larken stirred again and then stilled. Soren didn't know what time it was or even what the plan to get into the Manse was. Fisher only told them how to get to the Magnate, not how to get in or out.

Everyone still seemed to be sleeping. Soren had had a hard time drifting back off after Larken last woke up. He'd laid there, switching between praying and thinking of all the things that could go wrong. He was still awake when Hinlee and Brecker eventually woke up and started whispering to each other. The body could only get so much sleep, but since none of them knew when they would next be able to rest, they were all trying to take advantage of it while they could.

The windows had been blacked out for the whole flight, and it could just as easily be 3:00 in the morning as it could 4:00 in the afternoon. Soren's heart stopped for a moment. What if the hologram hadn't worked and they'd been caught? He had no idea where they were—only that the engine was off and that they weren't moving. Larken still slept soundly, so her supplement hadn't worn off yet. What if he'd only been out for an hour or two and they were trapped somewhere?

Then, the runners lit up again. Soren breathed a long, slow breath of relief. Loxly opened the door to the dark cockpit and walked over to Brecker and Hinlee first. He tapped both of their right boots and then moved to tap Soren's left one. He noticed Loxly left Larken's feet alone. Even on a mission, he didn't want to be the one to wake a sleeping Larken.

Loxly made his way through the cab, starting little fires of adrenaline-kindled energy as he went. Soren slowly rolled over, ignoring Larken's groan of annoyance. She snuggled deeper into his chest as the lights brightened.

"Larken."

"Fifteen more minutes."

"Get up, Peach," Delvon barked from the back of the Harpy.

Larken bolted upright and stared wide-eyed down at Soren—not Delvon. Crimson embers started in the apple of her cheeks and the flames licked down her throat to her chest. Even her ears reddened.

Soren couldn't help his Loxly-esque crooked smirk and asked, "Sleep well?"

Larken clambered over him so fast that she fell to the floor. She scrambled to her feet, muttered some unintelligible excuse, and then locked herself in the bathroom just outside the cockpit.

Candy lit into Delvon and Hinlee gave Soren a stern glare before asking, "Really? Like she isn't nervous enough already."

Soren had the decency to at least feel sheepish, even if he didn't let it show on his face.

Carl walked through the steady stream of snark flowing between his girlfriend and the bodyguard and past Soren. He knocked twice and Larken cracked the door enough to yank him into the bathroom with her. Candy finished with Delvon and led Levi to the other bathroom for a beard trim. When they emerged, Candy handed a razor to everyone with scruff on their face.

No one complained as she took charge and started bossing everyone around. Both Carl and Candy had been hard at work repairing the security uniforms, and the stress was starting to get to her. Delvon was able to learn that when a uniform was no longer up to code, the Manse sent them off to a facility to be burned. Ewan led a team and they were able to grab enough for this mission. None of them were sure they could get away with dressing as staff again, but it was better than just walking in as themselves. There were only a few masks that were able to be saved, so only the ones with the highest profiles would be given one to wear—meaning Larken, Soren, and the Tanner brothers.

Carl was still in the bathroom with Larken, and Soren began to feel guilty. They'd always teased each other before—he didn't realize this time would be any different. At least not yet, any way.

Things really would need to change between them.

Candy called for him after Delvon skulked out of the bathroom, looking naked without his stubble. Soren hadn't really bothered with shaving since leaving base. Before it was part of his morning routine; now he only did it if he managed to remember.

Loxly lounged on the bench Hinlee and Brecker had occupied during the flight, just as scruffy as ever. He'd stay on the Harpy again, ready to take off at a moment's notice. Soren had no idea who took the last watch, but he knew that there'd be no waking the sharpshooter for at least three days when they got back.

*If…if they get back.*

Soren let the door fall shut harder than he needed to as he chased the thought from his mind. There would be no *ifs*—there couldn't be if they wanted to make it through this. Soren lathered up his face and quickly rid himself of any facial hair. A sharp pain under his left ear told him he nicked himself. His eyes jumped from the spot up to his temple of their own accord.

True to her word, Jodi didn't leave so much as a scar… He just wished he could remember what happened after taking those pills. One moment he was in a room with Shadric and the smirking Medic, the next he was waking up in his bed in nothing but his boxers. He must have said or done something, because Shadric was the coldest to Larken Soren had ever seen him before they left.

Wiping off his face, Soren left his razor by the sink next to the others and reentered the cab. Candy and Hinlee waited outside the bathroom and pushed in as soon as Soren was out of the way. With the three women locked in their various bathrooms, the rest of them stripped and got into their uniforms. Soren's was a bit tight in his thighs, and Levi had to roll his pant legs up, but everyone else seemed to be okay.

Soren overheard Ewan volunteer to keep his team on the second floor and make the rounds to distract the Manse security from Larken as she moved toward the Magnate. Delvon refused, whispering that he wasn't willing to leave half the team behind when they needed to make their escape. There wouldn't be another way out, and once the security team realized what was happening, a witch hunt would start and Ewan, Breaker, and Hinlee would be the odd ones out.

Soren had to agree—it was best for them to all be together when everything hit the fan.

Carl knocked on his side of the bathroom door and peeked his head out. Seeing that they were all dressed, he opened the door fully and flooded the cab with the scent of dye and hairspray. Larken reluctantly emerged, sporting two brown braids and pale makeup. Thick gloss covered her lips, giving them a pouty expression. Soren tried not to stare but he couldn't understand how that amount of gloss stayed on her lips and didn't smear on the rest of her face. But it didn't stop her from being just as beautiful as always.

Delvon walked up to her and tilted her head to the right. He muttered something to her that Soren couldn't hear, and she rolled her eyes. The bodyguard huffed a chuckle and put something in her ear. Turning her face back to his, he tugged on a braid before trailing his hands down her arms until he could hold her hands in his. He brought them up and kissed the wrist of her left hand—no, not her wrist. He kissed a bracelet and then teased her as he showed off a matching black one on his own wrist.

Soren didn't know why, but until this moment, he'd managed to keep his nerves relatively under control. This small action on Delvon's part to try and cheer Larken up sent Soren's stomach plummeting to his feet. It was such a gentle moment between the two of them and for the first time, Soren was able to see the friendship Larken held close despite Delvon's tendency to be obnoxious. Would they have another moment like this when everything was said and done?

These could be the last hours Soren had with any of these people. Dread and anxiety washed over him in a way it never had before. Sure, there was a certain amount of nerves that came with getting shipped out, but it had never been anything like this. Before, he had the calm assurance that there would always be more soldiers to fight the Faithfuls. Soren may have been a Captain, but he was ultimately just a number in the Military District's database. Now things were different. So much rode on them for so many people. Who was there to come after them if they failed?

A styrofoam cup was pressed into his hand and he was encouraged to drink. Soren didn't even register the strong scent before the brew hit the back of his tongue. It was bitter enough to make anyone's chest hair fall out.

"You okay, Cap?" Loxly asked softly.

Soren's eyes leaked at the corners as he suppressed his cough. "What was that?"

The pilot shrugged. "Stolen contraband."

"I thought you weren't supposed to drink the coffee on an aircraft?"

"It was in a thermos," Loxly said. "We've got enough up front to keep ten bulls awake for three days."

Soren lost the fight and coughed a few times. It only made the acid coating his throat worse, and he regretted not paying more attention to what was in the cup. Loxly still did that sad puppy thing when he knew something was wrong with the pack dynamic.

When Soren continued to ignore his existence, Loxly said, "It's okay to be nervous."

Soren met his friend's eyes, finding an anxiety there that matched his own. Glancing over his shoulder at Levi, he thought about how close he'd been to losing his friend. He would never forget the fear in Levi's eyes as he thought he was dying, just like Soren would never forget the fear coursing through his veins as he watched. Soren decided to finally be honest about his feelings. What good were his unsaid words if something would have happened to his Second? If something were to happen to any of them? As uncomfortable as it was to be vulnerable in front of others, Soren knew that not having the chance to do it was much worse.

"It's not okay to be nervous—not for me. When I get nervous, things go wrong."

"Well, maybe that's just Maxim tellin' you that you should lean on Him more. If there was ever a time for it, it's now."

Soren really took Loxly in. He stood there, proud of the man he was and unashamed of his nerves. Soren didn't know if he'd ever given the man an actual compliment that didn't revolve around how well he did at training. He went back and forth, not wanting this to be goodbye but also not wanting to leave things unsaid. Soren's stomach tightened, just like it had before but he couldn't remember when. A thick lump grew in his throat and he tried to swallow it away. The lump wouldn't move and his tongue turned to stone. He couldn't speak, and that's when he remembered the moment he'd last felt like this. It was right before Larken left. He thought about that moment over and over again—hating himself for it. It was the moment he wished he could take back and do differently.

Now, he finally got that chance.

Soren pulled Loxly into a rough hug and said, "I'm really glad you sucked at school."

Loxly patted him on the back a few times before pulling away and coming to attention. His eyes were damp, but he didn't look away as he rasped, "It's an honor serving under you, Captain."

Boot heels pounded together all through the cab. Soren turned to find his Squad saluting him—Larken, too. For once, Delvon kept his mouth shut and gave him a nod of respect, one leader to another. After the fight, they seemed to have reached a silent agreement, and might even be able to be friends in twenty years or so. Only Maxim knew...just like He was the only One who knew what this mission's outcome would be.

# CHAPTER 32

"Okay, kid. Get over here so we can go through your check list one more time before you get off."

Larken's stomach twisted into a shape she didn't recognize. It was too swoopy and too angular to discern. It didn't help matters that she still reeled from waking up in Soren's arms. Subconsciously, she knew that she wasn't snuggled up to Delvon, but she didn't know who else would have volunteered to bunk with her and hold her so close. Vague memories of juice and gentle words drifted in her mind, slipping away again when she tried to catch them.

Jodi said before they left that Ezra packed a protein juice for her in a pack so she wouldn't go the full twenty-four hours without food. Larken thought it was weird that she wasn't as thirsty as she thought she should be. She wasn't completely aware of what exactly was in Ezra's concoction, but was glad for it because she didn't think she could stomach food at the moment.

Brown tufts of hair poked out from the two hair ties and danced over Larken's collar bones. She kept wanting to flick them away, thinking they were some weird hairy spider-thing and not her hair. The brown was a common Military color, and she hoped that she would look like all the other security guards that walked the halls of the Manse. Hair dye was all she could do since the idea of colored contacts freaked her out.

Larken bobbed and weaved through bodies to get to Carl. He looked her over one last time, tugging on the black military-style belt that felt so small compared to the one Carl, Candy, and Ezra had gotten her for her birthday. The black button-up sat squished under her bulky bulletproof vest that sported the words *Manse Security* in white block letters across the back. Carl unbuttoned the shirt cuff at her left hand and rolled her sleeve up. She was more than capable of doing it herself, but she knew that Carl was still shaken after watching her pass out on the last mission, so she kept her mouth shut.

The silver cuff caught the light of the cab and the fat aquamarine danced and glimmered as her wrist moved. Delvon had gotten a matching cuff in black with a noir-stained piece of wood in place of a gem—Ewan too. Larken wasn't sure if theirs had any fun tricks hers didn't, but they would at least have three chances to disrupt any minor frequencies. Larken didn't have to ask if the earpieces everyone was given would work when she turned the cuff on; Delvon would have already thought of that.

He could be smart when he wanted to be.

Larken ran a fingertip over the naked part of her right ring finger. Manse security were only permitted to wear wedding bands so she had to leave the ring Brecker got for her birthday back in her bungalow. She hadn't taken it off since receiving it and regretted not getting a few more punches in when she fought Dominic. Larken's heart stopped as Carl pronounced her ready to infiltrate—hopefully Dominic wouldn't be waiting for them.

Delvon started briefing everyone on the plan again. The weight of the earpiece the bodyguard slipped in her ear moments before sat heavy, and reminded Larken so much of the past year. Memories of gunning, Squad training, and everything else she'd donned an earpiece for.

It was so easy to ignore what was going to happen and just pretend that they were going to Field E. Larken closed her eyes and focused on that strip of ocean. Her hand drifted up to the pearl around her neck—forgetting the necklace wasn't currently there. She realized the reason she didn't move her hand wasn't because she needed Soren's comfort, but because Larken wouldn't be satisfied with only going to the ocean twice. There was still so much she wanted to do—wanted to experience.

They *needed* to make it.

"How was the flight, runt?" a voice crackled in her ear.

Larken's heart swelled as she lifted a finger to tap her ear piece. "Vallen?"

She rested her finger against her earlobe and listened as he promised, "I'll be right here with you the whole time."

There was the shuffling of a microphone and then Fisher chimed in. "Break a leg, Songbird. It's your time in the spotlight. Go ahead and shine your brightest."

Hot tears pricked Larken's eyes, and she glanced over everyone quickly. No one seemed to be able to hear what they were saying to her. Delvon watched her with his grey eyes and gave her a small nod. No surprise he was in on the secret conversation. Her whole family would be with her today. Pride surged through her as well as a confidence that only came after she completed one of Vallen's more difficult workouts.

*"You don't let anyone tell you who you are. You go out there with your head high and show them that you aren't someone who can be hidden away. You go out there and prove that you were born for this."*

Vallen's words filled her. He was right—this is what he'd been training her for all these years. He was the leader of the Faithfuls and had singlehandedly chosen her to follow in his footsteps. Out of all the people he knew, *she* was the one he wanted.

*She* was worth it.

"You okay?"

Larken dropped her hand and turned to find Soren standing behind her. Concern furrowed his brows and glinted a deep green in his perfect eyes. She grinned, forcing her confidence onto the grumbly Captain. "I'm perfect."

"Any questions?" Delvon grunted.

No one moved.

"Right. Let's go."

And with those three words, Soren pulled up his mask. The nylon material covered his nose and mouth while still managing to show off the majority of his freshly shaven cheeks. Delvon and Ewan followed suit as the Harpy's door opened and a set of familiar black steps reached out to the ground. Larken lifted her own mask and instantly understood how it was able to stay up. The nylon morphed to cover her mouth and nose, just like the earpiece fit in her ear. The apples of her cheeks were on full display as the material suctioned to her skin.

One by one, her team filed out of the cab, ready to greet tomorrow. They could only pray that when tomorrow came, the sun would be shining more brightly than yesterday.

# CHAPTER 33

B lack pixels surrounded her as Larken made her way down the steps. The lights were still out aside from the occasional floor lamp. It was like standing in an empty pool filled with abandoned aircraft. Using what they knew from the Military Manor, Delvon and Hinlee hopefully rigged the Harpy so it wouldn't set off any sensors inside the hangar. The cameras should also pick up the holographic image instead of the Harpy. And even though the lights were out, Larken still kept her fingers crossed that they weren't being watched. The hologram was all that could be seen, they would still be stepping out of the side of the fake Manse aircraft instead of an actual door.

Without making a sound, everyone moved to flank Larken. Loxly and the second pilot whose name Larken never caught stayed on the Harpy with Carl and Candy. Candy had given her a quick squeeze before she headed out into the hangar, promising to have more self-control than Carl if Larken were to puke everywhere again. The words still danced in Larken's head, and she grimaced as Ewan and Delvon stepped into the spots to her left and right.

Instead of walking behind her like he normally did, Soren took up the spot in front of her. Levi was the one who brought up the rear. No one said anything, but they'd all made the same unspoken agreement: Levi would be protected at all costs. Larken tried to pretend it was because he'd been shot last time and not because her friends cared more about needing an uninjured medic in case something happened to her.

Jodi had offered to come—volunteering Ezra as well—but Delvon had pointed out that there wouldn't be a need for her. Levi would be fine and either Carl or Candy could call them like last time if something happened. More bodies weren't needed; it would only draw attention. Besides, Delvon claimed that this time they'd have a secret weapon and wouldn't even need medical attention. Larken knew he was full of it, but with the new wave of stress washing over her as Soren took his first step, she couldn't get her mouth to open and insult the bodyguard.

No one seemed to be making any noise except for her. They all stared ahead, stone-faced, gripping their tech guns. Her hands grew slick around her weapon as the tips of her boots scuffed the cement floor of the hangar with each step she took—almost as if the ground was pleading with her not to go. Larken's stomach roiled worse than it had after she'd been shot with the tranquilizer. She wanted so badly to give in to her fear and stay put. She couldn't understand why it was always her, or how she'd been so confident only fifteen minutes ago and now felt no braver than a spooked hare.

Hot and cold flashed across the back of her neck as nausea and anxiety warred over her stomach. Larken's breathing picked up and turned ragged while the tech gun dug into her palms painfully. It was too much—all of this was *too much*. Her confusing emotions, the way her stomach sloshed as if she were on a dingy trapped in a storm, the flashes of heat and the sudden chills, and—

"Sing in your head, Songbird," Fisher ordered calmly. "Sing the words and hold the notes."

Larken stared, not realizing she'd stopped moving and everyone was now watching her. Embarrassment flushed her face, and she took a step back. Levi grabbed her right shoulder and kept her in place. The wrongness of it being Levi behind her instead of Soren only added to the jumbled mess inside her.

A guitar chord cut through the madness, sounding in her earpiece. Larken stilled—too afraid to move and break the sound. It was her only lifeline, and she prayed that the fading note wouldn't abandon her in her time of need. A second chord joined the echo of the first, and then a third. Larken would know the musical fingerprints anywhere and she had no idea how she would ever thank Shadric for stepping up and helping. The melody to *Nuovo Amore* filled her and she gasped a silent breath after the first stance she mentally sang.

As if he couldn't help himself, Shadric started singing. A voice deepened by age joined his and harmonized Jon the stable boy's part. Larken wanted nothing more than to be wherever they were so she could sing with them. Estelle's part filled her and Larken kept a tight hold on her tongue so she wouldn't sing and give their position away. Eventually, the song ended, and her breathing evened out. Her panic attack was finished, and she was once again filled with strength. And even though her hands still shook slightly, Larken stepped out of Levi's reach and nodded at Soren.

She was ready.

As Soren turned around, Larken sent up one last prayer and followed. Hinlee walked to Soren's left and Brecker to his right. Ewan and Delvon fell exactly one step behind Larken, giving the couple the chance to do the same with Soren. Larken was then in the middle of a tight, well-armed circle. She couldn't help but wish that Loxly was coming with them. She could really use a hand to hold as Soren reached out for the metallic doorknob. One twist and then their lives would never be the same again.

Larken didn't know if the same weight was crushing Soren and he was just better at hiding it, or if he really wasn't bothered by what was happening around them. Either way, he wasted no time pushing the door in and stepping into the Manse. He held it open for all of them, and Larken caught a quick wink as she passed him. She could see it in his eyes—the mission in Stars had followed him into the bright hallway.

Larken returned his wink.

If he could fake confidence for her, then she could fake it for him, too.

Even though there were no windows, Larken could sense the darkness outside. Humidity had somehow found its way in and clung to every floor runner and wall hanging that pinned the hall, reminding her of the storm brewing outside. It took Larken a moment to realize the pink flowers on the wall weren't holograms, but wallpaper. Looking around, everything that didn't have to be updated wasn't. Larken thought it was rather charming. It made the prison a little more homey.

Ewan nodded to Soren and broke away from the group. Hinlee and Brecker turned to the left and followed him, leaving only Delvon and Levi standing with them. Larken reached for her left wrist, but Delvon's hand shot out and caught her before her finger could brush the aquamarine.

*Not yet*, Larken reminded herself.

Soren headed the opposite way from Ewan, and Delvon let go of her before walking off. The two men didn't wait for her, but she knew they wouldn't let her fall behind, either. They were playing to the cameras that followed their progress. As far as the security team knew, they were just a group that got in and split to get to their morning posts. At least, that's what Larken hoped.

From what she could remember of the map, Ewan, Brecker, and Hinlee would be walking past the guest rooms and the sitting area. Since they were on the first floor, that whole side of the building *should* be empty aside from the occasional security guard. This meant that Larken's group would be going past the library and the office area. Larken didn't know how crowded the library might be, but if the offices on the second story belonged to the staff, and the offices on the third to security, then that meant that there was a good chance that the people who ran everything media related, from the Manse lawn to the Magnate himself, worked in there.

Larken tried to ignore the security cameras and how her friends were doing. Instead, she focused on the wallpaper. The thick strip that held the flowers was about as tall as her forearm. A white-pink-yellow sort of watercolor shade filled the rest of the wall in blotches. Pictures of waterfalls, mountains, and fields occasionally dotted the wall. There was a very noticeable lack of end tables and statues—leaving them with no chance of cover if they were to get caught. The halls were completely bare of anything, and the only adornments were the pictures.

Rounding the corner, Larken spotted a set of beautiful double-wide glass doors. On the other side of them sat shelves and shelves of paper books. She almost gasped and stumbled into Levi as she unintentionally gravitated toward the library. Levi nudged her forward, silently reminding her to act like she'd seen this place before. Larken shook herself and forced her head to get on straight. She needed to stop acting like an impressed tourist and more like a bored security guard.

Down the hall past empty offices and a left turn later, their group just caught sight of Ewan. He gave the security guard to the right of the stairs a nod before starting up them. Larken had been a bit nervous about sticking out with a mask, but the woman standing to the left of the stairs wore one as well. Both of them held the same tech guns that their group carried, though the man's grip wasn't as tight on his as the woman's was. Hinlee climbed the stairs behind Brecker and the man Ewan nodded to let his gaze follow her. It was a good thing Brecker had gone up first. He wouldn't have blown their cover, but he most certainly would have had a lot to say about it on the way back to Camp.

Soren took his first step into the entryway. Larken kept close behind him, hiding from the security camera trained right on their little group like a giant, emotionless eye. Larken ducked deeper into Soren's back trying to go unnoticed. It didn't matter where she stood or what she did, the camera only seemed to follow her as they moved across the entryway over to the stairs. Panicking, Larken scratched at her nose in what was hopefully not an obvious excuse to check her mask. The nylon was still there, and so were the brown braids that hung at her collarbone.

"Guy working the desk must think you're cute," Delvon teased in a whisper.

"Must be," Larken agreed as she took one last opportunity to take in the entryway.

The floor tiles and the decorative pillars were the same yellow-gold color a lot of old paintings used for sand. The color was so rich and sunny that Larken wanted to sprawl in its hue like a fat cat. The lack of front windows was unnerving, but as Larken took a closer look, she noticed glass sheets covering walls in random spots. One of them flickered to life out of the corner of Larken's eye and showed a sprawling meadow. There were so many interesting things about this place that Larken could have spent hours exploring.

Soren took the first stair, pulling her back to the present. She followed him up and let Delvon and Levi fall into step behind her. Her eyes glanced over the woman before darting to the man on the right. Larken caught him mid-perusal and he gave her a cheeky wink when he met her gaze.

A flush the likes of which hadn't been brought out since the first time Dominic flirted with her rose up Larken's neck and face. She quickly looked away and then ran into Soren. A proud chuckle followed her up the steps and both Delvon and Levi crowded closer.

Delvon yanked on one of her braids and rasped, "Can you not?"

"What do you want me to do?" Larken hissed back.

"Tell Carl to stop doing you up and make you ugly."

"You should have seen the dress he wanted to send her to the opera in," Levi added unhelpfully. "Loxly said it was beyond scandalous."

"Trust me—I've already seen her do *femme fatal*. She doesn't need to do it again."

"Will you two shut up?" Larken whisper-shouted, making Soren huff out a small laugh.

The whole interaction distracted Larken long enough that a small jolt of shock went through her the moment they all spilled out onto the second-story entryway. The same soft yellow-gold followed them up into the room past the pale marble steps. A hush washed over them as they joined Ewan, Brecker, and Hinlee. Subtle birdsong and a distant creek sounded from unseen speakers hiding behind the thick plant life.

"What in the skies?" Hinlee muttered.

Larken couldn't help but agree. It was like nothing she'd ever seen before. Long planters held giant, spiraling dragon trees with thick tufts of snake plants trying to reach up to their limbs. Some of the trees hit the ceiling while others were short enough that planters of green and gold devil's ivy could hang above them. Instead of the hot humidity Larken had come to expect with greenhouses, this room was dry and cool. Again, she found herself wanting to stay and look at everything. There was no way these plants could be real, right? They were in a room with no sunlight, and they were all *thriving*. They had to be fake.

Delvon must have noticed the amount of time spent gawking because he cleared his throat and took up his post by the door behind them. Levi followed suit and moved to the other side. Larken's heart rate picked up again and a bead of sweat formed at her temple as she flicked her gaze up to the camera. It was trained on her just like the one on the floor below. She turned her attention to Ewan who gave her an understanding tilt of the head.

Using the camera's current angle to his advantage, Ewan passed his gun to Brecker and bent to tie his boot. His fingers never reached the laces. Instead he traced a circle over his cuff. Larken looked away, not wanting the camera to follow her attention, and peered at Soren instead. He was still pretending—still trying to push away the memories that danced behind his eyes. Larken reached out with her free hand and grazed the inside of his wrist. He jumped slightly, hand gripping his tech gun tighter. Her eyes crinkled at the corners as she offered him a kind smile, this time giving him the same silent promise he'd given to her all those times.

*I'm right here, and I won't let go.*

Ewan's words stole them away from their moment as he whispered, "We're good."

Larken lifted her gaze to the camera once more to find it twisting and turning as it spun around, trying to catch any bit of visibility. At least the cuffs worked—they could all be grateful for that small mercy. However, now all the Manse security knew that something was up.

Delvon didn't bother with the boot-tying pretense as he traced a clockwise circle over the smooth wood in his cuff. Larken did the same to her aquamarine as the others reached up and double-tapped their earpieces.

Larken had just lifted her finger from the stone when Delvon said, "Ewan, you head out first. Deckard, you're two minutes after that. Any longer and they might get here before we start, and any less, they won't have time to think that it's just a single wire."

Soren nodded, taking an ever so small step closer to Larken.

Hinlee and Brecker both offered the group a small smile before they set off after the younger Tanner brother. And just like that, they were separating again. Only, this time, Larken and Soren would be leaving Delvon and Levi behind, too.

Sweat slicked the back of Larken's neck as she waited for the two minutes to pass. They were even longer than Vallen's workout minutes. The seconds were hour-long heartbeats that pounded loudly in Larken's head. Then suddenly, it was time. She took one staggered step and then another. In her mind, she knew what she needed to do, but it would seem her body wasn't quite ready to follow instructions yet. Soren waited as patiently as he knew how, which still wasn't very patient. The muscle in his cheek twitched whenever he looked at her, telling her that he was gritting his jaw.

Something dark flashed across his eyes before Larken could close the distance. He did it for her, taking two large steps and pulling his left hand from his gun. Soren wasted no time grabbing Larken's right hand from her gun and tangling his fingers with hers. She almost gasped and demanded an explanation, but then remembered the Manse security couldn't see anything.

Soren yanked her to his side and brought his face down close to hers. She watched as his eyes shifted from their hard gold hue to the green one she'd always preferred. "This time I'm not letting go."

Hot tears pricked Larken's eyes, and she nodded. He seemed so confident in his words, and on the surface, Larken chose to believe him. He was always there when it really counted. It was the after part—when everything was over and calm—that kept her from fully trusting him, though. Even still, she could have melted right then and there at his words. It was only knowing that Delvon and Levi were there that kept her together.

Soren didn't ask if she was ready before jumping in; he just took the right turn in the hall and led them out past the plants. Larken tried to focus on his callused hand in hers and not where Ewan, Brecker, and Hinlee were. Had they reached the library yet? Or were they taking their time and hadn't even reached the offices? Soren's long strides were a bit quicker than they usually were, and Larken needed to jog slightly to keep up.

When they rounded the corner Larken tried to pull her hand away, but Soren kept a firm hold on it until the last possible second. Laughter and the scent of generic microwaved food escaped past the shut door leading to the second-level sitting room. Larken flexed her hands around her tech gun. Breaks at the Military Manor were staggered so there was always someone working. Her mother ordered the staff out of sight whenever possible so that it seemed like the building cared for itself, but was that the case here? Would the two of them run into a steady stream of Manse servants leaving the guest quarters once they rounded the next corner? Or was it possible that they were all currently shut away in the sitting room, enjoying their breakfast?

*Maxim,* Larken pleaded silently, *help my nerves. I'm going to make a mistake if I don't calm down.*

A loud crash exploded from behind the door they were now passing. Larken nearly screamed as she jumped and dropped her tech gun. Everything went quiet and then there were roars of laughter as muffled voices heckled someone about dropping the glass pitchers of juice they were carrying. Larken grabbed her heart and let out the scream in a long, slow breath through parted lips. Soren bent and retrieved her gun for her.

He offered her a small smile. "Alright?"

"I will be."

"Everything okay on your end?" Ewan asked, the concern thickening his brogue.

Soren brought his hand up and pressed his earpiece before answering, "Some of the staff are a little too excited about their breakfast."

Larken accepted her tech gun with shaking hands. Soren spared a few seconds to rub a hand up and down her back while they waited on a response. Ewan didn't say anything more, so Soren ushered them on. They rounded the corner, and the door to the guest rooms sat open down the hall. No one seemed to be coming from it, so they didn't slow. Soren only took a moment to peek around the corner before giving the nod of *all clear*.

It would seem that everyone was indeed enjoying their breakfast together before starting their workday. Maybe the team would get lucky and it would be the same for the next floor. Maxim knew that having all the security hidden away and eating would be a big help for them.

Soren and Larken hurried along the hall, and Larken took a second to peek into the guest quarters. A long hallway sat on the other side with multiple doors, as if it were a hotel. The same glass meadowscapes sat in between various doors, giving a false sense of life to the windowless building. After spending so much time outside with Vallen growing up, and then at Camp, Larken wasn't sure if she could ever live in a place like this. She picked up her pace to catch Soren.

When they got to the Magnate, she would have to ask him how he did it and if having a three-story library filled to the brim with paper books was a fair trade.

# CHAPTER 34

S oren and Larken hit the library doors just as the trio did. Ewan offered Soren a nod that was much more respectful than any his brother would have given, and Hinlee grinned at Larken.

"We just finished our second lap," she said. "Levi and Delvon headed out after we got back to the entryway."

"They should get here after we get back," Brecker agreed. "You should head on in. No sense in waiting for us in the hall."

Soren felt Larken stiffen in excitement next to him. He'd known from the first moment they realized what exactly was in the library that if anything was to mess up their plan, the temptation of paper books would be it. Larken wasn't able to hide her longing as much as she thought.

"See you soon then," Soren grunted before pulling one of the double doors open for Larken.

Her eyes were already on the books as she walked past him, and her shoulder brushed against his chest. He wondered if she even noticed. Did she realize that even that small bit of contact was enough to practically seize up his heart? No, not even a little bit. Her teal eyes were wider than he'd ever seen as she looked over the shelves. What must it be like for her, seeing all of this? Soren knew she'd turned to books in her times of sorrow and stress, so what was she thinking with these forgotten pieces of history in front of her?

Without pulling her gaze from the first shelf, she set down her gun and peered closer at the spines. She walked like that for a ways down the aisle. Soren didn't think even getting attacked would pull her focus. Then, when she got halfway, she paused. Larken was so small standing between the two giant shelves that stretched up around her. Her lips parted ever so slightly, and she reached a tentative hand out to one of the books. But right before her finger grazed the spine, she balled her hand into a fist and wrapped her arms around her middle.

The room around them was older than anything Soren had ever seen. The red and brown hues played off each other like warm apple and cinnamon. Shelves stood taller than him by a good three feet and were filled to the brim with priceless paper volumes. All of it was amazing and something he likely would never see again...and yet Larken was the only thing that held his attention.

Gently, Soren set his gun down next to hers and joined her. At first, he didn't notice the change in her, but as he got closer, he could see that her awe had shifted to sadness in the last few seconds. Unable to help himself, Soren placed a gentle hand on her shoulder.

Without prompting she said, "My dad used to read me that book before..."

Soren didn't look up to where she indicated. He only watched the complicated wheels turn in her mind as she tried to find the right words.

Eventually, Larken faced him and met his eyes with her deep teal ones. "What if we can't do it? What if we fail and everything we had before—all the people we loved before—they just—"

"Hey," Soren murmured. "Hey now, don't think like that."

"How can I not?" she rasped, tears welling in her eyes. "This whole thing has been a mistake, Soren. I'm not the right person."

Soren strongly disagreed with her, but he kept that to himself. If they were going to be able to move on and finish the mission, she needed to get her fears out *before* the security team realized the dead zones were moving up to the third floor and toward the elevator.

"I mean, look at me. I'm a mess. I can't make up my mind about how I feel, and I keep bouncing between one extreme to the next. I feel frivolous and stupid."

Soren did what she asked and looked at her—*really* looked at her. Her brown braids didn't fit her pale skin, nor did the stress that furrowed her brows.

"It's just your anxiety. I keep bouncing around, too."

"Not like this," she argued. "Not like I am. I keep thinking that nothing can stop us and then the next second I'm afraid that Dominic might be waiting for me around every corner. Even now I'm scared that my mother somehow has this place bugged and is listening to this conversation."

Her breathing was picking up again like it had in the hanger. Soren had to do something. He hated that panic attacks had somehow found a way into her life, and he couldn't help but feel he was partially to blame.

"I'm going to mess up. I'm going to mess up and get you all killed. I'm going to get *you* killed, Soren."

Soren tugged his mask down first and then hers. He cupped her face and forced her to meet his gaze. "Breathe."

"What?"

"Breathe, Larken. You're okay. I know it feels like you're in another crash, but look at where we are."

"I can't look," she whispered. "Soren, I can't see a way out. They picked the wrong person and I'm going to let everyone down like I always do."

A tear escaped past her lashes and Soren used a thumb to wipe it away.

"Shadric said that I held the key to a better tomorrow, but I can't even see past the next five minutes."

"Would it help if I said I couldn't see that far either?" Soren offered a small smile, feeling braver in this moment with her than he had since getting off the Harpy.

"No." She huffed a sad laugh. "How am I supposed to lean on you if you don't know what you're doing either?"

She had no idea how right she was. He wasn't supposed to be doing this. He'd promised himself to only be her friend and give her the absolute best chance at success that he could. Friends didn't act like this with each other. Friends didn't ignore dangerous situations to remind them how much of a friend they could be. And friends definitely didn't stare at each other the way Soren was staring at her now.

Suddenly, it all hit him. Memories of their time together twisted into a dart and stabbed him in his heart. The beautiful poison spread through his body, tightening his every muscle.

It was Larken.

It was always only ever going to be *Larken.*

He was there, holding her in her room even though he didn't know what to say as she asked why her mother hated her. They were back on the couch as she shared her deepest secret with him of how she injured her shoulder. She was in that black dress, a single tear sliding down her cheek as she translated the words of that stupid opera. On the bench in the garden she clung to him like he was her only lifeline. The same happened in the crash and on the hoverbike as he rescued her from her wedding. Everything brought them to this very moment, and the force of it was so dizzying that Soren almost dropped to his knees.

There was never going to be any other life for Soren outside of Larken. She had wrapped herself around him so completely that if something were to happen to her, his heart would be worse than the shriveled black thing she had breathed life into. If he had to go back to the way life was before this woman crash-landed into it—

Doubt clouded her eyes and she bit her lip. "I just don't understand, Soren."

"What?"

"Every time we're about to crash, you promise you'll never let me go and that you'll be there to protect me. Then, when we don't crash, you pull away like I'm diseased or something."

She swallowed thickly and Soren followed her throat's slow bob with his eyes, unable to tear his gaze away.

Larken was quiet for so long that Soren started to think that maybe she meant for him to say something. But then she admitted, "Out of everything—my mother, Dominic, and failing... the thing I'm most afraid of—the thing I've *always* been most afraid of—is that when I eventually do crash, you won't be there."

Soren's heart was wrenched from his chest. No, she couldn't be afraid of that. How could he have let this happen? How could she be afraid of the one thing he knew to be true of himself?

Bile rose to the back of his throat. He needed to say something— to apologize. It was all so stupid now. Why didn't he just say something before? Maxim knew he had plenty of opportunities. Every time they were forced together, each fight his feet didn't want to walk away from, all of the moments he assured her that she mattered and said nothing more.

Larken was his everything—there was no denying it any longer. He would do whatever it took to keep her safe.

He would do whatever it took for her to know that she was loved.

His tongue went fat and his throat closed like it had when she told him to ask her to stay back in the dorm room. He wasn't ready to admit his heart then, just like he wasn't quite ready now. But Maxim take him if he let her think for one more second that he wouldn't crawl on bleeding hands and knees across broken glass to get to her.

"I will *always* be there for you, Larken. I promise you."

Another tear slipped down her cheek. "How can you be sure?"

He was done waiting.

Soren brushed the tear away just as he had before, slipped his hand to the nape of her neck, and brought his lips to hers. Larken gasped around his mouth, and he used the opportunity to deepen the kiss. It'd been a long time coming and he told her everything he hadn't been able to with his mouth against hers. She was timid at first, but once he slipped his tongue past her lips, she became bolder and demanded more from the kiss. Soren was only too willing to give it.

They could have been there like that for seconds or for hours, he didn't know. Soren only knew that when they eventually broke apart, he wouldn't be able to keep the promise he made himself. When it came to Larken, he was now going to be selfish and do whatever he could to keep her. He didn't care if that meant stealing her away from all of this or wearing a tie every day as he faced the world as a bumbling Luminar—he was done letting her go.

Larken shook as she panted slightly. Soren wrapped his arms around her and rested his chin atop her head. There were so many things he wanted to say to her, but now it really was the time for silence. Larken needed to process the offer he'd just given her. She needed to remember that he was still an option, even if he'd been behaving like a poor one.

Larken eventually lifted her head off his chest and met his gaze. Her cheeks were still flushed, but a shy smile played at her lips. She opened her mouth to speak and then the library doors opened.

*Thank the skies Loxly is stuck on that stupid aircraft.*

Larken must have had the same thought because her shy smile turned into a grin.

"Pull up your mask before Hinlee sees you," Soren teased.

Larken's flush deepened a bit more, but she did as she was told.

Soren lifted his as well and fetched their guns. Ewan let the glass doors fall closed just as Soren passed Larken's tech gun to her. He'd never let her know, but he was still on edge after their moment together. It wasn't enough—and there was no way he was going to let anything happen to them when he knew what was waiting for him on the other side.

"Ready, Peach?" Delvon asked as he looked her up and down. The man narrowed his eyes, clearly knowing something was off with his friend, but thankfully not saying anything.

Those two words seemed to bring Larken back to herself. She stiffened again, her spine going straighter than Soren thought was possible. He reached out and placed a gentle hand on her back. He already knew what she was thinking—she'd just told him. And she wasn't wrong to have those fears. Everything would change once they went up those stairs.

They would split just like they'd planned. Soren and Levi would get Larken to the elevator by way of the offices while everyone else ran around the other way to distract the security team. Then, hopefully enough of the security would be taken out and they would all be able to take the elevator down to the Magnate.

Together, they took a collective breath. A copper staircase stood ready before them. Spiraling up to the third floor, there was enough room for maybe two small people to walk side by side. Soren's eyes drifted to Larken again, unable to stay off her for long. She glared at the stairs and then eventually nodded. It seemed to be the que Brecker was waiting for and he stepped forward. The Scout was the first up the stairs and was followed by the rest of them. Soren took up his usual spot behind Larken and had to duck more than once so he wasn't hit by a copper rail. Their boots all screamed a too loud cacophony as they tried to move as quietly as possible.

They all spilled out onto the third floor, their footsteps still echoing behind him. Together they made their way through the shelves toward the glass doors. Soren sent up a prayer that they would all make it out alive and stepped closer to Larken. She jumped as a monstrous rumble of thunder shook the room around them. Lighter books shuddered on the shelves while the glass screens on the walls rattled. The one closest to them sparked in and out of focus, the image bouncing between that meadow and a not-so-fun circus theme.

It would seem that the storm had finally caught them.

As if to answer his thought, rain pelted the side of the Manse with a ferocity that Soren couldn't help but admire. With the raindrops determined to bore holes into the Manse, they reached the glass double doors and spilled into the hall. Again, Delvon was the last one out. His face was set in a deep frown, and he only waited long enough to give Larken a brief nod before heading off with Ewan, Brecker, and Hinlee. Soren fell into step at Larken's right, leaving Levi to bring up the rear. The field-medic's brow furrowed, and he clutched at his tech gun tightly with both hands. He would never admit it, but Soren knew his Second felt responsible for what happened with Larken and the tranquilizer.

Soren wished they would have had time for goodbyes, but they were fighting the clock. The security team would know where they were going now—there was only one place left for them *to* go.

Either they would succeed and change the world, or they would all die trying.

# CHAPTER 35

No sooner did Soren have the thought than the alarms started going off. His stomach soured and plummeted to his feet the same way it did whenever Loxly took off too fast. The blaring shook the halls and warred with the storm raging outside. To make things worse, the lights flickered on and off. Soren knew it wasn't a power shortage but a clever tactic to disorientate would-be assassins. It worked, too. As the three of them picked up their speed, Larken ran fully into him.

Soren grabbed her hand tightly—not willing to let this be the last time he touched her. Larken's palm suddenly slipped out of his as she cried out. Total darkness filled the hall as Soren reeled to face her. The lights came back on to reveal her sprawled on the ground over a bit of bunched up runner and her tech gun a good hundred feet or so ahead of them.

Larken stared at him with round, terror-filled eyes as Levi rushed for the gun. Soren brought his hand up to tap his earpiece to tell the others—what, he didn't know. The words died on his lips as a group of twelve or so guards appeared behind Larken.

His stomach churned with the fear of combat he always got on the frontlines, and his eyes dropped to Larken in time to see her mouth the word *Soren* before the lights went out again. Shots rang out, challenging the boom of the thunder. Something hot and fast nicked Soren's cheekbone and he dropped to his stomach. His harsh breaths were caught by the runner he and Larken now shared, and each inhale reeked of dust and age. Soren didn't have time to wonder how often the runners were cleaned or how old they were. He could only grope for Larken's hand in the dark and pray that Levi hadn't been shot again.

On cue, a woman cried out and Soren half-crawled, half-sprang forward. He crushed Larken between him and the floor, not caring if he accidentally kicked her in the face. His own chin hit the heel of her boots painfully. There was another cry—this time a man's—and Soren tensed. The lights had only been out a few seconds and yet it felt like he'd been in the dark for hours.

The gunshots slowed and the lights blared to life. Soren fought a wince and caught sight of a masked woman clutching her knee. A man with curly brown hair cropped close at the sides bent over her. Another man had two women working on him as he bled freely from his clavicle. The security group shouted over each other, and Levi let off two more shots from behind them now that he could see again. A man dropped his tech gun as Levi's bullet went through his left wrist and into the bicep of the woman behind him, and another woman went down as she clutched at her side.

It was like a sick sort of déjà vu. That first day when Larken's aircraft went down, Soren had been sitting around, mentally complaining about how much trouble she was going to be. And instead of crowding around the television with the rest of them to get a look at the *Military Sweetheart*, Levi played darts by himself—hitting all the vulnerable spots on a silhouette he'd stolen from the range.

Soren hated irony and didn't waste any more time with it as he scrambled to his feet and yanked Larken up by the back of her bulletproof vest. He used too much force because she stumbled when her feet hit the floor, but Soren paid her no mind as he aimed his own tech gun. He let Levi take the ones still firing and took the others for himself. It was high stakes gunning and Soren was in the lead. Each shot that found its mark sent out an arc of orange static, rendering the whole muscle numb and useless for the next few hours. Thighs and hips were on the top of Soren's list, ensuring that whoever went down stayed down.

The lights went out again and Soren stilled his hands. Each stretch only lasted about a minute but with the adrenaline pumping through his veins, he would have believed it if the gaps lasted years. Another shot sounded and the bullet whizzed from behind, over Soren's shoulder and past his ear. He didn't know if it was Larken or Levi, but whoever it was, they missed. A retaliation was fired and clipped Soren's left shoulder. Air stung the fresh wound, but that was the worst of it. And unless the outside of the bullet was laced with poison, he'd be fine.

Then, nearly as soon as the lights went out, they came back in full force. Well, Soren assumed it was in full force—black smoke billowed around the hall and engulfed the security members. Its dark tendrils crept out to them, and Soren turned. He ran, grabbing Larken's hand again as he did, and let Levi play lookout.

Darkness hit again and Soren stopped. Larken yanked out of his grasp and fired off three more shots. He used the opportunity to reach up and press his earpiece. "We've been found."

"So have we," Hinlee shouted in his ear over heavy gunfire. "A whole group of them and Ewan lost his—" Hinlee screamed and the line went dead.

"We need to get out of here!" Levi barked.

Soren didn't need to be told twice. He found Larken's hand once more and was off the moment the lights came back. The constant change was giving him a headache, and Larken stumbled again. Soren looked over his shoulder to make sure she was okay with the pace he'd set, only to find tears slipping down her cheeks.

"We need to get out of this smoke," he ordered.

"How?" Levi asked like it was the stupidest thing he'd ever said.

Soren only growled, his heart beating to the point of combustion.

They rounded the corner past the offices when the glass wall separating the cubicles from the hallway exploded. Shards shattered into millions of tiny pieces and crashed onto the floor. Larken skidded as she stepped on a pile of it and her feet went flying out from under her. Levi moved quick enough that the back of her head landed on his boot instead of the glass covered floor.

Splinters still ended up in her hair, dancing in the light like crystalized snow. The lights went out just as Soren knelt. He missed the spot he'd planned to place his knee and hissed as thousands of cuts tore into his skin. Soren once again found himself groping in the dark for Larken.

Shouting filled the area between the gaps of the blaring alarm and bouts of thunder. Soren's fingers brushed either a shin or a thigh right before he was ripped away. Two bodies crowded around him and yanked him to his feet. The one to his left kneed him in the back of his thigh and jabbed him in the tender spot between his shoulder and neck. Numbness spread down his arm and caused him to drop his gun.

The lights came back to reveal two men with block, goggle-looking glasses holding him. They could clearly see in the dark and had the advantage. Levi fought with another security guy, his tech gun missing completely, while four more stood over Larken. All their guns were aimed directly at her heart, and her chest heaved as blood ticked rapidly through the vein in her throat.

Soren had failed her…

It was over and he'd failed them all.

"Please," Larken pleaded behind her mask, "you don't understand."

"We understand perfectly, *Cadet Hale*," a familiar voice mocked.

Soren squinted, blocking out everything the best he could, and used the time he had to take in as much of the men he was able. Darkness swallowed them just as his stomach twisted. Soren knew exactly who these men were.

Only a miracle would save them now.

His mind raced as he prayed for more darkness. These men were all about the show—they wouldn't dare do anything in the dark that Larken couldn't see. Plan after stupid plan flirted around in Soren's mind like a sugar-hyped hummingbird. His body was in overdrive, and he needed time to sit and think of something. Since time was exactly what he didn't have, his mind offered up what it could.

Lights blinded them once more and one of the men reached up to touch his headpiece. "Good news, sir. We've got her."

Larken sent a pleading look to Soren, begging him to do something. He did the only thing he could think of and growled, "I knew this would happen."

"What?" Larken asked in raspy disbelief.

"You were always more trouble than you were worth. I should have just let Squad 22 take you when I had the chance."

The man fighting Levi chuckled darkly as Larken's eyes widened ever so slightly in understanding. These weren't regular guards that had detained them—it was Braves's old squad.

Larken's lip trembled under her mask, and she let the stress tears she'd been keeping back for weeks fall. "Soren, how could you—"

"If you all want her so badly, just take her. I'm over all of this, to be honest."

"Soren!" Larken cried out, her voice reflecting her breaking heart. She tried to get up—to go to him, but the men all shifted around her.

Her tears overtook her as she stole the show. She lamely fought the men around her and managed to get to her feet. She stood there, nothing more than a weak, sniveling girl. She yelled and cried so much that her words weren't distinguishable, and reached her hand out past the guards that held her at bay. Even Levi's fight slowed so the two could watch the performance.

"Women," the man said rolling his eyes.

Levi answered him with an uppercut to the jaw.

"Soren—*please*. Please!"

He only shook his head, silently telling her not to move yet.

The seconds ticked by, and they could all tell that Squad 22 was getting bored with the show. Larken only needed to hold the spotlight a little longer, just until—

The darkness hit and Soren made his move. He brought his

hands up and jabbed his thumbs under the nose pieces of the glasses. Soren yanked them up over their heads and surged forward out of his captors' grasps. They grappled after him in the dark and Soren helped himself to a fresh set of eyes. Instead of the clear picture he expected to see, all Soren could make out were thermal images.

*I can work with that.*

Soren stuffed the second pair of glasses into his pocket and scooped up his gun. In quick succession, he smashed the butt of it in both his assailants' temples. They crumpled to the ground like the pitiful snakes they were. Soren aimed and shot Levi's sparring partner's knee—successfully downing him. Levi paused, not daring to move now that the blows subsided and he couldn't see.

Larken screamed and Soren rounded on the others. All four men had her surrounded—doing what to her, Soren didn't know. He fired off two more shots and was careful not to hit them anywhere that would do any permanent damage...even though everyone in Squad 22 deserved it. Each bullet found a spot in the middle of the soldier's backs and successfully numbed their trapezius and deltoid muscles. Guns fell to the runners, making that same muffled clatter sound that Soren's had, and he used the opportunity to hit them in their thighs.

Soren had just enough time to fumble with a replacement magazine before Levi's new friend used the wall to pull himself up. The magazine clicked into place and Soren aimed for the man's second knee. He pulled the trigger just as the lights blared back to life.

Crystal clear images greeted him once more and Soren's mind only took a second to adjust from the thermal imaging. Hopefully the transition would be just as smooth for the others once they got their glasses, as well.

A clap of thunder roared and shook the world. But as wild and unruly as the sound was, it couldn't cover the gut-wrenching cry that spilled from Larken. Soren reeled, gun already aimed. The two remaining men held Larken tightly and Xander Fig, Dominic's Second, flashed Soren a vile smirk as he pulled an emerald dagger from the right side of Larken's abdomen. Soren's eyes zeroed in on the spot and he was momentarily frozen. A too-large gash split open the front of her bulletproof vest, right where the contour of her stomach was.

Dampness started slow, then quickly spread. Soren lifted his eyes to hers, not able to believe what he was seeing. Larken's lips were parted as she stared at him in shock. Blood soaked though the black vest and sat about the size of Soren's extended hand. Her knees buckled slightly, and she was forced to lean more into Fig.

The man looked ready to purr.

Realization of what was happening kicked Soren into overdrive. He yelled and shot off two rounds, hitting him once in each shoulder while Levi ascended on the other man from behind. Fig only laughed as he stumbled off balance and fell. Soren shot him again, once in each leg.

Larken gasped, claiming Soren's attention. She stared at her left hand while the right still clutched at her middle. Larken teetered and Soren was there in an instant.

"He stabbed me," she said, dumbfounded.

She lifted her hand enough for Soren to get a quick look. He ignored the way the blood sent his stomach twisting and thanked Maxim that it wasn't too deep. Larken would need a heavy-duty dermis gun at the least and some stitches at the most.

"Yes—but you'll be okay. Levi's here." Soren said his name the moment Levi used the butt of a handgun to knock his guy out.

She wasn't paying Soren any attention and mumbled, "I've never been stabbed before."

Soren's eyes fell to the spot again. Blood seeped out between her fingers—not as bad as it could be but still bad enough that his stomach went sick. It was happening again. Larken was there, bleeding in front of him.

Why couldn't he ever manage to keep her safe?

"We gotta go!" Levi barked.

Larken nodded and Soren could see her jaw grit in pain through her mask. She tried to straighten, but she only got halfway before hissing and crouching back over. Soren gave Levi a single look and the field-medic rushed to his friend's side. He looped her right arm around his neck and bore the majority of the weight on her bad side. Larken still used her left hand to try and keep the blood in, but this was the best they could do for the moment.

The lights went out again just as Soren snatched the glasses off Fig. Soren only wasted enough time to steal all the others and place a pair on both Larken and Levi. It was slow going with Larken's injury and they didn't manage to get very far before the darkness dissipated. Soren had his tech gun up and at the ready. He scanned as they hurried across the runners. Levi helped Larken the best he could by giving her murmured encouragements Soren could just hear between the alarm and thunder.

They finally rounded the corner of the hall and Soren could make out the mat that sat in front of the elevator doors. That patch of green—the same color as the sprawling meadows—was their end point. All they needed to do was just get here without any more—

Gunshots sounded around them and sprayed the wall at the other end of the hall. The sheet of glass that hung there shattered and fell as Delvon barreled around the corner. His own tech gun was raised and aimed right for Soren only a moment before he realized who he was. The bodyguard sidestepped and turned, aiming behind him. Brecker rushed past Delvon into the hallway, Hinlee curled up into his chest as he carried her. Soren's stomach lurched and he almost fell to his knees.

*Maxim, please let her be alive.*

Ewan was the last to join them, dodging another round of fire and carrying Brecker's tech gun. Ewan's gun was nowhere to be seen and Soren was left to assume that's what Hinlee was saying he'd lost.

The lights went out and Soren jumped into action.

Soren slid up behind Delon and he called, "Oi, what're you doing?"

"Will you shut up and hold still?" Soren complained as he fought to get a pair of glasses on the bodyguard.

"What are these? Where did you get them?"

Soren only ignored the man as he moved on to Brecker. Soren used his opportune closeness to touch Hinlee's forehead. She moved into his palm and adrenaline-spiked relief shot through him. Ewan got his glasses last, and Soren ordered Brecker to the elevator.

"Levi and Larken will meet you there!" Soren called out over another rumble of thunder.

Brecker made a run for it, and then the assailants rounded the corner. Soren didn't know anything about these guards—or if they were even guards at all. He wouldn't have guessed that the Vigilants had impregnated the Manse without Vallen's knowledge, but it was something he would have to bring up to the Magnate. Clearly he wasn't safe here.

Ewan, Delvon, and Soren all took turns firing off rounds, and Brecker and Levi shouted at each other behind them.

"Oh, for skies sake! Just give me the stupid glasses, Brecker!"

"Hin—"

"Now!"

There was a moment of silence in the conversation before the lights came back and Hinlee spoke again.

"Good news is this thing isn't electrical. That would have ended things right here. I just need to rig it open and then—"

There was a rusty clang that echoed out over the alarm and Soren chanced a glance back. Brecker was helping Hinlee crawl into the elevator. He didn't entirely understand what was happening with the thing, but he was glad that the mechanic was figuring it out.

Another wave of bullets and darkness hit them, and this time Soren caught a well-placed shot to the side of his thigh. He felt it graze his skin, and he knew the wound was superficial enough that the bleeding would probably stop before they got back to the Harpy…if they made it back.

Something creaked behind them and Larken called out Soren's name. Collectively, the three men took a step back and then another.

"Ewan, get to the elevator and help Levi with Larken. She's hurt," Soren ordered.

Delvon, still bitter about being ignored when he asked about the glasses, demanded, "What's wrong with her?"

Soren ignored him again as Ewan ran past the both of them.

There was a bit of a scuffle behind them which ended with Larken saying, "Not until Delvon and Soren get here too."

The lights flared back to life as a roll of thunder shook the Manse. The alarm harmonized around it, and both Delvon and Soren gave the hallway before them one last look over. No one was there.

Together they turned, not wanting to stay and argue who'd go last. It was pointless when Larken was stubborn enough to make good on her promise. They would all need to be there, or she wouldn't move on to the next part of the mission. Too much bad had already happened; she wouldn't leave anyone behind when they were all so close.

As if the two couldn't help being petty, even in a moment like this, Delvon and Soren raced to the elevator. Delvon got there first and ushered his brother, who was still trying to reason with Larken, onto the elevator. It was small but appeared stable enough to hold the seven of them. Black wrought iron scrunched up at one side of the doorway, and Hinlee was already trying to pry it shut. It wheezed and protested, and she eventually had to give the job up to Delvon as she collapsed into Brecker, face pale.

Soren clapped Levi on the shoulder and gave him the okay to join the others. Levi didn't need to be told twice and moved. Larken let go of the field medic and reached her arms out, already asking for Soren's support. He wrapped an arm around her waist and noticed too late that someone was rounding the corner behind her. Soren tried to shield her—tried to do anything to keep her out of harm's way—but wasn't fast enough. In the blink of an eye, the lone security guard raised his tech gun and fired off a single shot.

Larken cried out loud enough to tell Soren that the bullet went through her vest, and she fell into him. He grabbed her and shoved his way into the elevator as if he was a bull. Delvon let the door fall shut and Hinlee fiddled with something for only a second before they started moving. The lights went out one last time as the elevator slipped down past the cement walls that covered their view of anything other than darkness.

"Brecker, stop. I'm fine," Hinlee muttered from the other side of the elevator.

Soren didn't know what was wrong, but it would seem Brecker had it covered.

Delvon shouldered his way over and got as close as he was able. "How bad is it, love?"

Larken only grunted and gripped Soren tighter. Soren felt around her as she gasped for air. Her face scrunched up as sweat broke out across her brow. The bulletproof vest would have slowed the bullet, so it couldn't be too deep—but that wouldn't make Larken any more comfortable. It was too crowded here; she needed space. Everything on her middle was wet, and he couldn't find where one wound started and the other ended. His only clues to where the bullet wound was were her whimpers of pain. Eventually, he found the injury on the left side of her back, diagonal from her stab wound. He was right, the bullet sat right past the vest, only deep enough to make Larken bleed. Once she was able to sit, the blood would slow—especially once Levi got his hands on her.

Relief flooded Soren. He had to fight not to hold her too tightly in her pain. Everything that had just happened hit him: the flight over, the kiss, the fighting—he could have lost her. He hated that this kept happening. Carefully, so as to not hurt her further, Soren pulled her in and pressed his lips to her temple.

"Stop scaring me," he ordered quietly.

"I'm banning guns," she muttered. "And bullets. Everyone will have to use sticks and rocks if they want to have another war."

"Sounds good to me," Soren agreed.

No sooner did the words come out of his mouth than the elevator began to slow. Soren's erratic heartbeat moved from his chest to his throat. He'd only ever seen pictures of the Magnate—

what would he make of them? Did he know they were there, or would he be surprised enough to call all his guards down to his rooms and have them executed?

Whatever the answer, they would find out soon. The elevator stopped and Ewan muscled the door on the opposite side open. All of them spilled out into a brightly lit room that housed no carpet or couches. Instead, soft, squishy grass covered the floor and comfortable-looking benches sat with vibrantly colored pillows. Each piece of furniture in this room was made of the same wood as the benches, and they all seemed to be carved by the same person. A large grey, brick planter sat in the middle of the room, reminiscent of a fireplace, but instead had white forget-me-nots spilling out over the sides.

And sitting there across the room waiting for them was the Magnate himself.

"Ah," he said, surprise coloring his features, "I wondered when it was going to be my turn, Miss Hale."

# CHAPTER 36

Magnate Edmar Wilmore held everyone's full attention despite the fact he seemed to be what no one had expected. Instead of rich finery, he was dressed in simple lounge pants with a well-worn housecoat. Larken noticed a hole near his collar above his breast pocket. Not only that, but he was barefoot.

Adrenaline slowly eased from her limbs and pain intensified across her abdomen. Blood trickled from her wounds and she sagged more into Soren as her knees wobbled.

"Please," he gestured to the benches around him, eyes still wide. "Fe-feel free to see to the wounded."

Delvon grunted, already annoyed. Larken rolled her eyes as a new wave of sweat broke out across her brow. She waited to see who would get to her first. Unsurprisingly, it was a three-way tie. Ewan produced a med-kit from who knew where and helped Brecker settle Hinlee on a bench, leaving Delvon, Levi, and Soren free to fawn over Larken like the mother hens that they were. They ushered her to the bench opposite Hinlee's and sat her down. Larken tried not to get too annoyed—or embarrassed. She wasn't making a great first impression.

"Let me put on some tea," Edmar murmured distractedly as he stood and set his book down.

Larken followed the motion with her eyes, watching with envy as the paperback book flopped closed and rested on a small table next to the Magnate's chair. It was a good distraction from the cramps starting in her middle. What she wouldn't give to take even one with her. She could have gotten lost in that library for hours—moving between the shelves, reading all the titles, touching all the spines, kissing Soren…

Larken jerked and turned her face away, knowing that the exposed apples of her cheeks were a bright red. After all their time together, after everything that happened between them, now was the moment that this idiot decided to share his true feelings. She'd never forgive him. Not for risking the mission by completely and utterly distracting her, and not for taking so *freaking* long to finally do it.

"Are you okay?" Levi asked, thinking her movements and discomfort were from her injuries and not the fact that Soren was so close she could lay her head on his chest.

"I've been shot *and* stabbed. What do you think?" she snapped a bit harsher than intended. A wave of pain from her back hit her, helping her cover her blush.

"We also beat the living daylights out of Squad 22. Even I'd take another bullet for that," he said as he tugged on the shoulder strap of her vest.

"Just cut it off of me."

Larken sat forward so the men could work and breathed slowly through barely parted lips. Soon she was once again down to her sports bra and bleeding in front of everyone. To make things worse, sleeping for twenty-four hours on the Harpy bench was starting to get to her shoulder. She didn't know how she was going to manage standing upright once this was all over. Not only that, but her panic was starting to set in again. They made it all the way here and no one was going to be able to stop Edmar from calling for help. He said that he was going to make tea, but what if that was a lie?

Ewan worked on Hinlee quickly, and Brecker held his finger to his earpiece as he mumbled steadily under his breath. Larken assumed he was updating Vallen. She scanned the room for cameras as Levi sterilized and numbed her—there wasn't room in either of the med-kits for a dermis gun. They had all voted to take antidotes in case any Vigilants showed up with their special bullets, and Larken was glad that, as far as she knew, they weren't needed. That didn't stop her growing panic, though.

Her heartrate picked up steadily and soon her breathing followed. Levi noticed right away, his hands still examining. His hard green eyes flicked up and met hers.

"Larken."

She silently told him to move faster.

He understood the order and got started.

Levi barely waited for her to get numb before he started on her stab wound. She kept glancing around, trying to figure out how similar this place was to the Manors. She wasn't able to see any cameras from where she sat, but that didn't mean the room wasn't bugged somehow. A luminary's private study was one thing; the personal chambers for the Magnate was another altogether.

Larken's anxiety eased some when the Magnate returned a few moments later with a large tray filled to the brim with a kettle and mis-matched mugs. "I'm sorry about the disorganization, but I'm not used to visitors."

Larken couldn't tell if he was trying to imply something or not.

He continued, "They never tell me anything unless it's absolutely necessary. I didn't even know you all were in the Manse, only that there was a chance you might show up eventually."

Levi gently pulled and tugged against her middle, stealing the majority of her attention now. Delvon was right there with a cloth to wipe away whatever blood got in the field-medic's way. Soren was only there for moral support...not looking at the carnage.

If it had been any other time, Larken would have teased him. But she knew the nightmares that haunted him—they found her at night, too. Larken would never forget the look in Soren's eyes as he told Loxly to leave Brecker behind, or the way Hinlee screamed for the man she loved.

A mug was offered to her before she had the chance to remember the horror that Levi endured. She didn't have time to think about how things could have been done differently or how it was her fault because she'd snubbed Dominic. Larken could only focus on the fact that the Magnate himself was offering her tea as she bled all over his expensive wooden bench.

He had a nice face, one that anyone could see used to be handsome. Age showed through his features some, and his hair was a light sterling grey on top and a dusty charcoal around his ears. No stubble covered his face, and his pale eyes were kind in a way Larken didn't know was possible for a man of his age in politics.

Larken accepted the bubblegum pink mug and shook her head stupidly as Edmar offered her sugar. It was all so weird. This man ran the country—by himself—and here he was, serving them tea in his pajamas. Of all the ways that Larken expected this to go, this wasn't one of the possibilities she'd thought up. And judging by the expressions on everyone else's faces, Larken wasn't alone.

"We better make this somewhat quick," Edmar reminded them. "I have the best security team in the country. Though, they clearly need more work."

Larken stared at the man openmouthed.

*Is he* joking?

As if to answer her, the Magnate winked her way after he passed off the last mug to Ewan. The Tanner brother set it on the floor and got back to work on Hinlee's exposed thigh. Larken couldn't see what exactly was wrong with it, but Brecker had helped Ewan cut her pant leg off before he checked in with Vallen.

Larken only briefly wondered why Vallen hadn't checked in with her instead, but seeing as she was liable to have another breakdown, she was glad he didn't. She was already bleeding everywhere; she didn't want to add stress crying to the mess, too.

With a soft groan, Edmar eased back into his chair. His toes flexed in the grass, and he brought a wrinkled hand up to rub at his eyes.

"I knew this day was coming," he digressed. "General Maxwell promised me that Maxim *would* make me see reason in the end—and now look. Half my country's on fire while you all lay injured in my rooms."

No one dared to speak, and the only ones still moving were Levi and Ewan. Larken desperately wished Loxly was there to help break the tension. He'd know what to say.

Edmar leaned back into his chair and took a turn taking in every single one of them before finally landing on Larken. "I guess all I can do at this point is thank you."

Larken blinked slowly and swallowed past a dry spot in her throat.

"Thank you for not giving up," Edmar said.

She nodded.

"Now," Edmar said, his demeanor changing form an old man enjoying the rain to the sole ruler of Koraythea, "tell me your plan. Only rumors have reached me, and I'd like the truth."

"Rumors?" Levi asked, pausing in his work and glancing over his shoulder at the Magnate.

"Yes, I've heard everything; from Miss Hale wanting to simply make a stand to her wanting to assassinate me." Edmar gave Levi a knowing smile.

Levi turned back to Larken and tied off the stitches. He motioned for her to sit up and moved around to the bullet wound on her back.

"*Assassination,*" Levi muttered sarcastically, only loud enough for Larken to hear.

Larken ignored him and yanked her mask down. She wanted the Magnate to fully see her as she told her story.

"I was always different," she started. "I was reminded about it daily. Thankfully, when Vallen first showed up in my life, I was so attention starved that I did everything he asked. His tasks started out small. They were just simple things like running a mile or perfecting a punch. But eventually, he got me to the point where I was ready for my mother to fully turn her back on me and send me to Base 14." Larken swallowed thickly. "And I'll always love him for that."

She continued, sharing what it was like living on base and about all of the attempts made on her life. "That was when I met the Faithfuls for the first time." She winced as she remembered shooting Shadric in the shoulder. "They'd infiltrated one of our training sessions and asked me to go with them. None of them recognized me, though."

Ewan covered a cough by clearing his throat.

Larken kept talking. She told Edmar about how she learned the difference between the Faithfuls and the Vigilants, and what her life was like after she was called back to the Manor. Soren interjected then and shared what he knew, and covered everything she missed and his side of things after Larken left base. Then she told Edmar what it was like after she'd been sent home again, and how she just barely escaped her wedding.

"Then I was brought to Camp where I became a Faithful. And now I'm doing this—trying to stop this stupid war my mother started just to keep a Title that never should have been hers."

Not once had the Magnate interrupted her. He didn't even take a sip of his tea as he listened. Edmar remained stone-faced the whole time and waited for her to finish.

With each word spoken, Larken's gut twisted tighter and tighter. She wished he would do something—give some sign that what she was saying resonated with him on some level. He had been so kind before and now she worried that perhaps he was just detaining them. But it didn't matter—once the dam broke open, Larken couldn't stop speaking.

She swallowed thickly. "And that's why we came here. We were hoping that you could help us," she finished.

Finally, Edmar's face changed the slightest bit as he asked, "And how would I help you, Miss Hale? What exactly is your plan?" He brought his mug to his lips and grimaced down at the cold liquid.

"We need to get rid of my mother. *And* Liam."

"And by *get rid of* you mean…?"

"No—" Larken shook her head vehemently. "—*no!* Nothing like that. Put them in jail, maybe, but I don't want them assassinated or anything."

Edmar set his mug on the little table by the book and clasped his hands together. He raised a silent eyebrow, waiting for her to continue.

"We just want to replace my mother with someone better. Someone who isn't Liam. Someone who actually *believes* in the Luminary ideals and lives for Maxim. Someone—"

"Someone like yourself, perhaps?"

Embarrassed heat flooded her cheeks, and she gave a small tilt of her head. A knowing gleam momentarily glazed over Edmar's eyes and he nodded in turn. He knew she didn't want this, but what choice did she have? This was what Vallen raised her for. Larken stepping up and taking charge would bring so much peace to so many people…so why didn't she feel better about this? Why did she suddenly feel so restless?

*Because I'm not supposed to be the Luminary…*

The realization hit Larken just as Levi produced a clean shirt from somewhere. Larken tugged it over her head as guilt ate away at her stomach. As soon as they got back, she would have to pull Vallen aside. They needed to choose someone else. Vallen raised her to do great things…but being Luminary wasn't one of them.

She swallowed thickly, wanting very much to run away. Something stilled her, though. It wasn't the three men standing around her, and it wasn't the way Edmar stared at her. It was something else…something *more.*

A small smile curled the Magnate's lips as he asked, "What would your life as a Luminary look like?"

He used that tone again—the one where Larken couldn't tell if he meant something else other than what he was saying. Larken swallowed thickly as she panicked. She didn't want to lie to the man, but she couldn't just say nothing, either.

Then, as if he could read her every thought, the man winked at her.

"Things would be the same, I guess," she said slowly. "I would probably keep to myself mostly. I'd encourage the District to foster relationships with Maxim by leading by example. I'd give military funding where I saw fit. And I wouldn't start any civil wars."

He dipped his head. "Good to hear."

Larken told him the truth—or, at least, the truth she had planned on giving. Guilt twisted her stomach and she almost caved and backed out right then. But a small smile curled Edmar's lips and he silently urged her to speak the words she needed to put voice to.

"I promise, I'll do whatever is best for the District."

"Wonderful." Edmar scratched at his chin, covering a knowing smile as he did. "And the future Luminar?"

"Undecided." Larken took a deep breath and prayed that Fisher's advice was the right one to follow. "I've decided not to rush into anything or try and impress anyone by having all the answers. I plan on seeking a husband that will not only help me be the best version of myself, but will help the District as well."

"I appreciate your honesty. And to be honest myself, I find I agree with you. Trogar wasn't much older than you when he rushed into marriage with your mother. It makes one wonder what could have happened if things were different. Not that I begrudge your existence," he added.

Larken offered him a smile. He didn't know—or he was choosing not to believe in rumors.

"I don't mean to put you on the spot, Miss Hale," Edmar said, "but can you tell me a bit more about your relationship with Maxim? I'm curious about what you mean when you said you would lead by example."

"I—" her voice caught.

Soren reached out and grazed her back with his fingers and Larken could feel the eyes of all her friends on her. She closed her eyes, frantically searching for the right words. What could she say? What *were* the right words?

Larken's eyes snapped open and she blurted, "I don't know."

Edmar raised his eyebrow again.

"No. I mean—I don't know, but I try. I try to be the best I can." Larken shook her head. "I'm not perfect and I don't pretend to be. I struggle with things just like everyone else. But, a very good friend told me recently that me trying is enough. Me being *who I am* is enough. I want to live a life that I'm proud of and I try to do that every day. All I can do is my best and that's all I can promise you and the Military District. I'll try my best and I'll lean on Maxim when my best isn't good enough."

"Thank you." Edmar gave her a smile that melted all the icky feelings inside her gut into a puddle of peace.

She'd done it. Larken didn't know what was about to happen to her—especially since she now knew she needed to discuss everything with Vallen—but whatever she was supposed to do in this moment, she did it.

A clap of thunder roared so loudly, it reached them all the way where they were. As soon as the sound faded, the elevator behind them began to ascend. The security team must have been able to fix whatever Hinlee had done to it, and they were now officially out of time.

Edmar hopped to his feet and ushered them all up. "Quickly, through the back door. I may be Magnate, but you're still wanted criminals."

He led them all to the back of the room, Brecker carrying Hinlee once more, and waited until Delvon was through before closing the door behind them. The Magnate turned on a light, revealing a stone room, and then slapped his hand against a screen on the wall. The stone wall in the back of the room lifted slowly. The grating sound had Larken clenching her jaw and the waft of freezing air forced her to clap her arms around her. Soren immediately moved in and pulled her to him for heat.

The storm sounded louder than ever and Larken's heart jumped to her throat. The hangar was exposed as the wall made it up halfway, but the Magnate didn't let them wait. Without a goodbye, he shooed them under the wall into the freezing hanger. Brecker was first and he crouched with Hinlee in his arms; next were the Tanner brothers and then Levi. Soon, only Larken, Soren, and the Magnate remained. The wind, thunder, and alarm warred with each other, trying to be the one that was heard.

They were alone now. Larken should at least try to tell Edmar that she might not be the Luminary after all. She really meant it when she said she would do what was best for the District. The best just wasn't her.

Taking a deep breath, she called over the storm, "Edmar, I—"

"Be faithful, Larken! Live your destiny and joy will find you!" he shouted through a roar of thunder.

She nodded, knowing that he wouldn't hear anything more from her. Soren shielded her as they ducked and ran out into the hangar.

The wall screeched and then changed directions. Lights began to turn on and the hologram-covered Harpy sat at the end of the row from where they were. They ran, Soren eventually scooping her up so they could get there faster. Loxly's co-pilot stood at the top of the steps, waiting for them, and waved the team in one by one as if it would get them into the cab faster.

As soon as Soren barreled over the line, the co-pilot hit the button for the stairs, and they all fell into their seats. Harnesses were snapped into place and the co-pilot was shouting about the storm. Larken's panic settled over her like a freezing blanket. Her chocolates were in Levi's med-kit, and he was in the back of the Harpy. As soon as their eyes met, realization widened his eyes and he scrambled to unlatch his harness. The co-pilot yelled for him to stay put until Loxly got them out of the squall and into a gentler part of the storm.

The man ran into the cockpit and then they were off. Loxly wasted no time jumping into the air and getting out of there as fast as they could. The hangar's mouth sat wide open, allowing other aircraft to enter and escape the storm. Larken didn't see anything as they passed, she only knew that as soon as they were out past the lip, the wind buffeted against the Harpy and they were jerked to the side.

Her harness caught her and pressed a painful weight into her stitches. Cool dampness hit her middle whenever her shirt pressed against her skin, and she knew her stitches had ripped open. Larken's hands shook and she couldn't calm down. The world around her was a dizzy mess of storm clouds, thunder, and wind. Loxly fought against it, but they were still battered around like they were nothing more than a candle flame fighting to stay lit in a hurricane.

Memories of the nightmare she had on their way here assaulted her, and suddenly Dominic's voice was everywhere. He called her his and he reminded her that she wouldn't live long without him. Dominic was this storm and the storm was him. Their blackness was the same and there was no escaping it. It was all around her, and this harness wouldn't protect her for long.

A hand came out and touched her cheek. Larken jerked but stilled when she realized it was only Soren. He'd been there in her dream. He was in the crash, too. This wasn't a nightmare or some horrible vision. Loxly was flying the Harpy and Soren was here with her…just like he'd promised.

"I'm here," he assured, as if reading her thoughts.

Larken nodded, her eyes wide and suddenly damp.

Soren maneuvered the best he could and got as close as he was able. Bringing his arms up, he wrapped them around her, and Larken buried her face into his bulletproof vest. She shut herself away into the darkness and stayed there. She was still terrified, and she still didn't know what was going to come next, but Soren was here. He was her rock as the Harpy jerked and bobbed through the storm. He was here, and this time, Larken knew that he would never let her go.

# CHAPTER 37

oxly had landed about fifteen minutes ago, but Soren couldn't bring himself to wake Larken up. She snuggled into his chest, just like she had so many times before—just like he was hoping she would do from now on. They'd done it. They'd gotten to the Magnate and then out of the Manse mostly unscathed.

Up in the air, they'd needed to wait for the storm to calm down so Larken could get her meds. But once she was able to take her seatbelt off, she admitted that her stitches had ripped open. Loxly passed off the controls when he heard that and rushed into the cab. He went to Hinlee first to make sure she was okay before devoting the rest of his free time to Larken. She harassed him mercilessly as a coping mechanism for her stress and he gladly took it, even threatening to help Levi patch her up. Soren had gripped one of her hands while Loxly took the other between both of his, kissing her knuckles every so often.

It was then that the guilt of the last month or so hit Soren. How much time had Loxly and Larken been able to spend together? Larken was readying herself to take over a District and lead a revolution, while Loxly had to sit back on the last three missions. It wasn't right for the two of them to be separated—not when Loxly was the older brother that Liam *should* have been.

Once Larken was patched up and Levi convinced them that she wouldn't die before they reached the safehouse, Larken was given her chocolate. Delvon was the one to update Vallen, and Loxly kissed his friend's forehead before passing her off to Soren. The sharpshooter returned to his seat after checking in on Hinlee again, and it was smooth sailing back. The storm stayed behind them as if Maxim Himself was covering their tracks.

When they'd landed, Hinlee was rushed off to surgery. Ewan had done what he could on the Harpy for her, and even Levi helped once Larken was out. The bullet Hinlee had been hit with was embedded in her femur, and even though it wasn't life threatening, it still needed to come out. Ewan prepared her for the worst after they'd gotten out of the storm—she might have a limp after every-thing was said and done. Hinlee only grabbed Brecker's hand and said that she didn't need to be able to walk perfectly to fix engines.

If everything went perfectly though, Hinlee wouldn't ever have to touch another engine again. None of them would have to use any of their special skills if they didn't want to. Soren knew that he wasn't going to pick up another gun for a long time—and Larken had another thing coming if she thought Soren was going to ever let her fight in another war. She'd scared him too many times already, and now he wouldn't ever be able to get the image of her bruised and stitched up abdomen out of his mind.

Soren's hand drifted up over her side and traced the bullet wound on her back with his fingertips. He was there that day when Vallen made her promise that she wouldn't get shot. This made three times now.

Three times that she could have been taken from Soren forever.

He tightened his hold on her as much as he dared and kissed her temple. Larken stirred and slowly blinked her unfocused eyes open. She peered up at him under dark lashes and then a pale blush touched her cheeks. Soren traced his way back over her side and up where he brushed a wisp of hair behind her ear. Larken's own hand came up to his chest and then to his cheek.

"You got hurt," she whispered.

"I did."

"I'm sorry I didn't notice."

"You were busy getting stabbed and shot. It's okay."

Larken lifted her head and kissed the scratch on his cheek. He let his eyes fall closed and leaned into the feeling of her warm lips on him. She pulled back too soon, and Soren had half a mind to demand more attention, but she sat up.

Larken barely lifted her arm as she grabbed at her shoulder. It popped loudly and she gasped in pain as her arm fell like a dead fish. Soren winced but pushed away his squeamish belly and got to his feet. He couldn't help but stare at her shoulder as he helped her out of the Harpy.

Bright sunshine that didn't match the season surrounded them. Green grass reached up to the clear blue sky and danced in the breeze. Larken closed her eyes and took a second to breathe in the fresh air around them before they started walking.

"Where are we?" she asked.

"Do you remember when we would ditch you at the Manor so you could go dress shopping or whatever with Carl?"

"*Yes*," Larken grumbled.

"This is where we would come. It's also where Vallen was the night of the opera."

Larken stared out across the field, completely missing the hatch. Soren laced his fingers with hers and redirected her to it, saying, "Let's get you to the med-bay."

She nodded and stared out across the grass as he crouched to punch in the code. The hatch flew open, revealing the now-familiar ladder leading into the secret bunker.

Soren hopped in first, went down a few rungs, and then held a hand out to help Larken in. "I promise there's no centipedes down here."

She grinned and took his hand.

He helped her, bearing her weight when she couldn't and ensuring that she didn't fall. Every time she moved her shoulder wrong, she had to stop and catch her breath. Her middle wasn't much better—she couldn't twist or turn to look around her. Soren stayed with her until her feet hit the ground.

Larken faced him and looked up past his shoulders and head to the florescent lights above. He stared at the way they reflected in the black of her eyes. The hatch slammed shut like it always did and caused Larken to jump out of her skin, and Soren smothered a chuckle as he wrapped his arm around her and led her down the hall. The rooms were the same as before with the heavy doors and the little windows. The only difference was that this time, there were actually people inside them claiming their bunks and joking around. Soren and Larken would be rooming with Carl and Candy while the rest of the Squad was together. Soren didn't know where Delvon would be, but he didn't really care. The man would probably just end up in a chair outside their room, anyway.

For always griping about being a bodyguard, the man didn't really seem to have an interest in changing professions.

Instead of taking a right at the end of the hall, Soren went left. Larken leaned heavily on him, her eyes drooping and her breaths starting to come in shallow pants. His heart skipped a panicked beat. She needed medical attention sooner rather than later, so Soren scooped her up and carried her the rest of the way. Past more rooms they went and then past the small cafeteria and kitchen. Soren hurried all the way to the med-area, trying not to jostle her too much.

He learned that Jodi was still finishing up with Hinlee, so Soren flagged down Ezra. The Medic didn't bother hiding his relief when he said, "Larken."

"Ezra." Larken smiled sleepily. "Would you mind helping me? I seem to have injured myself slightly."

Soren sighed deeply, keeping his opinions to himself.

Ezra only quirked a dark brow and smirked. "Slightly?"

"If Vallen is getting whatever report you write up, then yes. Slightly."

Ezra chuckled and gestured to an open door down the hall.

"There's a bench in there. Why don't we go take a look at you and then I'll decide what to put in the report?"

Soren wasted no time getting Larken set up on a familiar-looking black bench. He didn't leave the room when Ezra got to work adjusting her, but the informational notes on the side of a box of gloves had suddenly become the most interesting thing Soren had ever read in his life. Larken grunted every now and then as *pops* filled the room and groaned as Ezra helped her lift her shirt up over her head.

The bruising was much worse than it had been the day before when Levi patched her up on the Harpy. Soren couldn't tear his eyes away as Ezra cut the stitches and disinfected the wounds again. Crusty blood clung to her skin, refusing to part with her. Soren couldn't blame it—she'd lost so much blood already. He knew from his training that the amount wasn't dangerous, but it didn't seem that way in the moment. He had to keep reminding himself over and over again that if it was as bad as it looked, Levi would have used Loxly for a mini transfusion on the Harpy.

After everything was cleaned, Ezra waited for Larken to meet his gaze before asking, "Do I need to get a dermis gun out?"

"No."

Ezra then got to work. It took about two hours to stitch Larken up and pump her full of antibiotics in case she picked something up at the Manse or on the Harpy. During that time, Vallen sent out a message saying that there was to be a meeting later in the evening. Soren didn't say anything, wanting Larken to focus on getting treated. She perked up almost immediately after, though Ezra still insisted on setting her up in a wheelchair. Larken looked to Soren to side with her, but he frowned, silently telling her to get in the chair. It was an old model, one that was all black metal and giant wheels— nothing like the hoverchairs they used now. Larken only sighed as she sat in it and then thanked Ezra for the help.

Soren set an alarm to go off ten minutes before the meeting Vallen wanted to have. He didn't want to forget to watch the time as he talked with Larken. They'd missed so much time lately and he wasn't willing to miss any more if he could help it. After he put his communicator back in his pocket, he pushed her out the door and through the halls of the bunker. He did a better job of explaining where everything was since she was able to keep her eyes open now.

It was her first day at base all over again. Instead of speaking in an irritated huff, Soren took his time pushing the chair through the halls. He smiled, teased, and even chuckled a few times as Larken went through the Bunker with him.

How much time had he wasted being angry with her for making him crazy? Why hadn't he just acted on his feelings before? He'd been afraid of the other side of things, but now that he was here, there was nothing to be afraid of. Soren was actually happy, which was exactly what everyone implied would happen. Part of him was grateful for the hardships he and Larken had gone through—it made him realize how much he wanted this. But the other part was still kicking himself for being such an idiot.

Soren let go of one of the chair handles for a moment and grazed his knuckles down Larken's neck. She leaned into the contact like an affection starved cat, and he couldn't help but move closer and kiss the top of her head. He would make this work between them. He would see them through to the other side of this war and create a life of happiness and peace for her. Soren had been so wrong about her at the beginning; he owed her for not only that, but for bringing color into his dead, military-hardened life.

He blinked a few times, suddenly realizing that Larken had turned her head up and stared at him. Her teal eyes held a fierce seriousness to them that made his breath catch in his chest for a moment. His heart stalled.

*Did she regret the kiss?*

Soren swallowed thickly and grunted, "What?"

"Promise you'll take me to the ocean again." Her hand tightened on his. "I didn't have enough time there—I didn't have enough time with you. It was all I could think about before we went in."

His stomach melted into a warm puddle. Of course it was the beach. She got him all twisted up and panicky over the *beach*.

Larken continued to stare up at him expectantly.

"I'll give you a thousand oceans if it will make you happy."

She grinned.

Soren pulled his hand free from hers and placed it gently on her neck. He bent down, but just as his lips were about to touch hers, a whooping cry of excitement broke the moment. Their heads jerked forward to find Loxly wearing a teasing grin.

"So this must've been what Hinlee was talkin' about all those times. I thought there might be somethin' goin' on, especially after catchin' you in my room, but I figured Larken would've told me if there was."

Soren made a vow that if Loxly ever interrupted again, he'd kill him.

"Looks like the secret's out of the bag," Larken muttered.

"Was it ever in?" Levi challenged, joining Loxly's side. "Hinlee's going to be mad she wasn't the first to find out."

"What can you do?" Loxly asked. "We caught them first."

Soren tried his best to stomp down his blush, but he was redder than a boiled tomato. Crimson graced Larken's cheeks as well, so Soren did the only thing he could think of. Gripping the handles of the wheelchair tight enough to pop his knuckles, he pushed forward and left.

The two men left behind chuckled darkly at their expense and Soren knew that this new bit of gossip would spread through the bunker like wildfire. Delvon would no doubt corner Larken when he found out. He'd want to know why he wasn't warned ahead of time.

Which left Soren with a sick, guilty feeling in the pit of his stomach.

Laken could handle Delvon, but Soren needed to be come clean to someone else first.

Stopping abruptly, he turned the chair around and led it back to Loxly and Levi. The two men sobered, clearly thinking that Soren and Larken were coming back to cause them harm for the teasing, but Soren ignored them and went around to the front of the chair. He knelt and took Larken's hands in his.

"Loxly will take you to check in with Vallen. I've got something I've got to do really fast. I'll meet up with you again soon."

"Okay?" Larken tilted her head. "Everything alright?"

"I'm not sure."

With that, Soren was off. He had no idea where he was going, but he somehow knew he was going the right way. The hallways blended together until they became unfamiliar. It was the only place Soren hadn't been yet—having only been to the bunkers for short meetings—and the only place he could think where *he* might be.

A plastic eight-pointed star sat on the outside of the door he stopped in front of, and Soren took a deep breath before walking in. He'd been right, and Shadric and Fisher turned to face him. The room was the same as all the others, the only difference being the guitar stand and keyboard were pushed into a corner. As many chairs as would fit were crammed into the small space to give mini sermons when people were available to do so.

Fisher took one look at Soren and then excused himself. He clapped Soren's shoulder on the way out, and for some reason, Soren thought Fisher knew why he was there. The man wasn't blind…he must know what Soren thought of his daughter.

Soren slowly approached Shadric. The musician stood his ground and waited while Soren mulled the words over in his mind. He opened his mouth but the words he'd decided on weren't what came out. Instead, he said, "I don't like you."

"Yes, I am very aware of that fact," Shadric said with an awkward smile.

Soren wanted to deck him for that comment alone. Did he always have to be so easy-going and polite?

"What I mean is, I don't like—"

"If you're referring to my feelings regarding Larken, you should know that I don't much like you, either." Soren nodded. He opened his mouth to try again, but Shadric cut him off. *"But...you don't have to worry about it anymore. I'm no longer pursuing her."*

Soren didn't want to ask, but the question slipped out, anyway. "Does this have anything to do with that day Jodi drugged me?"

"It has everything to do with it." Shadric rubbed the back of his blond head and his smile turned sad. "The way you talked about her—I knew that I wasn't the one who truly deserved her. She would be happiest with you by her side and me as just a good friend. And because I love her, I'm letting her go."

Soren didn't know what to say. He felt bad that he couldn't remember what he'd done or said, but he appreciated the honesty. He was also glad that Larken wasn't losing her friend because of this.

"Someday I'll move on, but until then, I'll be keeping a small distance. I want you two to have the best chance you can have—without distractions."

Soren nodded. This man was open and honest about his feeling regarding Larken, and he wasn't ashamed about them either. Soren envied him for that and had to admit that maybe he wasn't so bad after all.

"I do have one favor to ask though."

"Sure."

Shadric grinned. "If you two *do* decide to get hitched down the line, don't even think about asking me to sing at the wedding."

Soren cracked a small smile. "If you think I have the same music taste as Braves, then you're as dumb as I originally thought."

Shadric barked out a laugh and motioned to the door with his head. "We should probably head to the conference room. It should be getting close to—"

Soren's communicator went off in his pocket with his alarm. He pulled out the device and cleared it before shoving it back in his pocket.

Both men stood there awkwardly before Soren summoned up enough strength to put his pride aside and say, "Thanks...Shad."

# CHAPTER 38

arken's cheeks still burned. Loxly wouldn't give it a rest; he kept going on about how he'd known from the moment he'd walked her to that first lunch with Dominic. It didn't matter how much she kept reminding him that the only thing he did was talk her down from punching Soren in the face. Out of everything, this was the good news they decided to fixate on.

The closer they got to wherever they were going, the less Larken cared about what Loxly and Levi talked about, focusing instead on the growing pit of anxiety in her gut. Soren said during their time together that Vallen was prepping for a meeting—the *last* meeting. They only had a few days here before they shipped out to the Manor.

The green field above them made it hard to believe that they were in the heights of autumn and would be hitting winter sooner rather than later. The Night of Masks was just a few days away and Larken could only pray that Carl was ready. It would be the biggest night of his career. Not only did he have to dress and style each and every soldier, but he would somehow have to hide weapons and some sort of protection underneath the outfits. Larken herself would have to spend every moment she could in her heels once she was fit to walk. It wouldn't do to trip in the shoes Jodi bought her.

One hall turned into another until they were suddenly at a door. It was so plain, so unassuming, and yet Larken found herself afraid to go in. Not that she had much of a choice; she was in a wheelchair and Loxly didn't know anything about her inner turmoil. None of them did.

Even if she'd had the time to talk to someone between her sudden realization and this moment, she would've kept it to herself. Everyone had put so much hope in her—how could she be selfish and say their efforts and their trust were all for nothing?

Levi went ahead and pushed the door open without ceremony. Larken bunched up the hem of her shirt, trying to keep her stomach where it was supposed to be. Shadric's team, as well as a few others, lazed around the room and paid them no mind. Vallen seemed nonchalant, but Larken knew better. She could tell how tense he was by the way he held himself. His dark eyes snapped up to meet hers. He stared for only a few seconds before his frown deepened. She knew he knew.

He jumped to his feet and marched over to her. Without a word, he commandeered the chair from Loxly and wheeled her back out into the hall. He went a ways down so no one walking in would overhear and parked her. Coming around, he crouched in front of her like he used to do when she was a child. His knees popped loud enough to make her cringe, but he paid them no mind.

"I know that look."

That was all it took. They weren't kind words, but they were familiar. They were all her body needed to fall apart. Even though no tears came, Larken's face crumpled, and she curled into herself. Vallen had his arms around her immediately and held her to him tightly as if that alone would transfer the weight she carried to his shoulders.

"Vallen," she croaked through the exhaustion that suddenly weighed her down so completely, "I can't—"

He jerked away, a hard expression she couldn't read on his face. "Don't say it. Not yet."

Larken shook her head, throat going tight with pain. The words needed to come out—needed to be heard. "I tried. I really *tried*. I was going to go all the way, but then I was there in the Magnate's sitting room and—"

It was Vallen's turn to shake his head. "I know, runt. I know. I've been through this, but trust me when I say that you'll want to sit through this meeting before you make any decisions. Don't say something you can't take back just because things are hard right now."

Larken swallowed thickly, trying to compose herself. He was right—he *had* gone through this. She didn't know the specifics since there hadn't been any time to ask, but he wasn't born Blade. Vallen somehow became the leader of the Faithfuls, and for the first time, Larken had to wonder if it was something he even wanted. Again, it surprised her how similar their lives were.

"I promise when everything is done, I'll bring you right back here before Carl can get his hands on you. I know I've been distant and distracted, but please trust me on this one."

He'd never given her bad advice before. Of course, there were plenty of things she hadn't agreed with—mostly the whole *being dead* thing—but everything worked out the way it was supposed to in the end. Every promise Vallen made, he kept.

She could make this one last promise for him.

Larken took a deep, slow breath before nodding. Vallen kissed her forehead and stood. He went behind the chair and turned her just as Soren and Shadric reached the door.

Her stomach fell and she dropped her eyes. Ever since the kiss, she hadn't given Shadric a single thought. A different kind of guilt washed over her, and she couldn't bear to put on a brave face for the singer right then.

Vallen pushed Larken into the room and parked her between Soren and Delvon without prompting. Everyone that absolutely needed to be there was, and Vallen asked Brecker to close the door. Brecker gave Hinlee's hand a squeeze before doing so. She sat in a wheelchair that matched Larken's and seemed incredibly perky for just having surgery. She must be able to handle anesthesia better than Larken. That, or Jodi gave her something to be able to sit through the meeting.

Vallen didn't bother with a chair and sat on the edge of the table with that same tense posture he had before. The hair on the back of Larken's neck stood up and she realized that Vallen wasn't anxious about her decision—he was nervous.

Something bad had happened.

Something bad enough that he knew it would change her mind about her decision.

He took only enough time to glance over everyone in the room before saying, "Four hours after you left, the Magnate was assassinated."

No one breathed. Larken's ears rang in the silence, not believing that she'd heard him right.

"I don't know much, but this video is all over every news station in the country."

Vallen stood and moved out of the way of the television behind him. He turned it on, and the Magnate's face filled the screen. Vallen played the video. Edmar cleared his throat into the microphone before moving back to sit in the same chair he'd been in during their visit, still wearing his housecoat. This recording must have happened only minutes after they'd left.

Edmar cleared his throat again and said, "I'm sure you'll all wondering why I'm sending out an emergency broadcast after being silent for so long. Well, the short answer is that I was biding my time. I was waiting until I, myself, could figure out what *I* believed was right. And now I know."

Larken balled up the hem of her shirt again.

"As you all know by now, there was a break in. The fugitive Larken Hale and her team managed to get past our security and all the way to my personal quarters where she found me like this." He spread out his arms to show off his disheveled appearance. "She was not violent, nor did she try to cram ideals down my throat. Instead, she did something far worse."

Soren reached out and grabbed Larken's hand as her stomach fell past her feet.

Despite what she thought, they'd failed.

The Magnate shook his head, taking his sweet time to elaborate. "Believe me when I tell you that it would have been kinder for her to kill me. Instead, she forced me to take a good long look at myself and the state of this country." Edmar sighed. "I'm sorry to say that I despise what I saw."

Larken hissed out a breath when she realized the pounding she heard was from her oxygen-deprived lungs and not the video.

"District has gone against District for too long. The military has gone unchecked for too long. Maxim has been ignored for *too long*. Miss Hale may have joined the Faithfuls, but she's the only one who's tried to get all the Districts to see eye to eye in over twenty years. I have failed as Magnate, and for that, I am sorry."

Edmar cleared his throat again, this time bringing a hand up to wipe at his left eye as well.

"Miss Hale proposed this while she pleaded her case: strip her parents of their titles and give her the title of Luminary. She swore that she would bring peace, and I believe her. However, I also believe that she would make a very poor Military Luminary."

The Magnate stared at the camera in a way that had Larken feeling like he stared directly at her.

Edmar cracked a half smile. "That is why I've decided to name Miss Larken Hale my sole heir."

Hinlee and Candy gasped—they were the only ones that visibly reacted. Larken fought to keep her mouth from dropping open. His parting words drifted back to her and hit her in full force.

*"Be faithful, Larken! Live your destiny and joy will find you!"*

Larken could see everyone in the room turn to look at her out of the corner of her eyes. She ignored them and squeezed Soren's fingers to the point of breaking. She wouldn't react. She would remain as stone-faced as Vallen taught her to be. Larken had to remind herself to breathe and didn't dare let go of Soren's hand. She kept her gaze on the screen, and she was glad she did when she was one of the few that didn't jump at the loud bang emitting from the video.

"Where is she?" a muffled yet familiar voice demanded.

*Dominic.*

Larken's heart stopped—she knew what was about to happen. She didn't want to believe that he had reached this point—that Dominic had become so unhinged that the fires were no longer enough and killing came this easily to him. She didn't regret leaving him, but Larken couldn't help but feel responsible for everything he did.

Especially this.

Edmar stared at a spot just over the camera and grinned triumphantly. "She's chasing tomorrow."

There was a rage-filled shout and then three gunshots. Larken tried not to flinch, but couldn't help squeezing Soren's fingers again. Edmar still grinned despite the bullets hitting him in his chest and the crimson spreading over his housecoat. The camera rattled and then fell to its side before going black completely.

Again, no one said anything.

Vallen didn't move right away, but when he did, it was enough to break the dam. Chatter broke out around them, and Larken wanted nothing more than to curl into herself and hide until she could make sense of everything that was happening.

She'd been named heir.

No—not just named. Edmar Wilmore was dead.

Larken was the Magnate of Koraythea.

She didn't need to be Luminary. She needed to *find* one.

*He really did know that I didn't want that life,* Larken thought. All of his knowing smiles and winks flashed before her eyes. As soon as she gave her first answer, he had this planned for her.

Louder and louder the conversations got, each one trying to be heard over the other. Questions of what was going to happen now, and of what this meant for the final stand, danced around the room. Larken's hands shook with nervous energy that turned her stomach bitter. Air grew thin—there were too many people in this room. In this *underground* room.

Soren dropped her hand and stood. He came to attention, silencing all conversation. Staring straight ahead and looking every bit the solider the military turned him into, he announced, "My glaive is yours, Magnate Hale."

Loxly, not to be outdone, followed suite. "My shotgun is yours, Magnate Hale."

One by one her squad—her *family*—stood and pledged themselves to her. Well, everyone except Hinlee, who just pounded a fist on the table twice before swearing her fealty. Delvon waited until they were finished and then was on his feet pledging himself as well. Larken shot a glance over to Vallen. He said nothing, only swallowed thickly and gave her a small nod.

He'd shared what he needed to. She was now free to make her choice.

She closed her eyes, taking the time she needed to ground herself. In her mind, she didn't see a building with no windows. Instead, she walked along the beach, hand in hand with Soren as a giant Manor sat behind them, surrounded by forest. The Capital would be a place of politics, the Manor by the sea would be their home. Larken would use the skills Vallen gave her to watch and listen. She would use the life lessons her family taught her to avoid favoritism in the Districts and spread the power evenly. And she would use the gift Edmar gave her to keep the peace and have the private life she'd always wanted.

The path she saw was so clear now that it was in her mind, she didn't know what else she could do but chase after it.

*You're gonna change things, Larken. And with Maxim with you, you won't lose.*

Opening her eyes, she met Vallen's. She nodded and the room filled with cheers.

Shadric had been right in a sort of roundabout way. Larken did hold the key to a better tomorrow, and hopefully, so did the rest of the Faithfuls.

# CHAPTER 39

Carl helped Larken out of her chair and onto her bunk, and she slumped back on the mattress, trying to get as comfortable as she could. She'd spent most of the last thirty hours sleeping, but she was wrung dry. Physically, her meds were starting to wear off, and emotionally...well, things had been more difficult than she would have liked.

Vallen was true to his word and took her to that same spot in the hall to discuss her new title. Larken was glad he hadn't let her quit before she knew the whole story. She couldn't explain it, but thinking about being Magnate just brought this gentle peace to her that she craved more of. She didn't know if it was Maxim's guidance, or the thought of a home away from the Military District by the sea, but it was something she couldn't give up on now.

She'd choked up when Vallen had taken her in his arms and told her how proud he was of the strong woman she'd become. He always knew she was meant for great things. He even charged her with proving it when he left her standing alone in the dorm all those weeks ago. It was crazy to think that it'd only been a few months since this all started. Just a few months after so many years of war.

Carl fiddled around the room for a moment and then stole the pillows from the three other bunks. He helped her sit back up and then stuffed them behind her so she would be more comfortable. Larken let herself relax, and as she did, the tension eased out of her tight muscles. Soren had been injured as well, but there was no way she was climbing that stupid ladder just to sleep on the top bunk. Not that she was probably going to be able to sleep at all until they drugged her and loaded her up into the Harpy for their trip to the Manor.

The small room sat windowless and sad round her. Dark grey paint covered the chilled walls. Larken broke out in goosebumps as a scent reminiscent of her old room at base surrounded her. The florescent lighting made everything look damp, and even though she knew that the walls were dry, she still tried not to touch them. She sat on one of two bunkbeds that were pushed to opposite sides of the room against the walls. Only a single nightstand that held a skinny lamp sat between them.

Her body ached, and she momentarily regretted her decision to keep the scars. Jodi had said something after the meeting about stopping by with some miracle drug for her ailments. Larken hadn't been told anything other than an *"Ask Soren"* when she tried to get more information. And of course, Soren didn't say a single thing.

Carl brought her back to the moment by nudging her left knee and sitting down on the bed. It was only now Larken realized how much he'd let himself go for her sake. His navy hair, though styled, had grown into a curly mess that resembled Loxly's hair more than his own. The left side of his shirt collar sported a hole *and* a small stain that could have once been cocktail sauce. Stubble had started poking through on his jaw, but it was nowhere near as noticeable as the dark bags under his eyes.

She was going to suggest he take a nap instead of doing a trial run, but he said, "I knew you could do it. Didn't I say I did when we were trying on wedding gowns?"

Larken grinned. "You may have mentioned it."

"*Mentioned* it? Kid, I called you a warrior and gave the best pep talk of my *life!*"

"Is that what you call it?" Larken teased.

Carl bent forward, rolling his eyes. He pulled a familiar box out from under her bunk and opened the lid to reveal a pair of black pumps. Scooting back, he lifted one of her feet and slid a heel on. "It would seem we've come full circle."

"Prissy Star."

"Prissy Star indeed." Carl slipped her other shoe on and let his hand linger for a moment before meeting her eyes again. "You know, I thank Maxim every day for Dominic. I know he made your life miserable beyond measure, but if he wasn't trying to impress you with his connections, I never would have met you. And I have to tell you that I am very glad that I have."

Larken knew that her friends were starting to influence her because Carl's admission didn't make her anywhere near as uncomfortable as it would have before this whole thing started. There was once a time she probably would have kicked Carl out so she could be alone with her emotions. Now, she was able to admit, "Me too."

Carl left it alone and stood. He walked over to his travel case in the corner of the room. Larken hadn't noticed it before but recognized it as the same one he brought to the dorm the day of the opera.

He wheeled the caboodle over and quirked his lips. "You don't get options this time."

"I was so looking forward to trying dresses on with my stab wound."

"Will you get over it? So you were stabbed—big deal."

"I've never been stabbed before! I didn't like it!"

"And I used to hate the color red, yet here we are. Move on, will ya?"

Larken pulled a pillow out from behind her and chucked it at him.

Carl caught it full in the face before grinning and saying, "I'm not giving that back."

Larken couldn't help a grin of her own. She didn't know how it was possible, but she was actually having *fun*. Each time Carl took her out or did her up, it was either for her family or for Dominic.

This was the first time it was all about her. She was wearing *her* shoes, the mask *she* chose. Even now Carl was about to show her a dress that he made specifically for her. It was like what her birthdays were always supposed to be. Except this time, the political statement she was going to make in the Military Manor ballroom was very different than the ones her mother spun for her as she grew up.

Carl sat on the bed again and opened the caboodle. Larken noticed the pearl hairpin Fisher gave her right away. It rested in a clear drawer at the top by itself. She wanted to ask if she could wear it, but she also didn't want it to get ruined so she kept her mouth shut. Carl took out the same baubles he'd used last time. He lit them and let the baubles float aimlessly around them. He reached deeper into the caboodle and produced a thin lavender case, then lifted the lid, revealing the mask Larken would wear the next time she saw her mother.

Black lace spiderwebbed across the velvet lining of the box. The gold fabric caught the silver inlays of the mask, as did the light from the baubles. The silver shone and then passed the light onto the diamonds that graced the lace. It was dainty, simple, and perfect. There would be no hiding her eyes, no hair dye, no fancy illusions.

Just Larken.

She would march on her mother, wearing her differences proudly, and force her to see what her life had become. The unwanted daughter with the blonde hair now held all the power that was slowly slipping from her grip. There were no more nerves holding Larken back, and she knew there wouldn't be again.

Was she still afraid? Yes. She was afraid that her friends wouldn't make it and that something might happen to Vallen, but the nerves of failing were gone. The hard parts were over. All that was left was fighting for what was right, and Larken had spent her whole life doing that. And she didn't just fight—she won.

Carl held the mask up to her eyes so he could see how much of her face showed through. He then set it down and pulled a few pale colored pallets out of the caboodle. He readied a long, skinny brush and brought it down across her eyelid. As if he couldn't help it, he started humming *Wanting You*—or more specifically, the line about Larken's blue-green eyes. He'd teased her about it the first time he did her up, too.

If Larken wasn't stretched out on her bunk, she would have kicked him.

Once he was finished with the color testing, he stood and put the makeup away. He wasn't going to put much on, just enough for her to be performance ready for when she faced her mother. Carl might not be able to shoot like Loxly or fight like Brecker, but he could help anyone find their inner confidence. He would never know how much this moment meant to her.

Carl pulled free a garment bag and turned to face her again. "I know you aren't going to put it on until we get there, but I wanted to show it to you before everything hit the fan."

Larken held her breath in excitement.

Carl unzipped the bag and pulled the dress free. She couldn't help her gasp and brought her fingers up to her lips. Everything about the dress, from the silhouette to the color, was impeccable.

"You like it?" Carl asked, uncharacteristically doubtful.

"Carl...it's perfect."

# CHAPTER 40

Dominic blew a puff of blue smoke at the mirror before squashing the butt of the cigar in the ashtray. It sat to the right of the sink, just in front of the bar of soap that held scars of when he'd missed the tray. His fingers lingered on the remnants for longer than he wished. This would be the last time he smoked. After he had Larken, he'd stop all of the habits she hated.

Dominic sprayed some product into his hands and worked it through his hair. He'd let it get too long. Bringing a comb up, he brushed his blond hair out of his face. The three scars glinted silver in the light that shone from above the mirror. He wouldn't be able to keep them after they were married. It wouldn't do to have the husband of the Magnate be marked up like some spurned lover. He would have to be perfect for the media—especially once he announced his new title as the Military District Luminary.

Yes, Dominic had big plans for the future. Once Deckard, Tanner, Barlow, and every other confidant Larken had was dead, he would betray Cornella. He would claim self-defense when it came to Larken's friends and prove his worthiness by killing Cornella himself. Then, after she was all alone, Larken would turn to him. She would finally see what he'd been trying to show her this whole time.

They were perfect for each other.

Dominic had it all planned out. He knew that Larken was going to make her big stand tonight. His old squad was under strict orders to make sure that she was separated from the rest of her group. They knew that if they failed this time, it would mean their deaths as well. They'd warned him too late that Larken was at the Manse. His squad wanted to impress him by catching her before they said anything. Then the fools let her go.

She'd managed to make it all the way to the Magnate because of his squad's failure. At the time, Dominic thought everything had been ruined. He hadn't known when he pulled the trigger that she'd already been named heir. Would it have changed anything? No. He still would've killed the Magnate to give Larken her new life.

It's what he promised her, after all. A new life away from the family that didn't want her.

And no one in this world wanted her more than him.

Dominic buttoned up his white shirt and frowned. He was thinner, too. The shirt didn't cling to him like it once did. He'd been smoking too much and not working out enough. He would have to change that, as well—not just for Larken's sake but for his, too. It wouldn't do her any good for him to put himself in the grave right after they were finally together.

All of the pieces were finally starting to fall into place. This time his plan *would* work. Larken would be put somewhere safe, and Dominic would take care of the rest. Originally, he wanted to save Deckard for last. Now, he would be the first to go. There would be no messes this time for Dominic to clean up.

*Everything* would go his way.

Dominic slung his red tie around his neck and tied it. Making sure it was perfect, he donned his black suit jacket. He brushed off all the invisible dust from the lapels and pulled his mask from the pocket. It was the same shade of blood red as his tie. He gave himself one last look over and then his eyes drifted over to the ashtray. After tonight, everything would be over.

Larken would be his, and Dominic Braves would *finally* get what he deserved.

# CHAPTER 41

Cool air circulated through the cab but sticky sweat still dripped down Soren's back. He thought he might be sick from all the knotted-up stress in his stomach. Larken seemed to be fine—she joked and laughed with everyone, trying to lift their spirits.

She had woken up about thirty minutes ago and seemed fine. She claimed that, *"They were headed to their deaths anyway, so what did it matter if they crashed?"* Her reasoning was sound, but Soren caught her small jumps whenever they hit harsh winds. Delvon had looked at the forecast and, thankfully, it wouldn't rain, but the winds were going to be insane. After the bodyguard finished briefing them on the weather, Larken beat Loxly to the *winds of change* joke. Loxly then made everyone cringe by saying he was going to change her nickname to *Phoenix* since little birds didn't rise from ashes. He then got boo'd into the cockpit where he'd stayed ever since.

Soren honestly didn't know if pretending everything was fine was working for Larken or not. He only knew that if Loxly's co-pilot hit one more spot of turbulence, he would be sick.

The stupid tie didn't help. It slowly choked him and felt more like a noose than a fashion statement. It was the same tie he'd worn to the opera, the same one he'd worn in the fight after. The suit he spent so many hours shopping for finally had a practical use he could be proud of. And, of course, Loxly paraded around with his nose in the air reminding them that he was the one who talked everyone into buying one.

The door to the cockpit sat open so the pilots could hear everything happening in the cab, and Soren could see Loxly's suit jacket hung over the back of his seat. Soren didn't even pretend to think about what was going through his friend's mind. Loxly had shared a long goodbye with Rich before they set out for the Manse. They both knew that it was quite possibly the last time they'd ever see each other again. Soren envied his friend for that. He didn't have anyone that would be waiting to hear what happened to him. Everyone he loved was right here.

Vallen pressed his arm up against Larken's back as Carl did her makeup. All three sat on the bench Soren had shared with Larken on the way to and from the Manse. Soren wished he was on the bench with her now, holding her and asking her what she was really thinking. He couldn't even begin to imagine what was going through her head.

Carl's magic baubles floated around his head, shining light on Larken's upturned face. Everything had changed and yet this moment was so reminiscent of their first flight together. Vallen held the same steady strength he always did, but Soren assumed that this time he was feeling emotional pain at the thought of losing Larken, instead of the physical of getting shot twice. Back then, Larken had tried her best not to seem weak. Now, everyone here knew *exactly* how strong she was.

She'd overcome so much since that first flight. Her time at base had changed her, just like it had changed him. Soren wasn't the same man he once was, and he was so thankful that he wasn't. Guilt twisted his stomach, reminding him of everything he'd done in Cornella's name. He thought he was doing the right thing—that he was doing Maxim's will. Then Larken came and turned his world inside out. She'd changed him so completely that he couldn't help but accept that Maxim did bring them all together for such a time as this.

Losing his heart along the way was just a beautiful accident.

Loxly got up and slipped into the bathroom behind the cockpit for a few moments. He came out clean shaven and Candy jumped on him, wielding a brush and a handful of mousse before he had to take his turn flying again. It would be the last pilot change. When Loxly got up out of that seat next, it would be after he landed on the Military Manor's front lawn.

The media wouldn't be on them—it would only be concerned about who was wearing what, so they were going to go in through the front door. When Larken was asleep, Vallen had explained that the press didn't wait outside the front doors; instead, they waited just inside at the bottom of the grand staircase. There they took pictures as the guests claimed the stairs and walked the pathway. All routes on the first floor were blocked off. To get to the ballroom and gardens, the guests would walk up the stairs, down the hall, and then back down the stairs that held the ballroom doors at the bottom, allowing everyone to make a grand entrance.

Soren thought it was an elaborate waste of time, but Delvon pointed out if they landed in the hedge maze, they would get shot down before they got within a hundred feet. At least this way, they would have the protection of the media. Cornella was already losing her grip on her power; she wouldn't dare commit mass murder during the most anticipated televised event of the year.

Loxly whistled as he stared at himself in the pocket mirror Candy provided him. He gushed over how handsome he was for a good long while and then got back to work. Soren couldn't really blame him. If he had to sit as much as Loxly had in the last few weeks, he would do what he could to keep standing, too. Though, bragging about his good looks was maybe not quite how he would procrastinate.

Candy snapped her mirror shut and glanced around. Her eyes bounced from decorated body to decorated body. She paused on Soren and he watched as she took in his suit, hair, jaw, and even the knot that held his tie. Candy moved on, catching sight of a not-primped-Brecker. The Scout was helping Hinlee try and stand in her heels. A set of black flats hung off the fingers of his right hand while she wobbled and clutched his left shoulder.

"Hin, there really isn't any shame—"

"Yes there is! Do you know how much these cost me?"

Soren's lips twitched as he looked down at her impossibly high red heels. Hinlee wobbled again and this time her face scrunched up and she clutched at her thigh. The action caused her to trip and Brecker grabbed her around the waist before easing her down on the bench behind her.

Hinlee hunched forward, defeated. Brecker pulled one shoe off and then the other, replacing them with the flats. He grinned up at her and asked, "Would it make you feel better if I wore them?"

"Like your fat feet could fit." Her smile was sad, and she huffed a deep breath. "I just wish I got the chance to wear them at least once. I never would have bought them if I'd known—" Her voice caught.

Brecker placed a hand on her thigh where she'd been shot. He pulled Hinlee in for a deep kiss, breaking his no *kissing in front of the squad* rule. Everyone gave them as much privacy as possible, but they could all still hear him say, "You're perfect. I'm the Scout, so it's *my* job to go ahead and make sure everything's okay. Trust me when I say, Hin, I'll *always* come back for you. No matter how fast you walk."

Hinlee wiped away several tears and said, "I love you more than the stars in the sky."

Brecker cupped her cheek. "I love you more than the sun is bright."

Soren's eyes drifted over to Larken. Her fingers played with the pearl at her chest—the one he'd gotten her so long ago. He wished he knew what she was thinking. Were nerves finally setting in? Or were Brecker and Hinlee making her emotional? Even though Hinlee's limp wasn't as bad as Ewan had warned, it was still there.

She would always have that reminder of how things could have gone—just like Brecker would.

Candy waited only long enough for Hinlee and Brecker to finish their moment before she was on him. His hair received the same treatment as Loxly's, and he didn't do nearly as much grumbling as Soren expected.

Carl pronounced Larken ready and helped her up off the bench. The two made their way to the bathroom, and Carl grabbed the garment bag off the hook he stuck on top of the door. They shut themselves away so he could once again work his magic. Soren hoped Larken had enough time to adjust to her heels—he wanted her to have that extra layer of protection.

All the while, Candy had been dancing around in her pink ones, loving the secret danger they held.

She paused in front of Delvon and winked before asking, "What do you think?"

Delvon sucked on a tooth and grunted, "It's better on you."

Candy beamed. "You think? I thought it was fitting—you know? Larken wore it to fight the cause, so I wanted to, too. Though, I'm not sure how much fighting I'll do."

Soren took in the tight pink dress wrapped around Candy's slim frame. He didn't even want to think about why Larken had worn it. Hinlee didn't share his reservations and asked what the two meant, and the story of how Larken used it to try and trick Braves came out.

If Soren felt sick before, it was nothing compared to how he felt now. He couldn't get the image of Braves slobbering over Larken in that dress out of his mind.

Soren tried to distract himself by remembering his own moments with Larken. The one that his mind stuck on was when he chased her in the water. Even so, the sick feeling never subsided, and the longer Larken was in the bathroom, the worse it got. Every second more Carl spent getting Larken ready was another second closer to almost certain death. The prayer committee was hard at work even now, Rich leading them as he asked for protection over his son.

Fisher would be sitting in the one happening back in the bunker, praying equally as hard for his daughter.

Did Trogar know what was about to happen? Would Wardell be at the party tonight? Or did Cornella have enough sense to keep him out of harm's way? They had to know that tonight was the night. It made the most sense. If Soren was on the other side, he would be prepping for an ambush and trying to convince his Lumina of how irresponsible continuing with the celebration would be. But he wasn't there. He was right where Maxim had placed him. It was just one more thing Soren would never be able to pay Larken back for. He hated to think about what would have happened if Vallen hadn't selected his squad for Larken to join.

Not wanting to keep things unsaid, Soren cleared his throat. Everyone stared at him, but he only met Vallen's intense gaze. "I— we—never thanked you, sir. For bringing Larken into our lives."

Vallen took him in for a moment before moving on to the different members of Squad 19. Loxly even poked his head around his seat for a few seconds to nod his agreement.

"Do you want to know why I selected Squad 19?" Vallen asked.

"Larken said it was because we lived in the same dorm you used to," Levi answered.

"That was a major factor, yes, but not the only reason." Vallen swallowed thickly. "I read through all your files and each of you had something that Larken could relate to if she decided to open up. I knew that being with you, she wouldn't be alone.".

Hinlee sniffed and wiped at her eyes again.

"So, Deckard, I believe it is I who should be thanking all of you."

There were only a few seconds of silence before Larken cleared her throat. She stood just outside the bathroom with Carl at her side. Both Candy and Hinlee gasped, and Soren's lips parted. His breath caught in his chest as he stared at the image that was Larken Hale.

She was a vision of glossy skin and black fabric. Triangle straps held the dress up, capping over the tops of her shoulders and stopping right before the dip of her arm. The gown hugged her in all the right places while not looking like it would hinder her fighting. The front of her hem hit the spot right under her kneecaps, while the back landed in the middle of her calves. Soren didn't know what Carl put on her arms and legs, but they looked softer than butter.

Wheat waves cut off at the middle of her shoulders and Soren noticed a hair tie around her wrist. She would go in proud, elegant, and then hopefully come out the victor. Carl fastened a black weapon belt around her middle and was careful to avoid the sheathed sword on it. Soren spotted her handgun as well as the dagger Wardell got for her. The silver hilt of her sword glinted in the light of the cab just as Soren's glaive did. His eyes momentarily dropped to the weapon and to the teal cloth that he'd knotted together just under the blade.

The previous night, when Candy was helping Larken in the bathroom, Carl had pulled out the cloth. At the time, it was perfectly folded and Soren thought it was a pocket square. He'd been wrong, and Carl told him that they had extra from the Manor that he didn't feel right leaving behind. Soren didn't remember Carl packing it the night of the rehearsal dinner, but then again, his mind had been somewhere else then. Carl told him that it could be used as a tourniquet if Soren wanted, but that the fabric should go to him.

Soren's heart squeezed as he reached out and trailed his fingers across the cloth. It was the same color as Larken's eyes. He would only use it if he absolutely needed it. Until then, it would serve as a reminder of who he was doing this for. It was a token Larken didn't even know she gave him, and he would wear it proudly into battle.

Candy rushed to Larken, pulling Soren's attention back to the present. She produced a tube of lipstick from who knew where and popped the cap off with a wink. "Told you it would be a good idea to bring it."

"My signature color, right?" Larken teased.

"You know it, girl."

Larken stood still as Candy applied the lipstick, though her eyes drifted over to Soren. It was only now he realized he hadn't seen her biting at her lips recently. Either she'd started doing it in private or she'd been too stressed to. However, the longer he stared at her lips, the less he thought about her nervous habit and more about what happened in the library. His lips twitched into a smirk and a slight blush colored Larken's cheeks.

She was thinking about it, too.

Carl put him on the spot by motioning him with his head. Soren pushed to his feet, nausea momentarily forgotten, and headed over. Carl pulled a set of cases free and handed them to him. The lavender case was thinner than the black one, but Soren still needed to use both hands.

He glanced down and brushed his thumb over the top of the lavender one as Carl said, "We'll be landing in about ten minutes, and I've suddenly forgotten how to tie a knot."

"What?"

Carl was already ushering everyone over to where the masks were getting handed out. Someone had closed the door to the cockpit, giving Larken and him as much privacy as possible in this little corner of the Harpy.

Soren understood.

Carl would never know what this gift meant to him.

What having this last moment with Larken meant to him.

Soren pulled Larken into the corner gently and blocked her with his large frame. His stomach flipped for a different reason now. She was right here—so close, and yet her mind was worlds away. She stared up at him, doubt in her eyes.

She cast a quick glance to where the others were and sucked in a shallow breath. "I know we don't talk about things, but if I don't tell you that I'm scared of losing you, I'll explode."

Soren balanced the cases against his middle and brought his free hand up to her cheek. "Not talking about things was a stupid rule."

Larken clutched at his wrist with both hands, digging her nails into his skin. "*I can't lose you.*"

Soren traced down her jaw and let his fingers land on the pearl. "You won't. No matter what happens to me—*to us*—I'll always be with you."

She nodded, eyes going glossy. Soren peeked over his shoulder and then quickly pressed his lips to hers to prove his point.

He pulled back and rested his forehead against hers. "I—" his voice caught for a moment, but he pushed through it, "I'm scared of losing you too, Larken."

She sniffed.

"I'm scared of losing you and turning into the man I was. I'm scared of you being taken away from me and not being able to help you. But mostly I'm scared of not having the time to tell you all of the things I should have been telling you all along."

She leaned back, silver lining her lower lashes. "What things?"

"I hate the music you listen to." She laughed, but he continued, "I hate it so much and I get so angry whenever Hinlee blasts that playlist you made for her. But I can never get those stupid songs out of my head."

"You really hate my music?" Larken smiled and stole his breath away.

"Absolutely."

"I kinda guessed that."

"You should have—I wasn't subtle about it. But—" His breath hitched again. "If listening to it meant I could spend the rest of my life with you, then I would never listen to anything else ever again."

Larken's grin faltered a bit and she sniffed again. She lifted up to her tiptoes and pressed her lips to Soren's.

He wanted so badly to stay there and deepen the kiss, but the descent had already started. They really didn't have enough time together. Soren swore to himself that he would do whatever it took to make it up to her.

He offered her the cases holding their masks, and she took the top one and opened it. They shuffled a few things around, and Soren waited for her to turn so he could tie her mask on. She did the same for him, and he was forced to bend back awkwardly so she could reach.

Once she finished, he moved to face her again. He pressed his forehead to hers and breathed in the smell of grapefruit one last time before the world as they knew it ended. "We will be together again, Larken. Whether it's in this life or the next, we *will* be together."

"Never let go," she reminded him.

Soren opened his eyes as Loxly landed the Harpy. The door opened and the stairs descended off to the side. Larken stared up at him, her eyes so blue in that moment he could drown. Vallen took up his sword and handgun, encouraging the others to follow suit. They were officially out of time together.

Maxim help them all.

"I'll never let go."

# CHAPTER 42

The stars hinted at their presence as the clouds blew past them in their hurry to find clearer skies. Wind tugged at the hem of Larken's gown as well as her hair. She was thankful for the hair tie Candy had slipped her—it would seem she would be needing it sooner rather than later. Not that she could fault Carl for not thinking of it. He never had to fight anyone with hair flying everywhere.

The grounds were uncharacteristically quiet and somewhere in the close distance, the wolf hybrids could be heard whimpering in their kennels. They were always put away during the party because they scared the guests. Larken almost wanted to let them out to add to the chaos, but she wouldn't risk any of them getting hurt, even if they no longer knew her.

Loxly traipsed down the Harpy stairs seemingly without a worry in the world, while shrugging into his jacket. He slapped the black button on the side of the aircraft to hide the stairs and shut the door.

Without missing a beat, he asked, "What are we all standin' around for? Don't we have a revolution to win?"

Larken grinned at her dearest friend and nodded. "Yes we do."

She took a deep breath—breathing in all of the familiar smells of the home she would never come to again. The grass, the kennels, the stables in the distance, and the overwhelming scent of her mother's yellow roses. Larken didn't know who the new Luminary was going to be yet, but before she passed off the title, she would burn every single one of those rose bushes.

Larken's eyes snapped open, and she glared up at the home that brought her so much hurt, grief, and anger over the years. If she could, she would burn it to the ground, too. This place—this *empty home* didn't deserve to stand. Neither did Cornella Hale. She took too much. Cornella stole, and lied, and murdered. She needed to be stopped, and Larken was the only one who could do it.

Larken unsheathed her sword. She cast one last look around her before taking a step forward into what could be the final hours of her life.

Her friends followed suit and equipped their weapons as well. Soren wrapped both hands around the handle of his glaive, just as Loxly held up his shotgun. Levi had three med-kits strapped to him and held his tech-gun close. It was quite the sight, seeing them all in their finery, carrying their favorite weapons. Hinlee was a vision in her pastel purple and pink gown that showed off her legs and fanned out behind her in a tulle train. The train was made to come off and act as a tourniquet if needed.

Carl's outfits had little things included in them to hopefully make the fighting easier. Loxly, Levi, Brecker, and Soren all had suits already, but those who didn't got Carl's special treatment. Hinlee had her train, Delvon's and Ewan's cufflinks exploded, and Larken's gown was made of the same stuff her Manse security vest was. Carl claimed to be inspired and hoped the bulletproof material would help protect her at least a little bit. Whether it did or not, Larken knew one thing for sure.

After tonight, nothing would be the same again.

Larken led the way up to the Manor. She didn't need to slow any; the servants waiting to open the doors had sensors that alerted them when someone was coming. The doors opened wide and soft, and murmured conversation met her.

As soon as Larken crossed the threshold, all noise stopped. She'd expected a frenzy—flashing cameras, shouts, security trying to detain her, but there was nothing. Only openmouthed stares. Cameras drooped to the floor and the men and women behind them watched her in disbelief as she walked in with her fellow Faithfuls.

It was the exact opposite of how they sent her out during the TONES Festival.

Everyone seemed to take a collective step back as they filed in. Larken reached the stairs and didn't dare look at any of them as she climbed the first one. The eyes watching her had her more rigid than her sword's blade and more on edge than she should have been. If anything went wrong tonight, it would be these people that suffered —the unseen ones like the reporters, the party goers, and the staff. All their deaths would be on Larken. She could only pray that the majority of them would be smart and get as far away as possible once everyone realized they were there.

Every year, the Manor wore the same decorations for the party. And in the years prior, they never failed to amaze Larken. The same blood-red runners guided the guests to the ballroom at the end of the hall. Old velvet drapes hung from the ceilings, covering paintings, photographs, and other modern touches. Little hovertrays held waxy yellow candles and floated around, casting everything in a vampiric glow. The Military Manor had fully embraced its gothic roots like it did every year, but Larken didn't see any of it as she took her first step down the hall.

She passed by everything in a daze, as if she were a long forgotten specter that wandered the halls of the Manor. Carl taught her a trick in the bunker after she was healed so she didn't wobble in her heels as she led the way. But that didn't change anything. She tried searching for the confidence Carl had hoped to give her by helping her, but none of it mattered. She was still a stranger in this place, and just as unwelcome as if she really were a ghost.

Before, Larken would have spent months looking forward to this event. Not because of the party, but because she could at least pretend people didn't know who she was behind her mask. But the moment at the front door just now told her how wrong she'd been back then. Larken was lost to society for the better part of a month and despite that, she was still recognized under her mask. It was just something else that fueled her rage.

No one said anything behind her as they made their way forward. Larken didn't know if it was because they were too nervous to speak, or if they thought speaking would break her focus, but either way, she was glad for it. She silently poured her heart out to Maxim. He was the only One that could help them now.

*Please,* she pleaded. *Please, if it's true and I have been called for this very moment, be with us and see us through to the tomorrow You promised. I can't live in the dark anymore and I need the sun to rise and chase away my mother's shadows.*

Larken didn't have time to fall to her knees or to do anything else. The stairs that would take them down to the ballroom sat only a few feet away. At the bottom, there would be a set of double doors. They were now the only thing that separated them from Cornella.

Larken faltered, unable to help herself, but picked up her pace once more. The fear inside her of facing Dominic and her mother kept her distracted enough that she didn't think about what would happen if she tripped down the stairs. A single, rough hand reached out and quickly squeezed her shoulder. It was the only support Soren could offer as she crested the stairs. Larken stepped down the first one, and then a second. When she hit the halfway point, two men in yellow masks reached out with glove-covered hands and opened the doors.

Time slowed as Larken moved. The haze she'd been walking through got thicker and muddled her concentration. None of this made any sense. How could things have changed so drastically after she got into the Vixon with Vallen? She was supposed to still be on base, fighting in a war she had nothing to do with. How did she even get here?

*Does it matter?* Larken asked herself.

*No.*

Larken's heel hit the floor too soon and her second one followed. She was here and there was absolutely no turning back. With a deep breath and the power of the Faithfuls behind her, Larken marched confidently forward and stopped just past the double doors.

Hundreds of candles floated in the air, their light playing off the blood-red decorations. The room held a delicious orange glow because of it, and Larken couldn't quite stomp out the little jolt of comfort it gave her. The black cats her mother always used for the party slunk around and demanded attention from the partygoers. The androids came in all shapes and sizes but were covered in the same black fur. Their green eyes were all programed to have the same cat-like intelligence, and for the first time, Larken wondered if the felines were just for show or to spy on the guests. She never would have known if Vallen hadn't mentioned Estelle had a camera inside her. Perhaps this was how Cornella kept her thumb over so many people. After all, what did a drunk guest care if their secrets were spilled in front of an innocent black cat?

At first, no one noticed them. Larken watched the party go on as people laughed and danced. One couple in particular caught her eye. They had matching masks with green and orange feathers that stuck up high over their heads. The man's suite jacket and the woman's dress held the same plumage. Little sparkling lights jumped from feather to feather, surrounding them in faint golden rings as they spun around.

Then there was a gasp followed by the shattering of a glass. Everyone looked to where the commotion was and then stopped what they were doing. The feathered couple faltered mid-spin and stared openmouthed. There were a few more gasps as the music faltered and then died out altogether. Larken hefted her sword as she scanned the crowd.

She first caught sight of her father over at the bar on his usual stool. He appeared more sober than Larken had seen him in years. He grinned at her and gave her an approving dip of his head. That alone almost broke her. Swallowing past the lump in her throat, she kept going until she found who she was searching for.

Larken didn't register Liam standing off to the side in his blue suit and mask, or Dominic in his black suit and red mask. She only saw Corella Hale glaring daggers into her from across the room. The woman was as stunning as usual in a deep emerald ballgown with a matching yellow and gold mask. Her hair was still pulled back into its signature twist, just as her lips were stained their usual red.

She sneered, and the fear that Larken expected to feel wasn't there. Instead, there was only a deep sorrow for the woman who let such ugly emotions lead her to this awful darkness. That, and a surge of courage Larken could only credit Maxim for.

Larken lifted her chin and grinned, riding that burst of confidence and refusing to be meek for the first time in her life. "Hello, Mother. Miss me?"

# CHAPTER 43

"Well, if it isn't my ungrateful daughter. Or should I call you *Magnate Hale* now?"

Larken gripped the hilt of her sword tighter.

The crowd parted as smoothly as if it were water, and Cornella stepped down from the stage. She seamlessly placed her champagne flute on a tray that a terrified staff member held. Larken didn't know his name, but even with the mask, she recognized the older man. He'd always smiled at her when he saw her. She stared at him until he met her eyes, then flicked her gaze to the hidden door next to the stage. The man nodded ever-so-slightly and backed effortlessly into the crowd. He must have understood her silent order completely, because he encouraged other staff members, and even a few guests, to follow him.

Larken knew she wasn't going to get another chance, so she held her sword out for the person nearest her to take. Instead of Vallen or Delvon reaching out, like she expected, Carl took the weapon nervously. Larken glanced at his face and saw it was stony, but his hand still shook as he wrapped his fingers around the hilt. She sent as much silent confidence his way as she could and then brought her hands up to her hair. She pulled it up into a bun as Cornella prowled forward. The woman moved as if she was some horrible spider-cat-hybrid that was finally catching its prey.

Cornella smiled, barring her fangs behind red lips. She had done the same thing in Larken's nightmare right before she pushed her. It was only when she stood a few feet away that Larken realized her mother's mask had little yellow roses around the border.

She had a sudden vision of tackling her mother to the ground and whacking her in the face repeatedly with that stupid mask.

"Don't you think you're a little too old to be playing pretend?" Cornella asked in a hushed voice that still carried throughout the room. "You should know by now that no one wants you. Not as the Magnate, and not as a Hale."

Larken tried not to let the words affect her. She always knew her mother felt this way, but hearing them for the first time from Cornella's own lips…

Cornella noticed Larken's hesitation and smirked. For a moment, Larken didn't do anything. She took in the people and masks around her, and her eyes drifted back over to the bar. The yellow mask her father wore had been pushed up on his forehead like a pair of sunglasses, and his familiar brown eyes followed her every movement. When he caught her gaze, he smiled again and lifted his glass to her.

Larken's childhood hit her in full force as the pink liquid quivered in the whiskey glass. When he was sober, he would throw Larken princess parties. He would dress up with her and bring her down to the bar. There he would have one of the kitchen staff come over and fix them some pink lemonade to drink. It happened so rarely that Larken thought those moments nothing more than a dream. But Trogar was there, sober, waiting for his little girl to change the world.

Larken turned back to her mother. "Please, Mother. You've done enough. Stand down."

"You think a little brat like you can tell me what to do?" Cornella's lip curled. "You—whose only accomplishment was *ruining my life?*"

"You did that all on your own, *Mother*. All I am—all I ever was—is the woman *you* turned me into."

Larken's words found their mark and Cornella seethed, "You've never been a Hale. You've only ever been a Fillmar."

"I'm more of a Hale than you'll ever be," Larken said, holding her right hand out for her sword and pulling her gun free with the left.

Carl made to hand it back, but a gunshot sounded from somewhere in the crowd. Larken stilled as screams filled the ballroom. No one moved as fear surrounded them with its dark embrace. Larken searched frantically, trying to find the shooter. She couldn't, but she caught sight of a man in a yellow mask moving his lips with a finger pressed to his ear. She narrowed her eyes, trying to make out what the man was saying.

"Larken, move!" Dominic shouted.

She didn't even think. She lurched to the right, only for her handgun to catch the bullet meant for her heart. It flew back out of her hand and exploded. The bullets that were never supposed to mix did, and erupted in smoke, fire, and bright light. Chaos broke loose as Larken steadied herself and pulled free the dagger Wardell gave her. Guests screamed and shoved each other to get out of the ballroom. More people than Larken could count in the confusion pulled out their weapons and charged into the smoke—their yellow masks a beacon that named them as Vigilants.

Larken couldn't see any of her friends and panic gripped her heart. What if one of them had gotten hurt from the explosion?

She turned back around just in time for a large man to collide with her. The man continued on as if nothing had happened, but Larken hit the ground hard. The glass dagger went skidding out of her hand and into the smoke. Cornella's laugh sounded over the panicked screams and Larken turned her face to her mother. She snarled and got to her feet. Using her thumb, Larken made sure the ring Brecker got her was pointing straight out and marched up to her mother. Cornella's smile faltered as Larken pulled her arm back and punched her in the face.

With a scowl still on her face, Cornella whipped back around to face her daughter. Larken stood her ground and gave a Delvon-like feral grin. A sharp angle in the bridge told Larken her mother's nose was broken. Blood trickled from both of Cornella's nostrils in thick rivulets down and around her lips to her chin. Crimson dripped down to her chest and landed just above the dress's neckline. Cornella didn't seem to notice as she disappeared back into a crowd of yellow-masked Vigilants. Larken rushed forward but was scooped up by two men she didn't recognize immediately.

"It's been a while, Cadet Hale."

Larken's middle burned as little flames danced around the scar on her stomach.

*Dominic's Second.*

Soren never told her his name, but that didn't change the way her side tingled.

"I'm afraid that we didn't get to spend anywhere *near* enough time together," he said, pressing his fingers into the spot where he stabbed her.

Larken lunged and shoved, trying to get away. She managed to pull her right hand free and punched out. One guy was caught in the eye, and another one in the mouth. Larken felt more than heard a tooth go loose and the man backed away, choking on his blood for a moment. People screamed and ran as a few gunshots sounded from behind her. She didn't know what was happening with her friends, but she knew that no help would come for her in the next few minutes. She brought her fist back again, only for it to be caught by the Second.

He dug a finger into the weak spot at her wrist and her hand went numb. The Second yanked her to him and Larken stumbled over her feet. She fell into his chest and he used his other hand to grip her neck. He rubbed his thumb back and forth over her jugular.

"Do you know how easy it would be to kill you right now?" he asked. "All it would take is…one…little…" he pressed into her skin hard enough to make her head pound, "touch."

Larken tried to think, but it was like moving a spoon through thick molasses. She groped at his hip, trying to find a weapon of any kind as she rasped, "You can't kill me. Dominic would never allow it."

The Second's hand tightened around her neck. "You think I answer to that lunatic? That I just come running whenever he snaps his fingers?"

"You're all pathetic," Larken wheezed out. She gave up her search for a weapon and clawed at his hand.

"What do you know? You have no idea what Dominic has planned for you." He tightened his grip again and the pounding in Larken's head doubled. "You should be begging me to kill you."

Finally, he let go, and Larken gasped for air. She crumpled a bit as she went dizzy. Her forehead ended up pressed to his chest and her shoes came into view. Thinking quick, Larken kicked her foot against the Second's leg. He only laughed at her feeble attempt to fight back, but she didn't care and kept kicking until she felt the latch go loose. She brought her knee up and waited for the heel to fall off. Larken slammed the hidden dagger down in full force onto her captor's foot.

Dominic's Second roared and released her. Larken wobbled on the blade tip and fell into the other man that held her. In one swift motion, he hoisted her up over his shoulder and stripped her feet bare. Larken fought the action but used her new vantage point to take in the scene behind her.

The smoke cleared enough for her to see Brecker and Hinlee standing back-to-back, shooting tech-guns loaded with who knew what. Enough Vigilants encircled them that Brecker didn't seem to want to leave Hinlee to fight on her own. Loxly stood in the back by the doors and took careful aim with his shotgun. Glass littered the floor around him, as well as rubble from the pillars that flanked the double doors. Chunks of stone had been blown from the white columns and blocked the doors. Ezra, Jodi, and Candy stood by with handguns and med-kits, waiting to help. They took aim when they could but mostly just stood back with tight grips on the kits.

Shadric's team had already disappeared into the masses while other Faithfuls stood on the other side of the doors and fought to get in.

Carl was nowhere to be seen and Larken could only pray that he was somewhere safe. Her sword was missing too, and panic gripped her insides. She sought out Vallen—hoping that he might somehow have it, but he didn't. Both Vallen and Soren had five Vigilants on them apiece. They fought tooth and nail, using whatever opening they could to try and get to Larken.

Vallen held his handgun and sword, aiming for thighs and feet in an attempt to down as many people as possible. Whenever one person fell, another was in their place a second later. Soren, on the other hand, slashed out with his glaive. The moment was horrific and terrible, but Soren's movements were as beautiful as ever. The fierce scowl on his face didn't soften as he swept and cut. The teal sash Carl gave him was knotted under the blade and only added to the beauty of it all. Soren was meant to use it as a tourniquet if he needed, but he had wanted the cloth where he could see it. He hadn't told Larken why and she hadn't had time to ask before they set out.

"Larken!" Vallen shouted, bringing her back to her senses.

She wiggled and fought, trying to get down. The man that held her reached up and slapped her rear end and surprised her so much that she stilled.

"Always wanted to do that!" he joked—to who, she didn't know. Larken could only assume more people came to help him with her. There were too many of Cornella's soldiers and not enough of them. They were getting overwhelmed.

Larken grabbed a handful of the man's hair and yanked it back as hard as she could. It was a mistake. The man cried out and jerked before he lost his balance and fell backwards—Larken still in his arms. Larken threw her hands up to protect herself as her world tilted, but strong hands caught her waist before she could fall any further. For the briefest moment she thought that maybe Vallen had gotten to her.

She'd been wrong.

The Second pulled her back to him once more. Larken kicked out, trying to get at anyone within reach. Her shoes laid uselessly on the ground. Around her, guests screamed and rushed to whatever exits they could find. People in yellow masks ran around, the coverings marking themselves as the enemy. Security guards fought as well, picking and choosing their sides. Larken no longer cared if they wore a mask or not. If anyone in this moment chose to side with her mother, then they would share whatever fate was destined for them all.

Together, the remnants of Dominic's old squad gathered around Larken and her captor. The Second had a tight grip on her bicep and yanked her after him. The pushed and shoved through the crowd, ignoring how much she fought, and soon had her out of sight of her friends. She called out to them—to Vallen, Soren, Delvon, Loxly—to anyone who might be able to hear her over the fighting. They took her past the bar, and she looked around frantically for her father.

Trogar had abandoned his stool and drink and was helping people escape through the hidden door behind the bar. He caught sight of her just as the last person disappeared, and his mouth fell open. Larken couldn't hear him, but he mouthed her name and turned to get to her. A Faithful caught him before he could get very far. The two shouted at each other while Trogar threw his arms around and pointed at Larken. The Faithful wasn't very patient with him. As poor a leader as he had been, he was still the Luminary and needed to be protected.

Trogar shouted her name once more, and this time Larken heard him faintly over the chaos around her. The Faithful reached his limit and escorted Trogar out of the ballroom.

There was a bang, and Larken jerked so she could see what was happening. The doors had been successfully forced open and Faithfuls spilled into the ballroom. The screams and shouts only got louder as the fighting increased. Soon there was a Faithful for every Vigilant, and only the bravest of the party guests watched on from the shadows. There were even a few reporters and cameramen that seemed to have a death wish as they got as close as they could to get the perfect shot.

One braver than all the rest jumped out in front of their little group and called, "Magnate Hale!"

Larken watched in horror as Dominic's Second raised his gun and shot the young man in the chest. He stared down at his chest as blood spread across his white button up, then looked back up to Larken. He dropped his camera and then staggered a step. Larken screamed, unable to pull her eyes away from him.

Dominic's Second spun her around and blocked the sight before her.

"He didn't *do* anything!" Her voice caught as the image played over and over in her mind. It was happening again—just like when that young pilot who was just trying to fly Larken to base. People were dying because of her. "What's wrong with you?" she demanded, trying to stay on top of her emotions.

"He got in my way."

"I thought you didn't answer to Dominic?" Larken challenged.

"Shut up," he growled, lip quivering in anger.

She shook her head. "You're so full of it. You talk big but when it really comes down to it, you're nothing but a puppet. Do you even have thoughts of your own or do you just believe everything you're told to belie—"

The Second used the hand holding the pistol to punch her in the jaw. Larken bit her tongue and stumbled into the man next to her, despite the tight grip still holding her bicep. Her ears rang, and her jaw and cheek throbbed. She didn't dare lift a hand to cover the pain, though. Instead, she lashed out. She fought with renewed vigor, scratching and kicking at everyone who got too close. The man who caught her fall tackled her and she latched on to him. Before they hit the ground, she sunk her teeth into his right ear.

"That's enough!" the Second called out. "Just get her out of here!"

The men worked together to scoop Larken up despite her thrashing and screaming. She had no weapon, no way of escape.

The members of Squad 22 moved in closer, each one grabbing ahold of one of her limbs. She was trapped and would be handed over to Dominic at any moment.

Only, the Squad 22 Captain was nowhere to be seen.

Neither was Cornella.

# CHAPTER 44

S oren shouted and grunted as he fought off the onslaught of Vigilants. He didn't miss the fact that Squad 22 had carried Larken off, or that Liam had ducked out of the ballroom with the others. For someone who had been raised to take over the *Military* District, he looked ready to either cry or throw up. Cornella let her group of guards whisk her away to the top of the stage where she stayed and watched from the shadows.

The irony had Soren gritting his teeth and lashing out that much harder. She'd played the part of director, moving armies here and starting fires there. All of it was some grand scheme just to stay in the spotlight she was never meant to have.

No wonder Fisher dumped her.

Larken screamed, stilling Soren's heart as ice filled his veins. Frantically, his eyes darted to the spot he last saw her. She was gone. Panic gripped him in its oily clutches as his lungs protested his next breath. He kept searching, but she was nowhere to be seen. Soren looked over his shoulder and yelled, "Vallen!"

"Go!" he ordered. "We've got things handled here."

Soren didn't need to be told twice. He cut down the man in front of him and didn't even wait for the skewed mask to fall and hit the floor before Soren hopped over the body and ran. All around him were crazed people, either fighting or fleeing. A few stupid ones stayed to watch. A cameraman laid dead on the ground a few feet ahead. Soren almost ignored him, but caught sight of a group of Vigilants near the body rushing out of the ballroom. They were suspicious enough that the hair on Soren's arms stood up, so he followed them.

It was slow going getting through the crowd of fighters. No one was evenly matched, and it only added to the confusion. There could be three Vigilants to every one Faithful, or five Faithfuls to every two Vigilants. Weapons of all sorts swung through the air while gunfire acted as the composition to the fighting. Soren bobbed and weaved, dodging what he could. It wasn't until he stepped on the blade of a sword that he skidded and fell to his knee. A topaz mace swung back over a Vigilant's head as he took on two Faithfuls and went right through where Soren's face was a few seconds ago. Soren's heart fell down past his stomach and he moved his foot out of the way so he could get a good look at the sword that saved his life.

A familiar carbon infused crystal blade stared up at him.

Soren growled deep in his throat as he snatched it up. He scanned the ballroom quickly for any signs of Carl, but the stylist was nowhere to be found. Soren surged to his feet and quickly helped his fellow Faithfuls cut down the man with the mace. He didn't wait around after slicing through the back of the Vigilant's thigh and ran for the door.

Soren charged into the hall the group had gone through. The floating candles, blood-red curtains, and runners spilled into this hallway, as well, and Soren vaguely remembered there being a bathroom down this way from back when Vallen gave them the Manor breakdown. The Vigilant group was nowhere in sight, and there was no sign that Larken was even with them. Despite that, he couldn't just turn back without at least checking. He would rather waste three minutes in here than the alternative.

He only got three steps in before a smarmy voice drawled, "It's so like you to follow her."

She was here, and Braves had no idea that he just helped him.

Soren gently tossed Larken's sword onto the bunched up hem of one of the velvet curtains. He gripped the handle of his glaive tightly and got into a readied stance. "Get out here, Braves, and face me like a man."

"You'd like that, wouldn't you? You're nothing but a murderous heathen."

"I'm not the one setting fires and drugging innocent women."

A dagger flew out from behind a crimson curtain and missed Soren's head by a few inches.

"You're a Captain. Shouldn't you know better than to let your emotions get the better of you?" Soren couldn't help the jab. He already knew Braves was unhinged, but he was glad to know that it was now affecting his fighting.

Braves came out from where he was hiding, a crazed sneer on his face and a dagger in each hand. Looking at him, Soren almost felt bad for his fallen comrade. He'd lost weight and Soren could tell his eyes were sunken even with the red mask in the way.

Another feeling of déjà vu washed over him. They'd been here before, back when Soren walked out of Connie Dayton's office. Braves was waiting for him then, too. Only that time, he'd been trying to—

"Where's Larken?" Soren snarled.

"Finally safe from *you*," Braves answered triumphantly. "She's on her way to the perfect life I promised her. The one that *Captain Soren Deckard* keeps interfering with."

"She doesn't want you."

"And you think she wants you?" Braves laughed. "You're nothing more than a mongrel. You're no better than one of those mutts she fawns over. Don't you get it?"

Soren's jaw ticked.

"She doesn't love you. She's *adopted* you. You're nothing more than a charity case to her. You were nice to her and now she's repaying you—that's all."

Soren knew what Braves was doing. The man didn't stand still.

He kept moving, hoping to attack the moment he found a weak spot. Soren just let him talk and work himself up, using the time to take stock of his enemy. Several dagger pommels poked up over a cumber bun that was the same shade of blood-red as Brave's mask. He probably thought he was being clever, wearing red instead of yellow. Soren had no idea why the man always seemed to be in red, but it didn't really matter.

Braves thought he would be the victor in this fight, but he was wrong. Soren was going to do whatever he could to stop him. The man had no idea how much his life was going to change in these next few moments. Soren didn't honestly know what was in store for them either, but one thing was for sure...

Larken would be leaving here tonight a free woman.

"Aren't you tired of being second best?" Soren asked. "Larken told me what you did, you know. What must it be like to know that the only way you could get to her was to take everything else away first?"

Braves slashed out with a dagger that Soren caught with the handle of his glaive. "Shut up!"

"Even then your plan didn't work out. Delvon and Shadric were there, waiting to take Squad 19's place."

Braves lunged again. This time, Soren missed the blade and Braves's wrist hit the handle instead. The Star shouted in pain and brought his other hand up. He stabbed Soren in the shoulder that had been patched up after his visit to the Manse. Soren grunted in pain, but Braves shouted over it.

"Just shut up, Deckard! You don't have any idea what you're talking about!"

"Don't I? How many times have you lied to her? How many times did you go behind her back and cut off another escape route?"

Braves seethed and pulled a second dagger free. He slashed out, catching more of Soren's arms and thighs than Soren would have liked. Soren got in his fair share of nicks and slices too, but he didn't dare stop talking.

"That's what you did. You trapped her. You kept her from being able to have any other option than you."

Braves feigned an attack from above and then ducked down to stab Soren in the back of the knee. Soren roared in agony, and his heart leapt up to his throat. He could only pray that Braves missed the artery back there and that he wouldn't bleed out before he got to Larken.

Soren's arms shook as he fought the pain, but he still forced his hands to move. He raised his glaive and brought the butt of it down on top of the soft spot between Braves's shoulder and neck. The Star grunted and fell back, leaving the dagger in place. Soren's leg wobbled horribly, but he pushed through it and managed to stay standing. He knew that as soon as his adrenaline was gone that he would be nothing more than a useless, bleeding lump on the floor.

Hopefully one that *didn't* die.

They continued to fight, dancing around each other and getting in blows when they could. Soren bided his time, knowing that the seconds he counted were everything. He didn't want to move too soon, despite the seconds feeling like hours.

Heaving, Soren grunted, "It's because deep down you know that she'd never choose you—that she never loved you."

"I said shut up!" Braves shouted, panting as if he'd just run ten miles.

"*She'll never want you,*" Soren gritted out as he jerked back and lunged.

Something in the air snapped and they no longer held back. Braves fought to kill him, and Soren fought to live for Larken. They lunged, slashed at each other with their blades, and moved in and out of each other's reaches. Soren blocked what he could, but needing both hands to wield his weapon, he couldn't do much to block his legs. Braves got in several more stabs, and even thought it wasn't the time, Soren made a note to rub it in Larken's face the next time she complained about her stab wound.

He needed to get back to her—he'd promised. His gaze flicked down to the teal sash around his glaive. Soren had a life planned for the two of them. He wanted to take her to the sea. They hadn't had any time to talk about what her being Magnate would mean for the two of them yet, but he knew that the ocean was where she belonged. He also knew that wherever she was, that's exactly where he wanted to be, too.

"You'll never have her," Braves hissed.

Soren let go of his glaive only long enough to punch him.

Braves's head jerked back, and his mask went flying. He barred his teeth and snarled as he whipped his head back around. Three white lines glowed in the candlelight, marring his left cheek.

Everything that Braves ever did to Larken gathered into a black ball and slammed into Soren's gut. He wanted to *take* her from him. Braves wanted to steal Larken away and never let her see the light of day ever again. The Star promised her love, but he only had suffocating darkness to give.

"I'll die before I let you kill her," Soren growled.

Braves yelled and threw a dagger at him. Soren deflected it, catching the blade with the knuckles of his left hand. Pain numbed them and the butt of his glaive dropped to the floor. Soren flexed his hand and gripped the handle tighter with the other. Braves pulled two more daggers free and used the opening to rush at him.

He clasped both hands around the pommel of the dagger and brought it up overhead. Soren lifted his forearm to block it. He caught the blade and shouted as it went through all the way. He didn't dare look up at the damage above him. Instead, he stared deep into the Star's eyes and the glaive went through Braves's chest.

The Star coughed and blood spittled out past his lips and freckled his chin. He gasped once—twice—before blinking slowly. "She's...mine..."

Soren used the glaive to yank the man forward. He got in Braves's face and growled, "Don't worry," he threw Braves's own words back at him, "I was just doing *what Miss Hale wanted.*"

Braves's eyes widened, hopefully remembering back to the very first time he tried to take her from Soren. The man rasped a wet breath in an effort to reply, but the words died on his lips as Dominic slumped onto the glaive.

Without thinking, Soren helped Braves to the floor and freed his glaive. Then he pulled out the dagger in his arm and tossed it to the ground next to the Star. Soren yanked his tie free and tied it just above his knee before pulling the dagger out. His leg still wobbled dangerously. It would give out any second, but he pleaded with it to hold him until he could get Larken back to Vallen. He didn't care what happened to him after that.

Larken just needed to be safe.

Soren scooped up Larken's sword and ran the best he could down the hall. Thankfully, it didn't take him long to hear voices. He reached the end of the hall and turned right.

The group poked and prodded at Larken, nicking her with daggers or running the barrels of their handguns along her arms. They would have strict orders not to harm her, but Soren was willing to bet they were trying to scare her as much as they could get away with. She was so small standing there against the wall with a bleeding lip and no shoes. Even from where he stood, Soren could see her mind working behind her eyes. She was looking for a way out of this despite everything. Soren was glad for once that she didn't try and fight back. He couldn't imagine what those five, full grown men could do to her.

Soren didn't wait to assess the scene—his leg wouldn't allow it. He got as close as he could before lashing out with his glaive. Soren caught the man closest to him in the neck, successfully taking him to the ground. Using Larken's sword, he caught another on in the back of the thigh. Confused shouts sounded around them and Larken leapt for Braves's Second. The man didn't even know he was officially Captain now as Larken produced a handgun from somewhere on him. She barred her teeth as she pressed it against his stomach, right where he stabbed her, and pulled the trigger.

He cried out and fell. Larken didn't waste any more time on him, as if she knew that ignoring him would be an even bigger blow than ending his life. Soren handed Larken her sword and together, the two of them incapacitated the rest of Squad 22. Once she was able, Larken rushed to him and wrapped her arms around him so tightly that he gasped out in pain.

"Careful," he grunted. "I have it on good authority that bleeding out on a woman and dying is a pretty stupid thing to do."

Larken pulled back and took him in. Her eyes went wide as they looked over his injuries. "What *happened?*"

She grabbed his arm since it was the first thing she saw and looked over the stab wound. Larken undid his tie and retied it more securely under his elbow.

He ignored her question. "Is there a different way to get to the ballroom? We can't go back the way I came."

She dropped her gaze to the small puddle of blood on the floor. "Soren—"

"We don't have time to talk. I need to get to Levi." He shifted his leg back so she couldn't see. Pain shot up his thigh and his leg nearly gave out then. "Or anyone else with a med-kit. I'm not picky."

Even though he knew Larken was more than capable of seeing to his injuries, she didn't have anything to patch him up with. Nor did he want her seeing him like this. She would only blame herself.

She nodded, the worry never leaving her eyes. "Through here."

Larken grabbed his injured arm and wrapped it around her shoulders. Soren tried not to lean on her too much, but was grateful for the support. She helped him to the door and twisted the knob. When she pulled it open, screams spilled out into the hall. Fifteen or twenty party guests huddled together, quivering in fear. Larken gently pulled Soren to the side.

"You all need to get out of here. Now," she ordered.

The partygoers didn't wait around to be told again. Skirts, suit jackets, and masks all rushed past them. Larken waited until the passage was clear before helping Soren in. The door fell heavy behind them and Larken led them through the dark. She helped him get to the other end of the passage and then fiddled with the door. He heard her fingernails scrape against the wood as she twisted the knob, then she pushed her free shoulder into the door and shoved it open.

She helped Soren out and they took in the ballroom. The smoke had nearly cleared, as well as most of the guests. Neither Ezra nor Levi was in sight. Instead, Carl sat about a hundred feet away, trying to stop the bleeding of a man who already seemed to be dead. Soren's heart immediately went out to the man. As soon as Larken saw, her breath hitched.

Soren wobbled and his knee buckled. He was going to have to tell Larken.

"Go get Carl's med-kit."

"Soren?"

"I can't—" he collapsed. Landing hard on his bad knee.

Larken fretted over him, trying to find his injury. She was wasting time and she didn't even know it.

"Larken. The kit!"

She gave him one last worried look and rushed over to Carl.

She dropped to his side and set her sword down. Larken gingerly pulled Carl's hands from the body. Soren kneeled between two potted plants by the secret door, but even from there he could see the tears on Carl's face. Larken reached up and cupped his cheeks. His horrified, wide-eyed expression crumpled, and he buried his face into her shoulder. The med-kit laid off to the side, unattended, and Larken looked back over at Soren with a torn expression. She didn't know just how badly he was hurt, and now she didn't know who to help.

Vallen used his sword to cut through a Vigilant's stomach and then shot them as they fell. Spinning, he caught sight of Larken in the center of the ballroom. The man moved slower than he had before Soren left him, but still fought to make his way to her. Soren gulped a deep breath and pushed all the strength he had to his leg. He needed Carl's med-kit. Then, if he was lucky, someone would be able to help. Larken could, but Soren wanted her to get to Vallen before—

Cornella held her gown in fists as she stormed down the stage steps. Larken didn't notice, her focus still on Carl. Soren pushed to his feet and smothered a cry as his leg fully crumpled under his weight. His glaive skidded across the white-wood floors away from him. A tech-gun he didn't recognize sat several feet to his left, closer to the bar than to him. Fear for Larken turned his blood cold and he tried crawling to it, but the back of his thigh protested the motion, and Soren hissed out a breath of pain. He watched as Vallen lifted his handgun and pulled the trigger. Soren didn't know if it was his imagination or if he could really hear it, but the empty click echoed all the way over to Soren. Everyone was too far away stop her.

Soren could only shout, but as he opened his mouth, Cornella reached her daughter.

*No. No, Maxim. Please, not like this…*

Larken placed a hand on the back of Carl's head just as her mother reached out. Soren couldn't look away. He was going to watch her die and he couldn't do anything to stop it. Cornella grabbed ahold of Larken's bun and yanked her back. Larken cried out and brought her hands up to her hair. She twisted and thrashed, trying to break free. Soren dug his nails into the floor to try and pull himself forward, but his hands only slid against it pathetically. He brought his good knee up to his side in an attempt to push himself toward the gun, but his bleeding knee only had the other slipping and sliding. This was how it was going to end for them.

They might as well be worlds apart.

Larken swept out with her leg and tried to reach her sword. Carl barely had any time to realize what was happening before a Vigilant appeared behind Cornella and shot him. Soren flinched at the sound. Carl's left shoulder jerked and he went sprawling to the ground. Candy screamed somewhere in the distance and Larken stilled, shock covering her face. Soren's throat went tight as he realized that this was probably the last he was going to see Larken. Vallen doubled his speed and Soren could only pray that the man could do what Soren was unable to.

# CHAPTER 45

arken's feet slipped and slid against the ballroom floor as she fought Cornella's death grip. She was only now just realizing how much blood was on the ground around her. She let go of her mother's fingers and started punching at the woman's wrist blindly. The ring connected with flesh and Cornella released her grip enough that Larken could get away. Her hair fell in chunks from her bun, but the hair tie still clung to what it could.

Cornella hadn't dragged her very far and Larken lunged for her sword. A hand grabbed onto the back of her skirts and she stumbled back. Vallen stood out of the corner of Larken's eye, reloading his gun.

"Vallen!"

He looked up just as something sharp and excruciating stabbed Larken's left shoulder. Larken screamed and Cornella yanked her back by her hair again and pressed a topaz dagger to her throat. Larken's own blood dripped from the blade and onto her neck.

"No one move!" she ordered. Then she turned her lips to her daughter's ear and said in a voice only Larken could hear, "You were a disappointment then, just like you are now. How many times do you need to injure that shoulder of yours before you learn?"

The weight of everything she'd done wrong leading up to this moment came crashing down on her.

The ballroom floor was suddenly cold under her feet. Larken's gaze drifted first to her abandoned heels and then to her sword. Carl bled freely only a few feet away, and a puddle was slowly overtaking her blade.

"Cornella, don't do this! Let her go!"

The blade dug deeper into her throat, almost enough to draw blood. "Drop your weapons, *General Maxwell.*"

Vallen bent slowly, setting his sword and handgun on the ground. He kicked them away and before he stood up, Larken caught sight of Loxly standing behind him, shotgun aimed just over Larken's shoulder. Delvon stood off to Loxly's left, hands empty and twitching. Larken knew the bodyguard well enough to know that as soon as he had an opening to get to her, he would.

Vallen held his hands out and took a step forward. Cornella stood her ground and pressed harder on the dagger. The pain that should have been there was dulled by the one in her shoulder, but still, a warm trickle made its way down Larken's throat.

Vallen stilled again, following the blood with his eyes.

Cornella yanked Larken a step back so they stood between two of her men. The Vigilants both held tech-guns and shifted them to Larken's head. Cold breath escaped past her lips and her ears rang. Everything was muffled and Larken knew that this was the end. She'd failed.

This time, there would be no saving her.

There would be no tomorrow.

Vallen opened his mouth, but Larken couldn't make out a single thing he said. Her mother laughed behind her, but her words were muffled too. The only sound Larken could make out was her own heartbeat.

In a haze, Larken took one last look around.

Hinlee sat in a corner tying her train around Brecker's arm. Ewan had a bit of her train on him, too. He leaned against the wall behind them, putting pressure on his thigh. Levi sat close by, holding Candy back as she cried and watched Carl bleed all over the ballroom floor. Shadric and his team were all in a group and being held at gunpoint. The five of them were outnumbered two to one.

As for Soren…he was still by himself, hurt and unable to move. That part hurt her the most. The pearl was a heavy weight around her neck, reminding her that the one man who was so afraid of being left alone was now going to die apart from his friends.

Larken closed her eyes and was at that spot again. Her new home stood behind her as she watched Soren wade knee deep into the waves. They were supposed to be there. They were supposed to have their chance.

A single hot tear worked its way out of the corner of her eye.

It was all over.

*Maxim, please don't let us suffer.*

Slowly, Larken was able to force her eyes open. Something had changed, but she couldn't quite put a finger on it. She looked around the ballroom again, and then a third time. She was halfway through her fourth when she realized that the tech-gun that was just out of Soren's reach was now in his hands. No one had so much as shifted, and Larken couldn't figure out what had happened until a slight movement by the bar caught her eye.

A familiar hand reached up and slowly pulled the whiskey glass of pink lemonade back. Larken had no idea what her father was doing, and she honestly wasn't sure she if was glad to see him. She didn't want him to get hurt any more than her friends, but he still had the power of the districts on his side. He could do more away from here and safe than if he died right along with the rest of them.

Unable to hear Larken's silent pleas to find safety, Trogar reached his hand back and then flung the glass up over the bar. The glass exploded on the wood floor and Cornella cut Larken a little deeper in surprise. Loxly used the opportunity to shoot the man to her right. He crumpled and Cornella's grip loosened just enough that Larken risked raising her arm and elbowing her mother in the stomach.

Cornella dropped the dagger as the wind was knocked from her lungs. Larken escaped her grasp and rolled away. She'd barely stopped moving before Delvon dropped on top of her.

"Stop trying to die, Peach," he grunted in her ear. "You're the Magnate, don't forget, and you're making it incredibly hard to keep you safe."

Larken ignored him as she watched her mother internally combust. Her cheeks went red and she scowled down at Larken. Larken fought Delvon and tried to get to her sword, but Delvon only crushed her closer to the floor and grunted, "Let someone else handle it for once, will ya?"

Blood still covered Cornella's face, though it looked like her nose had stopped bleeding. She turned to the man at her left with a closed-mouth scowl and yanked the tech-gun out of his hands. The guard wasn't expecting it and stumbled a step back.

Larken readied herself for the impact. Delvon pulled her closer and dipped his head into her neck. He was feeling guilty too, she knew it. He was asked to do one thing, and up until now, he'd been able to do it. Larken had truly been safe with him.

Cornella aimed at Larken and sent a scathing glare her way. Then a cruel smile twisted her lips and she lifted the gun and pulled the trigger. She never broke eye contact and there was a small explosion from the barrel of the tech-gun. Larken pushed against Delvon, needing to see who'd been hit. She shoved him off of her enough to turn.

Vallen staggered back—falling to his knees as his hand went to his chest.

*No. NO!*

Larken shrieked and clawed at the ground as her eyes burned. She didn't care that she was injured and didn't have a weapon— Cornella was going to pay. All Larken's life she'd been neglected, abused, and tortured by this woman. Never before had Larken felt this level of animosity for Cornella. This time, she'd gone too far. Vallen was all Larken ever had that brought her happiness in this Manor of hatred and lies. Cornella couldn't get away with this. Her mother only dropped the gun at its owner's feet before throwing her head back and laughing.

"You're too easy, my dear. I honestly don't know how Captain Braves couldn't figure you out sooner."

Cornella lifted her hand and moved her index finger around in a circle. The Vigilants moved, putting themselves in front of Loxly, Soren, and anyone else who had a weapon. Larken only barely registered what happened as she stared in horror as Vallen slumped forward. He threw a hand out to catch himself, but it slipped in his growing puddle of blood and he hit the ground. Larken fought Delvon again and managed to slip through his hold. In the confusion, he kicked her sword away and she watched helplessly as it skidded closer to Vallen. Larken gritted her teeth and searched frantically for something else to use. Delvon scrambled after her, demanding that she come back. Larken ignored him as her rage over the last twenty-one years filled her.

"I figured out the Captain's little plan, you know," Cornella continued as if she hadn't just shot Vallen, that vile smirk she always wore on her face. "He built a house for you in Thresh. He was planning on taking you away. It's just a pity *all* of his plans failed."

Larken scooped up a dinner knife that had been dropped on the ground.

"He tried to kill Vallen first. Clearly he failed. But who would have guessed that the General was the leader of the Faithfuls, too? Of course, I'm just guessing here, but it all makes so much sense."

"Shut up!" Larken shouted.

"Now, is that any way to speak to your mother?"

Larken leapt in, sliced at Cornella's arm, and then jumped back just as a gun went off. The woman screamed as blood ran freely down her bicep. A bullet flew from the right through the spot that Larken had been standing. Cornella scowled down at her arm again and then back up at Larken. For the first time in her whole life, Larken saw fear there.

Larken lifted her knife again. The ballroom was mostly empty, and she stood far enough away from Cornella that a Vigilant could easily hit her. None of them did, though. She could only assume it was because they were afraid of what she would do to them if Cornella lost. And it would seem that her mother was having the same thoughts. The Faithfuls stood ready, waiting for Larken to give the order.

"It's over, Cornella," Larken said. "Give up."

"*Never.*" She turned to the man on her right and shouted, "Do something!"

The man gathered up his gun.

Larken lunged for her mother and shouted, "Now!"

A commotion broke out behind her as the Faithfuls started up the fight again. Shots rang out and Cornella threw her hands up in front of her face. She ducked and ordered, "Kill her!"

The Vigilant only hesitated for a moment, and then shot Larken.

First there was pain, then warmth. It would seem that the dress wasn't as strong as they'd all hoped. Larken stared down but couldn't quite see where she was hit. She brought her hand up and felt dampness right where her stomach was. She couldn't see the injury, but Larken knew that the bullet didn't go all the way through. She glanced up just in time to see Cornella lunge for her.

She shoved Larken back, and Larken fell, just as she had in her dream.

People shouted her name in the distance, but again Larken couldn't make out much. Not until she hit the ground.

Air exploded out of her lungs and she couldn't catch it again. Cornella laughed before scooping up her gown and grabbing her topaz dagger. She descended on Larken again, and two more shots rang out. Larken turned her head in time to see Delvon go down. His face was turned away and Larken couldn't tell if her friend was even still alive. Soren was supposed to be somewhere behind him over by the wall, but he wasn't there anymore.

Everyone was disappearing.

Larken tried to call out an order and demand someone help her fallen friends, but Cornella was on her again. She pried the knife out of Larken's hands and threw it away. Then Cornella yanked Larken up by the hair once more. Larken panted, still barely able to breathe. Her world went hazy in a dizzying sort of way that made it hard for her to keep her head up.

She lifted her head enough that she could at least see Vallen one last time before she died, but he was gone, too. A little red trail led off somewhere, but Larken was too tired to follow it.

"You took everything from me, you little brat, and now you're going to pay," Cornella hissed in her ear.

She yanked Larken's head back and held the dagger against her throat again.

"Get your filthy hands off my daughter."

Cornella spun, taking Larken with her. Vallen stood, bleeding everywhere, with Larken's sword raised high.

"You just don't know when to die, do you?"

"Sorry to disappoint, *Lumina*," Vallen grunted before he lunged.

Cornella screamed and dropped Larken. She dove to the side and stabbed Vallen in the thigh. Vallen grunted and Cornella ordered everyone within range to shoot him. He ignored the dagger and her words as he caught Larken just before she hit the ground. No one moved, causing Cornella to only get more irate. She ran around the pair of them and yanked the tech-gun out of her man's hands once more. Vallen held Larken close to his bleeding chest and used the sword to slash at Cornella's fingers.

Cornella dropped the gun, as well as a few fingers. Vallen panted, fading fast. Larken's sword drooped in his hands and her eyelids grew suddenly heavy. She breathed in Vallen's scent, ignoring the world around her. She would die here in his arms.

If Larken had known this was their end, she would have held him a little tighter when he first left her at base.

Cornella raced for the dinner knife and raised it with a crazed shriek. In one swift motion, Vallen turned and shielded Larken from Cornella's next move. She jumped for them just as Larken's eyes fell shut. Larken scrunched up her face and readied herself for impact. Vallen quickly tightened his grip on her and turned them around, putting himself between her and Cornella. There was a shuffle of fabric, a surprised gasp, and then the sound of a body slumping to the ground.

Vallen held Larken close to his chest. She cracked an eye open and found her sword clutched tightly in his fist. It was upside down with the pommel by his thumb and the crystal blade pointed down to the white wood floor. Blood ran down the side of it and dripped off the tip. Past that, Larken could see emerald fabric and more blood spreading across the floor faster than it should. She turned her face into Vallen's chest, not wanting to look.

It was over.

Pain settled over her body as well as her heart. She tried to fight it, not wanting to think about her missing friends, the people who may have died, or even what happened to her mother. She only focused on the house by the beach and joining Soren in the water.

The cold waves licked her feet first, then slowly moved up to encase her. She shivered as the sea welcomed her to its dark depths. At first there were shadows and sounds in the dark ocean, and a soft order to *hold on*. Then, there was nothing.

# CHAPTER 46

The tabernacle bells rang out, singing their joy and well wishes to the happy couple. The weather was surprisingly nice for it being the end of fall. The leaves were as orange and brown as ever, filling the world with a picturesque comfort. A small heat wave had rolled in, warm enough for people to shed their sweaters and jackets, and even Larken left her wrap in a pew to see her friends off.

The wedding was beautiful—everything Candy wished it would be. Wildflowers covered every available surface and were accented by wreaths made up of branches with orange and yellow leaves. Hinlee made a beautiful maid of honor, while Brecker stood up as Carl's best man. Seeing them up there together, Larken knew it wouldn't be long before they had their turn. Hinlee loved spring, so it would probably only be a few more months. Brecker still needed to pop the question, but no one anticipated a long engagement for them.

The pale lilac dress Larken wore was the same shade Candy had worn to her birthday party. Straps hung loosely off Larken's shoulders while the dress held itself up by cinching around her bust. The material was a soft tulle that caught every breeze that went by. All the women in the bridal party wore their hair down. Hinlee's hair was too short to style, and Candy didn't want to take the time to do updos for both her and Larken. Larken couldn't blame her. If she was the one getting married, she wouldn't want to do a single thing until it was time to walk down the aisle.

Soren grabbed her hand and laced their fingers together. Birds chirped overhead and the music started up. The two of them stood under the steeple, watching Carl take his new bride into his arms. Everyone else stood or found seats to watch the first dance. Brecker had found a chair for Hinlee by the Chins. Jing jumped up and down next to her father, her poofy flower girl dress bouncing with her.

The forest shared in their happiness and used the wind to kick up random leaves. They swirled around Carl and Candy in a beautiful display of autumn stars, and Carl pulled his new wife in for a kiss. Everyone cheered and clapped, just as happy to celebrate as they were. The ex-Faithful Camp had rushed to prepare the wedding. It was so soon after everything was over that a lot of the residents hadn't even had time to go back to their home districts yet. Though, quite a few of them decided not to go at all.

Life was simpler in the woods.

Larken agreed, but her heart belonged to the sea. So much so that somewhere south of them, the building process of Larken's new home had already started. She used the same team that repaired and replaced parts of the Manse when the building needed it. She'd brought up a map of Koraythea on the giant screen in the Manse security sitting room and pointed at a random spot by the sea. No one except the builders would know where her home would be, just like she wanted. Larken didn't really understand how it would all work out, but Delvon assured her that she would finally get the privacy she'd always wanted.

Even though Larken was trying her best to get away from it all, there were a few things she needed to deal with in the Capital. Still, for the first time in a long time, Larken didn't care about what happened next. There were, of course, things she needed to see to. Liam needed to be found and new Luminaries needed to be chosen, but it didn't need to happen now. It didn't even need to happen tomorrow. Larken could take a break—they could all take a break.

Apparently, all the Vigilants had dropped their weapons and pledged themselves to Larken after Cornella fell. The process of weeding out the military bases and making arrests had already started, but Larken delegated it to someone else. The Faithfuls had won. They had created a better tomorrow, one that everyone could look forward to. The war was over, and at least for now, there was happiness.

Larken could still remember waking up to Trogar's and Fisher's faces. They had crowded in around Ezra who was shining a light into her bleary eyes. Vallen laid in the bed to her left and never took his eyes off of Ezra's hands. Larken would never forget what he'd done for her—what he'd said. He called her his daughter. It was the best title she'd ever been given.

Soren tried to hide it from her, but eventually had to tell her about what happened to Dominic. She tried to feel bad, laying there in the recovery wing, but mostly she was just sad for the situation. What had happened to the fun-loving womanizer to give him such a horrible end? Larken had felt responsible for a few days, but after speaking to Fisher about it, things slowly got better. They had been in the same situation in the end—both trying to outrun their crazy exes.

Everyone else had their own recovery they had to work through. Hinlee still limped around, while Carl spent every free moment he had with a stress ball in his hand. He also had to start therapy after having a man die in his arms. Larken would never forgive herself for letting that happen to him. He was a stylist. His life was devoted to creating beauty. To have that happen to him—Carl was forever changed now.

Candy stood with him every step of the way. Larken didn't know how it was possible, but her love for Carl seemed to triple. Yes, it was hard, and he often got frustrated when he had to stop working on Larken mid-braid, but she was there to offer him whatever comfort she could. Candy was only ever patient and kind with him, and she currently looked up into her husband's eyes with enough love to get him through the next five lifetimes.

Larken looked up at Soren. His recovery was the hardest of all. He had to allow the Medic to be a little more invasive with their treatments than he usually would have. The tendon behind his knee was nearly severed, and Larken hadn't even known until she woke up. That didn't stop Soren from helping her with her rehab, though. The two of them spent a lot of time in the pool, slowly building up their strength. But now, he watched Carl and Candy dance with a small smile on his lips. She'd never seen him so relaxed, so carefree. Not even when he snuck her away for their day of fun at the beach. She squeezed his hand, and he shifted his attention to her.

Soren was so handsome in his suite. Carl picked it out so it fit him perfectly, unsurprisingly. The other one was beyond repair. Carl had tried to fix it for him, but the tears Dominic put in it were just too great. Nothing worked, so Soren had gotten rid of it. It made Larken a little sad that that bit of their history was gone, but Soren reminded her that there would be plenty more suits in his future. Though, if Larken got her way, it wouldn't be anywhere near the amount he was expecting.

Out of the corner of her eye, Larken could see others starting to dance. Shadric played with his band, his smile just as bright as ever. He wasn't singing, and something told Larken that he wouldn't for a long while. The war had changed everyone, and now that it was over, everyone wanted to start over.

Delvon stood by Levi, both with their arms crossed. Delvon didn't talk much about what happened and Larken didn't push it. He would share when he was ready. That didn't stop her from shedding a few tears on his behalf after she saw the scars, though. She'd been walking back to her room when she passed his and saw him talking with Ezra. He'd sat shirtless on his bed. His chest was shaved in two different spots and sported horribly distorted scars. As far as Larken knew, he hasn't been back to the gym yet. Not to mention, he was even quieter than usual. Larken was worried, but knew he would eventually come around.

Brecker pulled Hinlee up out of her chair and led her over next to the newlyweds. She hobbled a bit, but let Brecker gather her close with his good arm. The other was still a bit weak, but that didn't stop them from swaying to the music. Brecker went slow for her, making it that much more romantic. The memory of the moment they shared on the Harpy had Larken's heart melting all over again.

She nodded over to where they were, silently asking Soren to dance. He didn't move at first, but when he did, he didn't head for the other couples. Instead, he turned to face her fully and cupped her cheek.

"I didn't get a chance yet to tell you how beautiful you look."

Larken smiled, a warm fluttering starting in her chest and spreading everywhere. "You don't look so bad yourself."

Soren's lips twitched. "You know, I've been thinking a lot lately..."

Jing squealed as Loxly pulled her out onto the forest floor.

"Oh?" Larken teased. "Not too hard I hope."

Soren let go of her face and tapped his knuckle on her nose. He ignored her and asked, "Do you remember that night in the dorm?"

"Which one? There were quite a few of them. Like the night I almost burned the dorm down. Or were you talking about the night I told you about my shoulder?"

"No." A small smile twisted his lips as he thought about their time together. "Do you remember the night we were all playing cards?"

"Yes?" Larken answered, not sure where he was going with this.

"Before Lights Out, I won the round and you lost. Right before you went into your room, you said that you owed me an answer to a question."

Larken's cheeks went pink as she suddenly remembered. She nodded and waited for him to continue.

"Well, I've got a question for you."

Soren was grinning now. It flipped Larken's stomach over and a flock of butterflies fought to turn it right side up again.

He grabbed both of her hands and took a step closer to her. His smile dimmed as he stared into her eyes for several moments. The tip of his tongue darted out to wet his lips and he swallowed.

Somehow she knew that this, right here, was going to be a perfect moment—one that she would remember forever. Their outfits, the tabernacle, the autumn wonderland around them, and the way Soren's eyes glinted that beautiful shade of green that she loved so much. A breeze kicked up and pulled at her dress and hair. It was like something out of an old fairy story and she never wanted this moment to end.

Despite his nerves, he squeezed her hands and asked. "Do you love me?"

Larken grinned. She pushed to her tiptoes and kissed him, then pulled back only long enough to say, "Of course I do."

# 5 YEARS LATER...

Larken eased herself slowly onto the couch with Soren's help. He found a squat stool and slid it under her feet before he left to go greet everyone. He would never know how grateful she was for his help. Her feet were so swollen with blood that they were almost purple. Hinlee and Candy only laughed whenever she complained about it, but no one other than the men had any sympathy for her.

Absentmindedly, her hand moved up to rub her huge belly. Her little one recognized their mother's gentle touch and kicked her hand a few times. It was much different with Soren; he had a game he liked to play with the baby where he would tap one part of the belly and then the baby would kick the spot after. It was moments like that where Larken couldn't believe her heart could be so full.

Things couldn't be more different from the way they once were. Larken was Magnate, for one. She'd redone the interior of the Manse as much as Delvon allowed her to. He didn't get the promotion to Luminary's Champion like Larken had promised, but he was the head security guy of the *entire* country. The man would never rest—not that he was capable of it—and yet still managed to be a grump after all these years. Little by little he'd opened up about what happened on the Night of Masks, but there were still a few demons he kept to himself. He was still as protective as ever and things had only gotten worse after Larken told him she was pregnant. Apparently this child was destined to have many, *many* aunts and uncles—all of which were more protective than the last.

Zimena shrieked as she ran into the sitting room, her red curls bouncing with each step. Giggles spilled from her lips as Noah, Zion, and Loxly chased after her. Zimena was the spitting image of her father, even though she had Candy's hair. Noah, her older brother, was the opposite, though; his hair was Carl's natural blond. Noah was such a good brother, too. He didn't let anyone get too close to his baby sister—especially Zion, Brecker's exact copy. At the tender ages of four, three, and two, Noah, Zion, and Zimena were nearly inseparable. It didn't hurt that they all lived together at Brinestone.

Larken read the name in a book once and found it fitting for their new home. Of course, she and Soren occupied the master suite, but everyone else still had plenty of room to grow their families.

Levi, Ezra, and Jodi all became Brinestone Medics. They had plenty of work, what with all the babies, and there would be plenty more to come. Just two weeks ago, Ezra and Jodi announced their engagement, and Candy and Hinlee were already planning the wedding of the year for them.

Carl had been employed as the Magnate's Official Stylist, and Mr. Chin was brought on as Head Chef. Both Jing and his mother came to live with him in his little section of Brinestone. Jing was a lifesaver when it came to wrangling the children. She decided she wanted to become a teacher, and no one had a problem letting her practice. Now that she was ten, the extra set of eyes made life easier. She'd grown into quite the lovely young lady—one that Wardell had a hard time ignoring.

Loxly was hired on as Larken's chauffeur. Every time they went somewhere, he helped her find her wings again, even though they never went more than a few feet off the ground. He traveled back and forth a lot between Brinestone and his dad's farm. Someday he would take over the farm, but for now, he enjoyed the time he had in the sky.

Brecker and Hinlee went into retirement. They had too many scares involving the other and decided getting married and having a family full of love was the right choice for them. Larken couldn't agree more. Hinlee was pregnant again and waddled in shortly after Loxly scooped Zimena up and blew on her belly. Brecker set Hinlee up next to Larken before bending down and kissing Larken on the cheek.

Larken returned it with one of her own and waited for him to get settled before asking, "How was the flight?"

"Not as long as yours was, I'm sure," Hinlee teased. "But still long enough that Brecker had to stop a few times to let my stomach settle."

Brecker rubbed her small bump. She was still having morning sickness...all day long. Larken's heart went out to her. She only had it for about two weeks and then was back to training with Vallen.

It was something the two of them did together each day now that he was retired, as well. Their training wasn't as intense as it was before. Sometimes it was a walk, others it was a couple hours in the giant pool Soren insisted on being built. It was the one thing he'd always wanted as a kid that he wasn't going to deprive the growing Squad 19 brood. Larken hadn't realized at the time how much her swollen feet and belly would appreciate the reprieve, but she was thankful for the pool every day.

Vallen gave up his title of both General Maxwell and Blade. Now he was simply *Grandpa*, while Rich took up the name *Papa*. Fisher didn't know what name he wanted yet, but Trogar had his heart set on *Gramps*.

As if sensing where her thoughts were drifting, Hinlee asked, "Trogar stay behind?"

"Yeah. He thought it would be a good idea to have some one-on-one time with Wardell." It was the reason he gave, but Larken knew that being so close to the political side of things made him want to drink again. He'd been sober for the last five years, and she couldn't have been more proud. Wardell, too. He was over the moon that his dad had cleaned up and was getting his life back together.

"Fisher still having fun?" Brecker asked.

"Absolutely." Larken grinned, chasing the baby's kicks across her belly with her fingers. "He messaged last night and said he couldn't remember the last time he had this much fun on tour."

Hinlee twisted her face up. "Who's he playing again?"

"Estelle's father. The one that pokes fun at the mother the whole time."

Hinlee opened her mouth but was cut off by Zimena's shrill cry. Both women turned to look and found her sitting on the floor, pointing at the corner of an end table. Noah was on her in an instant, hugging and kissing her tears away. Larken melted and turned back to Hinlee so she didn't start sobbing her eyes out. Pregnancy was not ideal for keeping her emotions locked away—not that she had a reason to now.

Cornella was gone.

Larken didn't have to be strong anymore if she didn't want to be.

There was a lull as Hinlee watched Zion and rubbed her belly. Larken stared at the giant glass screen that once held vast meadows. Delvon had reprogramed the screens to show crashing waves so Larken could have a bit of home whenever she visited the Manse. Her hormones already had her so homesick that she could cry at any given moment. Larken's hand drifted up to the pearl that she never took off. They'd had to leave Brinestone about a week ago to make the meeting in time since they traveled by hovercraft. She constantly joked that the best thing about being Magnate was no one could force her to fly ever again.

Another pixilated wave crashed into the rocks. She missed Brinestone, the ocean, and all of her things—especially her bed and her pillows. The baby didn't bother her shoulder as much as Ezra thought they would, but she also got regular corrections and used whatever gave her the best lumbar support.

Soren came back into the room with Kinslee, Alex, Ewan, and Shadric in tow. Delvon and Vallen followed behind them.

Zimena babbled excitedly and called, "Gampa, Gampa!"

Vallen scooped her up and kissed her cheek.

Noah and Zion weren't far behind and were soon dancing under his feet.

Vallen made his way to the couches and let all three kids pile onto his lap. Zimena squashed her cheek against his in a drooly-looking hug. And as gruff as Vallen was, even he couldn't hide his smile.

Everyone quickly found seats where they could and waited. Carl, Candy, and Levi rushed in ten minutes later. The couple sat by Vallen, and Noah jumped into his father's lap. Levi was the last to find a seat. He dropped into it, saying, "Sorry, one of the kitchen staff slipped and cracked their head on a counter. I was there when someone came for help."

"It's okay. We haven't started yet," Soren said, pulling Larken close.

She rested her head on his shoulder and took in everything around her. Their lives had all changed so much over the last five years.

"How are renovations coming?" Brecker asked Ewan.

"We finished last week, if you can believe it," he answered, brogue just as strong as ever.

"About time," Delvon muttered.

"Well, there was quite a bit of..." he paused, not meeting Larken's gaze, "*damage.*"

"Is that what you're callin' it?" Loxly asked with a laugh.

Ewan's ears went a slight shade of pink. "Well, that sounds better than saying our Magnate burned my house down."

Hinlee sighed and adjusted until she got comfortable. "A fitting end, in my opinion. I only lived there for a few weeks and even I hated it. Who can blame her?"

"Liam," Levi coughed.

Everyone laughed.

It was no secret Liam was bitter about the situation. He was caught breaking into the Military Manor the week after Carl and

Candy's wedding. Liam had the bright idea after a day of drinking to simply lock himself inside and keep his future title that way. When Larken had been asked if she wanted to press charges, she said, "Absolutely." The immature part of her had wanted to order that every single creepy crawly thing she could think of be put in his cell, but she didn't think a petty act of revenge would make the best impression on the country.

Shortly after that, Larken got started on renovating the Manor. She burned down all of her mother's roses, just like she promised. Ewan wasn't really a fan of the white tile and open spaces, so Larken burned the Manor down, too. The only thing that survived the fire was her grandmother's fountain. Larken had the garden at Brinestone filled with wisteria, dahlias, forget-me-nots, and strawberry bushes…and there, in the center, Larken's grandmother stood, sword held high and water flowing from her clay pot. There the fountain flourished, running water for the children to play in, just like Larken used to.

One by one Larken met the eyes of her Luminaries. Kinslee still led Gadget. She'd kept her word and the District turned over a new leaf. Maxim was first and foremost, just as she promised. Morgan had stepped down and passed the title onto Alex the previous year. A far as Larken knew, Morgan still took his afternoon stroll through the gardens with his wife every day, and their daughter, Eudora, was still driving them all crazy.

After the fighting had stopped and the Vigilants swore their allegiance to Larken, she asked Ewan to be the Military District Luminary. He gladly took the job, honored that he would be chosen out of so many. Out of everyone, he sought Larken's and Vallen's advice the most. Each time he showed the vulnerability of not wanting to make the wrong decision, Larken grew more and more sure of her choice. As for Star District, Larken thought it best that Narcissa and her son Charles didn't keep their grand titles. Fortunately, Shadric needed a break from music. Larken made the offer and he accepted. All four of the Luminaries were now people Larken could trust to help run the country, and she was glad of it. They provided her with the life of peace she'd always hoped for.

The meeting started and Larken snuggled deeper into her husband's side. She would try to stay awake this time, but they all gave her grace considering her current state.

She never knew how perfect her life would turn out. If she had, she wouldn't have fought Cam, her old stylist, so hard that morning he'd practically yanked her out of bed to get ready for the TONES Festival. Maxim truly had a plan for Larken, one she didn't ever dare dream of. All of this was thanks to Him, and she would forever be grateful. Despite that, Larken still abolished the Festival. People were still free to join the military if they wished to, but no more children would be sold or donated ever again.

Maxim had brought them all so far, Larken almost couldn't believe that her life had turned out this way. She now knew kindness, friendship, and love. The best part was that Larken didn't have to be afraid that her mother would take it all away from her. Everyone had told her that Maxim would see her through, and He had. She would never doubt Him again.

Soren reached over and placed a hand on her belly. The baby kicked him, wanting to be close to their father. Ewan talked in the background about the new Military Manor, but Larken could care less. She looked up at Soren and smiled.

"Are you happy?" she whispered.

"Beyond words. You?"

Larken tangled her fingers with his so they both cupped her stomach. "More than you know."

# ABOUT THE AUTHOR

C.C. Urie is a Multi-Genre Christian Author who lives in Michigan. Her whole world revolves around her family, and her favorite time of year is when the leaves start to change. She's always had a love for reading, and enjoys sharing her stories with others. Her true calling in life is using her books to help spread the Good Word and show others how God has changed her life for the better.

# OTHER BOOKS BY THIS AUTHOR


**The Divine Courage Trilogy**

Defender

Betrayer

Vanquisher


**Hearts of Deadgrove**

Southern Charm

www.ingramcontent.com/pod-product-compliance
Lightning Source LLC
Chambersburg PA
CBHW021343310726
48971CB00001B/263